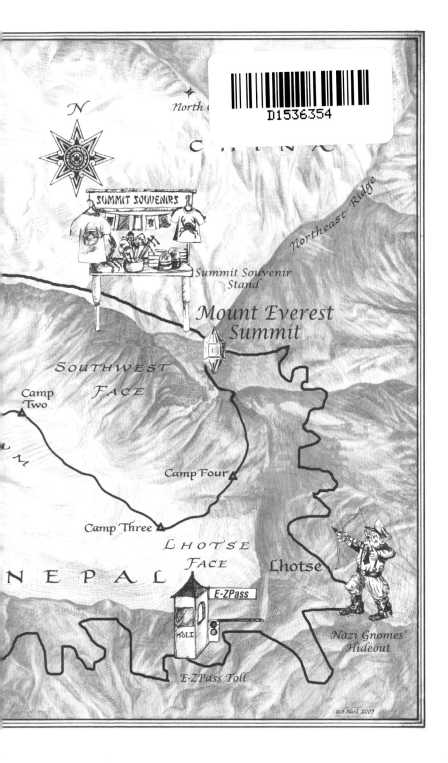

INTO
HOT AIR

INTO HOT AIR

MOUNTING MOUNT EVEREST

CHRIS ELLIOTT

Illustrations by Amy Elliott Andersen

WEINSTEIN
BOOKS

Map copyright © 1997 by Anita Karl
with additional illustrations by Amy Elliott Anderson

Copyright © 2007 Chris Elliott

ISBN: 978-1-60286-007-0

First Edition
10   9   8   7   6   5   4   3   2   1

To all members of Mountain Maniacs' fall 2006 expedition, but especially to my fellow thespians. I hope I got all the facts right. It would've been a lot easier if someone had returned my calls.

INTRODUCTION

Ever since Jon Krakauer made it sound so appealing in his 1997 best seller *Into Thin Air*, thrill seekers, novice climbers, and disabled people with something to prove have all flocked to the Himalayas with one shared ambition: to stand atop the apex of the planet, look out at the spectacular view, and . . . snap a couple of snapshots . . . I guess.

But why would I, a relatively sane guy with a perfectly fine, authentic-looking G.E.D., make the dreadful decision to climb that dumb-ass slag heap of a mountain? Well, it all began with my great-uncle Percy.

In 1924, when asked why he wanted to climb Mount Everest, George Leigh Mallory coined the celebrated phrase "Because it's there." But earlier in the year, when faced with the same question from a group of distinguished adventurers at New York City's famed Explorers Club, Percy Brackett Elliott coined the not-so-celebrated phrase, "Because horsey horsey, he don't stop/ He done let his feet go clipetty-clop." He then he broke into an ambitious gallop, tripped, banged his head on the podium, and fell into a coma. His Everest attempt would be delayed a full year, until surgeons could devise a way to plug the gaping hole in his noggin, eventually sealing it with a handful of abandoned athletic socks and a quart of latex primer (linen white). It was never quite clear whether or not he was completely out of his coma before he made his attempted climb.

In those days the borders were closed, and unless you had the patience to file the proper paperwork, you were denied access to the mountain. Uncle Percy had no such patience. Instead, he resolved to fly to Everest and climb up from wherever he crash-landed. He built himself a plane based on instructions from a toy model (actually of a boat) and christened her *Ever Rest*. The aircraft was the first of its kind ever to be constructed entirely out of yeast paste and horsehair—the only building materials available at the time, due to the silica famine of 1923 (so no fiberglass). But, oh, was she a sight to behold! On December 1, 1924, he pushed the single-engine biplane out on to the muddy runway behind the Elliott barn in Brooklyn Heights, waved good-bye to the curious onlookers, and then went back inside. Apparently he had lost interest in the whole adventure, and it would take another week before the idea appealed to him again.

And so, on December 8, 1924, armed with only a fingernail clipper, some meat lozenges, and a jar of petroleum jelly, Percy Brackett Elliott took off from Love Field in Brooklyn Heights and headed east toward the Himalayas. And then on December 7, 1941, the Japanese bombed Pearl Harbor. (That has nothing to do with this story, but I thought it was worth remembering here, as I'm writing this on Veterans Day.)

I never met my great-uncle Percy, and there are those, like my grandparents, who insist that he was completely out of his mind. But from the time I was a child I've felt a strong kinship with the man, especially since my grandparents often remarked on how much I reminded them of him. (Apparently we both liked to stick beans up our noses.)

In 1999 an expedition to retrace Mallory's efforts discovered his perfectly preserved body on a windswept cap sheaf, 28,000 feet up the south approach to the summit. He was lying face down just below the Hillary Tit. He had broken his right leg and his left arm, and all the vertebrae in his lower back were crushed. The assumption was that he had choked on a frozen hunk of bangers and mash.

But what about Uncle Percy? Had he made it? Was he the first person to stand on the roof of the world and shout out at the top of his lungs "Hey, all you mo-fos, you can kiss my big white ass!" (or whatever would have been appropriate back in 1924)?

Sadly, Percy never returned home to tell his tale, and no climber has ever come across a single shred of evidence proving that the Elliott/Everest expedition even existed. In fact, some conspiracy theorists claim that my great-uncle wasn't even in the Himalayas in the winter of 1924, but was in Washington, DC, trying to secure a patent from the war department for his inflatable underpants.

Alas, my great-uncle's name faded into obscurity. That is, until about a year ago, when I received an anonymous package in the mail. Assuming that it was either a dirty bomb or live Maine lobsters, I let it soak in warm, soapy water for a week before opening it. When I finally unwrapped its contents my life changed forever. Pushing aside the putrid lobsters, I discovered my great-uncle Percy's diary! Here was the whole sordid, seedy (and extremely soggy) detailed chronicle of the 1924 Elliott Mount Everest expedition—at least up to the point where it abruptly ended with the curious entry:

Farewell all. I leave now for afternoon tea with the jub jub bird and nasty old Mr. Bandersnatch.

At last, now there was evidence!

The mysterious diary could not have surfaced at a better moment in my life. My brief marriage to famed fashion designer Vera Wang had ended abruptly in an ugly custody battle over my collection of vintage 1980s Girbaud pants, and my one-man show as Ethel Merman had just closed Off Broadway due to numerous complaints by the board of health.

With the overwhelming success of my first book (*The Shroud of the Thwacker*, Miramax, $22.95), my next book was highly anticipated, and yet I had been frittering away my days by submitting falsified documents signed "Yours truly, Peter Stuyvesant" to the New York Historical Society and writing made-up participatory journalistic articles in the vein of the late, great George Plimpton—mostly for my own amusement, but for some legitimate ink-testing laboratories as well. After the diary's arrival, however, the prospect of writing a book about climbing Mount Everest loomed in my imagination as a participatory journalistic adventure that I might actually participate in.

I would retrace my great-uncle Percy's expedition, prove that he summitted the mountain before anyone else, and solve the mystery surrounding his disappearance! Hopefully, I would find his perfectly preserved frozen body somewhere up in the Himalayas and return it home for a proper Elliott burial—complete with marching bands, dancing dogs, and bearded ladies (they're my second cousins—the dogs, that is).

Those were my reasons—simple enough, I thought—but in reality far more complex than I could ever imagine. And so excited was I at the prospect of climbing Mount Everest that my enthusiasm clouded my judgment. Not only did I ignore the potential danger, I neglected to ask the most important questions of all: who was the anonymous person who sent me Uncle Percy's diary in the first place—and why?

PART ONE

Too bad it's so cloudy.

—Sir Edmund Hillary
The Summit, 1953

THE SOUTH APPROACH
28,000 FEET

I had been climbing for so long that I was aware of nothing anymore, except the struggle to put one foot in front of the other without collapsing under the weight of the man on my back. Camp Four had to be close, but there was no way to tell for sure. A freak storm had taken us by surprise a few hours prior—first charging over the Pumori Peak and then bearing down on Everest with an almighty vengeance. I couldn't see my hand in front of my face, let alone the rest of our fellow climbers. We had already lost four people, and as far as I knew Michael and I could be the last ones alive. I braced myself as a gust of bitterly cold wind rushed through the holes in my tattered parka. The cold chilled my bones and sent my muscles into painful spasms. Then I sneezed and my nose shot off my face.

"Goddamn it. Not again!"

At that exact moment, a huge column of snow corkscrewed twenty feet into the air and coiled around me like a snake. My nose twirled around inside it like a flying prune, blowing just out of reach each time I scrambled to catch it. Michael groaned.

"Put me down, put me down. I need to rest."

Rest? Rest from what? I've been carrying your fat Academy Award–winning ass all the way up from Base Camp! But I didn't say what I was thinking, I just thought it to myself, because I was so delirious that I thought that if I thought it out loud, he might hear it. So I kept the thought inside, but then I thought, *He probably heard me think it anyway, the jerk.* (That's the kind of logic one uses in the thin air at 28,000 feet above sea level, especially when one was borderline re-tarded before even starting the climb.)

"Oxygen. I need oxygen. Give me your oxygen!" he demanded.

"Did you happen to see where my nose went? It blew off again."

"Just put me down, will ya?"

I allowed him to slide off my back and onto the snow. His eyes, glassy and pale, glared up at me. I could tell he had reached his per-sonal "wall." Either that or he was filling his snow pants with an-other load of what the Tibetans called Himalayan ying yang. That was just one of the unpleasant side effects one experiences at high altitude, along with pulmonary edema, cerebral edema, hypother-mia, freezing of vital internal organs, swelling of bosoms, and shrink-ing of penises—none of which was mentioned once in *The Idiot's Guide to Climbing Mount Everest.* (Its only warning was to abstain from singing "The Happy Wanderer" above the "Death Zone," "as it may pester your fellow climbers." A-duh! I had quit crooning "Valderee, Valderaah" by the end of the first week and had been belt-ing out "Sweet Georgia Brown" nonstop ever since.)

Ahead of us, barely visible through the blizzard, was the wind-swept crest of the peak itself. We had come so far and were so close, but I feared Michael was not going to make it, and for the first time in this punishing enterprise, I felt a twinge of sympathy for the man.

"Stop sightseeing, lunkhead, and give me your goddamn oxygen, now!" he shouted.

By *twinge of sympathy,* of course I meant, "What ungodly atrocity had I committed in some past life to earn such a loathsome com-panion?"

Michael had managed on his own up the steep ridges of the

Lhotse Face, across the slippery crevasses of the Khumbu Icefall, and around the prickly pinnacles of Krakauer's Terse Hemingwayesque Prose, but recently he'd given up, and in a moment of deeply regrettable "team spirit" I'd agreed that, yes, we would "carry each other." But that agreement was not working out the way I had imagined. I suppose Michael felt that as long as he had strength enough to ride piggyback on me, then by God he was going to make it to the summit. In a way, it was hard not to admire that plucky, old-fashioned, "I don't care about anybody else except myself" approach to life—it's a uniquely American quality that I believe many of us in this great country have lost.

I unscrewed my last canister of compressed gas and attached it to Michael's regulator. He immediately began to breathe more easily. I, on the other hand, began to experience a feather-headed consciousness far more fuzzy than the one I live with every day. I glanced over the steep drop to my left, struggling to make out some sign of the rest of the team. I couldn't see anyone. However, I could see in the distance several small, gray, gnomelike creatures scurrying about—a clear sign, according to *The Idiot's Guide*, that my brain was hemorrhaging and that I had about three minutes to live.

Lost in a hypoxic stupor, I became aware of a gentle voice whispering in my ear.

"Chris . . . Chris . . ."

Could it be? Was it my great-uncle Percy? Had I finally found him? Was my quest complete? Had he survived up here on Everest all these years, or was this his spirit come to guide me to Camp Four?

"Chris," said the voice, "you will go to the Degaba System. There you will meet a magic goat who will help you."

"Huh?"

Actually it was not Uncle Percy at all, but Tzing Tzang, our *sirdar* (or "big Sherpa on campus"), screwing with my head again. Our Sherpas, although an amiable band of hard workers, had all turned out to be insufferable smart-asses.

"Hey No Nose, looks like your boyfriend want to make big gravy with you," Tzing Tzang shouted, as he shook me back to consciousness, attaching a fresh supply of oxygen to my regulator. ("Make gravy" was Sherpa slang for sex.) When I opened my eyes, Michael was on all fours pointing feverishly at his rear end.

"I'm seeing gnomes," he yelped through his mask. "I need dex. I need dex now!"

Apparently I wasn't the only one whose brain was hemorrhaging. I turned to Tzing Tzang and said panting, "Where are the others? Did they make it?"

"Uh no, they all died."

My jaw dropped in sheer horror as the helplessness of our situation began to sink in.

"No, just pulling your leg," he said. "They're right behind me—I think—hard to tell. Maybe they *did* die. Hee hee hee."

Then he pulled out a syringe of dexamethasone—a powerful steroid that retards the hallucinatory effects of hypoxia—yanked down Michael's pants, and jammed the needle straight into his commemorative tattoo of Cesar Chavez. The big man was instantly energized. He shot up, took one look around, and scrambled back up my spine like he was ascending the summit itself.

"Grab my camera," he ordered, and then yowled, "Yee haa!" as he spurred me on with his sharp crampons. "On to Camp Four, Silver!"

A moment later, Duncan Carter, our team's intrepid leader, appeared by my side. "Hey, A-holes!" he shouted, "this storm's getting worse. Chop chop! Camp Four is just ahead!"

Our fellow climbers shuffled past, their eyes lifeless and deserted, like the bewildered survivors of a major catastrophe, while

I slogged along under Michael's immense weight. I saw Yorgi, the blind Russian, feeling his way about with his cane, but my friend Wendell, who had been guiding him, was nowhere to be seen. (Wendell, for the unlucky few of you who missed out on my last best seller, *The Shroud of the Thwacker*, is my longtime best friend. And more important, he was hauling the bag of Oreos we were going to chow down on when we got to Camp Four.)

"Yorgi," I heaved. "Where's Wendell?"

"Zee ran off, I don't know where. I'm blind, remember?"

"I'm right behind you," grumbled Wendell.

"Oh, thank goodness. For a second there I thought you'd left us."

"No such luck."

"Isn't this exhilarating, Wendy?"

"Yes, I love freezing my ass off on a godforsaken mountain with no hope of ever getting back alive."

"Oh, come on, it's not so bad. Hey, I know what would raise your spirits—why don't you carry Michael for a while?"

"Uh, no thank you. You're doing fine. I'm better in a supervisory capacity anyway. That's it, keep carrying him. Good, you got him. Keep going . . . Oh, I so wish I was dead."

Despite Wendell's despair, it never occurred to me to attempt Everest without him by my side. I didn't do much without Wendell. We were baptized together, barmitzvahed together, and even had our butt-cheek implants done together. (It was cheaper that way; we were going to have the left ones put in next year—if we survived.)

"We're almost there, Wendy, and then we can enjoy our delicious Oreos. Just keep thinking about those Oreos. That's what's keeping me going. Oreos, Oreos, Oreos. Mmm, mmm good."

"Ah, yeah . . . right," he said strangely.

Hand over fist, foot over foot, we made our way to Camp Four, a ragtag collection of tents perched precariously on a sloping ledge, and our final resting spot before the assault on the summit in the morning. I gently deposited Michael's king-size posterior on his king-size inflatable Sealy Posturepedic mattress and paused in the hatchway of his L.L.Bean colonial style tent (an exact scaled-down replica of his mansion outside of Detroit), half expecting a tip. As soon as I realized that none would be forthcoming, I bowed and shuffled across the spindrift, taking one last look-see for my nose before collapsing from exhaustion inside mine and Wendell's Wal-Mart Family Fun tent.

"We made it!" I cried, but Wendell, shivering in his flimsy bag, only grunted.

Outside, Duncan was still barking orders. "It's not over yet, A-holes! Everyone to your tents. Tie yourselves down to something—like the snow, I guess. This is going to be bad—real bad."

The fierce nor'easter intensified, pummeling our tent as I zipped myself into my Peanuts (Wendell wished he had one too) sleeping bag.

"Oh, Wendell, I know it's been a long haul, but just imagine, to-morrow we'll be standing on the summit of Mount Everest, looking down on this whole godforsaken world, pissing in the snow, and suck-ing back a couple of ice-cold egg creams—my treat!" (I just assumed there'd be some sort of concession stand up there or something.) "Which reminds me. What do you say we dig into our cookie stash?"

But Wendell seemed distracted, staring down at something in his hands. "I think the Sherpas must have got into the Oreos," he mumbled.

I saw that he was holding an empty bag.

"Sherpas, my ass! You ate them!"

"I wanted my last few minutes on earth to be happy ones."

"You're a pig!"

"You're an idiot!"

In a flash we had our hands around each other's throats.

(I'd like to say that it was the strain of the climb that was causing us to act irrationally, but it was just that we both really like Oreos.)

Wendell's fist made contact with my jaw, sending my oxygen mask flying. Then my fist made contact with the center pole, causing our Family Fun tent to collapse on top of us.

"Give it to me!" I gasped, squeezing his neck as hard as I could. "I know you have another cookie somewhere in your parka!"

"If I do, it's mine!" he wheezed. "You owe me because we're all going to die on this stupid mountain!"

"You wanted to come!" I yelled as we thrashed back and forth.

"Are you kidding? It was your stupid idea!" he said, throwing me down. "This whole dumb climb was all about you and your dumb midlife crisis. You and your divorce, you and your career, you and your crazy great-uncle."

"At least I have a career! Because of me you get to hobnob with celebrities."

"Celebrities? Ha! B celebrities, at best."

"Oh yeah?"

"Yeah!"

Out on the col, Tzing Tzang noticed the mound of vinyl bouncing up and down and shouted, "Quit making gravy, boys, and tie yourselves down!"

We stood up and then Wendell threw something really hard at me that bounced off my forehead and nearly knocked me out.

"Ow, wait. Time out! That really hurt!"

"It was supposed to, asshole!"

At first I thought it was a rock—the kind that they heat up and use for foot massages at fancy Beverly Hills salons—but after I rubbed it on my feet for a bit, I realized that it was my frozen nose.

"Wait, wait, Wendell," I said, trying to fit the proboscis into the gaping hole in my face. "It doesn't fit. Wendell, this isn't my nose!"

"On to Camp Four, Silver!"

"So what? It'll work, won't it?" Then he put me in a headlock and started to strangle me.

"Don't you see, Wendell? Our search is over! We've finally found Uncle Percy! Sort of . . ."

Wendell finally stopped pounding me. "Really?"

Suddenly, from all around us, came an ear-piercing racket. It sounded like a freight train, hurricane, and earthquake, all rolled into one big, thunderous stink bomb.

"Avalanche!" shouted Duncan from somewhere out on the col.

The frozen ground beneath us began to shake and Wendell looked alarmed.

"Some vacation, huh?" I said. "Isn't this funtastic!!"

Then the ground gave way and Wendell tumbled into a widening crevasse. I grabbed his hand, but it slipped out of his glove, and then he was gone.

"I still have the last Oreo, asshole!" he shouted as he fell out of sight. Then I blacked out.

CHAPTER ONE

One month earlier, Grandpa shuffled into the kitchen, clutching a large framed portrait in his arms.

"Here's the last known photograph of your great-uncle Percy."

"Well, hello there, Mr. Handsome," I said, studying the black-and-white photo. "I can definitely see a family resemblance." The intense-looking man in the photo was in his early fifties, sporting a salt-and-pepper beard and a stern expression. He was also covered in tar and feathers and wearing a lady's wig.

"Was it Halloween?"

"No . . . he was probably out West selling some more of his useless 'Pep-Tonic.'"

A steam of tears moistened Grandma's cheeks. "Poor Uncle Percy. How I miss him so."

"Your grandmother is so grateful that you're going to finally bring Percy back to Brooklyn Heights, where he belongs . . . You'll be leaving soon, right?"

Stalwarts of support, my sweet grandparents seemed especially eager for me to climb the tallest, most dangerous mountain in the world. I suppose they were just anxious to get me out of the house. After all,

I had been living with them ever since the breakup with Vera (and actually quite a bit during the marriage itself).

"That's right," whimpered Grammy. "They're tears of joy," and she leaned over and gave Gramps a little peck on his cheek.

"Eewww! Get a room, you two!" I said, averting my eyes. "As a matter of fact," I continued, "I don't even have a clue how to get started. I mean, don't you need a guide or something?"

Through her tears, Grammy said, "Oh, I cut this out of the *Pennysaver* for you." She pulled a clipping from her apron.

"'Mountain Maniacs,'" I read. "'Come and get your Ya Yas off in the Himalay . . . yas.'"

"Classy," said Gramps, pulling on his suspenders as I read on:

If you dream of exciting exploration . . . One of our trained professionals will be happy to guide you and your friends up Mt. Everest—the tallest mountain in the world, in case you haven't heard. There you can stand at the apex of our planet, twenty-nine thousand feet into the stratosphere . . . look around and . . . take a couple of snapshots or something.

If you think you have what it takes—mainly the cash—then hurry in and meet our friendly, licensed mountaineering experts at Mountain Maniacs magnificent corporate headquarters, located just half a mile west of Route 9, adjacent to the Woodbury Mall, right behind the Carpet Warehouse.

"So you can leave now, right?" Grammy asked.

"Too bad this is way over in Jersey. You guys know I'm still not allowed to drive."

Grammy said, "Actually I've already called your charming Negro friend Wendell, the cab driver. He's going to take you there tomorrow."

Percy Brackett Elliott

"Yeah, but won't I need climbing equipment or some—"

"Gotcha covered," Gramps said, throwing a tarp full of junk on the table. "Cleaned out the garage. You got Christmas lights, brake fluid, bicycle pump, rat poison, and a box of six-penny galvanized nails. Everything you need."

I mused out loud, "Do you 'spose it's very much like Brooklyn? Mount Everest, I mean."

My grandparents rolled their eyes behind my back. (You may be wondering how I knew that since it was . . . behind my back. Well, their dry old eyeballs make a very specific sound when they roll. It kind of sounds like someone whispering, "Our grandson's an idiot.")

As I gazed through the greasy window to the bustling street below, I continued to cogitate. "I mean, people are people all over the world, right? 'The child is black, the child is white, together we learn to . . . bite the bite.' Does the moon not shine over Bangladesh as well as Brooklyn Heights? Oh, dear, sweet Savior, what invisible power compels me, as it compelled my great-uncle before me, to confront its staggering countenance? Perhaps to truly understand, we must first go back to my childhood and answer some of the lingering questions that only . . ."

"Okay, well, look, Chris . . . ah . . . it's about time for your Grandmother and I to start drinking, so maybe you should be on your way, huh?"

"Yes. Yes, you're quite right, Gramps. There'll be plenty of time for us to debrief upon my return. So, as the Katmandu locals say, Adios, amigos!"

CHAPTER TWO

The next day, as we crossed the George Washington Bridge in his cab, I could tell that my friend Wendell was upset. Maybe it was that he was missing a day of work to drive me to Mountain Maniacs, or maybe my decision to sit in the backseat had him a tad piqued. (But I'm sorry, if I'm going to be driven around, I want to be driven around in style.)

"You comfortable back there?" His eyes shot daggers at me in the rearview mirror.

"Yes, thank you," I answered back, "would you mind turning the music down, please?"

He did the opposite.

"That's perfect," I said.

Although I was familiar with the seminal events of Percy's life, something about the true nature of the man had always eluded me. For instance, I knew that he was born on a ship. It was during the doomed Franklin Expedition to discover the elusive northeast passage. The H.M.S. *Terror* became trapped in ice in Baffin Bay, and all 129 crew members perished—all save for one golden-haired child, presumably the progeny of one of the "comfort ladies" Franklin had brought along to keep the crew happy. Inuit Eskimos discovered Percy and raised him until the age of twelve, when they auctioned him off to the Elliott family, on vacation from Brooklyn Heights.

But how did he accomplish all the things Grammy claimed he had? At one time or another he had been a traveling salesman, an inventor, a collector of fine art on velvet, and a burlesque stripper. And what had inspired him to climb the mountain solo in the first place? I opened his diary and flipped to a page at random:

> Dear Diary,
> Let me begin by saying that I have no idea how I've accomplished all that I have in my life, and if anybody knows what the hell inspired me to climb this wretched mountain solo in the first place, I'd love to hear it.
>
> Percy Brackett Elliott

I could only hope that unraveling the mystery would provide the backbone of my next best seller, kind of like I did with *The Shroud of the Thwacker* (except without me getting stranded forever in the distant past while my cloned double continued to live out my life in the present). I presumed this story would be less eventful, but presumptions are always just that—presumptions—although sometimes they can be postulations. And I suppose there's always the chance that they could be presuppositions, but usually presumptions are just that—presumptions. (Although for the purposes of this book, let's call them ass-sumptions.)

"Hey, Wendell, there's the Carpet Warehouse. We must be close!"

We pulled up to a dingy storefront. In the windows were faded cardboard cutouts of women in bikinis advertising suntan lotion.

I read the sign, perplexed: "Duncan Carter, Bail Bondsman and World Famous . . . Bounty Hunter?"

Wendell eyed the small print under the sign: "—and Mountain Maniacs, Inc."

"Oh, yeah, this is the place," I said, relieved.

A little bell over the door jingled as we went inside.

"Hello?" I called out. The décor screamed retro Katrina chic—water-stained cardboard boxes everywhere, garbage strewn across the floor, and wanted posters of unsavory types on the walls.

"Are you A-holes back already?" called a voice from somewhere in the rubble. "I told you I would have the money by Friday!"

I peered into a small, dirty bathroom, where a gangly man in torn jeans was boiling water on a hot plate on the back of the toilet.

"Umm, Mr. Carter?"

"Yeah, yeah yeah, look, I said I . . ." He pulled something steaming out of the pot with a pair of tongs and looked up at us. "Oh, sorry. I thought you were someone else."

His skin was worn, covered in pockmarks, wrinkles, and pleats, and his spaghetti-blond hair seemed oddly unnatural. He was wearing a "Free Tibet" baseball cap and a T-shirt that read, "I like to snatch kisses and vice versa."

"Yeti femur," he said, holding up a scalded bone with the tongs. "All that's left of him anyway. Pangboche: nineteen hundred and eighty-two. On a secret mission to bag a live specimen, but things went terribly wrong. The first attacks came at about four in the morning. Next day I crawled out of my bivouac over to my best friend, Herbie—miniature golfer, bosom's mate. I tapped him on the shoulder and he upended like a top. Yeti had gotten him from the waist down. I'll never put on a pair of snowshoes again. So seven men went into the mountains, one came out. The yetis took the rest, December second, nineteen hundred and eighty-two. Thank you, thank you very much. Nobody does Quint like me."

I swallowed hard. "So that's a real yeti femur, then?"

"No, A-hole, it's a ham bone," he said, regarding my dumb-founded expression with equally dumbfounded eyes. I didn't understand what the hell he was talking about.

"I'm making bean-and-bacon soup," he explained. Then he threw the bone back in the water and shook his head. "We got a live one," he mumbled.

"Oh, I see," I said, still not understanding.

Then Duncan stared at the wall for a second. He seemed to be off somewhere else.

"Um, sir?" But there was no response. I waved my hands in front of his eyes. "Sir!"

Wendell and I felt awkward and uncomfortable, and as we always do during such moments, we began to giggle. We tried to hold it in, but it burst out through our noses with simultaneous snorts. Suddenly, Mr. Carter sparked back to life.

"Sorry about that. I kind of space out sometimes. Bad case of altitude sickness in 'ninety-six. Name's Duncan Carter, Mountain Maniacs, Inc.," he pronounced, extending his hand in the overly formal way that teenagers do.

"Hi," I said, shaking his hand, "Chris Elliott, big-time actor . . . in the . . . acting . . . world, I guess you could say . . . if you were going to say something . . . or not."

"Yeah, man, cool. I recognize you from that dumb-ass movie you were in. You know, the one with the boat. What was the name of it?"

"*There's Something About Mary*?"

"No, that was the good one. What was the really stupid one?"

"I don't know," I said, "they're all kind of . . ."

"*Cabin Boy*," said Wendell.

"Yeah, that's it. Man, that was stupid. Stuuuuupid!"

I stood with a frozen smile on my face while Wendell and Duncan shared a hearty laugh. After he let go of my hand, Duncan loaded his palms with Purell and rubbed them vigorously.

"Nothing personal, just got a little germ phobia. And a teeny fear of heights."

"Mr. Carter," I began, "we came here for—"

"Yeah, yeah, yeah," he interrupted, "who you want me to track down?"

"In a way, I guess you could say I want you to help me track down . . ." I paused for dramatic effect ". . . myself. You see, I've just gone through a rather nasty divorce, and on top of that, my one-man show as Ethel Merman closed, so now I'm searching for that next big thing in my life—the big boom-ba, you know what I mean?"

"Nope."

Wendell jumped in. "He's been reading this dumb diary that his crazy uncle wrote and now he wants to climb Mount Everest—it's stupid!"

"Oh, a mysterious diary, how interesting. Fellas, if I had a nickel for every A-hole who came in here with their long-lost uncle's journal wanting me to help them go find his frozen body . . . not like climbing Everest is hard or anything." He sighed. "Well, let's take a look at it."

"It was sent to me *anonymously*," I bragged, handing him the diary. Duncan read out loud in a mocking voice:

Up early this morning. Left an offering of candied dung and fried leather at the Gumboo shrine. The hill men assure me that such a fine offering will secure me safe passage through the Langbu corridor. High hopes of finding a route to the summit today. If I make it to the top, I shall place the sacred Golden Rhombus back where it belongs, and then finally the "peoples" shall be tranquil, and all shall be right with the world.

His tone suddenly changed and he now seemed interested.

Maybe if I have the time, I'll take a couple of snapshots before climbing back down. Oh well, as the Tibetans say, Adios, amigos.

P.S. Lost my nose to frostbite last night. The wretched thing blew off like a rotten apple. I wonder who, if anyone, will ever find it. (Wouldn't it be funny if it were one of my descendants, climbing the peak to locate my frozen corpse! Ha!)

Percy Brackett Elliott
Everest
Dec. 1, 1924

"Percy?" Duncan's bloodshot eyes lit up. "Your uncle was Percy Brackett Elliott?"

Duncan began to flip through the diary madly.

"Is this some kind of joke?" he muttered, astonished. "This looks like it's actually the real thing."

"What's a Golden Rhombus—his butt?" Wendell asked.

"I don't know," I said. "Maybe back in nineteen twenty-four they replaced rotten butts with gold ones, just like teeth. What do you think, Mr. Carter?"

"Huh? What about your butts?"

"Look, we're sorry we bothered you, Mr. Carter," said Wendell. "My friend here is kind of like Lucy. He comes up with these hare-brained schemes from time to time. But he doesn't know the first thing about mountain climbing. We'll just be on our way and—"

"Hey, wait, not so fast," said Duncan, suddenly serious "So, you want to try to find his body, or what?"

Wendell was exasperated. "A second ago you just said—"

"Well, yeah," I interrupted. "I was kind of thinking that."

"Why?"

"Why? Um . . . 'cause . . . *tch tch tch* . . . um . . . cause he's . . . family?"

"That the only reason? I mean, there's no other reason you want to find him? No . . . hidden agenda or anything? Let me put it to you this way: You're not looking for anything specific . . . besides his body . . . like anything that might be small or shiny?"

"Well, no, of course not. Why?"

My answer seemed to excite him. "Oh, no reason. Just wondering. That's all." He closed the diary, took a deep breath, and walked to the display windows. "The Himalayas are beautiful this time of year, you know." He ran his fingers up and down the edge of the cardboard, bikini-clad cutouts. "Rolling hills, big mounds of rocks, craggy peaks. One doesn't just climb Everest, you know. One must make love to Everest."

Wendell rolled his eyes as Duncan continued, "The first time I made love to the mountain, I was merely a lad, not much older than you are now. How old are you?"

"Forty-five."

"Oh, well then, I was considerably younger. But the point is, 'Once you go schist, you never . . . um . . . ah . . . you . . . never . . . res-ist!' That's it! It's like another planet up there. You're on top of the world. The thrill of adventure, the lust for glory. Few are lucky enough to seek it. Your uncle was one of the few."

Wendell turned to me. "Oh, come on, Chris, you're not really going to do this. Mr. Carter, you don't seriously think he's going to climb Mount Everest? He gets winded when he takes a shower."

"That's why I hardly ever take 'em." At that Wendell and I gave each other high fives.

"Oh, he'll be fine. It's much easier these days, with all that new Gore-Tex stuff." Duncan riffled through mounds of papers. "Okay, we got the standard release forms that you'll need to sign, and then there's the matter of the fee, and we'll have to get equipment ordered right away if we're talking about a fall expedition, and . . ." He stopped and looked out the windows. "Um . . . were you guys followed, by any chance?"

"No," I said. "I can't even get people to return my calls."

Duncan continued to shuffle through the mess on his desk. "So, as I was saying, I'll need a down payment, and then—"

"How much is all of this going to cost?" I asked meekly.

Duncan looked back and forth between Wendell and me. "How much you got?" Then he laughed. "Just joshing. But seriously, you're in the movies, right?" He took a scrap of paper and wrote a figure, then mumbled to himself something about interest and loan sharks and burial fees, crossed it out and wrote a larger figure. Wendell and I gasped.

"Sixty thousand dollars?" I said.

"That's ridiculous," said Wendell. "You could buy Mount Everest for less than that!"

"There is no way I can get my hands on that kind of bling-blang-walla-walla-bing-bang!"

"I smell a shoot-the-bull, Chris. This guy's just trying to rip you off!"

"Look, boys, there's a lot of expenses with climbing Everest. You gotta pay for yaks and Sherpas and food and equipment—I swear, I'm a straight shooter!"

Suddenly a car alarm went off outside and Duncan crouched down, aiming a large canister of pepper spray at the door. After a moment he stood up, looked at us sheepishly, and added, "Sorry, fellas. You, uh . . . never know when uh . . . an angry ex-con is going to come gunning for you."

I searched my pockets and Wendell reluctantly searched his. We pulled together about twenty-three dollars and a couple of Oreos. I

"Nobody does Quint like me."

felt like a failure. "I'm sorry, Mr. Carter. I don't think I'll be able to afford it."

Duncan leaned back in his chair with his hands behind his head. "Well, you're famous, uh . . . sort of, right? Why don't you hit up some of your rich celebrity friends?"

Wendell snorted and I chuckled nervously.

"Well, see, I don't really have too many celebrity friends, per se. For the most part they're all just jealous of me . . . on account of all of my unrealized potential, dontcha know?"

Carter stood up. "Listen, the window of opportunity for a fall attempt on Everest is closing real fast. You don't want to get stuck up there in a freak storm or an avalanche or anything. If we're gonna go, we godda go like yesterday. I'll give you forty-eight hours to come up with the cash—otherwise you're gonna have to wait till next year, and I can't guarantee I'll still be in the business." He looked over his shoulder. "Now do me a favor and wait until I'm in the bathroom with the door shut and locked before you leave. And if anybody asks you, you came inside and nobody was home. Or better yet—I was dead."

It was quiet in Wendell's cab as we drove back to Brooklyn. I couldn't wait a whole year to go to Everest! This was the kind of decision you have to make on the spur of the moment, or else you run the risk of reconsidering.

Wendell eyed me in his rearview mirror. "So what now, Lucy?"

CHAPTER THREE

We were still tucking in our shirts and straightening our ties when we arrived at the Jacob Javits Center on Thirty-fourth Street. Rushing in, I paused briefly to buy a raffle ticket for Larry David's Prius, and then we hurried over to the main exhibition hall.

A giant banner hung from the ceiling welcoming guests to the third annual Global Warming Summit and Boomps-A-Daisy Dance Off.

"This is it, Wendell," I said, "the movers and shakers, the people who make this world go 'round. You show them respect, and they'll respect you back. Unless you're obviously on your way out or, like, not a Scientologist or something."

"I can't believe you got invited to this," he said. "I thought you were banned from here ever since you got drunk and took that Hummer Sea-Doo™ for a joyride through the dancing waters at the boat show."

"Well, it all depends on how you define *invited.* If by *invited* you mean 'received a gilded invitation in the mail,' then no, I wasn't invited. But on the other hand, if you mean 'swiped an invitation off the desk of one's local AFTRA representative, after one made her go searching for the files pertaining to one's delinquent dues payments,' then yes, I was clearly invited. Now who should we hit up first?"

The place was jammed with movie stars, writers, celebrities, politicians, and reality-show freaks. In the center of the room, tuxedoed UN dignitaries stood with cocktails in hand, rubbing elbows with glamorous Hollywood types. On the outer rim, lesser-known celebrities (mostly voice-over actors and soap-opera stars) sat on folding chairs like freshmen waiting for that special someone to ask them to dance. The round dining tables were adorned with 'environmentally friendly' centerpieces (called flowers), while PR people in convention booths represented every country and concern in the world.

The band had just finished a rousing rendition of "Enjoy Yourself, It's Later Than You Think," and now Al Gore was taking the stage. He was obviously blotto, and he began babbling on and on about saving the world from utter destruction or some such nonsense.

"Look, people, I'm serious," he yelled, spitting into the microphone, "WE'RE ALL GOING TO DIE. Like, SOON."

"And you're sure *you know who* is supposed to be here?" Wendell asked, scanning the glitzy rabble. "I don't see her."

"A bit anxious, are we? I think maybe someone's got a cru-*ush*!"

"No, I just happen to be a fan of her work. And her, uh, politics. She's very active in the PETA organization, you know. She once spent a week chained to a raccoon. How can you not admire that?"

"The only thing you admire is her hot little bod."

"Just promise not to embarrass me. And stick close. I'll need you to introduce—"

"Regis!" I called out.

"—me to her," he finished, but I was already on my way to the buffet table, where Regis was having his ear talked off by Kofi Annan. I pried him away.

"Looked like you needed a little rescuing there, am I right?"

"Well, actually no, I was quite interested in what the former sec-retary-general was saying. Now if you'll excuse me—"

"Hey, don't you recognize me? Chris Elliott! I did your show once in the mid-eighties and was never asked back, remember?"

"Right, now I remember. That was the one we couldn't air because of all the racial slurs."

"Right, right. That was me!"

"Sure. So, what are you up to now, Cliff?"

"Well, as a matter of fact, I'm mounting an expedition to the Hi-malayas and I was wondering if you'd like to come along. See if I can get—"

"Jeez, that's great. Good luck with that." And then he sidestepped quickly away and jumped into a photo op with Katie Couric and Kreskin in front of the Serbia/Montenegro booth.

Wendell sidled up to the buffet. "Well, that went well."

"He must have had his hearing aid turned off."

"Hey, isn't that your old boss by the punch bowl?"

"Oh, yeah. Hey, Dave!"

"You believe these weasels?" Dave mumbled, spiking the punch with Night Train. "Imagine having to talk to them day in, day out. Welcome to my life, buddy."

"Dave, this is my friend Wendell."

"Ah huh. Where you from, Wendell?"

"Um, New York City."

"Ah huh, and what do you do for a living?"

"Oh, ah, I'm a cab driver."

"Oh, a cab driver? Well, that must be pretty exciting?"

"It's all right."

"Yeah, yeah, now let me ask you something: Being a New York City cab driver, do you ever just, you know, just give your horn a good honk?"

Wendell looked embarrassed. "Well—"

"You know, just a good 'honk'? You really like to sit on it, don't you? You just like to sit on the damn thing, don't you? And give it one of these: HONK!"

Wendell laughed. "Well, yeah, I do."

"That's what I thought. Well, that's great. Nice talking to you, Wendell. Thanks for coming by." And he walked off.

"Dave, wait, I wanted to talk to you about a really exciting opportunity!"

"I don't have the time right now, buddy. I just came for the clams." And with that he was gone.

"Jeez. After all the times I saved that guy's show with my insanely brilliant writing . . . ."

"Chris, I don't think this is working out," Wendell said. "Can we at least go look for—"

"What about those drag queens over there?" I pointed at the booth marked Campaign for a Free Tibet, where two guys gussied up in orange dresses stood behind a table full of pamphlets.

"Those are monks, Chris. They're holy men."

"Wow, I've never heard that one before, but don't worry about me. I'm fairly secure with my sexuality—pretty much. They won't turn me."

Wendell ditched me as I approached the monks. "Hey, how ya doing, fellas? Long way from Greenwich Village, aren't ya?" And then I laughed like a hyena (a spotted hyena, actually).

They clasped their hands together and bowed.

"You know, fellas, every now and then in a man's life, even in a gay man's life, he's faced with a crossroads. Does he go left? Or does he go right? Or—and this is very important—does he go *up*?"

The two "monks" nodded their heads sympathetically, but obviously had no idea what the hell I was talking about.

"Okay, look, I'll be straight with ya—pardon my French—my

name is Chris Elliott, and I'm trying to get some people to climb Mount Everest with me. You see, I had this great-uncle, a guy named Percy, and—"

"What did you just say?" asked the taller of the two.

I sighed. "I said, 'Hey, how ya doing, fellas? Long way from Greenwich Village, aren't ya?' And then I laughed like a hyena, a spotted hyena, actually, and—"

"No, no, about your uncle."

"Oh, I had this uncle Percy—"

"Percy Elliott?" asked the shorter one.

"Yes, and you see—"

"Percy Brackett Elliott?"

"Yeah, that's right," I said, a little surprised at what a popular guy my uncle was turning out to be.

"You are Percy Elliott's great-nephew?"

"But of course he is," said the smaller of the two. "The resemblance is amazing!"

"What's it to you two?"

"Nothing, nothing," said the taller monk excitedly. "You will excuse us please." And they rushed off, leaving a sign out on their table that read:

GONE FISHIN' (FOR THE ENLIGHTENMENT OF ALL BEINGS)

"Jeez, who peed in their Post Toasties?"

On stage, Al Gore was being led off in tears. The emcee (a cloned hybrid of Billy Crystal, Whoopi Goldberg, and Robin Williams that Monsanto, Inc., rents out for these sorts of gigs) took the microphone.

"Big hand for Al, folks. Thanks for the heads-up on that end-of-the-world thing. Next up we've got someone with a brighter view of the future—probably because he's not nearly as good at math." The hybrid smiled in a terrifyingly inoffensive way. "So, in case you're looking at this crazy, messed-up world and wondering, Who's the boss? I'll tell you who's the boss. This next guy's the boss, that's who!"

The crowd chanted "Bruuuce!"

"No, no, no," said the hybrid. "Not Brussssss, you idiots. Tony! Tony, come on out here!"

The former sitcom star made his way to the center of the stage.

"Heyaz folks. Thanks for the ovations. Wow, what a thrills it is to be heres. Ain't it beautifuls? And all for a worthys cause, too— dats what it's alls about, rights? The first time I heards about global warmings I said, 'dis ting is gonna come back to bite us all in the asses,' and I was rights! It bit us all in da asses, just like TiVo bits us all in the asses with da residuals, rights?" There was a smattering of applause, and for some reason Kofi Annan laughed out loud.

"TiVo!" Kofi said, shaking his head. "You tell it, brother!"

I retreated to the men's room. Standing at the porcelain urinal, I could hear Tony up onstage, singing "My Way," and the lyrics seemed especially apropos.

> *Yes, there were times, I'm sure you knews*
> *When I bits off, mores than I could chews*

What was I thinking? How could I convince a bunch of celebrities to climb Mount Everest with me? It was never going to work. I had definitely bitten off way more than I could 'chews.' "I'm just a big, fat failure," I mumbled. "Failure, failure, failure." I started to bang my head against the wall. After about ten bangs, I was interrupted by a deep, gravelly voice.

"Pitiful stream, son. You should get your prostate checked."

I whipped around and splashed all over my trousers.

"Lauren!" I shouted.

"It's been a long time, blue eyes."

"What the hell are you doing here?"

"Well, you know, I do still get invited to the occasional fête."

"No, I meant here, here!"

"I saw you come in."

"Yeah, but it's the *men's* room."

"So?" she was leaning her shoulder up against the tile wall, sipping a Booker Noe's and eyeing me up and down.

"So . . . that means it's just for men, not women."

"Oh, that's a bunch of malarkey. I've never played by the rules and I don't plan on starting now. You know me." She downed her bourbon and hurled the glass against the far wall, smashing it into a thousand pieces. "Just let 'em try to kick me out. 'Men's room.' Ha! the question is what are *you* doing here? I didn't realize you were interested in global warming."

"Well, I'm not really. I'm just . . . well, I had this uncle who climbed this mountain, and I thought if I could go find his frozen corpse, that it might, you know . . . well, make me a better person? No, that's not it, um . . . what I mean is, it might . . . be cool? No, um . . . well, it's like, um . . . ."

"Still looking for that 'something' in life, aren't you?" she said, shaking her head.

"I guess so," I muttered, and I started to cry. "Oh, you always did know how to get to me. Didn't you?"

"It ain't that hard, kid."

I had first met Lauren—or Betty to her friends—many years before in a summer-stock production of *Kiss Me, Kate*. She may not have been quite the star she used to be, but she was still a fiery dame. She was wild, to say the least, and that was one crazy summer, let me tell you—a summer I'll never forget. It was actually Lauren who had given me my third elbow, after a painful arm-wrestling match one night after the show. I assumed she had the hots for me—

especially the night she broke my arm—but whether she did or didn't, she always made me feel a bit unbalanced.

"Now, finish up and stop crying," she commanded. "I know what you're up to and we have to talk."

I hurriedly shook the dew off the old lily pad, zipped up and flushed. As I moved to the sink I could feel her piercing movie-star eyes burning holes in the back of my head, the small of my back—and the nape of my ass.

"So, I hear you're looking for some suckers to go mountain climbing with you, is that it?"

"Uh, yeah . . . I don't suppose you'd want to come along, would you?"

"Climb Mount Everest? Old dame like me?"

"Yeah, sorry. Bad idea. I guess I'm desperate."

"Desperate? Oh, well, thank you very much."

"I didn't mean it that way . . . I just . . . oh, forget it."

I was rubbing my hands together beneath the cold running water, keenly aware of Lauren gliding up beside me. I turned off the faucet, smiled awkwardly and dried my hands.

"Let me tell you something, kid. You've got guts," she said, wetting the tip of her long index finger with her tongue and then flattening some flyaway wisps on the top of my head. She took a long drag off her cig, then stamped it out and straightened my collar. "You always reminded me of Bogie." She put her craggy hands on my shoulders and turned me toward the mirror. "You have his strong chin and his faraway eyes"—I jutted my chin out and squinted my eyes—"his gruff but lovable demeanor"—I made my best "gruff but lovable" expression—"and his unbridled, masculine sensuality"—I lowered one eyebrow, curled my upper lip, and made a "come hither" look to beat all "come hither" looks. Then I growled like a wild tiger.

"But what you don't have is his smarts," she said, abruptly pulling away to check her makeup in the mirror.

"What do you mean?"

"You've got all the finesse of a lead balloon."

"I don't understand."

"You're dumb, kid. As in *stupid*."

"I'm still not following you."

"Think about it," she said, applying bright crimson lipstick. "What do us celebrities care the most about?"

"Tax exemptions?"

"No, you twit. Ourselves. I've been watching you tonight. Every time you open your mouth, out comes a reason why *you* want to climb that damn mountain. You never talk about why the mountain is *worth climbing*. You've got to make this adventure seem so hot, so majestic, so 'it' that they'll do anything to get some of that glitz to rub off on them. I mean, this is Mount Everest, for crying out loud, right? Who wouldn't want to climb it?"

"You're sounding interested."

"As I said, I don't like to play by the rules, but even for a tough old broad like myself it seems rather daunting. But then again, dreams are meant to be pursued. And when you're out of dreams, you settle for whims. And when you're out of whims, you drink until you get one. Bogie taught me that, among other things . . ." She seemed far away for a moment, then she snapped back. "All I know is that ever since we starred in *Kiss Me, Kate*, I've seen a fire inside you—a fire that I would hate to see extinguished simply because you can't come up with some cash."

"You knew that's all I really wanted, huh?"

She smiled slyly. "How's the old elbow?"

"All three of them are fine." I lifted my arm and showed her.

"Now, think! What would make it irresistibly enticing to our celebrity friends?"

"Hmm," I paced back and forth, rubbing my chin. "Celebrities, enticing . . . celebrities, enticing . . . celebriticing . . ."

Suddenly the door to the men's room swung open.

"Out of order, use the ladies' john!" she barked, and slammed the door in whomever's face.

"I just don't know," I said, and that helpless, impotent feeling that I used to get in math class and when I was in bed with Vera started to seep back in.

"Think! Why are we all here tonight?"

I started to have an idea, and as I always do when I begin to get an idea, I started to shake uncontrollably. (The doctor says it's because the tubes in my brain are too small for big thoughts to get through.) "Is it . . . publicity?" I asked, quivering.

"Smart boy! It took you long enough," she said. "Now, stop shaking."

"Sorry."

"Mint?"

"No thank you, I'm in training."

"And what manner of publicity do well-meaning, high-profile personalities find simply irresistible?"

Again I thought for a moment. *Manner of publicity . . . manner of publicity . . . ?* Suddenly it hit me like a ton of bricks. "A cause!" I blurted out, and I snapped my fingers. "That's it. They need a cause—just like this whole global-warming racket."

"Exactly," she said.

"I have to convince them it's all for a worthy cause!"

"See, that wasn't so hard, was it?"

"Betty, I don't know how to thank you."

"Don't worry. I'm sure we'll think of something." She winked and laughed lasciviously.

I didn't like the sound of her laugh, but I gave her a hug nonetheless. "And you are coming, aren't you? Tell me you're coming. I can't do it without your share of the—I mean without you there by my side."

"My dear child, I'm eighty-two years old, I've lived through the old Hollywood studio system, World War II, and the advent of that ungodly *American Idol*—whoever came up with that abomination should be shot out of a Howitzer. I think perhaps I can handle the tallest mountain in the world. Besides . . ." She cracked her knuckles for several minutes, until I began to get sleepy. "God knows I could use the publicity myself. Now let's find us some suckers."

Out on the dance floor, there was still a little Boomps-A-Daisying going on, but generally the event was winding down. Lauren and I surveyed the slim pickings left in the crowd.

I saw her glance over at the Tibet booth, which, in the absence of the monks, was now being manned by Richard Gere.

"Don't even think about it," I said. "That huge forehead of his gives me the creeps."

"You seem a little picky for a person who's so 'desperate.'"

"I just want to put the right group of people together. I would hate to have to send someone home because they're not working out. That would just be too uncomfortable."

Wendell stormed up to us, obviously pissed off.

"That's it. I'm out of here. I finally found *you know who* and I just spent five minutes telling her about my passion for PETA-related issues, and the whole time she was just ogling that Tony guy, and then when she finally did notice me she said—and I quote—'Do you people have any more of those vegan paté hors d'oeuvres?'"

"Well . . . maybe she just thought you would have noticed?"

"And then she said she'd had a lovely time and told me to pass the word on to the rest of the waiters."

"Oh, okay, well, then she probably thought you were a waiter. But maybe she thought you were the headwaiter. That would be good."

"Well, I gave her a piece of my mind, that's for sure."

"What did you say?"

"I told her *Spider Man* was a baby movie with unsettling racist subtexts, and she ran off crying. I hate your celebrity friends."

"Wendell, I'd like you to meet Lauren, one of my actual celebrity friends."

"Hey, you're the one who slammed the bathroom door in my face!"

But Lauren didn't even acknowledge him. Instead she was eyeing Tony, who was walking toward us eating some pasta off a paper plate. "Now here's someone whose strength and stamina could be helpful."

She shoved me right in front of him.

"Tony, you know Chris Elliott, right?"

"Oh yeahs, what's up, Chrissys babys?"

"He has something he wants to ask you."

"Well, uh"—Lauren stuck a bony elbow in my ribs—"Ow. Uh, Tony, it's like this, we're gonna climb Mount Everest and I was wondering if you would like to come along? We could all die, and it's gonna cost you a pile of money, but I think it really could be a blast."

"Jeez. I don't know if I can, Chrissys babys. I gots a lot of banquets lined up."

"Oh, okay. Well, sorry to have—"

Lauren jumped in again, "I understand that you're the spokesperson for the national Wheat Growers Alliance, is that true?"

"Yeah, well, sees, we're all for the wheat, cause you grinds it into meal and mix it with water to makes the dough and that makes the pastas—and I'm campaigning to get people to make their own pasta at homes instead of that's storebought crap, 'cause you see, uh . . . yeah."

"Well, there you go," I said. "This would be a great way to draw attention to your cause."

"Jeez, you may be rights." Tony's wheels started turning. "Butz, uh, how, exactly?"

Lauren and I looked at each other.

"Because . . ." she said.

"Uh, because," I said, "there's going to be . . . a great big . . . pasta-eating contest. On the summit. If you win, you'll end up in the *Guinness Book*."

I was very proud of myself, but Lauren only sighed and shook her head.

"Reallyz?" said Tony. "Well, I'm inzies. Pudder dere!"

We shook on it, and then stood staring at each other uncomfortably.

"Who else are we gonna sucker in?" I whispered to Lauren, but Tony heard me, so I quickly corrected myself, "I mean, uh, encourage to join us on this entirely well-thought-out adventure."

"Hey. I know somebodys else. She's the most beautifuls, most generous persons in the whole wide worlds—I mean, she's just a casual-type friend'n everythin', but I bet she'd want to comes too. She's around heres somewherez." He pulled out his cell phone and punched in some numbers.

I whispered to Lauren, "It dosesn't sound like she's just a 'casual-type friend' to me."

Tony hung up and turned back, all excited. "She's lefts. Some goofy waiter got her all upsets. I'd likes to gets my hands on that creep, what's it."

Wendell was just walking up, spinning his cab keys on his finger, and hearing this, he ducked behind me.

"She's went to her farm upstate," Tony continued. "Hey, you know whats? It's only about an hours up the Taconics. Why don't we go up theres tomorrows and asks her? You guys games?"

Wendell whispered, "I think this guy's had one too many vodka Taconics."

"Yes, all three of us are game, Tony," I said, throwing my arms around Lauren and Wendell. "Tomorrow it is."

Lauren took out a fiver and slipped it to Wendell. "Be a dove and bring my car around will you, dear? Oh, and please inform the rest of the waitstaff that it was a lovely evening." Then to me, she said, "Shall I give you a lift home?"

"No, that's okay." I said. "I already have a cab waiting." And I winked at Wendell, who just grunted like a big old bear.

At that moment, deep in the bowels of the New York Public Library, a small desk lamp illuminated a cramped room. The smaller monk from the global-warming summit, whose name was Pong, stood on a ladder, running his finger along the spines of some dusty old volumes. After a moment he exclaimed, "I find it! Here it is!"

He pulled a large book off the shelf. Stepping down, he blew the dust off its cover—straight into the taller monk's face (whose name was Ping). The taller monk just stood there expressionless.

"What's wrong?" asked the smaller monk.

"Let me have that!" He sat at a table and opened it: "*Ghosts of Everest.*"

"Look in index," said the smaller monk eagerly.

"I know how to look something up . . . okay . . . page sixty-four, let's see." He scanned the page. "Nothing here . . . Oh, here it is. Oh, no."

"So it is not him, then?" There was a long pause. "Is it him or not?"

"It could be."

"What you mean 'could be?' Let me see it." The smaller monk went for the book, but the taller monk held it back.

"Listen, Pong, we could just put the book back on the shelf and walk away. We have very nice life here in America—baseball, hot dogs, HBO. You too young to remember, but nothing in the Land

"You remind me of Bogie."

of Snows but yaks and tourists. Are you willing to say good-bye to what we have forever?"

"I am willing to do all that the ocean of wisdom commands—whatever sacrifices that may entail. Are you willing, my brother, or have you decided that you are no longer worthy?"

"I'm just saying, is all."

The taller monk looked at his old friend, and then, giving up, he smiled sweetly and pushed the book over to him. The smaller monk adjusted his glasses and looked closely at the photo on the page. Then he gasped.

"The Rhombus has been reborn."

"Yes." The taller monk sighed. "I know."

The two left quickly, leaving *Ghosts of Everest* open to a chapter titled "Imbecile Attempts 1924 Solo Climb." Below the headline was a photo of Percy Brackett Elliott grinning a toothless smile and standing in front of an old single-engine biplane. He was holding his diary in one hand and a pair of inflatable underpants in the other.

CHAPTER FOUR

The next day, Wendell's cab again conveyed us across the GW, and once again I sat in the backseat, only this time I was flanked by Lauren and Tony. "Watch your speed, cabby," I instructed in a terrible English accent. "We wish to get there in one piece, yes?" Then I giggled like a hyena (a striped one with a gimpy leg who deep down inside wished he were a gazelle).

We drove up Route 87 for about an hour, until Tony finally said, "Yooz makes a rights right heres."

Wendell turned onto a dirt driveway and we passed beneath a large wooden sign that read ANIMAL CARE CLINIC. We went around a single-story farmhouse, past the formal entrance, and up to a side door with a ramp marked EMERGENCY.

"I'll wait in the cab," Wendell muttered.

"But don't you want to see—" I began.

"No."

"But you've got such a crush on—"

"No."

"And now she'll see that you're not a lowly waiter at all, but a lowly—"

"Shut . . . just *shut*, will ya."

"Sheesh. For a guy who drives people around for a living, you're being really surly."

An assistant greeted us at the door holding a cute little raccoon in her arms. On closer inspection, I saw that the raccoon had a patch over one eye.

"Oh, hi. You can go right on through. She's out back and she's been expecting you."

We went through a set of sliders into the backyard and stopped short at the sight that greeted us: There were literally thousands of animals scurrying and hopping about, and where they weren't running free, they were in large warrens marked ICU. In the middle of the lawn, across a veritable minefield of woodland creatures, was a gazebo, where, having her picture taken, was none other than our friend Kirsten.

Kirsten was one of Hollywood's hottest commodities, but to her credit she'd never let it go to her head. She was sweet and sincere in the wholesomest of ways, so much so that her school friends had nicknamed her "Sweet and sincere Kirsten, the wholesome one!" and voted her "Most Likely to One Day Be Internationally Renowned for Her Wholesomeness." In recent years she had been romantically (but wholesomely) linked with just about every leading man in Hollywood. In fact, *People* magazine even suggested that she had something to do with Vera's and my breakup—or at least I assumed that's what they meant when they wrote in a recent issue: "Hey, remember Chris Elliott? No, he didn't blow his head off! He was spotted eating out of a Dumpster behind the CPK on La Boheema." (I hate the way the rag magazines always talk in code.)

Lauren gasped. "Oh, my God, every one of them is deformed. It's hideous."

She was right. All the animals had some sort of problem. Some were missing legs, others eyes, and some were even more freakish: There were bunnies with rat tails, rats with bunny tails, and one horribly obese squirrel that must have weighed at least three hundred pounds.

"It looks like a scene right out of *Night of the Living Dead*," I said, "except with zombie animals instead of your standard zombie human beings. Note to self: Pitch *Night of the Living Dead Animals* idea to Weinstein bros. Maybe I could be the voice of the little, deformed seagull?"

Tony sighed with admiration. "Isn'tz shez greats? She doz so much promotional work for PETAs. Whatz an angel!" And with that he began to stride across the lawn.

Lauren and I tiptoed after him, being extra careful not to step on anything. It may have been my imagination, but it seemed like all the animals stopped and stared at us.

"That's perfect, Kirsten! Now hold up little Cotangus and make a sad face," directed the photographer.

Kirsten pouted and held up a bunny that had a big iron ring through its nose.

"Isn't it terrible?" she said, as we entered the gazebo. "Someone mated a cotton tail with an Angus bull, and this is what they got. His name's Little Cotangus. Get it? You put cotton and Angus together and you get Cotangus!" Then she giggled. "Isn't that cute?"

"Wowz, that's smarts. Whoze came up with that?"

Kirsten smiled coyly at Tony. "Oh, just little old me." Then she giggled and Tony winked at her, and then she crinkled her nose at him and then he blew her a kiss, and then bile rose in the back of my throat as I made involuntary retching noises.

"That will be all for today, thank you," she told the photographer.

Her assistant arrived with a tray of pink ladies.

"So now," Kirsten began, "Tony gave me the broad strokes of . . . is that right? 'Broad strokes?' It sounds so weird."

"No, that's absolutely correct, my child," said Lauren, pinching my arm nearly hard enough to make a fourth elbow.

"He says you're gonna climb some big mountain or something?"

"Yes, and we'd love for you to join us," I said. "We're going to climb Mount Everest."

"At Disney World?"

"No, no. Um . . . the Mount Everest that's actually in the Himalayas."

"Oh, right, where the Matterhorn is. Oh, look, here's Mr. Nubs," she bent down and picked up a legless porcupine and shoved it in my face. "Give Mr. Nubs a kiss! Come on, give Mr. Nubs his kissies!" I reluctantly kissed the spiky animal, and then Lauren pulled out several needles that had stuck to my lips.

We wandered up to a wire-mesh fence that corralled at least a hundred snarling, growling rabbits. Upon seeing Kirsten, they immediately hopped to the edge and gathered close to her.

She leaned down and opened a Rubbermaid container full of smelly raw chicken, pulled out a big hunk and threw it into the pen. The ravenous rabbits converged on the stinking poultry and ripped it to shreds.

"So, you're just gonna climb the thing and then what?"

"Well, maybe we'll learn a little something about ourselves, and once we're at the top, we could, uh . . . take a couple of snapshots . . . or something."

"Mmm . . . I don't know, sounds kind of . . . what's the word? Oh yeah, *silly*. Hey, here's little Ray Charles." She picked up a blind bunny and gave it a kiss. "Guys, I don't think I can take the time to climb an Everest right now."

"Oh, it won't take much time," interjected Lauren, "just a day or two. Besides, it's not '*silly*' my dear—anything but. You see, it's to raise awareness about the horrors of animal testing . . . on bunnies."

"It iz?" asked Tony. "I taught it was for the pasta?"

"Yeah, it's for both, didn't I tell you?" said Lauren, swirling her pink lady. "Does anyone have a smoke? I'm out."

"I hate animal testing," said Kirsten, squeezing little Ray Charles as she spoke. "I hate the way they strap them down and stick them with all those pointy, needle things." She was squeezing the bunny tighter and tighter as she spoke. "I just hate! hate! hate! animal testing!" At this point Ray Charles was squealing.

"But what's dooz the animals and the wheat growers haves in commons?" Tony asked, scratching his head.

Lauren huffed, "Don't you get it, guy? If people eat more home-made pasta, they have more energy to protest in front of the animal-testing labs."

"Oh, nowz I seez its."

"Shhhh everybody. Charley's gone sleepy time." Kirsten shoved the now lifeless, blind rabbit in my face. "Give Charley his nightie-night kisses."

This time I was really reluctant, but Kirsten's eyes narrowed.

"I said give . . . Charley . . . his nightie-night kisses!"

I closed my eyes, puckered up, and kissed the dead rabbit.

"So, uh, what do you say, Kirsten, are you game?"

"Well. . . . since it's for a worthy cause, and because I'll get a lot of exposure when the movie is released . . . I guess you . . . could say that . . . I'm in!"

We all cheered and Kirsten tossed the dead bunny over her shoulder into the pen, where the other rabbits pounced on it.

Tony did his best to hide his glee.

"That's just great!" I said. "But what do you mean by movie?"

"Well, it's going to be filmed, of course, right?"

"Well, actually, we haven't—"

"Of course it's going to be filmed," interrupted Lauren. "You can't go on a historic adventure like this without documenting it, now, can you?"

We had another round of drinks to celebrate and then worked out the money situation. It turned out that Kirsten was loaded and had enough to almost cover the whole expedition. Lauren and I were delighted, and as it was getting late, we thought we should head out, although Tony said he was going to stay behind and help Kirsten "feeds her cool zoos."

As we walked back to Wendell's cab, I whispered to Lauren, "How are we going to film the climb? We don't have a director."

"Never fear. I have just the guy for the job—and he happens to owe me a favor."

CHAPTER FIVE

The next day Lauren and I took a train to Michigan.

I was a bit skeptical about her choice of director. He had made some good movies, sure (at least I'd heard), but he wasn't exactly in the best of shape, and his weight could prove problematic on the mountain. But, as Lauren pointed out, it wasn't like I was going to have to carry him or anything.

We were invited to meet him at his new restaurant, and I was eager to sample the cuisine. He had opened it in hopes of bringing a little culture to his depressed hometown, but unfortunately, Bowling for Beluga, specializing in *foie gras* burgers and rare white truffles, turned out to be a bit more *chichi*—not to mention expensive—than Flint was accustomed to.

Our train pulled into town, and Lauren and I proceeded to walk through a bewildering hodgepodge of glum neighborhoods. From dusty windows above, spectral faces with hollow eyes peered through broken glass or pulled their shades down as we passed. A lone drunk lay unconscious in front of the old Piggly Wiggly, and somewhere in the distance two vicious junkyard dogs were having a go at it. Flint had been like this ever since GM shut down its plants, and my heart went out to its inhabitants. My mind raced with notions of mounting a big concert to save the community, but then we came to the restaurant and I got all giddy.

It was dark, with red velvet walls and elegantly set tables with flickering candles. The bartender motioned us through a set of velvet curtains and into another room, where a large man was enjoying a late-afternoon lunch. He beckoned us to join him.

"Smile," he said, holding up his video camera.

"Oh, for Christ's sake, Michael, put that damn thing down," said Lauren. "We've been on a train for five hours, and I don't have my face on."

"Take a seat!" he hailed, his boyish bangs peering out from under a baseball cap that read, "When Clinton lied, all that happened was his wife got really mad and made him sleep in the Lincoln bedroom, but when Bush lied, Powell quit, Katrina hit, and Rumsfeld . . . took a . . . um . . . shit . . . I guess. IMPEACH BUSH NOW!!!!!!!!"

"Can I get you two anything?" he asked generously.

"Well," I began, "where I come from, those froi groi burgers are all the talk, plus those . . ."

"Oh, right, you probably ate on the train."

He scooped the last spoonful of something exotic into his mouth and pushed his bowl aside.

"The famous white truffles?"

"These? Hell no, just a bowl of baked beans. The truffles are for paying customers. So what can I do for you two? You said it was important on the phone."

"That's right," Lauren began. "Chris has a very interesting idea. Chris?"

I made a show of clearing my throat. "Ah, I'm kind of dry—do you think I could get one of your famous Remy martinis?" and I winked.

"You know what the best thing for a dry throat is? A nice, tall glass of Flint tap water." He snapped his fingers and a waiter brought me a glass of yellowish liquid. I was getting the idea that Michael wasn't much into comping.

"Well, here's the deal," I said. "A bunch of us celebrities are going to climb Mount Everest, and we'd like you to come along and film the whole thing."

His reaction was quick and visceral. "Did you say climb Mount Everest? Haven't you ever seen those documentaries about the idiots who climb Mount Everest? They always come back missing a nose or toes or something something. I got enough worries with my hyperuricemia."

"Gout," explained Lauren.

"Besides, I don't quite see the populist angle."

"Well, it's simple," I began. "Celebrities fed up with big corporate monopolies—like General Motors, Halliburton, and Popeil—risk life and limb to climb the tallest mountain in the world— just to draw attention to their worthy causes. It's the story of liberal compassion triumphing over conservative ideology. It has everything: adventure, selflessness, and love." I snickered to myself. How could anyone buy this baloney? Pasta contests are one thing, but love and sacrifice?

"Besides," said Lauren, "remember, you owe me."

"I 'owe you'?"

"Democratic National Convention? Fleet Center? Third floor? . . . Back stairwell? . . . Spirit gum?"

Michael smiled wistfully. "That was a long time ago."

Lauren smiled back. "But it seems just like yesterday, doesn't it?" She reached across the table and took his hand. "You know, you still remind me a little of Bogie, around the eyes. Now there was a man who wasn't afraid to take a chance."

Michael thought for a moment. "Wait a second. Wait just a second." His brain began to percolate. "I think I see what you're saying. I'm feeling a title: *Famous People . . . on . . . Mount Everest!*"

"I love it," I said, "It's like *Snakes on a Plane*! Or cheese on a cracker!"

"You know what, this is big. This is not just a movie, this is a giant movie—this is an . . . IMAX movie! Just think of it, *F.P.O.M.E.: Hearts Too Big for the Big Screen*. And as the first IMAX filmmaker on Everest, I'd be legendary, which, uh, would be good for the cause."

"Well, actually, I think somebody already—" Lauren stamped on my foot under the table. "Ow!"

"What are the worthy causes?" Michael asked.

"Well, so far, it's just bunnies and pasta, but—"

"Perfect! This is what my work has been needing all along. Like me, my films deserve to be viewed in magnificent grandeur." He raised his fist. "With IMAX, my radical political perspectives will be too big to be ignored. The world will cower before my over-whelming compassion. Children will weep in the streets for fear of violating the social contract that binds us to one another in mu-tual care and support. Yes! And this young working-class kid from Flint will finally drink the blood of his enemies!" He slammed his fist down. "Guys, you got yourselves a director!"

"Wonderful!" Lauren said, and we all shook hands.

"We must celebrate!" Michael snapped his fingers and a waiter brought over a gold-rimmed mirror and some caviar. He took out a hundred-dollar bill and began to roll it into a tube.

"Now," I began, "on the issue of money . . ."

"Money's no object, my friend. I'd do this one for free. I'll just need the cost of equipment up front."

"Well, actually . . . you see, it kind of costs money to climb Mount Everest, and well, we almost have enough, um . . . but . . . see every-body's pitching in. My friend Wendell gave up all his Oreos and he's not even going."

He snorted a line of caviar off the plate and tossed his head back.

"God, that's good stuff," he said. "I wish I could help you guys out, but you see, the economy here has been really bad ever since those stupid white men at GM closed their factory. It's all I can do to pay for the shipping on the Kobe beef." There was an uncomfortable pause, and then he added jovially, "But we're not going to let money stand in the way of something this monumental. That's the way *they* think."

"Uh, great," I said, "so, uh—"

"So I'm sure you'll think of something." Michael got up from the table. "In the meantime, I'll start ordering the necessary equipment. You're Elliott with two T's, right? I want to make sure I get the billing straight. Thanks for bringing me this project, guys. I won't let you down."

Out on the street, I griped to Lauren, "Great, whatever he owes you just put us back in the hole! Now we have to pay for his share of the climb *and* his IMAX shit. Where are we going to come up with that kind of cash in the next"—I looked at my watch—"six minutes! My forty-eight hours are over, sister! Celebrities are so damn cheap! I'm so glad I'm just barely one."

At that moment, a black stretch limousine screeched to a halt in front of Bowling for Beluga. Three burly men in ill-fitting suits wearing sunglasses and earpieces got out and started frisking us.

"Mr. Elliott?" said their apparent leader.

"Yeah?"

"The president would like a word with you."

CHAPTER SIX

The limo was fat city. It had been forever since I had arrived at a gala in anything except Wendell's cab, so I spent a few minutes playing with all the automatic thingamajigs while the Secret Service men stared at me. The president didn't seem to mind, and waited patiently with his head down. In fact, he was looking a lot less cranky than usual. In fact—

"Oh, it's just you," I groaned.

"Martin, what the hell is this all about?" Lauren demanded.

"You should address him as 'Mr. President,'" said a bored-looking kid.

"Oh, for Christ's sakes, I'm not going to pretend he's the damn president. That was a TV show! This is the real world!"

The kid leaned over to Lauren and whispered, "Come on, please? I really need this job."

Lauren sighed. "Oh, fine. Lovely to see you again, Mr. President. Did you have a pleasant summer in Hyannisport?"

The former star of *The West Wing* nodded regally to Lauren. He was dressed in a blue suit with a red tie, and he looked every bit the part—except for one strange detail that I had never seen any made-for-TV president wearing: a strip of duct tape over his mouth.

Martin turned to me and mumbled, "Mmmmmmm."

"Sorry, Martin, I don't speak mumble. You got any nuts or anything in here?"

Martin's young aide interpreted for him. "The, um, president has been briefed on your Himalayan mission, and for reasons of national security, he thinks it is vital that he attend."

"Oh, that's sweet. You want to tag along, huh, Marty?" I couldn't help being condescending; after all, it was common knowledge that the man was a bit loony toons and truly believed that he was the president. The idea of bringing him along on a dangerous climb, where each member of the team would have to rely on each other, seemed ludicrous (whereas apart from that the plan seemed totally rational).

"May I be so bold as to inquire why the president's mouth is taped shut?" asked Lauren. "Not that I'm complaining."

The aide rolled his eyes. "The president is trying to show national solidarity with the plight of the homeless."

"He's right off his rocker!"

Martin gesticulated wildly at his aide—he was clearly upset with the explanation. The aide sighed and continued, "Specifically, the president feels that homeless people are underrepresented as . . . extras . . . in Hollywood movies . . ."

Lauren and I exchanged perplexed looks.

Martin mumbled for about ten minutes, moving his hands around as if he were delivering an inaugural address. "Mmmmmmmm mmmmm mm m mmmmmm!"

"The president wishes to point out how the homeless are the perfect choice for extras—because they work for food . . . "

"Mmmmm mm mmmmm . . ."

". . . and if we let them keep their costumes, then it's like a clothing drive."

There was a pause. Martin's eyes widened, and he gestured to the aide to keep going. "It's . . . ," he groaned, "synergy."

"Look, Marty," I said, "I appreciate your interest, but you really have to have your shit together to climb Mount Everest. It's not just something you decide to do on the spur of the moment, you know, like just because you're bored and your life is going nowhere and it's more respectable than blowing your head off. I mean—"

"The president would also like you to know that he would be willing to see to it that a large allocation of the national budget would be at your disposal."

Lauren and I looked at each other, intrigued.

"Well, that's a different story," I said. "How much are we talking about, Mr. President?"

"About seventy-five dollars," sighed the aide. Martin nodded.

"That's all?"

"Well, the limo is expensive, and we have a fake Oval Office to maintain."

Lauren and I conferred in hushed tones. "It hardly seems worth it," I whispered. "I mean, seventy-five bucks barely pays for the extra food."

"Yes, but look at it this way: it's still a bit more money, and if he's going to keep the dumb tape on his mouth the whole time, I don't believe he'll be eating much. We might come out ahead."

"Seventy-five dollars, huh?" I looked at Martin, sizing him up. "It's a tough climb, Mr. President, you're gonna have to keep up—there's no slackers on Everest."

Martin shook his head up and down excitedly, as if he knew all that.

"And there aren't going to be any special privileges, just because you're the president and all."

He clasped his hands together like he was pleading.

"Well . . . if you throw in a beach towel with the presidential seal on it, then I guess you got yourself a deal! Welcome aboard, Mr. President."

The limo pulled to a stop in front of the Flint train station and we all got out.

"Mmmmmmm," mumbled Martin, shaking my hand.

"The president would like to know your political affiliation. Are you a Republican or a Democrat?"

Lauren and I exchanged worried looks. The truth is I had no idea what I was. I hadn't voted since John Anderson ran for president, but it had nothing to do with not being a good American or anything; I just didn't want to get called for jury duty. The one time I served on a jury I caused a mistrial by continuously sneezing, "Bullshit!" during the defense's summation. The judge really called me on the carpet. I couldn't allow myself to go through that kind of humiliation again.

"Why, I'm an, uh . . . Independent, of course." Suddenly a passing car backfired and the "Secret Service agents" jumped into action.

"Gun!" they shouted, shoving Martin back into the limo.

"Wait for me!" shouted the aide. The limo sped off—with the young man sprawled over the trunk, holding on for dear life.

On the train back to New York City, I called Duncan Carter on my cell to give him an update.

"I've got five celebrities ready to go."

"That's very good," he replied. "Where are you with the money?"

"Well, see, that's kind of a different story. I'm close—just a few grand away—but I was wondering if you could give me just a little more . . . "

"It's all right, forget it. I have an idea how to raise the rest. Meet me tomorrow at three o'clock, on the corner of Seventy-fifth and

Fifth. Come alone—and make sure you're not being followed." And then he hung up.

"Well, it looks like it may be coming together after all," Lauren said, pouring a little bourbon from an old, sterling silver flask engraved with the initials HB into two paper cups.

"Was that . . . his flask?"

She nodded. "He gave it to me off the coast of Catalina." She paused for a moment, her thoughts far away, and then she came back to reality. "He said it always brought him luck. Seems to be bringing us some already."

I raised my cup to her. "Here's looking at you, kid."

We toasted each other and settled back in our seats.

"Thanks for your help, Lauren," I whispered. "I'm glad you're on board."

"Well, we make a good team, kiddo."

She placed her hand on top of mine, and Cat Stevens' music and visions of Harold and Maude danced in my head, so I gently pulled my hand away.

CHAPTER SEVEN

Twenty-four hours later I was standing on the corner of Seventy-fifth and Fifth. The wind was blowing hard, and I thought, *If this weather keeps up like this, it's going to be really cold up on Everest.* Suddenly somebody tapped me on the shoulder.

I screamed "Help! Mugger!"

"Shhhhhh! You idiot!" admonished Duncan.

"Jeez, you scared the squished bananas out of me!"

Duncan looked back and forth. "You weren't followed, were you?"

"I don't believe so. I don't have eyes in the back of my head, you know." I turned around to show him.

"Did you bring the diary?"

"Yes. Now, I've been thinking—"

"Great, let me have it." I handed it to him and suddenly he was marching down the street.

"Look, here's the shit," he barked. "I'm a goofy son of a bitch, but I do all the talk'n. *Capeesha-mondo?*"

"That doesn't seem fair," I carped. "What if I have to tell somebody I'm hungry or I'm out of rope or something?"

"I mean in our audience with the Great One. These guys can be pretty icy, but they've got a right to be—especially Him. There's a hierarchy in mountaineering and you gotta know how to speak their . . ." He stopped and stood frozen again, gazing straight ahead as if he were under a spell. A silly smile crossed his lips, giving him the dopey expression of a drunken monkey.

"Um, Mr. Carter, are you all right?"

Suddenly he blurted out ". . . language! Sorry about that—took another hiatus to Wacky-ville, but I'm back now." He took a pillbox out and swallowed a couple of pink ones, and then he continued on down the street.

"What 'Great One' are you talking about? I'm confused."

He directed me to follow him up the marble steps of an imposing Tudor town house. Only then did I notice the banner flapping in the breeze over the mansion's door. On it, a compass rose was embroidered in the center of a red-and-blue pennant between the initials *E* and *C*. It was the legendary Explorers Club, the infamous spot where my great-uncle Percy fell and hit his head so many years before!

I was impressed that Duncan was able to get an audience here, let alone with, as it turned out, none other than Sir Edmund Hillary himself, the first man to reach the peak of Mount Everest (supposedly).

"So you actually know this guy?" I asked, as we were ushered through some gothic archways into a dark, oak-paneled library.

"Shhhh."

"Ah, Mr. Carter," greeted Hillary, who was standing before a roaring fire, "still posing as a mountaineer, I see."

"Wow, and he even knows what you do for a living," I whispered.

Hillary walked over to a large globe in the corner of the room. Lifting the top of the sphere, he reached inside and extracted a crystal decanter.

"May I offer you 'gentlemen' a brandy?"

"Yeah, sure, why not?" said Duncan.

"Got any cranberry juice?" I asked.

Hillary's lip turned up in an involuntary sneer. "Please sit."

He poured Duncan and me each a goblet of French cognac, adding just a splash of Juicy Juice to mine, and then we sat in big leather wing chairs.

"Classy joint," said Duncan, checking out the library. "I can see why you people wouldn't want someone like me as a member."

"Your application was given the same consideration as anyone else's. If memory serves me, the members deemed you 'undesirable.' Or was it 'unstable'? Chin chin, gentlemen."

Sir Edmund Hillary had stood six feet tall in his prime, but now he was stooped by old age, chronic fatigue, and years of aping Groucho Marx for apathetic friends at cocktail parties. His ruddy face glimmered in the afterglow of the crackling fire, suggesting a life once replete with thrilling adventures and exciting derring-do, now replaced by the mundane tasks, humdrum social affairs, and endless hours of Internet surfing reserved for an old man with lots of time on his hands and the condescending title of honorary chairman of the Explorers Club.

Duncan downed his glass and cut right to the chase. "So you going to fund us or what?"

"This is the Explorers Club, Mr. Carter. We're not loan sharks." He spoke with a heavy accent that I took to be Ukrainian (but that I have since discovered was New Zealandic, whatever the hell that is).

Duncan said, "Not loan—sponsor. As in *give*?"

"My dear Mr. Carter, what could possibly possess me to do that?"

Duncan threw the diary on the coffee table. I noticed that Hillary tried hard not to pay it much attention, but something about it clearly made him nervous.

"A petty forgery," he said, regaining his composure.

"Maybe you should take a closer look."

Hillary's bushy white eyebrows bounced up and down as he adjusted his glasses and examined it closely. "You're the nephew, then? I knew your great-uncle."

"Really? Was he a cool guy?" I asked excitedly.

"Well, I suppose if you are a fan of complete unbridled lunacy, then yes, he was . . . ahem . . . 'a cool guy.' Perhaps even the 'coolest' of the cool."

"Wow! I knew it."

"He was full of heart, Percy was." His gaze drifted off into the distance. "But he was terribly misguided. He believed he could climb that ghastly mountain all by himself, and no amount of earnest beseeching could persuade him otherwise."

"I can save you the trouble of reading it," Duncan said, "There's nothing in there about whether he summitted or not, but as you can see—"

"Yes, I can see that he made it much farther than anyone ever suspected. At least to Camp Four on the south col."

"Do you think my uncle made it to the top, Your Highness?" I asked.

"Oh, I suppose anything's possible."

Duncan walked to the globe and helped himself to another brandy. "Think of what an amazing discovery it would be to find Percy's frozen remains and all the attention it would bring to the club."

Hillary snorted. "The members would never approve of such a ludicrous venture, Mr. Carter. It would sully our flag to have it planted by a no-goodnik, like yourself. It is more than just a symbol, you know." He gestured at the flag hanging over the mantel. "The color red stands for courage—*real* courage—and the blue . . . ah . . . the blue? Ah . . . well, the blue is just rather pretty . . ." A pained look crossed his face. "Carrying it is a high honor, bestowed only on legitimate explorers—not sightseers."

"Tell them it's the least they can do, considering poor Percy injured his head right here on the premises."

"Now you're grasping at straws, Mr. Carter. That was over seventy years ago."

"Yeah, nowadays, you'd get your snow pants sued off."

"There is no evidence that his injury affected his decision to climb, or his ability to climb, for that matter. The man was shouty crackers long before he hit his head. Something to do with lead poisoning, I believe."

"Lead poisoning?" I asked.

"Yes. Sir Franklin's dreadful expedition. Your uncle was the only survivor. The crew is said to have resorted to cannibalism. It's believed that it was lead poisoning from the ship's poorly canned food supply that made them do it, and I'm afraid it had a detrimental effect on your uncle's senses, as well."

"Wow, I guess there's more to that story than I knew."

Duncan was now spinning the globe, and I could hear the crystal decanters inside smashing to pieces. "Look, how's it gonna hurt the club to help fund one more little expedition?"

"Why does this mean so much to you, Mr. Carter? Could it be you're after something more than the summit? Something that might help resolve some of your current . . . financial difficulties?"

It suddenly felt like a giant elephant was in the room. (And it kind of smelled like it, too.)

Now it was Duncan's turn to look uncomfortable. "Come on, Edmund, everyone knows the Golden Rhombus is just a myth."

"There's that darn Rhombus thing again," I muttered.

"Only you don't think it's a myth, do you?" said Hillary, narrowing his eyes on Duncan. "Certainly you don't believe in its powers, but you think you can find it, don't you?"

"And what if I do?"

"Then you'll be a very rich man, but you won't be alive to enjoy it."

"Guys, could you please fill me in on exactly what the hell you're talking about here? I'd love to join the conversation."

"Ahem."

All heads turned to the attractive nurse standing in the doorway who had just cleared her throat.

"Excuse me, Sir Edmund. I hate to interrupt, but it's time for your colonic."

"Yes, yes, quite right, Mattie," said Hillary. "May I introduce Miss Matilda Soldane, my caretaker."

"Charmed, I'm sure," said Duncan, gallantly kissing the nurse's hand. "The name is Duncan Carter, world-famous bounty hunter and founder of Mountain Maniacs, Inc., and we were just trying to convince Sir Edmund here to fund our little celebrity expedition up to Mount . . ." He paused, zoning out again and staring blankly at the pretty nurse.

"Don't worry, he does this sometimes," I said. "It means he likes you."

"Everest!" Duncan finally pronounced.

"And, as I've already told them, it is out of the question. Come along, Mattie." Hillary locked arms with Nurse Matilda and began to walk out of the room, but then stopped and turned back to us. "Allow me to give you gentlemen a word of advice: You don't understand what you're dealing with. Everest is more than just a mountain. There are strange forces at work up there—otherworldly forces. Personally, I detest what's happened to her."

"Her?" I asked.

"That's right. It's a she, Chomolungma, the Goddess Mother of the World, and she is very much alive. Ever since climbing her has become a commercial venture, propagated by greedy fly-by-night companies, like your own little Mountain Insomniacs or whatever the hell it's called, she—Chomolungma—has taken the lives of over a hundred and ninety souls. And she will take more. This Hollywood Squares climb of yours is grossly imprudent."

"Well, sorry, old man," said Duncan, "but one way or another, we're going!"

Hillary's shoulders drooped.

"If there is no deterring you, then your only hope is to seek out 'the one who speaks her tongue,' my friend old Tenzing Norgay. You will find him in Labuse. I assume that will be your first stop before you cross the Khumbu Glacier."

"What are you talking about? Norgay died back in the eighties!"

"Seek out Norgay. He is the only one who can help you. Good day, gentlemen, and . . . God save you."

With that, Hillary and Mattie left, and Duncan and I stood silently in the library.

"What the hell did he mean by all that stuff? He acts like Everest is alive—and nuts."

"Relax, I got everything under control." Duncan pulled out the canister of pepper spray and shot a blast straight into his mouth, inhaling deeply until his eyes rolled back in his head. He seemed to be in nirvana, but spoke like he had just inhaled helium. "Listen, I was hoping it wouldn't come to this, but I know one surefire way to raise the money."

"How?"

"Don't worry about it. I'll handle everything. Now you just have to sign these forms and we're all set!"

He pulled out some contracts and I signed.

"Tell your worthless celebrity friends to start sewing their names in their undies. We leave in one week." Duncan slapped me on the back. "We're going to Everest, A-hole!"

"The Rhombus is just a myth."

It was a done deal. After signing the contracts, I felt as if a huge weight had been lifted off my shoulders. Now Duncan Carter was responsible for my life, and truth be told, I had been fed up with carrying the burden of responsibility for my own life for quite some time now.

CHAPTER EIGHT

Six blocks north in an unassuming brownstone, Ping and Pong, the two elderly monks, were waiting outside an office, being patted down by a bouncer-type monk (if there is such a thing). Satisfied they weren't packing any heat, the brawny holy man knocked three times on the door behind him. A voice from the other side called out "Yes?" and the guard opened the door. There, practicing his putt in the middle of the lavish room, stood a small benign-looking man in a red robe and yellow sash. His sparkly, bespectacled eyes lit up when he saw the monks.

"Friends," said the Dalai Lama, extending his arms to them. "I'm supposed to play with Tiger Woods next week, but I'm afraid I am a bit rusty." He handed his putter to the guard. "That will be all. Thank you, Bruno."

Bruno left and shut the door.

"Is the news true, then?"

"It is true, Your Holiness," said Ping, the taller of the two. "The Rhombus is reborn. We have seen him with our own eyes."

The Dalai Lama walked over to a big dharma wheel on the wall and gave it a spin.

"Then we must move quickly. It is a sign. Only with the Rhombus will we succeed."

"Yes, Your Holiness." But Ping sighed.

"I sense you are displeased, my old friend."

"I, uh, only wish the great day were already upon us, Your Holiness."

"Ha. You have always been impatient. You must learn to control such emotions. When you do that, you shall be at peace."

"I wouldn't hold my breath," mumbled Pong, the shorter monk.

"I only hope . . ." The taller monk paused and exchanged looks with the shorter monk.

". . . that this is the right road to travel . . . your ocean of wisdom."

"Now you seem cautious, not impatient."

"I am both, Your Holiness."

"This is an opportunity that must not be ignored. The Rhombus is the key to *Tanhakkhaya,* the extinction of thirst. And we have all been thirsting for a very long time."

"Yes, Your Holiness."

"Now, I must know the expedition's whereabouts at all times. They will be in great danger. As will we all." He offered them a stick of something. "Tantric gum?" The monks declined. "Good stuff. Launching it next quarter. 'Double your Karma, double your fun!'" He chuckled warmly. "Anyway, we will need the assistance of the Bodhisattva. I will rely on you two to make sure that he is properly embedded with the Mountain Maniacs. I myself will travel to the staging area in Labuse and personally oversee the final preparations for 'Operation Duhkha.'"

"Yes, Your Holiness."

"My friends, we must be judicious in all our actions from now on. Nothing must stop us, but in our strivings, we must never forget that the threshold between right and wrong . . . is always pain."

He hugged the monks. "Now go, and may the *prana* of *prajna* blow through the windmills of your minds."

Ping and Pong exchanged puzzled looks.

"It just means 'good luck.' I've been working up some new material. Okay, get out of here, you know what you have to do." The two left, and the Dalai Lama motioned for Bruno.

"I need a *dokuson* with the Bodhisattva as soon as possible. See to it."

"A doh-what?"

His Holiness sighed. "A meeting. Jeez, what religion are you, anyway?"

Down in the lobby, the two monks nodded politely to an attractive African-American temp receptionist as they traipsed quickly by the front desk.

"I'm driving this time."

"Oh no you're not!"

The receptionist was speaking loudly into her cell phone. "Hey, guess who I just saw? Richard Gere himself! Yeah, Mr. American Gigolo, walked right by me. You'd think a big star like that would be a little nicer about giving out his autograph. I mean it's physically impossible to do what he just told me to do! You'd have to be a contortionist or somethin'."

Once she was certain that the elderly monks were gone, her tone suddenly changed.

"Okay, listen up, this is Tinkerbell reporting in," she whispered. "The day we've all feared has finally arrived . . . No, really, I'm serious."

There was a pause.

"Friends," said the Dalai Lama.

"Yes, the little guy!"

Another pause.

"No, this is not a crank call. Get me Blue Folder at the Pentagon. If what I think just happened has just happened, then we need to act fast—and I mean like now!"

Duhkha: Stress, suffering, anguish, and pain—caused by that which is not stable.

CHAPTER NINE

On the morning of our departure, we savored our first bit of publicity when a small column appeared on Page Six of the *New York Post*:

IMBECILES TO SUMMIT EVEREST

What unlikely assembly of the famous (and not-so-famous) elite have conspired to top the most ostentatious of all publicity stunts (that championship trophy having been formerly awarded to David Blaine for spending three weeks in a fish bowl in Lincoln Center) by climbing to the top of the most ostentatious of all mountains? Well, I'll tell you. According to my dear friend Betty (that's Lauren to you peons), the plan was hatched at Bowling for Beluga—the 'in' spot for the crème de la crème of actors, writers, and reality show freaks. Apparently she and a band of celebrated derring-doers are now preparing to summit the thirty-thousand-foot-tall Mount Everest! Couldn't you start with something a little easier, Betty, like maybe a molehill? What has gotten into my dear friend's mind? She, along with Tony of *Who's the Boss* fame, "President" Martin, and sweet bunny-loving film goddess Kirsten you-know-who—oh, and that sucky actor from that movie I hated—are all joining forces with the Mountain Maniacs fall Everest expedition. And get this, the adventure will be documented beginning to end by that hefty filmmaker and weighty icon of liberal mores, Michael I-Swear-I-Don't-Hate-America himself. Of course, it's all for a worthy cause—a number of them, as a matter of fact. It would have to be, wouldn't it? "The climb is intended to bring awareness to Hollywood's staunch reluctance to hire the homeless in movies, to stop animal testing once and for all, and to encourage people to eat more homemade pasta, I guess." This according to my dear friend Betty. Well, good luck, old friend, and make sure you pack an extra pair of nylons. The Himalayas can be frosty this time of year!

—Liz Smith

On Pier 83, Duncan Carter sat in the wheelhouse of a chunky old tug, a relic from the now defunct New York Cross-Harbor Co. The green paint on its smokestack was peeling away, and the uncaulked planking along its hull hardly seemed seaworthy. Lucky for us the *Lady Jane* would only ferry us out to the handsome, seventy-foot-long *Princess V Luxury* yacht, moored just inside the mouth of the harbor. Apparently, Duncan had been granted its temporary use by an unsavory acquaintance in lieu of an outstanding bond warrant. It all sounded a little fishy, but however he had snagged it, I was happy he had. This would probably be the most relaxing and sumptuous leg of our journey—until we got to Base Camp, that is, where I heard they had just put the finishing touches on a fabulous new Four Seasons resort. I couldn't wait to try the *ahi ahi*.

Duncan's plan was a simple one, and his itinerary took into account the expedition's limited budget. We would eschew flying altogether and cross the Atlantic in the *Princess* yacht, entering the Mediterranean through the Strait of Gibraltar. The Atlantic crossing would be dicey this time of year, as October was the height of hurricane season—and the fog season (and I think the iceberg season too)—but Duncan felt it was worth the savings. If time permitted, Michael was hoping we could zip down to Guantanamo Bay and visit the detainees (I was going to make brownies—and then eat them in front of them. Take that, Geneva Conventions!). Then, after a relaxing cruise, we would pass through the Suez Canal and into the Red Sea, shooting (literally) our way South to the Gulf of Aden and out into the emerald Sea of Arabia (better known as the Arabian Sea). Catching the Malabar currents, we'd whisk north through the Hershey Highway and around the tip of India so quickly that there would barely be enough time to shout "Sri Lanka rocks!" before we rolled into our first port of call: enchanting Calcutta. From there it would be a simple ten-day white-water rafting excursion up the Brahmaputra River, through Bhutan and into Nepal, crossing into Tibet during the dead of night and then back into Nepal during the light of day—arriving on November 27 at our final destination: the Labuse Lodge, located in gorgeous, downtown Labuse.

Duncan watched from the wheelhouse as two figures approached the dock: Michael and a skinny man who was pulling a dolly loaded down with numerous big boxes and hefty reels of cable.

"Lithium battery," said Michael.

"Check," said the skinny man.

"Color CCD videotape."

"Check."

"Beam splitter, reflex viewfinder."

"Check."

"Cartoni fluid head and underwater housing."

"Check."

"And fifty mags of seventy/thirty dual crystal film stock."

"That's a big check. Just sign here, sir, and you're all set to go."

"You gotta be shittin' me," Duncan called down. "You're gonna haul all that rubbish?"

"Is that gonna be a problem, Mr. Carter?" Michael asked.

"Yes, that's gonna be a problem. You're climbing Mount Everest, not flying the goddamn space shuttle!"

"According to your brochure," Michael said, "you provide all the Sherpas, bellboys, indentured servants, and undocumented workers required to carry our shit! Well, sir, this is my shit." Under his breath he added, "Along with twelve crates of Boston baked beans . . ." then louder again, "and I require it to be happily carried—that is unless you'd like me to file a class-action lawsuit for false advertising before we even get under way. I'm happy to do it, buddy."

"There's always one," Duncan muttered to himself.

Just then a lengthy stretch limo pulled up, with every conceivable assortment of matching monogrammed luggage strapped to its roof.

"Oh, Christ, what now?"

Lauren stepped out and began barking orders. "Garment bags, totes, and toiletry kits to the stateroom. Steamer trunks, duffels, and suitcases to steerage."

"Afternoon, ma'am," Duncan shouted down. "I see you packed light."

"Just a few trifles. A lady never knows when she may be called upon to gussy up. And you must be our brave Captain Carter?"

"At your service. I trust you had a pleasant ride down from the Upper West Side?"

"Yes, quite pleasant, thank you."

"Not too much traffic?"

"No, not much at all."

"Potholes?"

"Very few, actually. I think Mayor Bloomberg is doing a superb job of keeping our asphalt silky smooth."

"I'm so pleased to hear it," Duncan said. "Now"—and his tone suddenly became gruff—"grab two bags and your climbing gear, and tell your damn chauffeur to take the rest of that shit back up to your golden palace! There ain't gonna be any fancy cotillions on Everest. Now get your perfumed ass-fault on board." Then he emptied at least ten pills into his palm, tossed them back, and chewed them down.

"Let's go, A-holes! Chop chop. ETD in five minutes!"

"*Vroom!*" came a crackly voice through a bullhorn. "*Whoooosh!*"

Duncan slammed his head on the control panel of the *Lady Jane*. "What now?"

President Martin was arriving at the dock in "*Air Force One,*" a cardboard cutout of a plane that his Secret Service agents held in front of him while he jogged. The sardonic assistant followed behind on a scooter, making jet noises through a bullhorn.

"*Air Force One* cleared for landing," he said, with a noticeable lack of enthusiasm. "Agents, sweep the area or something."

The agents began to swarm the boat, which was apparently too much for Duncan, who emerged from the wheelhouse armed with a flare gun, yelling, "Off my boat, now!"

"Gun! Gun!" yelled the agents, and they tried to tackle Duncan but he just pushed them off. "Does someone want to tell me what this is all about?"

Martin, showing statesmanlike courage, walked straight up to Duncan and began mumbling.

"The president would like to know how you intend to make it to Everest in this piece of trash," said the assistant.

"What the hell do you have on your mouth, A-hole?"

Lauren sighed, "He's showing solidarity with the plight of the homeless."

"Say, she's a beautys, ain't she?" Tony was approaching the dock, arm in arm with Kirsten. (Are you thinking what I'm thinking?) "I's bets she rides the waves like butters."

"It reminds me of the little boat in *Cecil and Beanie Go to Sea*. It's so, like, storybook!"

"If one's reading Stephen King, my child," said Lauren.

"It's just a launch, people," Duncan said. "The real one's parked offshore—for, uh, legal reasons."

He pointed out to sea, where the *Princess V Luxury* yacht was visible just on the horizon. It was met with coos of approval.

"Swanks," said Tony.

The assistant translated Martin's mumbles. "The president needs a secure location if he is to safely transport the,"—he sighed—"nuclear football."

Martin proudly held up an oblong case, which was chained to his arm.

Lauren groaned. "What is that, a makeup case?"

Duncan was losing his temper. "You," he said to Martin, "stow your shit. And you two," he said to Lauren and Michael, "I don't care what you carry up, as long as you carry it your damn selves. And you"—he stuck a finger in the assistant's chest—"Are you paid for?"

"The, uh, national budget was only enough for one climber."

"Then get off my boat!"

"Wait, so does that mean I'm fired?"

Martin shrugged.

"Oh, how sad," said the assistant. "I guess that means I'll have to go on unemployment for, like, six months or something. Oh, well. I guess I can handle it." As soon as he was on the dock he turned and started to run away, letting out a "Yippee" as Martin saluted good-bye.

Next a rowdy voice with an unmistakable Southwestern accent bellowed "Howdy-do, everybody! Are we all ready to summit? I say, I say, are we all ready to summit?"

He was a burly middle-aged man with a bald head and big, black handlebar mustache. He stood on the pier with his legs spread wide apart and his hands firmly planted on his hips, wearing nothing but a skimpy black Speedo. His hairy abdomen hung over it, almost completely obscuring the swimsuit.

Duncan said, "Folks, say hello to Max Bullis of Austin, Texas. Max has summitted the Pumori Peak twice, the Matterhorn once—K 12 and even L 4—and he's done it all in that sexy little outfit you see him in there."

"Why on earth would you do such an asinine thing?" asked Lauren.

"Because he's a member of the Polar Bear Club! That's why!" pronounced Duncan.

"Among other things, little darling," cooed Max, slowly advancing. Lauren wasn't in the least bit fazed by his giant furry body. "I'm also a wealthy oil baron, a cattle rancher, a major fund-raiser, and one hell of a line dancer. Perhaps I can show you a few steps sometime?"

"Yes, well, before we do the electric slide together, your torso needs a good shaving."

Max released a booming guffaw. "By golly, she's got spunk!" he declared, slapping his knee. "We gonna have us a grand old time on this here excursion, little lady!"

Kirsten asked, "What's a polar bear club?"

"They're da guys dat jump into the ice-cold water for no reasons," Tony explained.

"You're so smart!"

"No, youz so smarts!"

Michael cocked an eyebrow, "'Major fund-raiser' for what, exactly?"

"Well, hell, boy, the Grand Old Party," Max said, clearly relishing the effect it was going to have on him. "What the hell else would I raise funds for? Poor people?"

"I knew it! I can smell a right-winger a mile away."

"*Ya zniyoo takia slova ketoria visegna pamogiyoo*!" came another voice from nearby. A young man with dark glasses stood on the sailboat in the slip next to the *Lady Jane*.

Duncan cupped his hands around his mouth and yelled, "Wrong boat, Yorgi! We're ten paces behind and to your left!" He turned to the group. "That's Anatoly Yakavich—or 'Yorgi' to his friends. He plans on being the first blind man to climb up . . . and then ski down Everest . . . on a Tuesday or something."

"The kid's got Brahman balls!" Max observed. Then he purred to Lauren, "Not unlike yours truly, missus."

"Lovely," said Lauren.

"*Til dulshen kricknut*," Yorgi muttered, traipsing away from the sailboat. "*E shapka pre lateet*!" He shook his fist at the sky and walked straight off the dock and into the Hudson River.

"Man's overboards!" shouted Tony.

"I got 'em! I got 'em!" yelled Max. And in true polar bear fashion, he dove straight into the icy water.

"I've got to get this on film," Michael said, hoisting the IMAX camera onto his shoulder while Tony and Martin helped haul the two men back onto the dock.

"*Spasibo*, my friend, *Spasibo*." The handsome Russian felt Max's face and then kissed him on both cheeks. (Are you thinking what I'm thinking?)

"Don't mention it," said Max. "Now that the Cold War is over, we're all com-reds, right?"

"That 'man on man' kiss is going to look great on a ninety-foot dome screen." Michael chortled. "Hee hee hee. You're gonna love it."

Max blustered. "If that little piece o' film ever sees the light o' day, you're gonna be pushing up cactus in my jalapeño garden. Do I make myself clear, blubber boy?"

"Well, I think we're off to a splendid start," announced Duncan, who then squirted some Purell on his tongue, shot some Dust-Off up his nose, and gave himself a blast of pepper spray. "Everybody on board, and I mean now!"

He rang the ship's bell and started up the *Lady Jane*'s cranky dual diesel engines.

"Put the damn camera down and cast us off, Michael!" he ordered.

"Wait, wait. Stop the boat," said Lauren. "We can't leave yet! I believe we're still missing a rather important member of our team."

"Oh, crap," Duncan muttered. "I forgot about that guy."

CHAPTER TEN

At that moment, Wendell's cab was speeding west on Twenty-eighth Street. As usual, I was sitting in the back, this time with Grammy and Gramps. We could just see Pier 83 and the *Lady Jane*, her engines belching smoke.

"Wait! Don't go!" I yelled out the window, "I'm coming! I'm coming!"

Wendell hissed. "Why is it that every time you go somewhere you're late?"

"Excuse me, Wendell, teatime snack is the most important meal of the day. And I'm sorry, but you just can't rush chipped beef."

"Stop bickering, boys," chided Grammy. "Did you bring your Dramamine, Chris?"

"Yes, Grammy."

"Extra grundies?"

"Yes, Grammy."

"Here, I made you a peanut oil and lard hoagie for the trip," she stuffed the sandwich in my backpack.

"Woman, why don't you just buy peanut butter like everyone else?" Wendell asked.

"Oh, I don't go in for that fancy stuff. Besides, that storebought crap is so expensive! Damned Saudis. Which reminds me, I made a tub of it for you two to take on your little campout."

"I told you I'm not going!" said Wendell.

"Had all your shots, Wendell?" Gramps wheezed out. "I've heard those Tibetan prostitutes aren't the most hygienic, if you get my drift."

"I just said I'm not going. What's with you people?"

"Don't forget to keep Uncle Percy on ice when you bring him back," Grammy chirped. "I don't want that smell in my kitchen."

"We won't forget. I mean, *I* won't forget," I said. "Wink wink."

Wendell's cab screeched to a halt at the pier and we rushed to the edge of the dock.

"You're gonna have to jump for it!" Duncan instructed. "I don't know how to back this thing up!"

"Ah, oh. I can't do this, I can't. I just can't."

"Sure you can," said Wendell. "Just take a running jump."

"Okay, if you say so."

I sprinted toward the edge of the dock and leaped off. I screamed bloody murder (I don't know why, it was just the first thing that came to mind) and soared into the air, and then I dropped like a lead balloon into the river.

"Help me! Help! I can't swim!"

"Wendell, save him," said Grammy, pushing Wendell toward the edge.

"Oh, shit, I don't believe this. Hold on. Hold on." Wendell took off his shoes and corrective socks and jumped in.

"Okay, buddy, hold on. I got you." He started to swim me back to the dock, but I grabbed hold of the life preserver that Tony had thrown from the *Lady Jane*, and suddenly we were being pulled toward the tug.

"Wait, no! We want to go the other way!" But it was too late. We were already being pulled up on the boat's deck.

"I'm not supposed to be here!" shouted Wendell. "Take me back!"

Duncan said, "Sorry, pal, 'reverse' don't work too good."

"But I can't go!"

"Sure you can, Wendy!" I said, as Lauren threw a towel over my shoulders.

"Here's Wendell's backpack!" shouted Gramps from the dock, and he tossed it onto the boat.

"My backpack?"

"I'm sorry, Wendy, I just couldn't imagine climbing Everest without you by my side."

"You bastard. Let me off! Let me off!" But the tug was already in the middle of the Hudson, where currents are much too strong for any swimmer.

"Wendell, we have a mystery to solve," I said, "and I can't do it without you. Remember when I couldn't find my readers and we spent a week putting the clues together and finally I found them between the pillows in my sofa? We were like the Hardy Boys!"

"Chris, that was a fun week, I admit it . . . but . . ."

"And remember when we traveled through time together and we ended up stranded in the nineteenth century? You got to become the first black president of the United States!"

"Oh, yeah. How did that ever get resolved, anyway?"

"Oh, you know . . ."

Wendell seemed to struggle momentarily, lured by memories of adventure, and then he shook his head. "Chris, forget it. It's stupid. It's Mount-freaking-Everest. Now let me off."

"Everest! Exactly! Think of the glamour, the fame . . ." I crossed my fingers and prepared my coup de grace. "Wendell Pierce, first African American to summit Mount Everest! Think how proud your mamma would be!"

Wendell rolled his eyes and sighed. I could tell I was starting to get to him. I wrapped a towel around his shoulders.

"You only go around once in life, Wendy," I said, "We gotta grab all the gusto we can."

Wendell glanced forlornly back at the dock and watched as Grammy and Gramps drove off in his cab.

"Plus, you'll get to spend two weeks at sea with the lovely Kirsten."

At that moment Kirsten walked up and dropped her bag in front of Wendell. She turned to me and said, "Have your porter take these to my room, will ya, Chuck?"

"So, what do you say, Wendy? Partners?"

He just grumbled, but I knew what he meant.

"Yay! Back together and better than ever." I held up my hand for a high five.

He reluctantly returned it. "But only because I know that if I'm not there you'll probably fall into some kind of *crevasse* or something."

"Hey, everyone, Wendell's on the team!" I couldn't believe he fell for that "first black man on the summit" thing, but then again, maybe he would be . . . I mean I've never seen any pictures or anything.

Wendell got to his feet and looked around the crummy boat. "So . . . we're going to Everest in this thing?"

Duncan shouted from the wheelhouse, "No sirree. We're going to Everest in *that* thing."

The second he pointed to the beautiful yacht, two black helicopters soared past overhead, followed by a fleet of Coast Guard and police boats with sirens blaring. They quickly converged on the *Princess V*.

"A-hem," Lauren said. "How exactly did you acquire the yacht?"

"*Princess V*, prepare to be boarded!" an angry voice announced over a megaphone.

"Are they looking for you?" I asked Duncan.

"Me? No, of course not! What have I ever done? Are they looking for you?"

"No," I said defensively, "although I did take some outrageous deductions this year."

"Uh, it's probably just a sobriety check. But best not to get involved in that kind of thing at this point. It could really slow us down." Duncan gunned the engines, and we blew passed the *Princess V*.

"Well, how are we going to get to Labuse now?" I asked.

"No worries, we can make it in this puppy right here. I'm a professional. Trust me."

At that moment, back at the Explorers Club, the old pendulum clock on the wall of Sir Edmund Hillary's bathroom chimed the five-o'-clock hour and then returned to its strident, rhythmic ticking. Hillary was so used to the sound that he had become oblivious to it. But now, as Nurse Matilda gently bathed him in warm water and saltpeter, he was startled when the pendulum abruptly stopped.

"It has begun," he said, his tired, craggy voice portending doom.

"Will we go, then?" Mattie asked, raising his wrist and scrubbing under his arm.

"We have no choice," he said hopelessly, and in his tired, yellowed eyes, Mattie recognized the raw chaff of fear.

Now on the upper deck of the *Princess V* yacht, the "temp" from the Office of Tibet stood with a stupefied expression on her stupefied face. Her CIA credentials hung from around her neck, and a menacing 45 magnum was strapped to her side holster.

"There's no sign of them, Tinkerbell," said a younger male agent, "and the skipper and crew aren't cooperating."

"Look, Resnick, you're new, so I'll let it slide. But 'Tinkerbell' is my code name. I'm not undercover right now, so you call me by my real name. Understood?"

"Yes, understood. Sorry, Captain Harding."

"A'right. Just don't let it happen again." Captain Harding gazed out to sea, taking little notice of the pathetic *Lady Jane* putting into the sunset right in front of her very eyes. "Now how the hell did we miss them?" After a moment of reflection, she turned back to the younger agent. "Get a jet," she said. "We'll head them off in Labuse."

High above the harbor, nestled in Liberty's torch, the two elderly Tibetan monks keenly watched the chaotic scene below.

"So the Americans get involved again," said Pong. "I wonder what side they'll be on this time."

"The Americans are on their own side," said Ping.

"At least the tug has escaped for now."

"Yes, for now."

"Do you suppose the Bodhisattva made it safely on board?" asked Pong. Ping focused his binoculars on the *Lady Jane*'s lifeboat. A hand stuck out from under its tarp and gave a thumbs-up.

"Yes, he made it on."

"But they will never survive crossing in such leaky boat."

"Have faith," said Ping. "It has all been fated. The Golden Rhombus will be returned to the sacred zenith and then all shall be stable in the world—not that I'm happy about it."

"Good . . . then can we go get some dinner now?"

"Mount Everest here we come!"

"Yes." They stood up. The taller monk looked down the steps leading out of the torch.

"Ugh. All those stairs. Whose idea was it we come up here anyway?"

"It has best view!"

"You just like it because it dramatic! You always hamming it up!"

"Maybe I help you get down stairs real fast, huh? How you like that?"

The two continued bickering as they descended.

Of course, I didn't know about the mysterious stowaway in our lifeboat, or about Hillary, or about the monks, or about the CIA's interest in our climb. But even with what I did know, I should have stopped everything right then and there. I could have called a halt to the whole doomed expedition. It was my last chance to alter the horrid course of events awaiting us. I could have eliminated so much heartache and prevented frostbite, hypothermia, hemorrhaged corneas—and yes, I could have saved lives. But luckily for us, my common sense prevailed.

"Sail on," I told Duncan, "sail on!" and everyone on board, even Wendell (sort of), shouted out with glee:

"Mount Everest, here we come!"

PART TWO

Higher in the sky than imagination had ventured to dream, the top of Everest itself appeared. Just one more bite of my bangers and mash, and then it's on to the summit!

—George Mallory
Everest, 1924

CHAPTER ELEVEN

In 1929 the International Hydrographic Conference, held each year in Monaco (and which really sounds like a blast to me—I'm gonna have to do that one of these days), unanimously adopted the "nautical mile" as the standard unit of measurement for maritime navigation, defining it as the average length of one minute of latitude running along the arc of any given meridian. It further determined that one nautical mile equals about 6,080 feet, or exactly 1,852 meters. So our trip would be a ten-thousand-nautical-mile voyage halfway around the world. But the *Lady Jane* had only made it about half a nautical mile—or three thousand feet—out to sea before a major storm broadsided us. Actually it was more like a shower—well, a sprinkle—that turned out to be just a busted waste pipe in the forward head, attributable to Max Bullis, whose "kids" (as he put it) "clogged up the pool." The explosion and the subsequent deluge was enough to short out the electronics, flood the diesel engines, and cause *Lady Jane* to leak like a one-legged hooker on a foggy day in old London town.

It would have been an abrupt and watery end to the whole expedition were it not for some quick thinking on Wendell's part. Using Grammy's peanut oil-and-lard mixture, he was able to caulk the major leaks and keep us afloat just long enough for the Coast Guard helicopters to arrive on the scene and pull us all to safety in rescue baskets. (They also rescued our luggage, IMAX equipment, and, un-wittingly, our stowaway, who, during the chaos, managed to slip un-detected into the duffel bag containing Yorgi's braille maps and skis.)

Later that night, Duncan met us all at Newark Airport and glumly shelled out the extra bucks for airline tickets ("That just means less undocumented workers to carry our shit," he groused), and we grabbed the Jet Blue Everest red-eye to Labuse.

Now, flying the same route as Percy had some eighty years before, I couldn't help but feel one with the man. Except of course our plane was a lot bigger, our cabin was pressurized, my seat reclined, and I could drink all the concentrated apple juice and Bloody Mary mix I wanted. When I tired of watching *Trading Spaces* (aren't those in-dividual TVs on Jet Blue cool? I was so jealous that Michael got to have two!), I nudged Lauren's bony elbow off the armrest, pinched Wendell's nose shut to stop him from snoring, and opened Percy's diary.

A piece of paper fell out, and as I picked it up I realized that it wasn't just a loose page, it was a letter! And not just any kind of letter—a love letter! It was from Percy to his mail-order bride—apparently written right after recovering from his coma. I raced through, scanning for dirty parts, but then my eyes settled on the word *Rhombus* and I began to read more carefully:

To my dear darling (whom I haven't met yet, but check my P.O. box for every day):

As I lay in hospital, unable to move or communicate but keenly aware of everything around me, I listened to the conversation between my young doctor and his busty nurse. "Did you try applying the tip of a burning cigarette?" the

nurse asked. "Yes, of course," said the doctor. "Needles
under the fingernails? Electrodes on nipples? Eddie Cantor
recordings?" "Yes, yes, yes," the doctor replied. "I'm not
incompetent, you know. There's just no hope. He won't
respond to anything. We might as well pull him off the life
support." (My doctor was not being totally honest, I remember responding quite favorably to the Eddie Cantor
recordings—in fact, I believe I was even able to whistle along
with "Toot, Toot, Tootsie, Good-bye.") But the nurse made
an impassioned plea for my life, and the young Dr. Kevorkian
(I believe his name was) reluctantly agreed to give me a few
more days before pulling the plug. Then my guardian angel
(in the guise of this stacked nurse) accidentally tripped over
the electrical cord to my iron lung—sending me soaring
forward on a rapid passage into the next world. And oh, my
darling, what a brilliant light I saw at the end of a long tunnel!
As I drew nearer, I glimpsed a homely prostitute with whom
I felt a familiar connection. She was riding a polar bear
bareback. "Gitty-up," she said, spurring the animal on,
"he's not supposed to be here, yet." The bear sighed like a
henpecked husband. "This is what I gave up life on the tundra
for?" he muttered.

Then the homely prostitute spoke unto me. "Percy," she said,
"it is in you to do what must be done. I made the mistake, but
now you must rectify it. Climb to the zenith and return the
Golden Rhombus to Chomolungma. It is in you to do this,"
she repeated, and then she was gone.

Suddenly I was transported back to my hospital bed, my eyes
wide open, my senses completely restored, and my hands
securely clamped on the breasts of the busty nurse leaning over

my prone body. "Doctor, he's alive!" she announced, "Oh, fine," muttered Kevorkian. And it was right then and there, my darling, that I dedicated myself to returning the Golden Rhombus, for I now know what it is. (And it is not my butt.) That's all for now—can't wait to open you.

Love and kisses,
Your horny dog, Percy

I felt a tear come to my eye reading this, knowing as I did that the long-awaited mail-order bride would arrive spoiled and have to be returned to sender. But what of his vision? Was the homely prostitute his mother? And if so, what mistake had she made? Whatever the near-death experience meant, my great-uncle now knew what the Rhombus was, and the revelation lit a fire inside him—a fire that would carry him all the way to the summit. (If he ever made it to the summit.) I thought hard on all of this—really, really hard.

"Stop that damned shaking," said Lauren, waking to the sound of my popping brain tubes.

"Sorry."

"Ladies and gentlemen, this is your captain speaking. If you look out the left side of the airplane you get a nice view of Mount Everest, the tallest mountain in the world, located in what is perhaps the most remote region of the world." He yawned. "But on the right there's a great view of the Six Flags amusement complex in Lhasa, boasting the world's tallest roller coaster, Big Bad Mamma Chomolungma."

I guess I shouldn't have been surprised when a number of passengers, including Wendell, rushed to the other side of the plane to catch a glimpse of the world's tallest roller coaster, but I slid over to Wendell's window seat and gazed out at the world's tallest mountain.

The rising sun illuminated her dramatically, and with our cruising altitude at about the same level of the summit itself, I was afforded a spectacular panorama that few have ever witnessed. Majestically situated in the southern region of the Himalayas, the thirty-thousand-foot-tall mountain is made of jagged schist, gray granite, and some glacial outcroppings of shale, limestone, and unsweetened rock candy.

It serves as a natural partition, separating the countries of Tibet and Nepal, although each year, due to excessive global warming and tectonic dysmorphia, it moves a staggering twenty-five feet east and is estimated to make landfall in the United States some time before the end of the century. (Geologists predict it will then most likely separate Malibu from Simi Valley.)

But those dry facts did nothing to prepare me for the sight.

She was magnificent.

A ribbon of stringy, nimbostratus clouds encircled the upper sixteenth of the massive mountain, allowing her jagged tip to barely peek through the fluffy white wisps. In every way she appeared like the true Goddess Mother of the World—albeit a Goddess Mother with a very small pinhead. Glancing below, I discerned three separate bands of climbers, all ascending at the same time. I assumed that the slow-moving procession of shimmering metal to the east was the "wheelchair accessible" route, while the swift-moving mountaineers speeding up the western col could only be the obnoxious E-Z Passers. A mixed bag of first-time climbers, family vacationers, and fugitive serial killers seemed happily stalled halfway up the bunny hill, but these "leaf peepers," as the locals called them, would all be off the mountain soon. We had been assured that by the time we started our ascent, Chomolungma would be all ours. (I can't remember why. Something about the weather.)

"Scared?" asked Lauren, back from checking out the roller coaster.

It would have been hard not to be. Since Everest was first conquered, back in 1953, by Sir Edmund Hillary and his trusty manservant Tensing Norgay, the mountain has claimed the lives of over 190 intrepid climbers. Each year the names of those most recently killed are somberly added to the *chorten* at Base Camp. (Do you guys even know what a *chorten* is? It's a stone shrine, okay? See, I know my shit.)

"Yeah, a little scared, maybe."

"You should be scared as all get out." Lauren grasped the wrist of a passing flight attendant. "Champagne for two, stewardess."

"Ma'am, we'll be landing soon," said the attendant, whose tone clearly sounded like she was there primarily for our safety more than anything else.

Lauren stared steely-eyed at the young woman. "Now, you listen to me, and you listen good," she began, her voice dropping as low as Everest is high, "I've been cut off by the best of them. Toots Shor, Vinnie Sardi, Wolfy Puck, and the top guy at Applebee's, so don't even try to start with your puny little 'I'm the top dog in the big dog show' crap. I've seen the act before, honey, and it cuts no bacon with me. You get my drift? Now, be a good little stewardess—which, by the way, is what you are—you're not here 'primarily' for our goddamn safety—and run along and fetch the damn champagne! And I mean like now!"

The frightened flight attendant quickly scurried down the aisle.

"You're a better man than me," I remarked. "When she cut off my apple juice, I switched straight to coffee."

"So, it's finally happening," Lauren said, scooting over to the window and looking out.

"Yep. We'll be standing on top of her head before you know it."

"I wonder if she knows we're coming."

"Um, jeez, Betty, I don't really know if the mountain, which is made out of dead rock, is aware that we're coming or not."

"Oh, don't be an ass."

"Hey, I don't make monkeys, I just train 'em."

The flight attendant set the champagnes down, and Lauren removed a cigarette. The nervous attendant looked furtively about and then, in an obvious violation of FAA rules, lit Lauren's smoke and dashed away. We clinked our glasses and sipped our bubbly.

"You can't pretend not to feel it too. Her presence?"

"Yeah," I said, "it's almost like she's beckoning me, the way the white whale beckoned Ahab, beckoning him to join the big stinking fish in their shared destiny. So, I guess you could say that Everest is my big stinking fish, even though I don't think a whale is technically a fish . . ."

"What do you really want from her?" she asked.

I sighed, "Oh, I don't know. At the global-warming summit, you said I was still looking for 'that something.' Well, maybe that something is just something I can call my own—something that screams, 'I did it and nobody else did.' Of course I know other people have climbed Mount Everest—a lot of them, as a matter of fact—so this probably isn't it." I blew on the window and traced the outline of the summit with my finger. "Maybe what I'm looking for will be waiting for me up there on the tip top, or maybe it won't. But I think just the getting there will bring me closer to what I'm seeking. And maybe that's enough."

"Ladies and gentlemen, this is your captain again. We've got about twenty minutes till we land, and I'll be turning on the seat belt sign soon, so if any of you need to drop the kids off at the pool, now would be a good time to do it."

Max Bullis stood up. "I call dibsies!"

A buzz of anticipation and excitement began to fill the plane. Michael was awake and already filming. "Smile, everyone! I want to get a shot of our arrival in Labuse."

Martin, stretching and yawning (as best he could with the tape on his mouth), leaned over and nudged Tony and Kirsten. He pointed wildly out the window and made the universal sign for "We're here, guys! Wake up! Look at Mount Everest. She's a tall mountain, isn't she? She'll be fun to climb, but I bet it'll be cold!"

"Wows, theres she is!" said Tony, pressing his face against the window, "I can't waits to get up to the top and dos a little two-steps."

Kirsten rubbed the sleep from her eyes and curled up on Tony's chest. "I had the most dreadful dream," she said, and as she spoke, everyone quieted down to listen. "I dreamt that we were all caught in a horrific avalanche close to the summit, and that we ran out of food and had to pick straws to decide who we'd eat first! It was horrible. Just horrible."

"There, theres nows. It was just a dreams, Kirsty babies. Just a dreams. Dats alls."

"I wonder what it could possibly mean?" I pondered.

"I've heard that when you have dreams about being eaten alive it means that you secretly have a fear of success," said Michael.

"There you goes. Sees? Youz just gots a little fear of success, dats all. I tink I gots one of those toos."

"Oh, thank goodness," Kirsten said, "because I was worried it was some sort of premonition or something."

"Nahs."

We all looked at each other for a moment and then joined in with "Nahs."

Below our feet, in the nonpressurized, pitch-black darkness of the baggage compartment, the temperature had plummeted to a staggering forty below. Ice crystals had formed on the crates and containers. The passengers' luggage seemed not so much stacked as huddled together for warmth.

The zipper on Yorgi's long black ski bag began to gradually un-zip. A moment later the stowaway, practically invisible in the dark-ness, slowly sat up. He seemed strangely unaffected by the cold.

He placed a small metal Rubik's Cube–like object on top of one of Lauren's steamer trunks and gave it a twist. Suddenly the bag-gage compartment filled with absolute white light (which was un-fortunately too bright for you to be able to see the stowaway's face). Two seconds later the illumination dissolved into billions of cas-cading orbs, as if the universe itself were in the compartment. Then a blue shaft of light shot out from the cube, generating a hologram of His Holiness, the Dalai Lama.

He was about ten inches tall, standing on Lauren's steamer trunk.

"Are you with the Maniacs?" he asked.

"I am, my master."

"Excellent. And no harm has come to the Rhombus?"

"No harm, my master, although I suspect sabotage was the true nature of the waste-pipe explosion onboard the *Lady Jane*."

"Interesting . . . the Republican?"

"No, he didn't help matters much, but I believe he was just in the wrong place at the wrong time. Most likely a surly longshoreman planted the bomb back at the pier . . . but he was obviously work-ing for someone else."

"Then this can only mean one thing: that our enemies are aware of our plan."

"But how?"

"Obviously a *yidam* has infiltrated our *sangha*. We must take ex-tra precautions."

"Yes, Your Holiness."

"You have done well, my little Bodhisattva. I will join you shortly. In the meantime try to find out who is working against us. The *yidam* is likely to take a human form; he could be anyone, anywhere. Stay close to the Rhombus, and make sure it remains safe."

"I dreamt we were caught in a horrific avalanche."

"Yes, my master."

"And bundle up, for Brahman's sakes! You'll be no use to me if you catch a cold."

And with that the Dalai Lama *gasshoed* (bowed), and the blue beam of light retreated back inside the Rubik's Cube and the hologram vanished.

Yidam: A wrathful deity.

CHAPTER TWELVE

"Tzing Tzang, how the hell are you?" hailed Duncan, as we stepped off the plane into the cold Himalayan air. The smell of harvested mustard, dried corn, juniper, and wet dog hung on the breeze. We were at sixteen thousand feet above sea level, and I already felt the effects of the exiguous Nepalese oxygen. (It made me horny.)

Duncan hugged the Sherpa. "You look ten years older and a few inches shorter, you son of a bitch."

The stubby man with chestnut skin and leathery hands was wearing the traditional *chuba* (or yak-lined overcoat tied by a piece of woven fabric). On his head he wore an old beat-up fedora.

"Everyone, meet Tzing Tzang. He's summitted many times: once using auxiliary oxygen, twice without any oxygen, and a few times using his childhood bong. He's our *Sirdar.* You have any problems, you go to him. Not me—*him.* Remember that."

"Thanks a lot, boss."

Sherpa means "easterner." Originally they were immigrants from East LA who settled in the lower Khumbu Valley of Nepal some six hundred years ago, and since the days of George Mallory and Percy Elliott, they have proved a necessary addition to any Everest expedition. Their natural facility to tolerate the thin air of high altitude (having grown up with all that smog), coupled with their unsettling eagerness to serve, made them ideal climbing companions. Unfortunately, Tzing Tzang seemed to be absent most of these meritorious qualities—or if he had them, they were masked by an unremitting cynicism.

"Hey, boss, looks like you got a bunch of winners this time," he cracked, not even attempting to hide his cagey smirk.

"Did you hear that, everyone?" I said, turning to my fellow climbers. "He thinks we're all winners! Yay!"

"Real professionals."

"Real professionals! Yay!"

"They look like bunch of rejects from Celebrity Fat Club."

"He says we all look like a bunch of rejects from . . . Hey, that's not nice. And I believe it's the Celebrity Fit Club, not Fat Club, so if we're not anything, we're not fit, not . . . not fat! So ha!" Wendell and I high fived each other again.

Duncan pulled Tzing Tzang away from our group. "Got my telegram, right?"

"Yeah, I got it. But I think you nuts."

"The goofy kid has the diary," Duncan said. "It will lead us straight to the Rhombus."

"And what about this bet of yours? I don't like sound of it. Too dangerous."

"That's none of your concern."

"It concern me if you go too fast—safety first, boss. Safety first."

"Yeah, yeah, yeah, safety first, don't worry about it. Come on. Let's go. Chop chop."

A caravan of three beat-up yellow Range Rovers with "Mountain Maniacs" scrawled on the doors awaited us. None of the undocumented workers loading our luggage seemed to notice that the ski bag grunted when it hit the top of the pile.

As we drove north, the asphalt gave way to cobblestones, and the bumpy road was lined on either side by healthy-looking poplars—and not-so-healthy-looking paupers. Fortunately, the boring topography was broken here and there by colorful prayer flags adorning the Arby's, Ruby Tuesdays, and Mazda dealerships along the way.

Above us, the *lammergeiers* (giant vultures) sailed along on invisible streams. The Tibetans use these vultures in their "sky burials." The body of the deceased is hacked into small pieces and then left on a sacred rock for the birds to devour. They believe that this ritual completes the circle of life, and there have only been a few rare occasions when they've accidentally hacked up a live person who just happened to be napping on the sacred rock at the wrong time.

As we rounded a sharp bend, there behind the golden arches lay the mighty Himalayan peaks—Makalu, Pumori, Lhotse, Laughing Cow, Brie, Bald Savalas . . . and towering above them all, the roller coaster—and then behind that, Mount Everest.

Labuse itself was a shit hole—literally. It was situated in a basin-shaped coulee, and with no modern plumbing to speak of, monkeys, yaks, *bosmytus* (cattle), *panthops* (sheep), and *yamyoks* (half-man, half-cow) evacuated themselves in long outdoor troughs, which flowed into and flooded the gulch with human and/or animal and/or half human-half animal excrement. The houses for the most part were one- or two-story affairs, constructed of stone and "crap," and the only hotel, the Labuse Lodge, was adorned with a myriad of hanging ochre icicles, its ragged burlap portière tie-dyed with the national colors of cocoa and umber. It was like Willie Wonka's chocolate factory, but I found out the hard way that the place wasn't made out of chocolate, or if it was, it was some sort of fancy Swiss kind.

"This place really used to be run-down," said Tzing Tzang proudly, as our caravan made its way through the cobbled streets. "But then Disney came in and poured a lot of money into the area and saved the economy. Everything you see here has been meticulously researched and recreated to approximate exactly what the town looked like about . . . a day or so before Disney came in to recreate it."

"So then, what was the point?" I asked.

"What do you mean?"

"If they made it exactly the same?"

"Well, it's not exactly the same. It's 'Disney' the same. All the cobblestones are made out of plastic polymers, the yaks and monkeys are animatrons, and what looks like shit dripping everywere is actually Swiss chocolate."

"I knew it!"

The lodge was like a movie set. It was dark, and a bunch of dusty old tables harbored a loathsome mélange of grody locals, either hunched over their poisons or fanning themselves with yak-tail flyswatters shaped like mouse ears. Butter lamps dangled from the rafters and cast a dim light.

"*Chaang* all around," Duncan said, bouncing in like he owned the place. He greeted the man standing in the center of the big square bar with a *gassho*. "Howdy, Chow, good to see ya again. It's been a while. Sorry about that little incident with your sister. Hope all's forgiven. Listen, any idea where I can find Old Norgay?"

Chow, the fleabag's proprietor, flashed a virtually toothless grin and eyed us with his one milky eye as we all took stools around the bar. "Well, well, well, if it isn't Duncan Carter? Back to lose some more climbers, are you?"

"You mean 'lead,' not 'lose,'" I said to Chow. "Duncan's our *lead-er*."

Duncan lowered his voice and leaned over to Chow. "Ixnay on the lost climberskees ay? I got paying customers with me. Cool?"

"Finally, a place where I can wet my whistle!" bellowed Max (still in his Speedo), while Michael zoomed in tight on his butt.

"Hey, Max, remind me again why our public school system is a 'failed monopoly.' I want to make sure to get your point of view on film."

"I'm gonna ram that camera down your throat if you take another shot of my derriere, Yankee boy."

"You should see this place, Yorgi," said Wendell, yanking him toward the bar. "It's like the frig'n Ritz."

"*Ya svedalto eto myo*! I do myself! Vindall, understand?"

"But you're freakin' blind. You need my help. I don't want you to walk into a wall or somethi . . ."

BAM.

"Oh, boy. Can we get some ice over here, please?"

"Order me a Booker Noe's, will you, darling?" Lauren said, checking her makeup with her compact.

"Speaking of, I'm famished," said I. "*Garçon!* A Labuse club, and a booger-nose for the lady, if you please!"

"Yaz—and I could goes for a big bowl of calsoneez!"

"Be careful now," said Kirsten, patting Tony's tummy, "I don't want you to lose your shapely figure." And then she giggled way too much.

"There'll be plenty of time to eat later, A-holes. We're here to find Old Norgay."

"Tenzing Norgay died back in the eighties," said Chow, chuckling. "Hey, Tzing Tzang, why you hang out with this loser? He nothing but trouble."

"Duncan's the boss," Tzing Tzang said. "Besides, I need the money. I'm working my way through beauty school. Now, where's Norgay?"

But before Chow had a chance to answer, Tzing Tzang grabbed his neck and pulled him over the bar. "You tell now, or else you die."

Kirsten gasped, "Tony, are those men fighting?"

"Yeah, it looks like it."

"Well, aren't you gonna do something about it?"

"Um . . . yeah, of course. I tink I should put on some musics to lightens the moods."

"He not here," Chow sputtered. "He dead. Nineteen eighty-six! He die! I swear!"

"That's not what I hear," Duncan said. "Now I'm only going to ask you one last time."

"Who wants to know?" barked a woman's voice and everyone stopped and turned around. Max whistled lasciviously.

A striking young Nepalese farm girl sidled up to the bar next to Duncan. Her hair was jet-black and braided with colorful beads, and she wore a long lambskin coat with a matted yak-fur collar. Attached to the rope around her waist was a small leather ammunition pouch, a coiled whip, and a sheathed Bowie knife (signed by the singer himself). She was handsome in an "I don't take any shit from anybody" kind of way, and she immediately smote me. (I besmite easily—especially if a sexy Nepalese farm chick is wearing big old Ugg boots.)

"Duncan Carter—Mountain Maniacs, Inc., and world-famous bounty hunter—wants to know."

"Your reputation precedes you, Mr. Carter," she said, "a reputation of unparalleled ineptitude, conspicuous alcoholism, drug consumption, and unrelenting womanizing."

"All in the past, sweetheart—except for the womanizing. I try to get in an hour every day, if I can."

"Norgay doesn't see just anybody. And not just anybody can see him. He takes on physical form only when he chooses. Seek him in the dirt and in the rain, and in the microscopic parasites living in the mattress pads of your Holiday Inns . . . but not here."

"Yeah, yeah, yeah, real spooky. But Sir Hillary told me he'd see me."

"Edmund sent you?"

"That's right."

"Prove it."

"He's wearing the ruby boots that the good explorer of the East gave him!" She looked at me like I was mentally defective (of all things). That made me really nervous, so I laughed out loud like a finback whale, which made Yorgi smack Wendell on the back of the head, thinking he was me.

"Ow. I didn't say it! It was him!"

"Jesus Christ," Lauren cried, "whom do I have to blow to get a Booker Noe's around here?"

Suddenly "Midnight at the Oasis" blasted out of the jukebox.

Tony began to sing along, "Put your camelz to bedz. Got shadows painted on faces, traces of romanz idée airz . . ."

"*Dancing* is so much more fun than *arguing!*" said Kirsten, cutting a rug with Tony.

"It's likes one of those old-time socks hops! Everybodies, congas lines!"

"Wee!" And at that we all joined in—the actors, anyway—holding on to each other's hips and mincing around the bar like complete morons. (Us thespians can't resist a conga line.)

The woman with the whip watched with disdain and disbelief. "Okay, enough. Stop!" she demanded, and then turned to Duncan. "I think maybe it's time for you and your little freak show to shuffle off to Buffalo or wherever you're playing next." To drive the point home, she pulled her coat aside, revealing the butt end of a revolver.

I screamed.

Suddenly a man's voice came from somewhere—almost, it seemed, from everywhere all around us: "It all right, Pamma. Any friend of Edmund's is friend of mine."

CHAPTER THIRTEEN

Tenzing Norgay (meaning the "Lucky One") and Sir Edmund Hillary (meaning "Big White Eyebrows Forever") were the first to summit Mount Everest, back in 1953. The two had, for many years, kept secret who it was who actually summitted before the other, but in 1980 Tenzing finally wrote in a letter to his son.

> Hillary stepped up first, and then I stepped up after him. And then the chicks we picked up at the "pimps and hos" party down at Camp Three stepped up after us.

Norgay was rumored to have died in Darjeeling in 1986, but his death was never fully substantiated, and over the years he had taken on the personae of a thaumaturgic being. There was even talk that he was capable of shape-shifting, levitating, and eating at Taco Bell without coming down with E. coli—and of course communing with Chomolungma. (There was also another rumor that this guy was a Vegas magician whom Disney had hired to entertain the tourists at the lodge—or perhaps he was just an animatron, like the yaks.)

But now, sitting in a booth, rocking in and out of the eerie light cast by the butter lamps, Tenzing Norgay—or whoever (or whatever) he really was—appeared every bit the necromancer.

"Sir Edmund says you speak the language of the mountain," said Duncan, slouched in the booth along with Tzing Tzang, across from Pamma and Old Norgay.

"If she wants to talk," the old Sherpa replied, rolling a cigar and lighting it. Then he threw his head back and laughed. "But she don't want to talk much these days. She not happy."

"What is it you want, Carter?" Pamma barked.

Norgay raised his hand. "Bop!" and then he lowered it slowly. "You must excuse my great-grandchild. As you can see, I've spoiled her. She speaks when she should listen."

"*The Godfather*!" Duncan was pleased. "Great movie."

"The sequel is much better."

"Definitely, but what about Part Three, huh?"

"Piece of crap. Don't get me started."

"Fellas, do you think we could talk business, please?" Tzing Tzang interjected. "If we're going to make it to Base Camp today, it might be good idea to get there before sun goes down."

"Here's the deal, Norgay: I want you to be our eyes and ears on the mountain. Base Camp supervisor. I don't really know who you are. You could be the great David Copperfield himself for all I know . . ."

Pamma jumped to her feet. "He is the great Tenzing Norgay, first Sherpa to summit Everest! Show some damn respect!" She pulled her knife from its sheath.

"Pamma . . . take a Zen pill," advised Norgay. "Go on, Mr. Duncan."

"I've seen enough shit on that mountain to know anything can happen, and I want to get back alive. Plus the Screen Actors Guild would have a field day with me if any of these putzes weren't around for the awards season."

Norgay leaned back, plunging his face into total darkness. Duncan squinted, but it was now impossible to see any aspect of the man (or spirit) he was speaking with.

"I know why you climb, Mr. Duncan," said the voice from out of the darkness. "The Golden Rhombus means many things to many people. To you it is simply a prize, but to the Tibetans it is much more than that. It is the lifeblood of Chomolungma herself—the Tibetan Holy Grail. It was believed to have been stolen many years ago and bestowed upon Percy Brackett Elliott, but the imbecile died in 1924 trying to return it to its rightful place. You see, to Tibetans the Rhombus and Percy are one and the same. He, the Rhombus; the Rhombus, he. You find him, you find the Rhombus."

"Sounds simple enough to me."

"But it is not so simple. You will be stopped—and perhaps even killed—or maybe a little of both. Ever since the Rhombus was stolen from the top of mountain, the world has been unstable. The only way to regain stability is to return the Rhombus to Chomolungma's peak. Then the Tibetans will have the power to do what they want—and what they want is very dangerous."

"The peak? It was stolen from the peak? I thought Percy found it somewhere up on the south approach?"

"No. No. It was the peak, the 'tiptop.' But Percy didn't find it. It was bestowed on him before he ever came to the Himalayas, by the thief who took it."

"I'm confused. If you're really Tenzing Norgay, then you and Hillary were the first ones to the summit, so how could its 'tiptop' have been stolen before you guys got there?"

A puff of white smoke appeared like an apparition from out of the black abyss and hovered over the table before dissipating.

"There was another, before us."

"What? Who? When?"

"The Rhombus is power beyond belief, Mr. Duncan. It is not to be toyed with. The threshold between right and wrong is always pain."

"Hi ya, fellas, what's the buzz? Tell me what's a-happen'n!" I sang, stumbling over to the booth, totally bombed. The high altitude coupled with the potent *chaang*, a beerlike concoction made out of rice millet, yeast, hops, and uncut cocaine, was affecting me in an almost hallucinatory way. I plopped down, burped, giggled, and then kissed Pamma on her braids. She promptly shoved me off the bench.

Norgay gasped, "It can't be you! But it is! You are him . . . there is no doubt about it. You are . . . him . . . No wonder they believe that you . . ."

He leaned forward out of the darkness, his once benevolent eyes now narrowed into unflinching beads.

"You are in great danger," he warned me. "You must not climb!"

A heavy silence hung in the lodge as everyone exchanged puzzled looks, but I just grinned and winked at Pamma and blew her a kiss.

Suddenly the butter lamps began to sway back and forth, slowly at first, and then faster and faster, and the mugs behind the bar began to rattle. A moment later, the floor was shaking.

"The *yidam*!" gasped Norgay.

"Is that a yes or a no?" asked Duncan.

The walls cracked open, the overhead beams groaned plaintively, and the ground rumbled with a furious violence.

"Earthquake!" shrieked Chow. "A real one! Not fake Disney one. Everybody out!" But before he had time to climb over the bar, a butter lamp fell from the rafters and smashed over his head, drenching him in hot fat. The aforementioned loathsome mélange of grody locals panicked, threw over their tables, and ran for the exit.

President Martin, Tony, and Kirsten beat a hasty retreat, as Lauren grabbed hold of me and dragged me out. "Come on, drunky!"

"Wait, what about the farm chicky-babe in the Uggs! She was hot!"

"Now we go, boss. We go now! Everyone to cars!" Tzing Tzang yelled as the place filled with smoke and dust, and the cacophony rose to a deafening din.

"I'll take the barley pop!" Max stuffed the keg of *chaang* under his arm and dashed for the door.

"Someone carry my camera. That's not my job!" demanded Michael, stamping his foot.

"Show some damn respect."

"Yorgi, come with me!" Wendell ordered, but Yorgi, as usual, would not accept his help.

"Nyet! Nyet!" he barked. "But, please to point me in right direction."

"There's no time to . . . oh, forget this." Wendell clamped Yorgi into one of his famous headlocks and pulled the Russian out.

Old Norgay clasped Duncan's wrist. "I will be your eyes and ears, but I will not help recover the Rhombus. For that, you are on your own."

"Agreed," shouted Duncan, as a huge beam came crashing down just inches away. Then he dashed for the door.

"Grandfather, we must leave, now!" Pamma struggled to wrench Norgay from the booth, but the placid Sherpa merely smiled, pulled out a magician's wand, and waved it back and forth a couple of times. Pamma sighed, "Oh, for God's sake, Gramps, you're not a real wizard," and she threw him over her shoulder.

Minutes later, we were back in our Range Rovers and racing out of town toward the Khumbu Glacier, when a shock wave rocked our vehicles. When we looked back, we saw that the Labuse Lodge had been totally obliterated.

"What the hell just happened?" I asked.

"Aftershock! Damn Disney people," Tzing Tzang muttered. "Fake shit very combustible. I told them it was accident waiting to happen."

As we sped away, I watched the column of black smoke get smaller and smaller and could only hope that Old Norgay and Pamma made it out alive—especially Pamma, who had already replaced Vera in my heart and soul as the woman of my dreams and/or my sick fantasies.

CHAPTER FOURTEEN

Uncle Percy's arrival in the Himalayas in 1924 had been no less eventful:

Dear Diary,
Blinding snow. Have lost all steering capability. Flaps useless. Motor dead. Can't control *Ever-Rest*! She's going down fast! Mayday! Mayday! Wait, I see a stretch of smooth ice up ahead. It's a perfect, natural runway. If only I didn't have to keep writing this damn diary I could free up my hands and possibly land this thing. Spinning violently out of control now—five hundred feet—dropping like a lead balloon—down—down—one hundred feet—difficult to write—forty-two feet—pencil needs sharpening—ten feet—sucking on my last meat lozenge (pork loin—not my favorite. The chicken tetrazzini is best)—three feet—good-bye, world, I hardly knew ye—down, down—one foot to go. I wonder if I should lower the landing gear? And that's it—the lights have gone out.

Percy Brackett Elliott
Khumbu Glacier, Everest, 1924

P.S. Could someone please get me an Alka-Seltzer?

When the lights finally came back on, my uncle found himself in the care of the gentle Buddhist monks of the Rong Shu monastery, who, after torturing him mercilessly (but gently, and probably for his own good) for about a week, slowly nursed him back to health.

A few days later he was strong enough to begin his solo ascent.

The Rong Shu monastery still stands today. It's situated on a noble promontory high up in the Manaslu cliffs on the Nepalese side of the border with Tibet, and it commands a spectacular view of the entire Tibetan plateau. On a clear day, looking west, you can see the majestic Karakoram Range; east, you can see past Everest all the way to Lhasa, the former capital of Tibet; and north of course is China, and the giant bronze statue of Richard Nixon trying to eat a potsticker with chopsticks.

The common perception is that Tibet had always been a peaceful little kingdom on a happy little plateau, where happy little peaceful people lived happily together in love and harmony, drinking *chaang*, smoking weed, and throwing wild key parties until the big bad communists invaded in 1950, but the truth is a little more complicated than that.

For centuries Tibet was not unlike ancient feudal Europe. The rich priestly class owned all the land and livestock and most of the platform shoes, and took huge cuts of the yogurt concessions and the mutton on-a-stick revenues, big moneymakers during the tourist season. The plight of the poor was justified as evidence that they had bad karma, or weren't spiritually enlightened enough, or had been practicing too much "solo gravy making" in their spare time. So when the People's Liberation Army took over, it was not met with overwhelming resistance only because some of the lower classes felt that in a way they *were* being liberated.

It was only after communist rule began to impose its own strict policies, like limiting sweets, banning improvisational comedy (which I happen to agree with, but that doesn't make me a communist), and burning all black satin underpants, that the Tibetans launched a rebellion (backed by the CIA and public television), which unfortunately failed.

After the rebellion, Mao came down hard on the people of Tibet, many of whom fled to neighboring Nepal. Fearing for the young Dalai Lama's life, his two most trusted monks disguised him as a traveling Jehovah's Witness and snuck him into India. He has not returned to his homeland since.

But now, standing on the balcony of the ancient Rong Shu monastery in Nepal, flanked by the same two trusted monks from his childhood, the Dalai Lama gazed out over the Tibetan plateau and mused.

"It is such a beautiful land. Such hardship. Such sorrow." The two monks, sensing his melancholic mood, simply nodded. Perhaps it was jet lag. (The three had beat us to the Himalayas in the Lama's private jet.)

The little man took a sip of tea. "I have been contacted by the Bodhisattva. He is secreted inside the blind man's ski bag." He walked to a table and picked up a gold scepter and bell, important symbols in Tibetan Buddhism that represent the alliance between "method and wisdom." "Take the *dorje* and the *drilbu*, my dear Ping and Pong, for you are both my method and my wisdom. With them we will defeat the *yidam*, and together we will walk the diamond path and drink from the untarnished well . . . yet again."

The two elderly monks exchanged puzzled looks. They didn't quite get that last one.

"Doesn't do it for you?" asked the Dalai Lama, who took out a notepad and crossed out some lines. "Oh, well, why muck around with a good thing?

CHAPTER FIFTEEN

We had traveled only about an hour before our caravan screeched to a halt at the edge of a great expanse of shimmering ice.

"Backpacks and crampons, A-holes!" ordered Duncan. "From here on out we walk!"

We all got out of the Range Rovers and readied ourselves for the first leg of our ascent, which would take us north on a seven-hour trek climbing at a relatively gentle gradient—but over rugged, denticulated schist and slippery glacial ice—to Base Camp, another two thousand feet up.

There were a number of Sherpas and porters there to help us with the heavy equipment.

Kirsten dropped her backpack in front of Wendell. "Here's my junk. I have to carry Mr. Pop-eyes." She held up a live bunny with big, bulging orbs. "I think he has 'grievous' disease or 'Gray's Anatomy' or something."

Wendell huffed, "Listen lady, I'm not . . ." but she was already skipping over to Tony.

As I helped Lauren on with her gaiters, crampons, and thingama-jigs, Duncan recited a half-assed safety speech: "You should each pick a partner and keep that person in your sight at all times."

We had already naturally coupled off: Wendell and Yorgi, Michael and Max, Tony and Kirsten, Lauren and me, and Martin and, um . . . America, I guess.

"Remember to wear your name tags at all times so I can identify you if your nose freezes off or some shit like that."

I started laughing, imagining Tony and Kirsten without noses! What fun!

"Hey, don't laugh," said Duncan, "it happens."

"Yeah, right," I muttered, "maybe to A-holes."

I was relieved that my old *Adam-12* knapsack felt pretty comfortable. It wouldn't pose much of a problem for me—at least not at this early stage in the climb. Secretly, I knew Wendell's *Barnaby Jones* knapsack was way too big and way too full of unnecessary junk, like his old Joe Namath Bullworker and his Apollo 11 commemorative coin collection, so I hardly felt any guilt at all about letting Grammy stick in a pair of my best dress shoes. *They're not that heavy*, I thought. *And besides, it's the least he can do for me, considering I'm the reason he's getting to climb Mount Everest in the first place!*

Tzing Tzang pulled me aside. "Yaks and monkeys overloaded. You need to carry Yorgi's skis."

"Jesus Christ! Heavier skis I have never felt! What are these, special skis for the blind?"

"The higher you climb," Duncan continued, "the more quickly your oxygen will be depleted. Be careful not to overexert yourselves. You're not used to the high altitude yet. You can easily become disoriented and lightheaded. If you feel this happening, try to focus on the . . ." He suddenly stopped talking, and a cold, deathly stare crossed his face.

"What exactly is he doing?" Lauren asked.

"There's something wrong with his brain or something," Wendell said.

"Yeah, but it usually doesn't last this long," I waved my hand back and forth in front of Duncan's face.

"Brave captain!" said Lauren, snapping her fingers. "Hello?"

"Oh, well," sighed Tzing Tzang. "I suppose we need to rest a bit anyway. It late. We sleep here tonight!"

He directed us to arrange our tents in a circle around the motionless Duncan.

As Wendell and I got cozy in our Family Fun Tent, he asked me, "What do you suppose all that stuff about you being in 'great danger' meant?"

"I think it was some sort of Sherpa blessing."

"But he said, 'You must not climb.'"

"He probably meant 'not climb, you must skip! It's more fun to skip than to climb!'"

Wendell sighed. "Whatever."

Outside, Duncan stood frozen, watching the sun until it disappeared over the—

". . . horizon!" he finally finished. "And lastly, once we start, there's no turning back, so if anyone's having second thoughts . . ." He looked around dazedly. "Um . . . guys? A-holes?"

As dusk fell, Captain Harding and her rookie partner, Resnick, stood in the smoldering rubble of the Labuse Lodge.

"The guy covered in butter says the earth shook, and the building collapsed and then blew up," Resnick reported, referring to his notebook. "Looks like an earthquake, plain and simple, but what are the odds of that happening right before we show up, huh?"

"Pretty good, I imagine, if that's what just happened," said Harding. She picked up a piece of twisted metal and held it to her nose.

"Calcium carbonate, ammonium hydroxide, and purified anionic acid. This was no earthquake—it was a highly sophisticated smart bomb."

"What kind of bomb is so smart that it impersonates an earthquake before it decides to explode?"

"Thermobaric seismicity-trembler, that's what kind. Probably a two-hundred pounder. Our country's had 'em for years. It's mainly used to cause political unrest, but it can also be a handy public relations tool—currying favor with hostile nations by making it appear as though we're a caring people who always send aid, even if the affected areas belong to our enemies. Little do they know that we actually cause the quakes in the first place."

"That is so screwed up."

"Don't be so naïve."

"But why would our government want an earthquake to happen here at the Labuse Lodge? We're just trying to stop these climbers, not eliminate them, right?"

"This wasn't us. We don't use anionic acid in our natural-disaster bombs." She thought for a moment. "At least we haven't for years . . ." Then she looked through her binoculars, scanning the horizon. "But this kind of technology is very expensive. Obviously someone feels even stronger about stopping the Mountain Maniacs than we do."

"Who?"

Harding lowered her binoculars and turned to her rookie partner.

"Get your *Mannix* knapsack, Resnick. We're going mountain climbing."

CHAPTER SIXTEEN

Dear Diary,

Upon the Khumbu Glacier, our garish sun radiates with analeptic ardor, but it is the sun's lustrous gleam, reflected in the sparkling pinnacles and dancing orbs that are the uninvited guests for whom this irascible ice—in fear of deportation to its baptismal depths—does most vigilantly incite to depart—that fills my soul with trumpets. I am reminded of *A Midsummer Night's Dream:*

> *A tedious brief scene of you, Pyramus*
> *And his love this be: very tragic mirth.*
> *Merry and tragical! Tedious and brief!*
> *That is, hot ice and wondrous strange snow.*

"Hot ice" and "wondrous strange snow," indeed! How grateful I am that I have taken on this journey. How my heart leaps at the prospect of that which awaits me. How my soul yearns for the summit!

Percy Brackett Elliott
First impression of the mountain, 1924

Dear Diary,
I've been climbing for about twenty minutes now and I want to
blow my head off! What the hell was I thinking? Forget all that
bunkum about wonderous strange snow. This sucks rotten eggs!

Percy Brackett Elliott
Second impression of the mountain, 1924

And I couldn't have agreed with him more. Of course, some of *my*
malaise could be chalked up to the fact that in addition to my own
backpack and climbing gear, I was also hauling Yorgi's ski bag—with
our mysterious stowaway tucked comfortably inside. At times I
thought I heard him breathing, but I just assumed that because of
the high altitude, my lungs had fallen out of sync with each other.
But even without the additional weight, I would not have been a
happy camper. The glacier was hell on earth.

A giant river of ice sloped upward, its surface scattered with cin-
ders, granite boulders, and half-eaten churro fossils—some dating
back to the Paleozoic era. Far above us was a fairway of steep and
slippery black ice, peppered with brittle outcroppings of irregular
permafrost. Giant ice pinnacles, artistically rendered by eons of ge-
ologic forces—and a local ice sculptor named Mishmash—protruded two hundred and fifty feet into the air, creating a natural
causeway known as the Phantom Alley. Shifting shadows gave the
illusion that the ice pinnacles were alive, and, as we passed by, I
even heard one of them speak.

"Hey, jerk-off," it said, "don't look now, but you're fly'n low." (I
thought it had been unusually breezy down there, even for the Himalayas.) I zipped up and thanked the pinnacle like a proper gentleman, and threw it a gingersnap.

The climb had begun pleasantly enough. We had emerged ener-
getic after a good night's sleep. Then with a hardy twelve-egg and

sausage "Everest Fool's Breakfast" from Denny's under our belts, we began our pilgrimage to Base Camp. For most of the day we hiked independently, free to visit with one another, but now as the sun bowed its head and the temperatures began to plummet, we were told to tether ourselves to our partners, clip our carabiners onto a safety rope, and follow along in a dutiful line (like kindergarten children, for Christ's sakes!) wherever Duncan and Tzing Tzang chose to lead us.

"This sucks," I remarked bitterly to Lauren, because we had accidentally tethered ourselves face-to-face and were compelled to schlepp sideways like a crab. But after about a mile or so, we fixed the problem. Besides giving me stereo breathing, a pounding headache, constant nausea, and an obstreperous ringing in my ears that sounded like Leo Sayer on helium, the high altitude had also put me in a really foul mood, which Lauren sought to remedy by teaching me how to smoke.

I could tell that the high altitude was also affecting Max and Michael, who seemed to be speaking in gibberish (a language common to cretins, simpletons, and the French—in addition to being a well-known side effect of altitude sickness).

"If more government is the answer, why the heck don't we just give all our millions to Washington and tell those folks up there to go fix everything for us! Ha, ha, ha, ha."

"You conservative Republicans just don't realize that a large percentage of Americans depend on subsidized programs just to survive!"

"Betty," I whispered, "I think they're speaking in tongues."

Right behind those guys, Wendell and Yorgi traipsed along the ice.

"Now, right in front of you is some ice. And about three feet ahead of that is some more ice, and . . ."

"*Nyak verxee*, Vindall! I get it—ice all around!"

"Watch it! There's some more ice up ahead! Gosh, it must suck to be blind. I mean, you just can't see *anything*, can you?"

And behind them, slogging forward over the alien terrain, Kirsten, cradling Mr. Pop-eyes in her parka, spoke in hushed tones to Tony.

"Do you suppose anyone suspects?"

"Nays. We've been subtles."

"Because it will never work if they find out."

"Yeahs. We'll have to be sneakys."

"All right then," and she put Mr. Pop-eyes in her pocket. "On three, then. One . . . two . . ."

"Three!" they yelled together, and let loose at us with the hail of snowballs they had been quietly collecting all morning.

"Hey, everybodeez, it's likes one of them old-times snowball fights!"

We all started throwing snowballs at each other. The sudden breakdown in order caused everyone to get tangled up in the safety line.

"What are you A-holes doing back there? This is Mount Everest, not a goddamn flea circus!"

High above us, the *lammergeiers* circled, oblivious to our reverie. They were used to such foolhardy visitors to the region. To them, we were simply a bunch of tiny black blemishes stretched out across the sweeping breadth of anguished ice—with one single straggler lagging far behind.

Separated from the fun, Martin breathed so heavily through his nose I could hear him. I have to say that my respect for the man was growing hourly, as with every agonizing step his staunch commitment to the plight of the homeless in motion pictures remained unchallenged. I have to say that because it sounds good, but honestly I thought he was a moron.

He must have heard something peculiar because he abruptly stopped. This caused the safety line to yank us backward and we all fell on top of each other.

Looking back, I could see Martin's eyes widen, scanning the surrounding pinnacles, crags, and drifts. He must have heard the sound again—this time from behind him—and he slowly started to unlatch the "nuclear football." He whipped around, but except for the ever-present laments of glacial ice fracturing and refreezing, there was nothing there.

He shrugged, relatched the football, and turned back around. Then suddenly:

"Grrrrrrrrrrrrrr!"

The noise echoed off the giant pinnacles. It was a wild animal— a large one, perhaps a *Panthera uncia* (that's smarty-pants for "snow leopard"). Although it would be unusual for the leopard to be up this high in the mountains this time of year, as they prefer to winter in Boca Raton. But what else could it be?

Martin jumped up and down and pulled on the safety rope and pointed in the direction the growl had come from.

"What's he trying to say? Just take off the damned tape, you imbecile," said Lauren.

Refusing to remove it, Martin continued to gesticulate wildly and point behind him.

"What is it, boy?" I asked. "Are you on fire? Stop, drop, and roll!"

"I've had about enough of you A-holes," yelled Duncan, stamping back from the front of the line. "This is no time to take a nap, princess." And he gave Kirsten a gentle kick in the ribs. (She was on her back making snow angels.)

"Everybody up. We're almost there!"

We brushed ourselves off and gathered our stuff together. Summoning our last fleeting bits of energy, we tramped on. But Martin remained worried and regularly glanced over his shoulder.

After about three more miles we crossed a large *neve*, or permanent snowbank. On the other side, haphazardly arranged across the ice, was a mass of multicolored tents. In the center of the camp, a number of Sherpas, porters, and valets chanted and danced around a *punja* pole, at the base of which was gathered a pile of backpacks, climbing axes, and rope. The Sherpas and porters believe that this *punja* ceremony appeases the gods of the mountain and blesses the climbers and their equipment, while the valets see it as an easy way to get out of parking yaks for about an hour. Directly in front of us was a beautiful white tent with a wraparound screened-in porch, to keep those pesky Himalayan mosquitoes at bay.

"Ah, finally—home, sweet home," said Lauren.

"Not exactly," said Duncan. "That's not our tent." To Tzing Tzang, he whispered, "How did he get here before us?"

"Who?" I asked. (The high altitude had apparently imbued me with superhuman hearing.) Duncan ignored me and addressed everyone else, "Um, folks, despite what we were promised, there seems to be another expedition on the mountain . . . It's no problem, though. Misery loves company, right? Our control tent is the little beauty right next to the big one there."

Our eyes fell on a small, beat-up, old army-surplus tent with a bunch of vultures sitting on top of it.

"What fun," I said excitedly. "It's like the bird house at the zoo! Not that that was my favorite part of the zoo or anything. Actually it sort of scared me, and it stunk."

"So who are these other climbers?" Wendell asked.

"Oh . . . um, you know, it's probably . . . just a bunch of virgins, or something," said Duncan.

Wendell automatically did a spit take (a literal spit take because he wasn't drinking anything at the time). "Virgins?"

"I believe he means first-time climbers," clarified Lauren. "Isn't that right, brave captian?"

"Uh, yeah. Whatever," muttered Duncan.

"Welcome to Base Camp!" hailed Old Norgay, stepping out of the Mountain Maniacs control tent with his arms open wide. I was disappointed because he was alone, but a moment later he was joined

Phantom Alley

by his great-granddaughter, her body language oozing with a sexy, jaundiced attitude and her face radiating with an acrid, sour sneer.

"Pamma! You made it! You're alive! Hip, hip, hooray!" I cheered, and sort of ran but mostly slid down the *neve*, pulling the rest of the Mountain Maniacs behind me.

Everyone's altimeters read 19,000 feet, 3¼ inches. I wasn't sure what mine read, because I had foolishly assumed that it was a specific type of thermometer—and at the moment I was taking my temperature and unable to get to it.

CHAPTER SEVENTEEN

In our storage tent the mysterious stowaway had shed Yorgi's ski bag and now sat on a low stool with a theatrical makeup case in his lap. He put a mirror beside him and tied his hair back with an elastic band. Next he took out a rouge pencil and some nose putty. Finally he taped a photograph of George C. Scott (as Fagin) next to the mirror and began to apply makeup.

It took him about an hour, but once the wig and pointy rumpled hat were on, the transformation was complete. There would be no way anyone would recognize him (as whomever he might really be) and you would have to be a complete boob-tube idiot to know he was made up as George C. Scott as Fagin from the low-rated 1989 TNT remake of *Oliver*. (Does anyone sense a "setup" here?)

A moment later, he was out mingling with the other Sherpas, pretending to busy himself at various chores while surreptitiously making his way toward the mess tent (the one with the giant illuminated Big Boy, happily serving a cheeseburger).

"There's got to be a morning after . . ." Kirsten sang into a microphone.

If we can make it to the shore,
There's gonna be a morning after
'Cause we can't take it anymore.

Oh can't you see the morning after,
It's snowing right now
but I think you still can see it.
It's a really cool morning after,
And it's waiting for us right outside the door . . .

Tony whistled and stomped his feet, then leaned over to Martin and whispered, "She sounds a lot better after post-production."

The mess tent accommodated a makeshift kitchen and two long tables, one reserved for the Mountain Maniacs expedition and one for the other expedition. Duncan wasn't exaggerating when he called them a bunch of virgins. They were twenty beautiful, tall, leggy blondes in snow-white parkas. Oil lamps swayed overhead as porters and Sherpas scurried about with jugs of *chaang*, pots of steaming tea, and bowls of tasteless mush—for us, anyway. The blondes were being fed lobster bisque and smoked sockeye salmon. Apparently Duncan had gone for the economy meal package.

"What on earth are all those pills for?" Lauren asked Max, who was laying medicine out in front of him.

"Oh, these? Um . . . well, these are just vitamins mostly," he said, and then he picked up a red one. "Now this is vitamin A—improves your eyesight." He picked up a yellow one. "This is C for my gums and muscles." Then a blue pill. "And this here is E. Hee, hee, hee. Spanish fly, know what I mean?" He winked at her, growled, and then licked his lips and barked.

"Subtle," Lauren replied. "And what are the rest of them for?"

He seemed not to want to discuss it. "Oh, just for a little condition I have. Nothing serious." And then he coughed. Lauren couldn't help but feel sorry for the hairy man, whose bare skin was already starting to turn a pultridudineous shade of purple. Max, sensing an opportunity, whispered, "You know, a lot of people say I remind them of Bogie."

"Mmm. Do they really, now? I was thinking more of Charles Laughton. Just pass me the salt, Max."

"There's got to be a morning after . . ." Kirsten continued singing, "and if we can make it to the shore, maybe we'll have a party at my house, and we won't let any losers through the door!" Wendell was screwing around with Yorgi, moving the blind man's bowl of mush a couple of inches to the right and then back to the left, and taking pleasure in watching Yorgi dip his spoon into thin air.

"Stop it, Vindall. I know what you do!"

"I'm sorry, man," said Wendell, "it's just so damn fascinating to be around a guy who just sees pitch black all the time."

Duncan grimaced and held his ears as Kirsten crucified the big finish.

"I say, we won't let no losers through the do-or!" Then she bowed dramatically and we all applauded.

"Bravoz," shouted Tony.

Kirsten blushed wholesomely, "Thank you, everyone, that's off my new album, *Screwed,* debuting next month. It's about losing out on love, I think."

Duncan stood up, clanking his mug with a spoon. "Thank you, Kirsten. That was . . . almost entertaining. And now I'd like to make a toast." He raised his mug. "Here's to our first day of climbing . . ."

Suddenly the tent flap opened, letting in wind and snow, along with a short gentleman with big teeth and a silly goatee. We all recognized him immediately. It was Richard Branson, the founder of Virgin Atlantic Airlines and a noteworthy adventurer in his own right. He nodded to Duncan and took a seat at the head of the virgins' table.

Duncan and Tzing Tzang exchanged worried looks. Duncan continued with his toast, obviously rattled. "As I was saying . . . Um . . . you all handled yourselves like real pros!"

We all cheered and drank down our *chaang*.

Branson cleared his throat. "Yes, chin chin, one and all," he said, accepting a martini from a Sherpa. "But tomorrow the true adventure begins, does it not?"

"What are you talking about, 'tomorrow'?" asked Duncan.

"Well, my dear fellow, tomorrow begins our climb in earnest: these lovely jewels and I up the west approach, while you and your matinee idols up the south. You haven't forgotten about our little wager, have you, old chap?"

"But we need to acclimatize first!"

The plan was to stay at Base Camp for three weeks, adjusting to the thin air before moving on to the next leg of our ascent: a five-thousand-foot climb through the deadly Khumbu Icefall (where at least one person always dies) up to Camp Two.

If you ascend too rapidly you run the risk of coming down with caisson disease—better known as "the bends" (gaseous nitrogen bubbles trapped in your tissues, often experienced by deep-sea divers or anyone attending a Clay Aiken concert). If you're not immediately put in a recompression chamber, you could suffer permanent brain damage and/or death. (But at least you'd be cured of this debilitating depression that keeps you in bed all day reading crummy books written by jerk-off actors out to make a quick buck.)

"Oh, I am sorry, old chap," said Branson, "but we've already acclimatized. You see I had a pressure chamber delivered to our suite at the Mickey and Friends Resort, in Labuse. We start climbing up tomorrow, but I suppose you'll have to stick around and get used to the thin air the old-fashioned way, yes?"

"But you said Base Camp was the jump-off point," protested Duncan.

"Yes, but I never said we had to 'jump off' at the same time. Now you'll have to climb at the double quick if you still want to win. Unless you'd prefer to forfeit everything right here and now."

Duncan thought long and hard about this, gazing down at our table and into each of our flummoxed faces.

"Ain't forfeiting shit," he declared, and he raised his mug to Branson. "We got a bunch of toughies here. We'll be fine. Three weeks is overkill anyway. One night is all we need. So here's to tomorrow. May the best team win!"

Branson raised his martini glass. "To tomorrow, then!"

Duncan cheered, "To tomorrow!"

We all halfheartedly joined in, "To, uh, tomorrow . . ."

For a few minutes, we merely spooned our mush and looked at each other glumly. Lauren finally spoke up.

"Brave captain, would you like to explain exactly what kind of 'wager' you have going here? I'm sure we'd all be quite fascinated."

Tzing Tzang shook his head. "What'd I tell you, boss? Rush, rush, hurry, hurry. This no good."

"You seem to be an expert at scheming, Mr. Carter," said Pamma, sharpening her knife. "I hope this won't increase the jeopardy your team is already in."

"Especially that one!" growled Old Norgay, pointing his crooked finger across the table at me and giving me the hairy eyeball. "He's in a lot of danger, in case I didn't mention it."

I stuck my tongue out at him.

"Well, hell, surfer boy, if you got a little bet on the side, I don't see any problem in that. As a matter of fact, I'd like to get in on it." Max removed a wad of cash from his Speedo and plunked it down on the table. "A little competition'll just motivate us all the more."

Michael coughed the word *capitalist* into his hand.

"Ain't nothing wrong with gambling, boy. It's as old as the hills and twice as dusty."

"I'll takes a piece of that actions too," said Tony. "Can you spots me one of them moist deuces, Maxy babys?"

"Tony, you know how I feel about gambling," said Kirsten, feeding Mr. Pop-eyes some mush.

"Butz Iz . . ." there was an awkward moment before Tony finally succumbed. "Ah, I don't like gamblings either . . . it's for lowlifez, rights?"

I made a whip-crack noise in the air over Tony's head.

"Relax everyone," Duncan said. "My business with Branson is my business, and it doesn't affect anyone at this table."

"Actually, brave captain, it affects everyone at this table," Lauren said. "And it isn't right for you to keep it a secret."

"Look, queenie, some things are just private. I guess being a rich movie star, living the glamorous life, you don't care much about that."

"Au contraire, brave captain, privacy is all us movie stars have to call our own."

"Yeah, well, your press agents are sure happy enough to spatter your dirt all over the rag papers." He pulled out a *National Inquirer* with the headline BETTY, BOGIE, AND ROBARDS IN PARANORMAL THREESOME.

"And one could only imagine how much it would be 'spattered' all over the papers if something were to happen to one of us as a result of your negligence, brave captain."

Lauren knew just exactly how to get under somebody's skin, and I pitied any skin (no matter what color, what nationality, or in Duncan's case, how many ticks were attached to it) that Lauren could manage to get under.

A blast of cold air made us all shudder. The door flap had opened again, this time admitting the unfamiliar Sherpa. He bowed and then made himself comfortable at the end of our table. I furrowed my brow, observing him closely. Despite being "unfamiliar," he seemed vaguely familiar to me, as well. He saw me looking and nodded weirdly.

So not only do I have Norgay giving me the hairy eyeball, but now there's this weird Sherpa making goo-goo eyes at me. Great! I felt like I did my first day at Rikers.

"Listen lady, I've had just about enough out of you!" Duncan barked, rising to his feet, "This is the real world, see? Not some make-believe, Hollywood land of fruits and nuts, okay? A man has to do what a man has to do. Maybe you don't have to worry about anything, but people like me, we have to worry about making ends meet, like how you're gonna pay for your monthly Netflix bill? Or who's gonna spring for your daily visits to the Erotic Bakery? Or where you gonna come up with the cash for all those jars of hand sanitizer and canisters of pepper spray? It ain't easy, sugar. It ain't easy!"

Michael nudged Max. "This is exactly what I'm talking about: the plight of the little guy."

"Oh, hogwash," Max shot back. "He doesn't have to buy fresh bosom bread every day. He could go to the 'Day-Old' Erotic Bakery—it's half the price." Then he coughed again.

Duncan said, "Look, it's as simple as this: none of you schlubs had enough dough to foot the bill. We wouldn't be here if I hadn't made the deal I did—okay?" He straightened up. "Now, I want everybody ready to move out at oh-six hundred. That means you too, queenie. Crampons and ice axes! And everybody better be sharp tomorrow. I'm not waiting for nobody. We got a mountain to climb."

As he stormed out of the tent, he stopped by the virgins' table and got right up in Branson's Kool-Aid. "And as for you, you supercilious, condescending, cocksure faux-Limey, I'll be waiting for you up at the summit! That's right, *waiting* for you!"

"I'll look forward to it . . . 'brave captain,'" chirped Branson, raising his martini one last time in Duncan's honor.

Duncan shot some pepper spray up his nose and disappeared into the snowy night.

We all sat there somewhat stunned for a moment, until I finally raised my hand. "Excuse me, but does anybody besides me think that Sherpa at the end of the table looks exactly like George C. Scott from that old TNT version of *Oliver*?" (For those of you who sensed a "setup" earlier, that was your big payoff.) And then I sang, "You gotta pick a pocket or two . . ." (and that was your big bonus). Kirsten joined in, and Tony and Michael each took a verse as we danced on the tables, pretending to be the Artful Dodger and Fagin and old Bill Sykes—what fun!

But not Lauren. She leaned over to Max and whispered, "I don't like this one bit."

"Hell, sugar," replied Max, "you only go around once, right?" And then he coughed again, and Lauren patted him on the back.

At that moment, I couldn't say what Duncan's true motives were, but regardless of the deal (or wager) that had been struck, presumably to finance our expedition, nothing was worth all the risks he would take and all the losses we would bear (my nose! hello? plus a couple of human beings, to boot).

CHAPTER EIGHTEEN

It would be a challenge for all of us to get to sleep that night. The anticipation of the icefall weighed heavily on our minds. Wendell and I had made our Wal-Mart Family Fun Tent as comfortable as possible, but I was still cold. Between the howling of the wind outside and the caterwauling of the creaky ice beneath us, I felt uneasy. I don't know why, but even Uncle Percy's usually comforting diary offered little solace:

Dear Diary,
Tomorrow I attempt the Khumbu Icefall. Just about everybody who tries it either dies a horrible death or loses a leg or an arm in the process—especially first-time climbers. I hope none of my descendants ever try following in my footsteps. It would be really stupid if they did.

Percy Brackett Elliott
Everest, 1924

It was the phrase *Dear Diary* that really freaked me out. I kept thinking, What the hell does he mean by that? Is he in love with it?

At about two in the morning, fed up with tossing and turning, I threw on my parka and stepped outside to have a smoke. (Thanks to Lauren, I was already up to a pack a day, and I had just started that afternoon.)

I nearly tripped over a clump of rags on the frozen ground in front of our tent. It was the Sherpa who looked like George C. Scott. For some reason he had decided to lay out his bedroll right at the entrance to our tent—almost as if he were guarding it.

I just shook my head. "Sherpas, gotta love 'em."

The earlier flurries had dissipated, and the sky was now crystal clear and black with a billion scintillating stars pasted to it like it had aced a whole lot of spelling tests. In silhouette the ever-present Chomolungma towered over Base Camp like a great hulking monster, her snowcapped peak just barely touching the cosmos. It was cold, the kind of cold that makes you really appreciate . . . um . . . warmth.

Prayer flags were strung from the top of a memorial stone *stupa* (remember that *chorten* I impressed you with by knowing about earlier? Well, here it is! Except now I'm calling it a *stupa*. Aren't I great?) I found both the sight and the sound disquieting, for some reason. (Maybe it was the list of all the dead climbers.) As I stood there smoking my tobacco, savoring every gratifying inhalation but cursing Lauren with every sputtering exhalation, I observed a dark figure settled on one of its lower steps.

"Can't sleep either, huh, Mr. President?" I said, making myself comfortable next to Martin and his football. I could tell there was something on his mind, and I figured maybe he needed somebody to mumble about it with.

"Smoke?"

He nodded, so I stuck a cigarette in his nostril. Having endured this duct-tape routine for any number of causes in the past, he was now an old pro at smoking through his nose. He would inhale through one nostril and exhale through the other, and he was even able to blow smoke rings, although because of a deviated septum the rings usually came out looking less like circles and more like Tony's homemade pasta carbonara.

"What do you think it all means, Martin?" I asked, gazing up at the stars. "Do you suppose there's a supreme being up there looking down on all of us? Or is life just one big practical joke? I mean, maybe we're all just one tiny speck of eye crust in some giant asshole's eyeball. Have you ever thought about that, Martin . . . Mr. President?"

I looked over and he was standing about ten yards away from me.

"Well, that's a hell of a thing to do to a guy—to get up and leave right in the middle of a guy postulating about the meaning of life. I mean, I think I was really onto something."

Martin held up his finger, signaling me to shut up and listen. He pointed toward the icefall.

At first I didn't hear anything, but then I listened more closely— and I still didn't hear anything.

"Ummm, was that the sound you heard earlier today, Martin?" I asked patronizingly.

He dropped his head and shook it back and forth, "no." Then he stamped out his cigarette and sulked back to his tent.

"Poor guy. Once the mind goes, the body follows. Damn this altitude sickness."

When I turned back around I found myself face-to-face with Old Norgay and Pamma.

"Holy Jesus! You guys scared the El Grande squished bananas out of me!"

"You must heed our warnings," Tenzing said. "There are mysterious forces at work here, the meaning of which are perhaps beyond

your comprehension, but you must know that you, more than anyone else, are in great jeopardy."

"Yeah, you mentioned that like twice already. Look, I may not be
the best climber in the world, but—"

"Listen to his words," said Pamma. "We are on your side. We are
trying to help you with your problem."

"I like the sound of *those* words, baby," I said, affecting my best
Hawaii Five-0 "come hither" swagger. "I got a lot of problems you
could help me with—both physical and mental."

"Do you know the story of your great-uncle's birth?" asked
Norgay.

"Yeah, yeah, yeah. His mom got knocked up by a randy sailor.
So what?"

He scoffed. "It was no sailor! It was . . ." He lowered his voice.
"A polar bear."

"What? Don't be ridiculous. Polar bears and people don't even
have the same blood type."

"Western scientific nonsense! The Rhombus doesn't follow your
rules!"

"Here comes that stupid rummy rumpus thing again. What does
the rhompus have to do with all this anyway?"

"Homely Lizzie—that was her name—was no ordinary prostitute!
She was cursed by the power of the Rhombus she carried. It
brought her to ruin. Its magic summoned a friendly polar bear from
a neighboring ice floe to aid her in her darkest hour. While the rest
of the crew consumed one another, it protected her, and then the
two . . . fell in love."

"Ew!"

"Your great-uncle Percy was the product of that union. And after
Lizzie bestowed the Rhombus upon *him,* she died in the arms of her
lover, but Percy survived to be rescued."

Well, I guess that would sort of explain Percy's near-death experience and also why he was so nuts all his life. Maybe it wasn't lead poisoning after all, but just plain old chromosomal damage . . . something else I would have in common with him.

"You don't understand. They think you are he: Percy reborn, reincarnated," Tenzing stressed, "which means they need you—or at least they think they do."

"Need me? Who? For what?"

He grew grim and looked up at the summit. "For 'sky burial.'"

"What?"

"Shhhhhh. Someone's coming," warned Pamma, and I turned around just in time to see Tony and Kirsten shuffling out of the "After Hours" tent.

"I just think a manz got a right tooz gamblez if he choozes, that's alls."

"Not any man who wants to be associated with me," said Kirsten curtly. Tony grumbled and kicked some snow.

"Oh, it's just the lovebirds, don't worry about them . . ." But when I turned back around—*poof!*—Norgay and Pamma had mysteriously vanished.

"Jeez, people sure do come and go in a hurry around here, don't they?" But then I realized that it was just that my eyes were closed, and when I opened them, I saw Pamma and Norgay walking back to their tent.

I shrugged off the encounter and slugged back to my hacienda.

George C. Scott was awake and holding the flap open for me. He nodded and smiled weirdly, and I smiled awkwardly at him, and we both glared at each other as I ducked down to go inside, but then I stopped.

"I'm sorry, have we met?"

"Ah . . . no, sahib. I've not had the pleasure," he said in a gravelly voice. "I'm . . . ah . . . Sherpa Flip Flop."

I frowned. "Flip Flop? Ummm . . . of the Wichita Flip Flops?"

He smiled and said, "Sure."

"Somebody close that damned door!" bitched Wendell. "It's as cold as a witch's tit in a brass bra in here!"

"Well, nice to have met you, Flip Flop . . . and . . . ah . . . thank you for opening my flap . . . Flip." I giggled at my own joke, but he just stared at me. (Like he was in love, for chrissakes.) "Well, we better get to sleep now, huh? We got a big day tomorrow. Nighty-night-night." With that I climbed back into the tent.

"Nice to meet you too," the mysterious Sherpa muttered, closing the flap. "Percy sahib."

Then he lay back down in front of the entrance to our tent and we all went to sleep.

CHAPTER NINETEEN

Where am I?

Climbing.

Don't look down!

Climbing.

What's on top?

Climbing.

The peak! I'm at the summit! I'm here! I did it!

The view is spectacular, I can see all the way to Brooklyn Heights. It's my grandparents' kitchen! Uncle Percy is eating one of Grammy's peanut-oil-and-lard sandwiches. What's he saying to me? I can't understand him. I think he's trying to warn me.

"I can't understand you, Uncle Percy! Swallow! Swallow!"

Grrrrrrrrrrrrrr!!!!

What's that sound?

Lizzie, the homely prostitute is riding bareback on Max Bullis.

"Honey pie, I'm not a real polar bear, I just belong to the club!"

"Put it back," she tells me, "fix my mistake and put it back. Your uncle tried, but he couldn't do it. But you can. It is in you—to do this."

I look down. My stomach is glowing. It's burning. It's throbbing. It explodes in a barrage of gore leaving a gaping hole behind.

But I'm still alive!

I put my hand in and feel around. First I pull out some guts, then a bent-up old license plate from Louisiana, and then a Patty Play Pal doll, and then something hard and small. It's a sparkling rock. It's pulsating, glowing, flashing red, green, blue and yellow.

"Put the Rhombus back," the prostitute says. "Put the Rhombus back!"

I brush the snowcap aside, and where the tiptop of Everest should conclude in a grand point, there is only a small vacant hole.

The rock fits perfectly into the hollow.

Suddenly beams of light shoot out of Chomolungma and up into the heavens—lightning bolts, static electricity—and then, with one giant explosion, I'm blown off the summit.

All is quiet now.

Where am I?

All is quiet.

Am I on a rock?

Yes.

Am I happy?

I don't know. (Who the hell am I asking?)

What's that?

Vultures! The *lammergeiers*!

"No! No! Get away! You don't want me! I'm still alive! I'm still alive! I'm alive! Alive!"

"Crampons and ice axes!"

"Alive! What?"

"Crampons and ice axes!" shouted Tzing Tzang, sticking his head into our tent and, thankfully, waking me from my sickening dream. I was hot and soaking wet, even though it had to be at least forty below. Our sleeping bags were covered with a thin coating of Jack Frost, topped off by a thick coating of hoarfrost. (The hoarfrost always likes to be on top.)

"What are you talking about? It's four in the morning!" protested Wendell, half asleep. "It ain't no frigg'n 'oh-six hundred!'"

"Branson left already. Duncan want to leave now! Duncan say 'chop chop.' Crampons and ice axes!"

Tzing Tzang exited, and we could hear him go from tent to tent, waking the others in the camp. Flip Flop Sherpa entered. He bowed and then began to prepare us some tea.

Wendell whined, "Man, I didn't sign on for no frigg'n Phnom Penh tour-of-duty shit. I mean, I ain't no jarhead. I ain't no front-line grunt, I ain't no . . . Hey, you okay?"

I must have looked pretty bad—out of breath, sweaty and flushed.

"Oh, I get it. It was one of *those* dreams, huh?" said Wendell, pulling off his dirty corrective socks. "Let's see, was it Vera this time, or Pamma? Or was it both? You dirty dog, you."

"No. It was a horrible nightmare." I sat up and looked my best friend straight in the eye. "Wendell," I said, "I'm scared. For the first time, I'm really, really scared."

I glanced over at Flip Flop, who put down the pot of tea and returned a frightful look. The stench of primal terror filled our tent, along with a number of other stenches.

"Plus, I think Max Bullis might be a real polar bear!"

At that Wendell threw his dirty corrective socks at me.

It was still pitch black out as we stood shivering at the far end of Base Camp, huddling and bracing ourselves against the icy wind. No one spoke a word. Beams of light from the small Petzl Zipka head-lamps on our half-dome helmets whipped about as we struggled to fit into our climbing harnesses. Tightening straps and buckling buckles was difficult in this kind of cold.

Because with each progressive ascent we would use fewer and fewer Sherpas and porters, we were all required to carry larger "expedition" backpacks now. But hoisting the hulking mass onto my back was relatively easy compared to connecting up with Duncan's main belaying system.

The process would have been mind-boggling at any time of day. First you would receive the yellow guide rope from the climber in front of you and hook your "bent gate" carabiner to it, and then you would slip the guide rope through the belaying loops sewn into your harness and attach your *jumar* (an indispensable climbing device that allows you to ascend a fixed rope) to the actual red belaying line itself. Oh, wait, maybe it's the other way around— well, it's one of those. Next, you would clip the *jumar* onto your safety harness, pass the whole rig though your self-locking Trango cinch, and finally secure everything with a slip hitch, clove hitch, a Flemish bend, and a double Prusik and/or Klemheist/Munter butterfly knot. Then, of course, you handed the yellow (or red— I can't remember which) rope to the climber behind you so they could do the same. This complicated procedure, known as the daedal belaying system, would allow Duncan and Tzing Tzang to climb ahead of all of us, securing pitons and guide ropes as they went. In theory, if one person were to fall, the red belaying line would go slack and the yellow safety rope would catch the climber without disturbing anyone else. Of course that was all in theory, and there were no redundant systems in place, so hopefully everyone was paying attention and secured the proper yellow (or possibly red) lines with the right Prusik (or maybe it was a slip hitch) knot.

Duncan removed the safety cap on a flare and twisted its base. A bright, white flame shot out, illuminating a thirty-foot swath of the tallest, meanest, baddest-looking wall of sheer vertical ice I have ever seen. Tzing Tzang lit another flare, as did Flip Flop, whose presence with us went unquestioned (he was just another Sherpa, after all).

"Stay close!" shouted Duncan. "This is the easy part!"

In the Mountain Maniacs' control tent, Old Tenzing Norgay was fumbling with the instructions to his telescope and tripod under the dim illumination of a kerosene lamp.

"Goddamn it," he said, and the tripod fell on his foot. "They make these things more complicated every year." Suddenly his Motorola X10 walkie-talkie crackled to life.

"Norgay, this is Duncan. Can you hear me? Check, check. Go to Channel One."

"This is Norgay. I read you loud and clear."

"Fine. I read you loud and clear too. We're just about to start."

"Roger. May the good spirits of the mountain be with you."

"Yeah, yeah, yeah, whatever. Just keep an eye on us and let us know what's happening with the weather, I don't want to get caught by a surprise storm. We'll check in with you when we're halfway up the icefall."

"Roger that. Over and out." Tenzing put the walkie-talkie down and continued trying to mount his telescope on the tripod.

"They're all going to die up there," huffed Pamma. "I don't know why you're allowing this to happen." She bundled up and left the tent.

As soon as Norgay was sure that his great-granddaughter was gone, he looked about furtively (almost as if he were about to do something sneaky and treacherous). Then he picked up the walkie-talkie and turned the channel knob to Channel Two (*not* Channel One).

"Base Camp calling Fidelity. Base Camp calling Fidelity. Come in."

A staticky voice replied, "This is Fidelity. What is the Maniacs' current position?"

"They starting out for the icefall."

"Idiots. They don't have a chance. Keep me posted. It's vital I know where they are at all times."

"Roger. Over and out."

CHAPTER TWENTY

Above Base Camp, the air is too thin to provide lift for even the most sophisticated Sikorsky S61 recovery helicopters, so once a climber has begun the three-and-a-half-mile ascent to the upper ridge of the icefall, he is beyond rescue. Since Everest became a mecca for first-time climbers, the icefall has claimed more than twenty lives—some under less than auspicious circumstances (a few have been found with cement shoes, bullet holes, and nooses around their necks, and some with notes blaming everything on those *Dateline* predator stings). In the tradition of the mountain, the bodies are always left where they fall. As seasoned climbers often quip, "Whatever happens on the icefall, stays on the icefall."

Personally, I thought it looked like the planet Krypton. It spills out from the lower third of Everest, draining onto the glacial col below. Because the water flowing beneath the thick ice is in constant motion, the crust is forever taking on strange and beautiful—but often per-ilous—configurations. Towers of ice will suddenly topple, or capacious chasms crack open beneath your feet as the glacial ice detaches from the mountain rock in an exploding cannonade of showering crystals. Some of these *bergschrunds* can be up to two miles deep, but any *bergschrund*, no matter how deep, poses a serious threat to all experienced climbers—and an even greater threat to burned-out dopeheads with a fear of heights who are looking for rhombuses and racing rich entrepreneurs to the summit. But luckily for us, Duncan had sent Tzing Tzang and a couple of reliable Sherpas ahead to secure aluminum ladders across the largest of the crevasses and to prepare Camp Two for our arrival.

The last forty-eight hours had taken their toll on all of us, both physically and mentally. Now, after enduring a fitful night in the frigid cold of Base Camp, we found ourselves jamming our crampons, pulling down hard on our *jumars*, and ever so slowly inching our way up the south approach to the tallest mountain in the world.

I was climbing about ten feet below Lauren and was amazed at how agile and capable she was—and at what a great-looking rear end she had. She was supposed to be a feeble eighty-two, and here I was a spry forty-five, and yet I felt like a broken-down old man. Every breath in was a mouthful of needles, and every breath out a mouthful of thimbles. It was only when the sun rose and I could see better that I realized the lid to Lauren's sewing basket had come loose.

Periodically, the red belaying line would go rigid and then slack off, as Michael traveled up and down the vertical wall of ice seated in a sling-and-harness contraption (essentially a dumbwaiter rig) that enabled him to remain parallel to us while filming. The extra weight required to raise him up and lower him down was redistributed amongst those of us who were actually doing the climbing, and I suspected that I was bearing the majority of the load.

"How do you like it so far?"

"Great, Michael!" chirped Kirsten, exerting tremendous energy in struggling to maintain her grip while cradling Mr. Pop-eyes in her arms and remaining perky and photogenic for the camera. "It's a little more difficult than I imagined it would be, but whenever I feel like I can't go on, I just remind myself that I'm doing it all for the bunnies! And then I just feel so good inside." As she flashed her wholesome smile, she was nailed on the forehead with a big dollop of dirty slush.

"Sorrys about thats, funny faces."

"That's okay, sweetie," said Kirsten, gritting her teeth. Under her breath she added, "For the bunnies . . . for the bunnies . . ."

"How 'bout you, Tony?" asked Michael. "Any regrets?"

"Hey, ask me when it's all overs, will ya? No, seriously, I couldn't be prouder. I want to give a shout-out to all my buddies back in Hell's Kitchens—to all the wiseguys, and the Westies and the whole gang from the neighborhoods. Hi ya, fellas, looks where I am now! Always said I was gonna make it to the tops, right? No seriously, God bless you for filming this, brother. It's a hell of a thing. And you know what's so great about its? No one's doing this for selfish reasons! Everybody here believes in sometings and dats what it's all about, right? It's like dat song says: 'What the worlds needs nows, is love, sweets loves.' Rights? Seriously, I'm a fan of all your works. Especially dat one where you eats all the McDonald's food and then you get all high on all that fat and cholesterol and shit, rights?"

"That wasn't me."

"No? Jeez, I could have sworn it was yoos. Well, you're doing a hell of a jobs anyways, so God bless ya, brother."

At the top of the rope, Duncan took deep and labored breaths as he pounded pitons into the ice and set the belaying rope.

"Don't look down. Don't look down," he repeated to himself over and over again. "You can do this. There's a nice tall can of pepper spray waiting for you at the top."

"And how fares the lovely Lauren on this auspicious morning?"

"Oh, for Christ's sakes, Michael, you look like Baby Huey in that thing."

"Somebody has to do it. Nobody will believe this without a record."

Lauren paused to light a cig.

"Well, are you ever going to climb yourself, or do you plan on riding that god-awful contraption all the way up to the summit?" Little did Lauren know just how prophetic her words were.

The day was clear and the view from the icefall spectacular. Looking down you could see all the way to Bhutan, and looking up you could see the peak—gallingly unattainable—set majestically against a bright blue sky. The picture-perfect-postcard sight gave little warning of the horror that we would all experience shortly—so you'll probably be surprised, or at least you would be if I didn't keep doing all this damn foreshadowing.

"Well, I'll tell you, Yankee boy, it's like this," explained Max Bullis, still naked except for the Speedo, his Scarpa G40 climbing boots, and his backpack and helmet, sounding upbeat despite the fact that his skin was beginning to turn black. "Whenever I get this high up, I can see the whole damn picture pretty darn clear, and when I get back down—if I get back down—" He coughed again. "I can bring some of that clarity to our crazy, mixed-up world. Oh, sure, we can argue over the gross rate of inflation and point our fingers at who we think is responsible—military cuts, welfare, faith-based initiatives, crime, education and all the rest, but the bottom line is, we're all the same. We all want the same things. We just have our own ways of get'n it, that's all. Hell, that's what makes horse races, right?"

Michael lowered his camera. I thought perhaps the two had finally found some common ground, a respite from the constant battle between left and right, a sign of a ripening friendship between apples and oranges. Or was Michael just disturbed by Max's words?

"What do you mean '*if* I get back down'? This is a sure thing, right?"

"Ain't nothin' sure in life, boy, which is why you gotsta make every moment count, and be free from government interference . . ."

And then the two were at it again.

Wendell yelled up at the bickering behemoths. "Why don't you guys just make out and get it over with?"

"Vindall, you climb like old lady," complained Yorgi, who kept ramming his head into Wendell's butt. "*Topomneet! Topomneet!* Hurry up!"

"Yeah, yeah. Keep your snow pants on, Ivan."

Suddenly there was a loud cracking noise.

"Look out below!" shouted Duncan.

Above, a colossal *serac* broke away and began a savage plummet down the face of the icefall. The monstrous hunk bounced off the ice wall at least three times, trailing chunks of glassy fragments and a swath of pulverized crystals behind it.

Flip Flop grabbed hold of me, slamming me flat against the ice.

"I got you, sahib," he said, just as the monolith flew past us with barely inches to spare. For something so big, it fell astonishingly slowly, almost floating to the glacier bed below, where it shattered into a billion pieces.

There was stunned silence as Flip Flop and I looked at each other, wide-eyed with relief. *That was a close one.*

"Perfect . . . and cut!" yelled Michael. "I'm out of film. I need to check the gate and change mags."

Flip Flop looked up and mumbled, "The *yidam* . . . That was meant for you, sahib."

"Me? Really? Then I guess I should go down and see if I can glue it back together, right?"

Flip Flop shook his head. "No, I meant . . . Oh, forget it."

"Everyone all right?" Duncan shouted down to us.

"Yeah, we're all fine!" But if not for Flip Flop I would have been squished bananas for sure.

We continued to ascend, silenced by a renewed awareness of the danger.

At about midday, halfway up, we stopped to have lunch on a tier, and Duncan pulled out his walkie-talkie and contacted Norgay.

"We got another three hours before we hit Camp Two. I'm gonna try to get there quicker," he reported. "The ladders are next. Over."

"Weather all clear. And, uh, the bearded one, is he all right?"

Duncan looked over at me. I was sitting a little ways away, contentedly dangling my legs over the edge of the icy perch and giggling while I massaged an egg-salad sandwich into my forehead. (The lack of oxygen affects everyone differently.)

"Yeah, that's a big 'roger.'"

"Keep sharp eye out for him, because he—"

"Yeah, yeah, I know: 'He's in great danger,' right? I got the newsletter. Listen, Norgay, we're *all* climbing this frig'n mountain, not just the fruitcake, okay? Expect the next contact when we make Camp Two. Over and out." Then he switched channels and spoke to Tzing Tzang. "Tzing, I want you to turn east and set the ladders on Viper Pass."

"That's not best route boss—over."

"I know, but it's the route Percy took. We might find *something* along the way, if you know what I mean, over."

"Big holes there, boss. Not best route—too dangerous."

"Just do it, okay? Over and out."

Down at Base Camp, Old Norgay relayed our position to Fidelity (whoever that was).

"Repeat—Mountain Maniacs halfway to Camp Two. Over and out." Then he dropped his walkie-talkie and stepped outside. Searching the camp with his eyes, he called out, "Pamma? Pamma?"

CHAPTER TWENTY-ONE

In order to cross the aluminum ladders, we were forced to lie on our stomachs and inch forward like worms, making sure that our crampons didn't get stuck on the rungs behind us. The first series of ladders were fairly easy, albeit awkward. (One of them was still covered with drops of wet paint.) On average, they only spanned about six- to ten-foot-wide crevasses and were sturdy enough to hold the weight of two climbers at one time, so we made quick work of them. Still, the lack of oxygen was playing havoc with my head. Duncan had stipulated that supplementary oxygen only be used past Camp Two, so although the ladder crossings were not particularly challenging, the lack of meaty air made it a punishing enterprise.

"I'm bushed," I gasped.

"Well, hang back then, dear child, there's no law that says you have to be the first. I just naturally always am."

Lauren was right. I unhooked my carabiner and sat down, catching my breath and relaxing as best I could. I waited till the end of the line and then hooked back on, buddying up with President Martin. Seeing this, Flip Flop retreated to the back of the line as well.

"How ya doing, Martin?" I asked.

"Mmmmmmm."

"Hearing any strange noises today?"

"Mmmmmmm." He nodded his head vigorously and pointed behind him.

"Don't worry about it, buddy. It's just the altitude. It does weird things to people. For instance, it makes me wash my hair with egg salad, of all things. I mean eggs, yes—but egg salad? How *de* classy."

We continued for another two hours, climbing ladders, belaying up slippery crags, and traversing over treacherous promontories. We were almost to Camp Two when our advance was suddenly impeded by a forty-foot-wide crevasse, the far side of which was considerably higher than the side we were all gathered on. The monster *bergschrund* was so deep you couldn't see the bottom. Four ten-foot ladders, laced together with climbing rope and bungee cords, formed a rickety, unstable aluminum catwalk.

"What the hell was Tzing Tzang thinking?" mumbled Duncan. He cupped his hands and shouted into the pit. "Hello?"

I replied, "Hi!" and giggled.

"Shhhhhhhh."

A moment later the echo came back, *Hello, hello, hello.*

"That's deep," he said.

"Maybe we should try jumping?" I asked. Yorgi smacked Wendell on the back of the head, and Wendell immediately smacked me.

"Listen up. This is going to be tricky. Take it slow, single file, and everybody stay frosty."

Duncan was the first one over. Then Lauren, then Yorgi and Wendell. Next, Max made his way across. His sweat was working in his favor, like a natural lubricant as he shimmied walrus-style across the swaying ladders to the other side. His flesh had deteriorated to such a degree that he left small napkins of dead skin behind him.

Next came Michael, who was surprisingly spry (probably because he hadn't been doing anything all day), opting to walk across instead of crawl. He got just about to the center of the makeshift bridge and then slipped, landing hard on his belly and dropping his IMAX camera into the abyss. It only fell about four feet, however, before it stopped, dangling in midair from Michael's harness. The bridge buckled under the repositioned weight, and the whole thing dipped in the middle with a sickening creak.

"Leave the camera!" shouted Duncan.

"No way! Pull me over!"

"Leave the frigg'n' camera!"

"No way! I am an *arteest*! I will not part with my tool!"

Resigned that Michael's mind was made up, Duncan and the others yanked hard on the yellow safety rope and slowly hoisted Michael and his camera across.

"That happens again, I'm leaving you *and* the frigg'n camera behind!" growled Duncan.

"Not unless you want to get sued," Michael shot back. Duncan did a slow burn as he turned menacingly to face Michael.

"You can't sue me if you're dead," he said.

Michael gulped. "Let's just agree to disagree, shall we?" Then he sidestepped quickly away.

On our side of the chasm, Kirsten was having a nervous breakdown. Tony's, actually.

"I can't dooz it. I can't dooz it!"

"Yes, you can. You have to. You have to do it for the pasta!" said Kirsten.

"Oh, screwz the pasta!"

"No, listen to me. You can do this. Mr. Pop-eyes and I will be right behind you," Kirsten assured Tony, but she was beginning to lose her patience.

"I cantz!"

"Oh, for crying out loud, stop being such a baby!"

"I can't helpz its!"

"Look, either I go in front of you, or you go and we follow behind you. That way we can make sure you don't fall off. What's it gonna be?"

"You promise you'll be rights behinds me?" he whimpered.

"I promise!" She gently wiped his tears away and gave him a playful nudge on his chin. "Funny face."

Ever so slowly the lovebirds worked their way across the tenuous supports.

It was getting late in the afternoon and the sun was dropping fast. A brisk wind now whipped though the cavern, adding additional sway to the already wavering bridge. Once Tony and Kirsten were across, I motioned to Flip Flop to climb onto the ladders.

"Please, sahib, you go first. Then I follow."

"No, no. Flip Flop, I insist."

"But . . ."

"Hey, I'm the sahib, right? You're the Sherpa. So, I'm the boss!"

Reluctantly Flip Flop began to cross. A moment later, Martin motioned for me to go.

"I thank you, Mr. President," I said and climbed onto the ladders.

"One at a time!" Duncan yelled from the other side of the breach.

Now alone, Martin was readying himself, when suddenly he heard the strange sounds again—behind him and close—and he began to panic.

"Mmmmmmmmm!"

"What's Martin saying?" I called to Flip Flop, who was just a few rungs ahead of me.

"I can't understand him, sahib. The wind, it's too loud!"

Martin jumped up and down, and then:

"*Grrrrrrrrrrrrrrrrrrrrrr!*"

This time I heard it too.

"What the hell was that?"

Suddenly the ladders buckled as Martin began to scurry across.

"Martin. Slow down!" yelled Duncan from the other side, but Martin was in a state of total panic.

He had reached me and was now climbing over me.

"Mr. President, that's too heavy!"

I heard a loud screech and a crack, and suddenly we were swooping downward. Flip Flop grabbed my hand, and I reached backward and clutched Martin's just as the back two ladders fell away. Flip Flop was the only one still clasping a rung as Martin and I dangled below him.

"I have you, sahib!"

"Martin, I can't hold you!" I yelled, stretched to the limit between him and Flip Flop. Max's sweat (and nasty skin goo) had made everything very slick, and I knew the president was going to go. "I can't hold you!" I shrieked.

We were still attached to each other by the yellow safety line, but when Martin's hand finally slipped out of mine—well, first his hand, and then the handcuffs, and then his stupid nuclear football—and he dropped, his dead weight yanked Flip Flop and me violently downward.

Then all was calm for a moment.

Swinging like a pendulum about four feet below me, Martin's intense actor eyes transmitted a pathetic plea. *Save my life! This was all your idea! Save my life!*

It was a look that I have not forgotten to this day (but if I try hard enough, I could probably forget by tomorrow). I didn't think there was any way that Flip Flop or I could pull him back up, and if he fell, he would take us and the ladders with him.

"Mr. President . . . Martin," I said, "you know what you have to do."

A confused look crossed his face, and he shook his head "no."

In such hopeless situations, a true mountaineer is expected to cut the rope and sacrifice himself in order to save the others. This is considered the noble thing to do. (Of course I couldn't be 100 percent certain that the situation was hopeless, but I couldn't take the chance.)

"You have to cut the rope," I said.

Martin's eyes grew wild, and he shook his head vehemently. *No!*

"So that Flip Flop and I can live!"

"Mmmmmmmmmm!"

"Yes, Martin, it has to be done."

"Mm mmm!"

"It's not that hard. Here, I'll show you," and I pulled out my Swiss Army knife and began to saw away at the rope. Martin became extremely agitated.

"I think it would be better if you did this—don't you think, Martin?"

Again he shook his head.

"Come on now. Don't be a wuss. You can do it. Think about your legacy. Look, either I'm gonna do it, or you're going to do it, but one way or another it's gonna get done. Now, what's it gonna be?"

After a long moment of deliberation, in which I really became fed up with his indecision, Martin's eyes finally surrendered, and his shaky hand reached up and took the knife from me. Then, watching me with a blend of total disgust, bitterness, and loathing—and a good passel of hostility, to boot—he reluctantly began to finish the grim work I had started.

"That's it. Very good," I encouraged. "Back and forth, back and forth. It's much better this way, Mr. President, believe me."

Then the rope was separated, and the beloved actor let out just a slight whimper as he dropped down into the dark, deep chasm.

"Noooooooooooo!" I cried. (Although privately I was relieved I wouldn't be joining him.)

Everyone screamed. "Martin!"

Then suddenly the ladders split apart—

The rope snapped—

Flip Flop and I plummeted—

I remember thinking, *This is what it all comes down to—my career is over and I haven't even been roasted yet!* when out of the blue a body slammed hard into both of us, and we grabbed on like baby chimps.

"Pamma! Where the hell did you come from?"

"Just be quiet," she commanded, wrapping her whip around us. "Stay still. I'll do all the work. I knew there was going to be trouble here."

Pumping and sliding her *jumar* (hot!) she hoisted us up until everyone could pull us to safety on the other side of the crevasse.

"Did you see what happened to him?" asked Kirsten, frantically.

"Him?" I shot back. "What about me? I think I just gave myself one of those rotor cuffs, or rotators cups or . . . the rotary clubs or something. You know what I mean."

"Where'd he goes?" asked Tony. "It was likes one of those old-times magic shows. He was there for a seconds and den he just disappears!"

"Where do you think he went?" asked Duncan.

"How 'bout it, boy, how deep is that there thing?" inquired the Texan.

"Martin, Martin! Martin?" everyone called out, but no answer came back.

"Mountain Maniacs to Base Camp!" Duncan shouted into the walkie-talkie.

"How fast can we get a rescue team here?" asked Lauren.

"We're too high up. Mountain Maniacs to Base Camp. Norgay, where the hell are you?"

There was no answer, only static.

"Great. He's probably off getting drunk. Thanks for recommending him, Hillary."

"He's not drunk. He's the brave Tenzing Norgay . . . ," Pamma began.

"Yeah, yeah, yeah. Sorry. I forgot. He's probably off getting *heroically* drunk."

We called down for at least an hour, but no response could be heard, save for our echoes and the eerie howling of the wind. Finally we gave up, and Duncan took charge.

"Look, everyone. It's getting dark. We have to move on to Camp Two unless you all want to freeze out here."

"What do you mean 'move on?' Aren't we going to go down there to rescue Martin?" asked Lauren.

"Lady, Martin's gone!"

I became hysterical. "That's not true. Don't say that. He just took a little fall, that's all. He's probably down there right now drinking champagne cocktails and watching *Hogan's Heroes* reruns. He can't be gone . . . He can't be gone . . . He—"

SLAP! (I hit myself in the face.)

"Thank you," I said to myself. "Although I wasn't that hysterical."

"Listen," said Duncan, "we've all just experienced something not so great here today. In fact, I'll even go out on a limb and say that we've experienced something pretty inconvenient. But this is the way things are on Everest. It's the law of the land. What happens on the icefall stays on the icefall. Martin knew the risks going in. We can't jeopardize more lives in a fruitless attempt to find his broken body. He's gone, people! We just have to face facts."

"Seems rather callous, brave captain, don't you think?"

"Lady, what do you want me to say?"

"Well, just that . . ."

It was the first time I had ever seen Betty speechless. But really, what could Duncan say? It was getting dark and there was no way Martin could have survived. Lauren ran her fingers through her hair and allowed Chomolungma's cold breath to cool her red-hot face.

"Well, hell, boy, perhaps a prayer is in order?"

"That's just fine, Max. And while we're taking the time to say a prayer for Martin, who's dead and gone, let's say one for the rest of us, who are still alive, because we still have to make it to Camp Two, and I say we go now!"

"Surely you can take the time to say a few words, Mr. Carter," said Pamma. "Or are you more concerned about how much progress Mr. Branson has enjoyed today?"

That jab seemed to genuinely hurt Duncan's feelings. "That's just great. That's just great," he said, throwing up his arms and stomping over to a rock, where he pulled out his Purell and pepper spray and began to imbibe.

"If we gonna leaves him heres, I says it's the leasts we cans dos," Tony pleaded. "I means, this guys wons Emmys's!"

Michael spoke up. "I'm not a religious man. In fact, I'm antireligion . . . well, not all religions, but definitely the born-again, *700 Club*, in-your-face crowd—and Christmas, too. I fucking hate Christmas. But I agree with Max—someone should say something."

All eyes turned to me. I didn't want to be the one to say anything. I hated public speaking. People always expect me to be funny, and I'm by nature a very serious person. But the truth is that this was all my fault. I figured I owed the guy something, so as everyone gathered at the edge of the crevasse and bowed their heads, I stood up and cleared my throat.

"Dear Lord, we are gathered here today to bid a fond farewell to an old and dear friend. Fester Martonelli Schinowsky, better known to all of us as His Holiness The President of the United States. Martin was born in 1940 in Butcher Holler, the son of a coal miner's daughter. After hauling garbage through his formative years, he went on a cross-country murder spree with Sissy Spacek that landed him in Los Angeles, where he became president, or at least thought that he had. Martin was an Emmy Award–winning actor with a long and distinguished career. Of course, I knew him best as Tad from the 1970s TV series *Bracken's World,* Episode Three, "Papa Never Spanked Me," but his credits also included the voice of Sly Sludge in *Captain Planet and the Planeteers, Apocalypse Now, The Missiles of October, JFK, JFK We Hardly Knew Ye, JFK in Vegas, Lee Harvey Oswald in Hyannisport, Why JFK Shot Himself,* and *Marilyn, Bobby, Teddy, JFK and Lee Harvey Oswald on PT-109: A Night to Remember.* But Martin was more than just an actor. He was an actor . . . *vist.* (Thank you, thank you very much.) He was involved in many worthy causes and charities around the globe, including Greenpeace, the Coalition for a Greener Tomorrow, Americans Against Concrete in General, the Save the Blue Channel movement, and of course the worthy cause for which he gave his life here today—I'm not sure what it's called, but it has something to do with getting more homeless people on TV for some reason. I think it's fair to say that Martin was more than just a friend to me—he was like a big sister, or a disturbed uncle, or a disgraced Catholic priest, but more than anything else he was a fellow celebrity. And oh, how he could flaunt his merchandise. No one could strut their stuff like Martin. And when he got out there on that dance floor, he sure could get down and funky, mister. And so in closing, I would just like to say that a great light has gone out here today. Perhaps it had been somewhat dim for a while anyway, but now it's definitely out. As he said in so many made-for-TV movies, 'Ask not what you can do for your country, but what your country can do for you.' So, let us not look to the past, but look to the future—our future, because Martin's future is now . . . in the past. Thank you, good night, and may Gawd bless."

The wind howled, and one by one each of us threw something of ours into the abyss as a sign of respect for our fallen comrade. Kirsten was first, throwing in a promotional copy of her new CD,

Then the rope was separated, and the beloved actor fell away.

then Lauren threw in Bogie's flask, Max tossed in one of his extra Speedos, Michael a can of baked beans, Tony his Jerome Kern sheet music, Yorgi his red-tipped cane, and Wendell his Apollo 11 commemorative coin collection. But I had nothing to give.

"Shall I play my drum for him?" I asked, but everyone was already walking away, hooking themselves back on to the guide rope and preparing to continue on to Camp Two. So I just gathered a heap of snow in my parka and dumped it into the ravine (It's all I had to give. I mean, I wasn't going to throw in my best dress shoes.)

It was a solemn, funereal trek to Camp Two. No one spoke a word. The worst had happened. Chomolungma had claimed one of our own, and we were all asking ourselves, How many more would she claim before this wretched adventure ended? And, Who would be next? And, How can I stop it from being me, even if it means recklessly sacrificing everyone else?

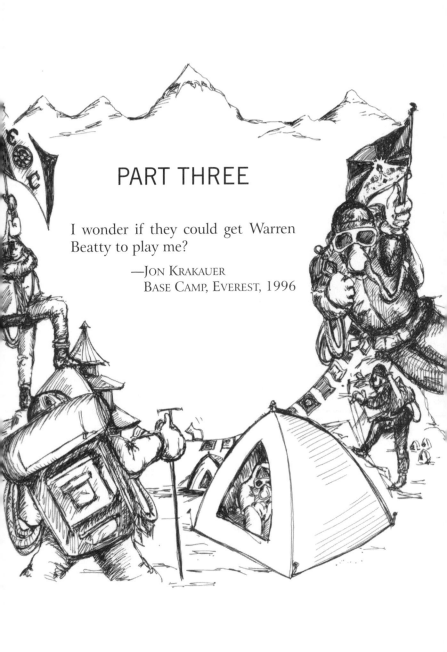

PART THREE

I wonder if they could get Warren
Beatty to play me?

—Jon Krakauer
Base Camp, Everest, 1996

CHAPTER TWENTY-TWO

At Camp Two, Duncan finally made contact with Old Norgay. The Sherpa was relieved to hear that his great-granddaughter was safe, expressed sorrow for the loss of Martin, and offered to inform *Variety* and the *Hollywood Reporter*.

Tzing Tzang prepared a roaring campfire, and we all huddled together for warmth. We were in shock, and it was difficult to forget the day's devastating events—at least until someone brought out marshmallows!

Down at Base Camp, Norgay heard a plaintive cry emanating from somewhere out on the col.

"Help! I need help here!"

Martin. He's still alive, he thought.

But it wasn't Martin. It was Captain Harding tramping breathlessly down the *neve*—her arms supporting the nearly unconscious agent Resnick.

"Where are you coming from?" asked Norgay, running out to meet them.

"Labuse."

"You ascended too quickly!" Norgay chided, taking hold of Resnick while other Sherpas arrived to assist Harding.

"Don't worry about me. He's worse off!" she said.

In the control tent, Norgay administered oxygen and shots of dexamethasone, but Resnick was not responding. His eyes were rolling back in his skull and his right leg was kicking spastically in the air. "I'll have the chipotle fried donkey, with a dirty—make that *filthy*—martini . . . and some matzo-ball soup on the side. Thank you. I'll order dessert later."

"Oh, boy. He's in real bad shape. He needs a Gamow bag fast."

"What the hell is a Gamow bag?" Harding asked, ravenously drawing oxygen from a mask.

It's actually not a bag at all, but a clear plastic chamber shaped roughly like a human body. When someone is suffering from HACE, high-altitude cerebral edema; HAPE, high-altitude pulmonary edema; or HARLS, high-altitude restless leg syndrome, they're placed in a Gamow bag, and air is pumped inside to simulate the atmospheric pressure of a lower altitude. The new bags are far more deluxe than the old ones, allowing a recovering climber to move his arms and walk around—basically like those cool biochemical hazard suits I had to wear around the house when I was growing up.

"How long will he have to be in this thing?" Harding asked impatiently as they zipped Resnick into the inflatable suit and began pumping in oxygen.

"Depends. Couple of days, maybe a week."

"A week! That's not going to work for us."

"What's the big rush? You don't acclimatize, you die! Haven't you ever climbed a mountain before? Who are you anyway?"

"That's not important. What's important is that I find the Mountain Maniacs. It's a matter of national security. Where are they?"

Norgay shook his head and muttered, "I guess you guys don't talk to each other much, do you?"

"What? What did you just say?"

"Nothing. Nothing. Mountain Maniacs already at Camp Two."

"Shit. That means we have to move now!"

"Lady, no way your boyfriend climbs tonight. His vital signs are stable, but he'll need to be in Gamow bag at least forty-eight hours."

"I'm sorry, Captain Harding," Resnick stammered weakly from inside the space suit. Then he kicked Harding in the face.

"It's all right, rookie. It wasn't your fault. I was pushing too hard. Just get better. We'll catch up with them somehow. Don't worry."

She tore open a candy bar and devoured it as she scanned the mountainside with night-vision binoculars.

"Just how far up is Camp Two?"

"Day's climb. You better not go tonight, lady. Too dangerous. They already lost one climber."

Harding grabbed Norgay by the collar. "Who? Who was lost?"

"The actor . . . um . . ."

"They're all actors, numb-nuts!"

". . . the Kennedy actor. Martin something."

She reflected on this. She had always been a fan.

"Please, lady, you need to acclimatize—otherwise . . ."

"Yeah, right. Otherwise I die."

At the supply table she picked up a walkie-talkie, an oxygen mask, and a half-dome helmet with a headlamp attached to it.

"Mind if I borrow these?" she said, strapping herself into a climbing harness and slinging a length of rope over her shoulder.

"Lady, you don't know what you're doing. Wait for your backup."

" 'Backup'?"

Norgay looked like he'd swallowed the proverbial canary.

The savvy CIA captain moved in on him, inspecting his features closely. "Have we met before? You a spook?"

"No, ma'am. I'm Sherpa . . . I meant to say your backup, uh, climber," he stuttered, pointing nervously at Resnick.

Harding's eyes narrowed on Norgay. "Just what do you know about the Mountain Maniacs?"

"Absolutely nothing, I'm just their eyes and ears."

"Yeah? How about Operation Duhkha? Know anything about that?"

"Huh? Operation what? No, nothing. I know nothing. I see nothing. I hear nothing."

Harding suspected Norgay was hiding something, but she didn't have time to do a proper interrogation. She was on an important assignment right now and nothing could slow her down. And that's the way Harding always was. Single-minded to a fault, she did everything by the book, and if she didn't have time to water-board someone as thoroughly as the law required, she wasn't going to bother.

Born forty-eight years ago into the racially charged cauldron of the South, the only daughter of a Baptist minister, Dana Harding had always lived with an unwavering righteousness. Even as a child she often refused to leave the table until she had made her parents force her to finish her black-eyed peas. The brutal slaying of her pet grasshopper at the hands of the Ku Klux Klan had hardened her at an early age, yet despite her personality (or lack thereof), she won her friends over with her sheer magnanimity and forbearance. Once, in her sixth-grade chemistry class, she held her palm over a Bunsen burner until her skin was scorched black. When asked what the trick was, she said, "The trick is not minding." (G. Gordon Liddy actually ripped that off from her.)

After graduating as head of her class at the police academy, she joined the CIA, where her talents were quickly recognized. Not only was she the star of their yearly talent show, but she was also recruited into the elite National Clandestine Division. This post allowed her to work closely with all covert agencies and required her to report directly to the higher-ups at the defense department, as well as the lower-downs at the offense department.

Lately she suspected that some of her colleagues were intentionally keeping her out of the loop. For what reason, she wasn't entirely

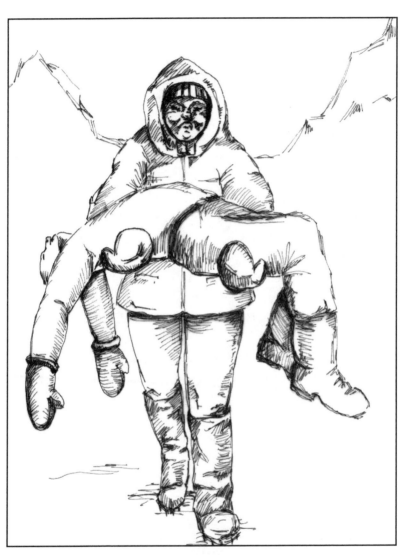

"He needs a Gamow bag fast."

sure. Maybe it was because her incorruptibility offended some of the shadier operatives, or maybe it was because she had a bad habit of botching missions at the last minute because she always forgot to take her gun's safety off. Being given the joke mission of preventing the Tibetans from reclaiming the Rhombus was a clear sign that the writing was on the wall. She had already decided that whatever the outcome, it would be her last case.

"Take care of my friend," she told Norgay, checking her falsies and the barrel of her .45 Magnum. "If anything happens to him, I'm gonna hold you personally responsible." Then she opened the tent flap and headed out for the icefall.

"Just call on Channel Three if you need anything—anything at all! Not Channel Two or Channel One!" Norgay shouted after her. "But Channel Three—Three would be just fine!"

After she disappeared into the darkness, he checked on Resnick, whose right leg was still fidgeting inside the inflatable suit.

"Excuse me, waiter. These are way overdone. I like my balls purple, thank you."

The old Sherpa picked up his walkie-talkie and switched it to Channel Four. "Base Camp to Blue Folder. Base Camp calling Blue Folder. Come in, please."

"Blue Folder—report. Over," said a new anonymous voice.

"I just had a visit from a Captain Harding? Over."

"Come back?"

"A Captain Harding!"

There was a long pause.

"Interesting."

"She was asking a lot of questions. Is she one of yours?"

There was an even longer pause.

"Don't worry about Captain Harding. Our people will deal with her. You just stick to the plan, Norgay, and you'll come out smelling like a rose. Blue Folder, over and out."

CHAPTER TWENTY-THREE

Camp Two was located on a marginally protected tract of powdery snow 21,000 feet up. It was quite a bit smaller than Base Camp—ten individual tents, two communal tents, and one "lovers' hideaway" tent. Despite Duncan's determination to beat Richard Branson to the summit, we would have to spend at least one week acclimatizing to the higher elevation, but he wasn't overly concerned, because somewhere on the western side of the mountain Branson and his virgins would have to pause as well. So now, as the campfire warmed his wrinkled cheeks, he hovered over Uncle Percy's diary with a flashlight, rapidly flipping through the pages.

"Poor Martin," I said, making myself a s'more. "I never realized just how dangerous climbing Mount Everest is. I mean, if I'd known it was gonna be this hard, I would have just written a book *about* climbing it without ever really doing it—just like my editor suggested."

"Martin probably would have appreciated that," Wendell said as he ignited the outer layer of his marshmallow and burned it until the liquid oozed out of its blackened craters. Then he popped the whole smoldering glob into his mouth (like a pig!).

"Yeah," I said, "but the late, great George Plimpton would have really climbed Everest, and I'm kinda of like the new late, great George Plimpton, aren't I?"

There was silence.

"Ah, what's the point?" I said. "We should just turn back, before someone else dies."

Suddenly Duncan looked up. "Huh? Go back? What are you talking about?"

"Well, give me one good reason why we should keep going?"

"Well . . . because! Because if we went back, you wouldn't find your dead uncle's frozen eighty-five-year-old corpse."

"Somehow that doesn't seem like fun anymore."

"And our brave captain would lose his little bet, wouldn't he?" added Lauren.

"Yeah, and that Rhombus thing-a-ma-gig that you came for, right?" I said, feeling my oats. "That's really why you want to find my Uncle Percy, isn't it?"

Carter and Tzing Tzang exchanged looks.

"Keeping more secrets are we, brave captain?"

"What is it anyway?" I asked. "I know it's not a butt."

"That's for sure," Duncan, stoked the fire.

"Well, then?"

"It's a rare gem, kid, an argyle diamond, to be exact. *Rhombus* refers to its shape. All sides are perfectly equal, forming an equilateral quadrangle—in geometric terms, a rhombus."

"Aren't all diamonds shaped liked that?" Wendell asked.

"Only after they've been cut. This is an uncut diamond. It was naturally formed—by nature, naturally, in the outdoors, where it's cold. It's said to have magical properties, and to be able to glow in the dark."

"Cool! Like Hot Wheels!"

"Plus, it's worth millions."

"And woe unto he who steals it," warned Pamma.

"I don't know about all that mumbo jumbo. I only know that the kid's uncle found it, and that if we find Percy, we find the Rhombus."

"And I suppose that's worth the death of a fine made-for-TV-movie actor?" Lauren sneered.

"It's worth whatever it takes, lady." Duncan dove back into the diary. "There's got to be a clue in here somewhere."

"Question, brave captain, if this Rhombus actually exists, and one finds it . . . well then, wouldn't it belong to our young Christopher here?"

Duncan snapped his fingers, and Tzing Tzang produced a contract.

"A mere waiver," said Lauren. "We all signed one!"

Duncan beamed. "There is a little additional paragraph in our young Christopher's 'mere waiver,' queenie. The frozen body is his, but all salvage rights belong to me."

"Is that good?" I asked, smiling like an idiot and drooling chocolate from the corners of my mouth (again, altitude sickness—sorry).

Tzing Tzang held the contract out, but Lauren declined it. Defeated, she shook her head in disgust and lit two cigarettes.

"Sorry, dear, I tried." She handed me one of the smokes.

Max, who lay on his naked back in the snow looking up at the stars, mused, "'There's enough in this world for everyone's need, but not enough for everyone's greed,' eh?"

"Shakespeare?" asked Lauren.

"No, honeybuns. Frank 'Never Despair' Buchman, evangelist and founder of the great Moral Rearmament movement. Brilliant man, a visionary."

"Wake me when he starts quoting John Birch, will ya?" said Michael through a mouthful of marshmallows.

I turned to Pamma. "Just what kind of power does this crazy rompus have?"

"Well, some people believe that it has power over life and death," she said weirdly, staring at the burning embers.

Suddenly our attention was drawn to a loud brouhaha on the other side of camp.

"I didn't mean it, sweeties! I was just thinkings out louds, that's all!" Tony was following Kirsten out of the "lovers' hideaway" tent.

"You're sick in the head!" she shouted. "Don't talk to me anymore! Leave me alone."

"Buts . . . comes backses!"

"Come on, Mr. Pop-eyes. This guy's a freak!"

The little bunny hopped into her arms and she marched off, leaving Tony standing in the snow all by himself. After a moment he glanced over at us and smiled sheepishly. Then he put his hands in his pockets and, whistling "Seventy-Six Trombones," scuffed back to his tent.

"Sounds like a little *trevogda* in paradise," Yorgi said.

"I hear that, high five!" but Yorgi missed Wendell's outstretched hand and slapped his face instead. I instinctually covered my head, but Wendell surprised me and smacked me twice on my cheeks, which made me squeeze his nose, which made him stick his fingers in my eyes.

"Gentlemen, vaudeville is quite dead, thank you very much," cracked Lauren.

"So Pamma, baby, if it has power over life and death, do you suppose if we find this diamond we could use its powers . . ." I paused for dramatic effect ". . . to bring Martin back to life? Woooooo!"

"Now, that would be a neat trick," observed Lauren.

Duncan snickered. "Come on, folks, this is the twenty-first century—not the Middle Ages, when you could get away with crazy shit like that."

"I don't know," said Pamma, "but its energy is said to be boundless."

"Then that's reason enough to keep going for me," I said. "All we have to do is find Percy, because he has the Rhombus, which is worth millions that I don't get to keep, right? Then we go back down to the icefall and haul up Martin, rub the Rhombus all over his naked body, and *bam*! We save him from everlasting torment in Hades—*ipso facto simplo*! Plus, we get to see Martin naked." (The high altitude was making me think clearer than I'd ever thought before.)

Pamma leaned in close to me. Naturally I thought she wanted to make out, so I closed my eyes and puckered up. "Listen to me," she whispered in a sultry voice, licking her thick lips, "your uncle didn't possess the Rhombus. He *was* the Rhombus!"

"We're not gonna make out, are we?"

"No."

I opened my eyes. "But what does that mean? Are you saying he was a walking, talking, human diamond?"

"It means that it was part of him. That's all I can tell you."

"Oh, I'm so confused," I said. "I don't think I'll ever understand what's going on." (But don't worry, Dear Reader, at some point you will. At least I assume you will. Other people always seem to.)

"Wait a second!" Duncan jumped to his feet with the diary in hand. "Listen to this. This explains everything!"

At that moment Flip Flop sat lotus-style in his tent communing with the little hologram of the Dalai Lama.

"What is your position?"

"We're at Camp Two, Your Holiness," Flip replied. "There was a close call with a falling *serac*, and then there is this." He held up a bent piece of a rung from one of the aluminum ladders. "It's obvious that the ladder was meant to break."

"The *yidam*!"

"Carter sent a group ahead to set the guide ropes and ladders. Surely one of them is the wrathful deity."

"Find out who. The Rhombus must reach the summit unscathed."

"Are you sure this is the right guy? He's, uh, really goofy."

"You think *he's* bad; you should have met his great-uncle. Now listen closely, my little Bodhisattva: When the idiot—er—Rhombus summits, we will execute our transmutation. Are you prepared?"

"I am ready, Your Holiness."

"And you are aware of the possibilities, that is to say, the consequences, what could happen . . . if something goes wrong?"

Flip Flop reflected for a moment. "Life is a wheel. I am certain that if that happens, I will come back—and hopefully next time as a better actor, right? Ha, ha, ha ha." The Dalai Lama laughed along with him.

The blue light pulsating inside Flip Flop's tent went unnoticed by those of us around the campfire as Duncan continued to read from Percy's diary:

> Camped out above Viper Pass. I'm certain I was visited by the hill people again last night. They're extremely quiet as they go about their mischievous work.

> I didn't wake once.

> The only sign that they were here was a feathered arrow, some yellow patches of snow, and of course my pants were around my ankles again.

Percy Bracket Elliott
Camp Two, 1924

We all looked at each other, perplexed.

"I don't see how that explains anything," Wendell said.

"I know. I just wanted to get everyone's attention," admitted Duncan. "But it *does* tell us that Percy camped out on Viper Pass. Look around people, this *is* Viper Pass."

"Who are those weird 'hill people'?" I asked. "They sound kind of creepy—like *Deliverance* creepy, if you know what I mean."

"Just hallucinations," Duncan quickly replied. Pamma glared at him and shook her head. "Now, I propose we form a search party tomorrow and scan the upper ridges surrounding the camp for any sign of Percy. I'll need some volunteers. Who's in?"

"'Night, everyone," said Wendell.

"*Dobry ootra*!" hailed Yorgi, and he was about to trudge straight through the campfire when "goodhearted" Wendell took hold of him and walked him back to his tent.

"See, you need to be with a seeing person at all times. You're practically helpless, man."

Max coughed. "Michael, my boy, why don't you and I continue our little discussion about John Birch and Frank Buchman over a nice bowl of Boston baked beans?"

"Sounds good to me." Michael said, and the odd couple got up and waddled away.

Duncan looked to Tzing Tzang.

"Uh, I should stay with the group, boss."

"You're coming with me."

"That's what I mean. I'm coming with you, boss."

"Well, of course I'll go!" I said. "I mean, I came here to find Percy, and if there's any chance—even the slightest chance that we could save Martin with this Rhombus thing, then we just gotsta do it, don't we? I mean, all the *West Wing* fans are going to be super-pissed. And those people are, like, scary obsessed."

"I'm going as well," thundered Lauren. "Bogie would have

wanted me to. Robards couldn't have cared less, but Bogie would've wanted me to."

"You're all crazy," announced Pamma, jumping to her feet. "One person is already dead. How many more have to die on this ludicrous adventure of yours? Read between the lines of that diary. There is danger all around us. Not just from falling ice and slippery rocks, lack of oxygen, frostbite, and altitude sickness, but also from the unseen forces of the mountain. Your uncle was aware of such forces and still he perished. Don't go looking for danger. Just don't."

Finally someone was being sensible, and we all let her words sink in.

"Let's do it for Martin!" I shouted, and we held up our marshmallow sticks and in unison cheered: "For Martin!" and then we whooped and hollered and formed a conga line and danced around the campfire like imbeciles. (Or at least I did, but I had my eyes closed so it was kind of like a party.)

It was midnight and Captain Harding had pushed her body to its limit. She had reached the perch halfway up the icefall where we had stopped to eat lunch earlier in the day, and now she radioed Norgay on Channel Three to tell him that she was going to spend the night there.

"How's Resnick's condition? Over."

"Improving. He sleeps like a baby. And you? Over."

"I've made myself a lean-to against the wind. It'll do fine."

"Sleep well."

"Let me ask you something, Norgay. I'm hearing strange sounds— like drums beating and animal howls. Is that normal for Mount Everest?"

Norgay laughed. "Just high-altitude hallucinations. Take some oxygen and all sounds go away. Sleep well. Over and out."

"Yeah, right, over and out." Harding put her walkie-talkie down and cuddled into her sleeping bag. She felt uneasy, so she took out her .45 Magnum and shoved it under her pillow.

Then she lay awake, breathing oxygen and listening to the strange sounds, which, despite Norgay's reassuring words, never went away.

CHAPTER TWENTY-FOUR

In a frigid cave below the Khumbu Icefall, the howling, drum beating, and flute tooting seemed loud enough to wake the dead, but they had little effect on the frozen bodies hanging grotesquely by their ankles from hooks on wooden poles—the remains of long-lost climbers, collected here for some terrible purpose.

One of the bodies, still barely alive, opened its eyes to the horrifying display. *Strange,* he thought. *Why do all these guys have their arms in the air?* Then Martin realized the terrible truth.

Is this hell or just another bad Star Wars *sequel? I don't remember getting an offer . . .*

He struggled to lift his torso enough to reach his ankles, but he was just too weak. The blood was rushing to his head and his eyes were throbbing, when he gradually became aware of another presence in the chamber. He couldn't see it, but he could hear its breathing—low and labored. Then it spoke.

"You're . . . you're not like the others. No, no, no. You're . . . you're special."

The halting, stuttering voice sounded familiar, but Martin couldn't quite place it.

The next thing he knew he was on the frozen ground, struggling to bring himself to his knees. When his vision cleared, there standing before him was the oddest combination of animal and human being that you could ever imagine.

Covered with short, grayish-brown hair, it was muscular but not particularly tall. In fact, it was rather stubby in stature. It stood like a human, but its features were more apelike. The head was disproportionately large for such a stumpy body, and its lower jaw protruded like a Neanderthal's. Its dark-skinned face was painted with stripes of yellow pigment, and it wore a yak-fur tunic, as well as a necklace of stones and claws. And in one hairy fist it clutched a climbing axe.

"I've been following you, you know," it said.

"Mmmmmmm?"

"Yes, that was me, '*grrrrrrrrrrr!*' I like to growl." said the ape-man, grabbing hold of Martin's ankles and causing him to flop backward. Then he started to pull him out of the chamber. "It, ah, it, ah, it makes me smile—growling does—like sugar. Although sugar's bad for your teeth, but I'm fixing that." The creature grinned wide, displaying a disorderly collection of yellowed teeth covered with bamboo braces, and then Martin passed out.

Most crypto-zoologists reject the notion of a half-man, half-ape wandering the snows of Mount Everest, although even Sir Edmund Hillary admitted that during his 1953 descent, he came across "a set of giant footprints that were either made by an undiscovered bipedal ape, or my ex-wife. Ha, no, just kidding. It was probably an ape."

In the United States, we know it as Bigfoot or Sasquatch; in the mountains of Mongolia it's called the Almas. In China it's the yeren, in Australia the yowie, and in Portland, Maine, it's "the people from away." But in the Himalayas it's called the yeti, or as the Tibetans say, muckamuck, "dirty man of the snow." (It's interesting to note that our term muckamuck, referring to a VIP or a "big-headed man," comes to us straight from the Tibetans.) At any rate, in all cases, a large hairy, bipedal hominid is described—although Mainers also report that it wears a New York Yankee's baseball cap and complains that there isn't enough meat on the lobster rolls.

The stubby muckamuck dragged Martin along a baffling labyrinth of frozen catacombs and through a beaded curtain into a large chamber constructed of blocks of compacted snow, like a giant igloo amphitheater.

The howling, drumming, and piping were deafening and only added to Martin's disorientation as the creature pulled him to his feet and smacked him back to consciousness.

"Just wait here," the hairy half-man shouted. "The chief will explain everything to you. By the way, my name is Harvey. Would—would—would you care for some yak urine?"

Martin wiped ice crystals from his eyes and looked around. It was like something right out of *The Island of Dr. Moreau*. (Except just different enough so that I don't get sued.) The room was bursting with hairy, big-headed hominids. They all seemed related to Harvey, but some were taller, some were shorter, and some wore different-colored face paint. Their weaponry and clothing seemed culled together from the pickings of a century of unlucky Everest climbers. Some held wooden walking sticks, others ski poles or modern ice axes. Some wore Sherpa fedoras while others wore half-dome climbing helmets with long-burnt-out Petzl Zipka headlamps.

A variety of livestock—yaks, serow goats, and wild schnauzers—wandered freely about, while mounted atop birch poles were the day's fresh trophy kills: snow leopards, Himalayan blue and red bears, and chu-teh monkeys. It was a bloody mess, and Martin nearly passed out from the stench. "Dirty man of the snow" was an understatement.

In the center of the high, domed ceiling was a circular opening, which allowed black smoke wafting up from a great fire in the middle of the room to escape, and around these blazing timbers half a dozen naked muckamucks with skeleton-painted faces danced crazily.

Martin noticed that the upper tier of the room was lined with open chambers—and in each chamber muckamucks were getting their teeth worked on by muckamuck orthodontists.

"I have to go in for a tightening next week," Harvey explained. He pulled open his simian cheeks. "See? He's yanking down my incisors and straightening my canines. We care a lot about our teeth down here."

The booming celebration stopped abruptly and an obese albino muckamuck began a slow and measured drumbeat.

"Ah, oh. 'Beat the drum and sound the brass—here comes the big horse's ass!' Hee, hee, hee, just joking. Good luck. I'll be—be—be—be right here." Harvey stepped back.

The crowd parted and an odd procession began to advance forward. First came little ones, perhaps children. Carrying baskets, they tossed a trail of blue Androsace blossoms, while one of them played a bamboo flute. When they reached Martin they bowed and peeled away, revealing a set of muckamuck acrobats who tumbled and cartwheeled their way straight for him. Behind them, bare-breasted muckamuck women with veils and chattering castanets did a seductive dance, bumping and grinding their way down the aisle toward Martin. One of them caught his eye and winked.

Next came a muckamuck on stilts, surrounded by clown muckamucks who threw wooden necklaces into the audience. *BANG!* A muckamuck dwarf came running out, chased by an organ monkey with a horn-shaped gun. Every time the monkey shot, the simian dwarf hopped up and down and covered his rear end with the backs of his hands. The crowd was in hysterics and banged their staffs and sticks together to show their appreciation. Lastly, a series of official-looking muckamucks—perhaps the seat of muckamuck power—paraded past Martin. Nodding politely, they all gave him the once-over and the hairy eyeball (although Martin was disgusted and threw the eyeball away).

A majestic, seven-foot-tall half-man, half-ape came forward, wearing a huge black headdress that had to have been designed by Bob Mackie. His long yak-skin cape was decorated with yellow handprints, and around his neck hung a fat chaplet of fireweeds. Over his shoulder was slung a thick coil of climbing rope embellished with crampons, carabiners, and pitons—and finally, on his feet he wore a brand-new pair of "muck boots" from Martha Stewart's gardening catalogue.

As he drew closer, his face, although obviously apelike in nature, seemed particularly expressive. His almond-shaped eyes were austere, yet perhaps . . . fraternal? Friend or foe, there was no doubt that this was the noble face of a chief.

All was quiet. He cocked his head, perplexed, and gestured to the duct tape covering Martin's mouth.

Martin shrugged, mumbled, and tried to laugh it off.

The pseudo-primate frowned, confused. He clanked his staff and walking stick together.

"He, ah . . . wants me to translate for him," Harvey told Martin.

"*Domshay ragoo Shawloo. Domshay magoo daboo,*" said the chief, with a scary, serious expression. Then he opened his mouth wide and displayed a beautiful set of white-painted wooden choppers.

"He, ah, he—he says, 'My name is Chief Shawloo. How do you like my caps?'"

Martin nodded his head enthusiastically. "Mmmmmmmm."

Harvey translated: "The stranger says your teeth are magnificent. You could be a movie star!" He turned to Martin. "I, ah, I, ah, I speak many languages. And my specialty is 'American mumble.'"

Chief Shawloo bellowed, "*Potala, shaba,*" and beckoned Martin to follow him to the fire pit.

The room was alive with murmurs and grunts as the community of big-headed *Quest for Fire* wannabes eyed the outsider.

Harvey whispered to Martin, "He likes you. I can tell. He—he—he thinks you're—you're—you're special. He has big plans for you."

"Mmmmmmm?"

"What? I didn't quite get that."

"Mmmmmmm?"

"Oh, you—you—you want to know how I learned your language! Well, I'll tell you, a great man taught me. The man who gave me my name." Harvey pulled out a framed photo of Jimmy Stewart and showed it to Martin.

"That's right. He used to visit us often. He was a big Sasquatch and yeti fanatic. Look—look—he even signed it for me: 'To Harvey, a pet like you, I'm happy to know. A friend you've been and never a foe, but alas sweet ape, please feel not low—but a pet like you, ain't nothing like my dead dog Bo. Love, Jimmy Stewart.'"

At the fire pit, Martin's jacket and shirt were removed, and Chief Shawloo dipped his hand into a vat of yellow pigment. Then he pressed his flat palm onto Martin's chest, marking him with the sign of the muckamucks. Finally, he presented him with a small wooden flute, which he hung around his neck. The room erupted with happy howls and rapid drumbeats, but Shawloo silenced them by raising his hands.

"*Pee shaboo ladee. Er macht shmata shtoo. Dee shna shaboo shto shmata macht!*"

"He says that we have waited long for the 'Toothless One' to arrive."

"*Fee laba dee do marta nacht!*" The chief circled Martin, pointing every so often to the tape on his mouth. "*Schmee gree baka ey maka bee. Shaboo laddee grav nee doo ee Shawloo!*"

Then the chief pounded his chest like King Kong and let out a monstrous roar.

The muckamucks went crazy, chanting, "*Shabay ee Shawloo! Shabay ee Shawloo! Shabay ee Shawloo!*"

Harvey spoke loudly to Martin, "He says that one day you will take his place as chief, and that it will herald in a new age for the muckamucks—an age finally free from gingivitis, multiple cavities, and impacted wisdom teeth!"

Shawloo, Chief of the muckamucks.

Martin shook his head vehemently "no." He would have liked to explain that he was just wearing the tape in protest of the way homeless people aren't used enough in the movies, but he was afraid that if he did, they would just hang him back up on a pole. Still, he had to find some way out. After all, he was president of the United States. He didn't have time to be no chief of no yetis.

"*Macht!*"

The crowd quieted down and Shawloo's voice became emotional: "*Et shlaby ya, doo, parta mait. Ee frachta bay doo Maita Schlaby?*" And with that he pulled a female muckamuck from the crowd. She was the same one who had winked at Martin, and the chief pushed her directly in front of him. "*Et ya frachta dee Maita Schlaby.*"

"He says this is his only daughter. Her name is Maita Schlaby. She is to be your bride."

Again the room erupted in loud jubilation as Martin very presidentially peed his pants. Maita removed her veil and revealed herself to be a stunning half-ape beauty (albeit with a huge head). Honestly, she really could have been a model in their world, if she had wanted to be. (Not that I would have found her attractive or anything. I'm no sicko, no matter what the monkey-keepers at the Bronx Zoo might have told you.)

She batted her eyelashes and licked her lips. Martin, horrified, politely mumbled, "Mmello mmmma'am," and then ran as fast as he could, smack into Harvey's hairy arms.

"Isn't it great?" said Harvey. "You get to live with us forever! Huzzah!" And all the monkey people cheered.

CHAPTER TWENTY-FIVE

The morning dawned bright and clear, but the cold was beginning to gnaw away at my nose, causing the incipient, ticklish pecks that I should have recognized as the early signs of frostbite. But at the time, I just assumed some cute little mourning dove must have gotten stuck in my oxygen mask and was making merry with my nose hair.

"Valderee! Valder rah, Valder ree, Valder ra ha ha ha ha ha. Valde ree, Valder rah, my knapsack on my back. Oh I love to go . . ."

"Will you shut up?"I almost didn't hear Duncan's muffled plea.

He was letting us use supplementary oxygen for the first time. Breathing the pure, thick air made climbing a pleasure, but it also made it a little difficult to understand what everyone was saying. Still, when Duncan pointed at me and made the universal sign for cutting someone's throat and drop-kicking his head off the side of the mountain, I realized that he'd had enough (and that's when I started singing "Sweet Georgia Brown" instead).

Those of us who had "volunteered" the night before now followed our trusty leader as he zigzagged through crusty snowdrifts at least three feet deep. In one hand, Duncan held Percy's diary, and in the other, a compass. Occasionally he would pause to check the position of the sun with his sextant. Then, after screaming, "I'm going blind!" and rolling around in the snow for a few minutes, he would get up and we would continue on.

At one point I saw something black sticking out about three clicks off to the east. (I've always wanted to say that. I don't even know how far a "click" is. The thing I saw was about three feet away.) I unhooked myself and set off to investigate. Up close, it appeared to be a piece of wood.

What would wood be doing up this far on the mountain? Perhaps a broken propeller blade from Ever-Rest?

When I picked it up, I saw that it was indeed a piece of petrified wood—"goofer," to be precise, a rare species of cypress commonly found in the Middle East ca. 2000 B.C. Brushing a bit of snow off one side, I was able to make out some partial Aramaic lettering, painted in gold leaf and still vaguely visible.

"Who the hell was 'oah'?"

"Over here!" shouted Lauren. "We've found something. Over here!" I chucked the worthless piece of wood away and hurried to join my friends, who were huddled over a find that I hoped would be more interesting.

Duncan was already digging the snow away from the torso connected to the frozen hand that extended out from the snowdrift, its blue fingers agonizingly bent backward.

"Is it him? Is it him?" I asked, excitedly jumping up and down.

"Don't get your hopes up, sahib," advised Flip Flop. "Lot of people die on this mountain."

"I know it's him. It has to be him! See, I have blue fingers too! And I can bend them backward too." I bent my fingers back until they cracked. "Ow!"

"Then I believe we've found your great-uncle, my dear," said Lauren, squeezing my shoulder.

"Not unless his real name was Ernst," announced Duncan. He was rifling through some papers in a small leather pouch. When we all looked down at the body we gasped.

Still half covered in snow but plainly visible was the unmistakable gray of a Nazi uniform. As if preserved in a time capsule, its epaulets and black leather chest belt and holster were still in perfect condition, and around the body's broken left arm was the classic red armband, glaringly antithetical to the blanket of pure white snow surrounding it.

Duncan read from an identification card. "Name is Ernst Videlhoff, doctor, SS officer, and . . . anthropologist?" He shrugged and threw the wallet and papers back on top of the body.

"Well, what the hell were the damn Nazis doing on Everest?" Lauren was especially disgusted by our find. She was the only one amongst us who had lived through World War Two, and those who did will never forget. (Or shut up about it.)

"How do I know, lady? I only know it ain't his uncle Percy."

"Maybe they came to the Himalayas to pick a bouquet for der Führer. *Sieg Heil!*" I said and stuck my arm out and took my black plastic comb and held it under the nose part of my oxygen mask, and then goose-stepped back and forth in the snow. I laughed like a hyena (because I hadn't laughed like one lately and I couldn't think of any other animal at the moment).

"They came on orders from Heinrich Himmler," Flip Flop blurted out, and we all turned and stared at him.

"It was a secret mission in nineteen thirty-eight, a ten-member expedition comprised of anthropologists, doctors, and experts in racial purity. Himmler believed that the true origins of the Aryan race went back to the peoples of Atlantis. His theory was that they were forced from their homeland by a natural disaster and migrated here . . . to the roof of the world."

"Cuckoo," I said, spinning my finger around my ear.

"He also believed that the Tibetans were the distant relatives of the German people."

"Oh well, that, of course."

"They spent weeks searching for clues, taking skin samples, measuring the average size of the Tibetan head, and teaching the lamas how to make the perfect bratwurst. In the end, however, they came up with nothing. On their last day, all ten members—plus a few pet schnauzers—headed up Viper Pass to play *Faust* on their glockenspiels, but they were never seen or heard from again."

"So the dirty Krauts froze to death. Serves them right," blasted Lauren.

"I don't think so," said Pamma, turning the body over and revealing three arrows sticking out of Ernst's back.

"Apaches!" I yelled, "run for your lives!"

"Pipe down," barked Duncan. "It wasn't Apaches."

"Then who? The Sioux? Hey, that rhymes! I'm a poet and I didn't know it. But my feet show it, 'cause they're Longfellows! Hee-hee-hee-hee." And then I sang, "I oughta be in pictures . . ."

Duncan looked at Tzing Tzang, who shrugged as if to say, *What the hell, go ahead and tell them, you've already told them everything else, you big motormouth.* "It was the hill people!"

At that moment a bitter gust of icy wind blew across our faces.

"What? You mean the creepy hill people that Percy wrote about in his diary? The little guys that he thought were cute little gnomes, but who turned out to be really nasty, inbred rednecks that snuck into his tent at night and did unspeakable things to him while he slept?"

"Yeah, that would be them."

"But I thought you said they were just hallucinations!"

"Yeah, well . . . I was hoping. The broken fingers are the giveaway. According to hill people lore, that's their calling card."

"Hill people have lore? There's lore about these people? That means they're real for sure! I mean, lore clinches it."

"Calm down, kid."

I started to panic and hyperventilate. "You lied to us! They could be around here right now, watching us, waiting for just the right moment to jump out and drag me away and make me squeal like a pig. I gotta get out of here . . . I gotta get out of here . . . I gotta—"

I tried slapping myself, but I was wearing my oxygen mask and slapping didn't work.

Tzing Tzang sighed and adjusted the valve on my regulator, allowing more oxygen to flow, and I immediately calmed down.

"Oh, that's much better. Thank you, Mr. Tzang," I said in a more than usually fey manner that even took me by surprise.

"Don't worry about the hill people. They're long gone from Everest," said Pamma, booting snow over the Nazi's body. "They supposedly migrated to West Virginia a long time ago." She exchanged looks with Duncan.

"Oh, thank God," I said, and then I wagged my finger at Duncan. "You!"

"Okay. Let's go," he ordered, looking at his compass, sextant, maps, and telescope. "If my calculations are correct, Percy's camp should be about three clicks off to the east."

We trudged on, marching endlessly across a blanket of white. As the day wore on, I began to notice little dark figures darting in and out of the boulders and snowdrifts all around us, but apparently no one else did.

"Did you see that?" I said.

"Just floaters in your eyes. Keep walking," Duncan ordered.

"But—"

"Just keep walking."

I slipped back to the end of the procession and hiked with my face pointed toward the sun. Then I heard a noise and turned to the side.

This time I definitely saw a pair of beady little eyes duck down behind a rock.

I took a deep breath in preparation to scream my head off, when all of a sudden I began to choke and gasp for air again. My vision irised down like the end of a silent movie and a moment later, it was if I were watching my whole life pass before me in slow motion: *There I was at one week old, eating my first Quarter-Pounder with cheese. There I was at two weeks old at my first ballet class (wearing my best dress shoes, of course). Oh, and there I was just three weeks old wandering the desert and being tempted by the devil—what an asshole—but we must have struck up some sort of bargain, because after that my career really took off.* (Bunk in, folks, because we got a long way to go—and it's all in slow motion.) *Oh, and there I was at four weeks old . . .*

"Stop!"

"What's the problem?" shouted Duncan.

"We have to stop! Something's wrong with Chris!" Lauren shouted.

"Just a little farther!"

"No, now! He can't breathe!"

"Oh fine."

Flip Flop was the fist to my side and yanked my oxygen mask off. Not only was my nose black from frostbite, but my face had turned a ghastly phosphorescent green.

"Carbon monoxide poisoning," he said. Then, without even thinking about it, he started giving me mouth-to-mouth resuscitation (which made his face turn green too).

"Oxygen! We need oxygen, here!" Lauren called out.

Duncan arrived with an extra tank of gas and Flip Flop hooked me up. I started to breathe again, but I was still jaundiced as an unripe tomato on a foggy day in old London town.

"We have to get him down to Camp Two," Pamma urged.

"What happened?" Duncan asked.

"They came on orders from Himmler."

Flip Flop picked up my old canister of oxygen and saw that it was totally empty. He examined the regulator, which had been turned up to full. Apparently when Tzing Tzang had adjusted it for me, he had carelessly opened the valve all the way, causing my tank to empty quickly of fresh air. For the last hour or so I had been inhaling pure, uncut carbon monoxide.

"Honest mistake, boss," said Tzing Tzang, not particularly concerned.

"Of course it was, Tzing," said Duncan, wrapping his arm around the Sherpa's shoulder. "You just had your mind on them hill people, right?"

"Yeah, right. That was it, boss."

"Well, that's a lesson for us all. We all gotta stay frosty on this crazy mountain." Then he attached a canister of pepper spray to his gas mask.

Flip Flop wasn't buying it though. He had found his *yidam*, and its name was Tzing Tzang.

It took us three hours to get back down to Camp Two, and Flip Flop carried me the entire way. The sun was setting fast and the temperature was rapidly dropping.

To our surprise, when we finally trudged into camp, all hell was breaking loose. Max and Wendell were trying to console Kirsten, who was in hysterics. "No! No! No! It's all my fault! It's all because of me! He told me he would do it. He told me he would. And he did it! He's gone! He went away!" Naturally, I thought she was talking about Mr. Pop-eyes, but apparently it was Tony who was now nowhere to be found.

CHAPTER TWENTY-SIX

"Foxtrot Three, Foxtrot Three. Tinkerbell calling Central Control. This is Tinkerbell calling Central."

"Patching you through to Blue Folder, Tinkerbell. Hold on."

Dana Harding had been climbing all day when her progress was halted by the same *bergschrund* that Martin had fallen into. As she sat dangling her legs over the edge of the abyss, she was surprised to find that her cell phone was still working, but since she wasn't on a hard line it would be more prudent to report to her superiors in code:

"This is Blue Folder. Go ahead, Tinkerbell."

"The M&M's are halfway up the cake."

"Has No-chin found his rump yet?"

"Cannot confirm. Will know more later."

"Any movement from the cute little dollies or any of those wild llamas?"

Harding rolled her eyes.

"Negative. No movement from the dollies *or* llamas."

"You must stop the M&Ms from reaching the top of the cake."

"It seems someone else doesn't like that flavor, either."

"Explain."

"Hot tamale."

"Just how hot?"

"Thermobaric, seismicity-trembler with anionic acid."

"We don't use that kind of Tabasco in our tamales anymore."

"We used to. Know anyone who's been playing with the blender?"

"Are you suggesting a rogue element within the kitchen?"

"It wouldn't be the first time."

"I'll let the chef know right away. Report back when you've made contact with the bowl of nuts—I mean, the M&M's."

Harding shut her cell phone and pondered the urgency in the man's voice. For the time being, she didn't give it much weight but just logged it into her photographic memory.

Now, since there were no aluminum ladders to help her cross, she gathered her gear, and pulled a grappling hook from her backpack. She attached a length of rope and hurled it over the gap. It caught in an icy lip on the other side, and she tugged several times to make sure it was firmly planted. Then she slipped the line through her safety vest, shouted "*Carabunga!*" and jumped off.

She flew for about three seconds before her weight yanked hard on the line and then the grappling hook pulled right out of the ice and she went plummeting below.

Luckily for her, her sleeping bag broke the fall, but she still landed with a hard bounce that knocked the air out of her. Gasping and heaving, she pulled herself up on her knees and looked back up at the wall of ice.

"Fuck!" she shouted.

A moment later the echo came back, "*Fuck! Fuck! Fuck!*" and she had to laugh. But when the echo fused with the sounds of drum-beating and chanting—the same sounds that had kept her awake all night on the ice shelf—she suddenly became serious.

"What the hell *is* that?"

As she stood up, she stumbled over Bogie's flask—next to it was the coin collection, Max's extra Speedo, Kirsten's CD, Yorgi's cane, the Jerome Kern sheet music, the can of baked beans—and my heap of snow. *But where was Martin's body?* Glancing back and forth between the intimidating wall of ice and the small opening at the back of the *bergschrund* where the sounds were coming from, she agonized over what to do. Yes, she was on an important mission, but if there was a chance that Martin was still alive, she knew it was her duty to investigate.

She unholstered her .45 Magnum, checked her crampons (as well as her supply of things that rhyme with "crampons"), stooped down, and began to crawl toward the mysterious sounds.

In Camp Two's communal tent, Flip Flop continued to administer mouth-to-mouth.

"Um . . . Flip . . . I think I'm okay now. Thank you."

"Oh, yes, sorry, sahib."

I was breathing fine on my own, and my complexion had returned to its normal pale chartreuse. Lauren was dutifully slathering my schnoz with Noxzema, which she claimed was a cure-all.

I sat up and Tzing Tzang came over with a cup of *chaang*. "Sorry about the old oxygen, kid," he said, and when he went to hand me the cup, Flip intercepted it.

"One moment," Flip glared suspiciously at the other Sherpa and took a sip and swished it around in his mouth several times. Satisfied that it wasn't poison, he spit it back in the cup and handed it to me.

"It's safe, sahib."

"Gee, thanks. Um, I'm suddenly not that thirsty."

Kirsten had regained her composure, and everyone had gathered around her.

"Tony and I had an argument. I can't tell you what it was about. I can only say that certain suggestions were made that I simply could not abide by."

"I think, for the record, we need to be a little more specific than that, Kirsten," said Michael, filming as per usual.

"That won't be necessary," huffed Lauren. "Go ahead, my child."

"He said that I don't respect him anymore on account of him getting all scared to cross the ladders and all, and that he was going to prove himself to me. And that's when he left."

"Left? Left for where? Where did he go?" Duncan pressed.

"To the summit. He said he was going to summit before anyone else, and that he was going to plant the *Who's the Boss* flag and do a little soft-shoe"—Kirsten hiccupped through her tears—"all for me." Mr. Pop-eyes' pop-eyes seemed to fill with tears as well.

"He doesn't even know the way to the summit!" said Duncan.

"That's what I said. I said, 'You don't even know the way to the summit,' and he said, 'What's to knows. It's ups, rights? I'll just follows the signs.' I begged him not to go. But I couldn't stop him." Kirsten began to bawl.

"There, there now, child. We'll just meet him up at the summit, that's all."

Kirsten looked up with bloodshot eyes, "Do you think so? Do you really think he'll make it?"

"Did he take his oxygen tank with him?" Duncan asked.

"No, just his pitch pipe."

"Then he's a goner."

At that Kirsten wailed even louder, and Lauren shot Duncan a death stare. He shrugged and mouthed, "Sorry."

Suddenly Max burst into the tent with a pair of binoculars.

"Good Lord, man. You must do something about that frostbite."

Lauren went rifling through her purse. "Now where is that Noxzema?"

Max's body was starting to look like one of Wendell's burnt marshmallows.

"You'll have to rub me down later, sweet cheeks. I've spotted our boy about twelve clicks up. He's on that craggy rock that Duncan says no one ever climbs because it's too dangerous."

"Baldwin's Five-o'clock Shadow? The fool! He'll never make it up that kind of rocky stubble. Give me those binoculars," Duncan commanded.

Stippled with slick, basalt outcroppings, and dark schist recesses, Baldwin's Five-o'clock Shadow was indeed a route to the summit, but not a route that any clear-thinking climber would ever attempt. Duncan gazed through the plastic window of the tent at a tiny black speck in the middle of a three-hundred-foot-high jut-out.

"I see him. He's stalled about halfway up on a narrow terrace. This is bad. It doesn't look like he can go up *or* down."

"Let me see. Let me see!" Kirsten grabbed the binoculars. "Oh, Tony, I'm so sorry. You don't have to do this for me. You may not be a movie star, and heaven knows I could have anyone I wanted, but there's just something about your base, boorish, brashness that I can't resist. Oh, yes, at first it was just an infatuation. I was curious more than anything else, really—curious to see what life for a TV celebrity is really like, but then I grew to understand and appreciate your complete and total classlessness. And Tony, you know that 'one' little suggestion that you had? Well, I've been thinking about it, and I've decided that if we can find a size that fits me, I'm okay with the idea. What's really important is that you know that I've never met anyone like you before, because I have managers and agents who keep me away from certain seemingly low-life elements in the business. But I'm so happy I ran into you at that global warming thing. You've changed my life, Tony-Baloney. So in closing, darling"—here Kirsten lowered her voice—"I want you to know that . . . I lo . . . lo . . . like you very much, you big lug, you."

Wendell handed me a tissue and I blew a loud foghorn into it. There was a long pause before Duncan finally spoke.

"Kirsten . . . sweetheart, those are binoculars. You can't communicate with them."

"Goddamn it. Then how the hell am I supposed to talk to the tool?"

Suddenly Duncan's walkie-talkie crackled to life. It was Tony.

"Hellos? Is anyones theres? Hellos?"

Kirsten grabbed it from Duncan.

"Oh, yes, sweetheart. I'm here. It's your little funny faces."

"Funny faces, is that you? I got myself in a little bits of a jams here, sweethearts."

"Yes, I know, my darling. I know, and I want to say a few things to you . . ."

Kirsten proceeded to launch, word for word, into the same soliloquy, and since we had all just heard it, we sat hunched over our beers debating Tony's hopeless situation in hushed tones.

Lauren said, "Losing one SAG member is bad enough. We're not gonna lose another!"

"Yes, we have to save him," I said.

"I would join you guys, but my feet are getting really swollen," Michael griped. He put his finger in his mouth, "I have a feewing I'm gonna need a piggyback wide up to Camp Twee." For some reason he looked over at me and winked.

"*Ya zniyoo*, I go!" announced Yorgi, pounding his chest. "I find him by smell. He wears the Axe Effect."

"Yorgi, you can't go," Wendell said. "It's time for you to face facts. You. Are. A. Blind. Man."

Yorgi's confidence finally seemed to be giving out. "But I'm . . . great skier . . . going to ski down the biggest . . . on a Tuesday . . ."

"Ah, yeah, well, we'll talk about that one later, friend."

"It all made so much zense at zee time," Yorgi said, shaking his head.

"No one's getting him," said Duncan. "It's too late in the day. We'd all freeze trying to get up there now."

"Well, we can't just leave him there," Lauren insisted.

"I'm afraid that's exactly what we have to do. We'll mount a rescue attempt in the morning, but not until."

"You mean leave him up there all night, boss?" asked Tzing Tzang. The experienced Sherpa knew better than anyone else that the odds of surviving a night at that altitude in the open air, with or without a pitch pipe, were next to nil.

"We have no other choice." Duncan shot a look at Lauren. "And don't tell me I'm being callous, queenie. That's just the way it has to be."

"You know there's no way he'll survive the night, Mr. Carter," said Pamma.

"You want to go up there and bring him down, sweetheart? Be my guest." Pamma didn't answer. "I didn't think so. He's just going to have to suck it up . . . at least until dawn."

Flip Flop lowered his head. "It'll be too late by then."

We looked at each other and let the sheer horror of the inevitable sink in. It seemed almost impossible, but not twenty-four hours after the tragedy with Martin, we were facing the possibility of losing yet another beloved member of our team. It truly felt like the expedition was cursed. Or were we just incredibly incompetent idiots? (*Impossible!*)

"And so in closing, Darling, I want you to know that . . . I . . . lo . . . lo . . . like you very much, you big lug, you."

"Ah, thanks, honeys. And FYIs, I thinks they got your size at the Penthouse Boutique in New Havens."

"Oh, okay."

Duncan took the walkie-talkie from Kirsten.

"Tony, this is Duncan."

"Hi ya, Duncan babys."

"Hi ya . . . ahem . . . Tony, we can't mount a rescue attempt tonight. I repeat, we cannot attempt a rescue. It's too late in the day, plus we're all really tired. You are going to have to spend the night up there, and we'll be up to get you . . . first thing in the morning. You can do this, Tony. You have to hunker down and protect yourself from the wind. It's going to get pretty cold up there tonight."

Duncan paused, looked into Kirsten's tear-filled eyes, and then over at all of us.

"Now Tony, I want you to listen very carefully to the next thing I'm going to say."

"Some subtlety is called for now, brave captain," advised Lauren.

"This is very important; if you have anything you want to get off your chest before you . . . you know . . . well . . . before we say good night, now might be the right time to say it. Not that you won't be able to say it tomorrow morning, but . . . just to be on the safe side, now would be a good time, if you know what I mean. Tony, do you understand what I'm really trying to say to you?"

"Nopes."

Max took the walkie-talkie from Duncan.

"Tony, this is Max Bullis."

"Hi ya, Maxy babys."

"I don't know if you're aware of this or not, son, but I'm an ordained minister."

"I knew it," grumbled Michael. "We got ourselves a 'born again.'"

"And I just want you to know, son, that you can tell me anything you need to, and I'll make sure that the word gets to the big guy upstairs. *Comprendez?*"

"Nopes."

"Jeez, this guy is thick," I muttered and grabbed the walkie-talkie from Max.

"Tony, it's Chris."

"Hi yas, Chrissy babys."

"Okay look, guy. I'm gonna give it to you straight up. You got about a snowball's chance in hell of surviving the night, but we're all acting like there's no problem so that Kirsten doesn't start panicking again, because quite frankly she's giving us all a headache. Got it?"

"Nopes."

"Give me that," Kirsten took the walkie-talkie from me. "Darling, it's simple. Do you have any last words?"

"Why do theys have to be my last words?"

"Because you might freeze to death tonight, my sweet."

"Oh, nows I gots it. Jeez, leave it to a dame to get through this thick heads of mine, rights? Well, let's sees. I don't got no regrets. Like the song says, 'I did it my ways.' I want to give a shout-out to the gang in the old neighborhoods and to the Westies. I probably won't ever get a chance to do a little soft-shoe up on the summits, so maybe you can do one for me, Kirsten babys. But just getting to knows all of yoos the way I have has made this whole thing worthwhile. Would I doos it all over again? No friggin' way! And if I could get my hands on Chrissy right now, I'd probably breaks him in twos."

Kirsten looked over at me, and, totally misreading her, I smiled seductively and winked. (After all, she was going to be back on the market soon.)

"No, I'm just joking, kid. I love all your work. Especially that *Homes Alones*. You were dynamite. But look, with this mountain deal here, at least I gave it a shot, right? Maybe I didn't get to the tops, but one guy's tops is another guy's bottoms—so I guess you could say that, at least I climbed up some guy's bottoms, rights?" It sounded like Tony was choking up. But then he blew a C major into his pitch pipe.

"Whether I'm rights," he crooned, "or whether I'm wrongs. Whether I . . ."

"Okay, Tony. Well I guess you probably want to get all tucked in for the night now," interrupted Kirsten.

"No, I'm fines. We could talk till dawn if you wants to."

Kirsten looked uncomfortable.

"Oh, well, yes . . . well . . . um . . . they're kind of giving me the hurry-up signal here. So . . ."

Duncan shrugged and whispered, "No, it's fine. You can keep talking."

"They're saying I shouldn't run down the batteries on the walkie-talkie, because . . . well, we'll need it for tomorrow when we . . . um . . . *rescue* you."

"We got plenty of batteries," I said, holding out a handful of double A's.

"So I'll say my good-nights now, my love. And I will see you in the morning. You can count on that."

Kirsten put down the walkie-talkie. "I'm sorry," she sputtered. "I just couldn't listen to him sing 'I Gotta Be Me' again. And besides, we had said everything we needed to say to each other, anyway." Then she ran out of the tent in tears.

Tony continued to broadcast, "I don't think there'll ever be enough time to say everything we need to say to each other, funny faces, buts I'm grateful for this opportunity, anyways. Oh, first off, just so you know, my will and all my vital papers, deeds, Barra bonds, et cetera, are in a safe deposit box at Banco Popular on Madison Avenue, and the key is under my bronze statue of Gene Kelly. Okay? Hello? Is anyone theres?"

I gently turned the walkie-talkie off.

A defeated morbidity (as opposed to our previous victorious morbidity) hung over all of us in the communal tent. It was like the terrorists had dropped a big feeling-down-in-the-dumps bomb.

"Darn it," I said. "Lost another one to Ditech Dot Com!" and then I tried to get everyone to laugh along with me. "Come on guys, buck up," I pushed, "he'll be fine. We'll just get him in the morning! Let's all set our alarm clocks for oh-six hundred. Crampons and ice axes, A-holes! Right, Duncan?"

Duncan dropped his head and walked out. "Yeah . . . right, kid."

"This has turned out to be one hell of a vacation," grumbled Wendell, as he escorted Yorgi to his tent. "Thanks for bringing us all along."

One by one, everyone skulked back to their tents, pausing only to shoot looks.

"*Et tu*, Pamma, *et tu*?"

All except for Lauren, that is.

"It's not your fault," she said, putting her hand on my shoulder. "We're all traveling on our own paths."

"Yes, my sentiments exactly," I responded, having absolutely no idea what the hell she was talking about. Then she left and I was alone. I looked out the plastic window and could just make out what I assumed was Tony tap-dancing up on Baldwin's Shadow.

Poor guy's gotta be lonely up there, I thought, so I switched the walkie-talkie back on.

"I gotta be mees. I gotta be mees . . ."

"Aahgg," I said and switched it off.

CHAPTER TWENTY-SEVEN

At 2 A.M. Duncan and his entirely untroubled conscience were sawing gourds like a big old Landrace after a long day at the Iowa Cattle Congress, when his walkie-talkie suddenly crackled to life.

"Oh, Goddamn it," he groused, fumbling in the dark. "This better not be Tony." He found his walkie-talkie and switched it on.

"Yeah. What is it?"

"Greetings, old chap. You're not asleep already, are you? Why, it's still the shank of the evening, old boy! Over."

"Branson," Carter moaned.

On the other side of the mountain, comfortably situated on the western *cwm*, Branson's Camp Two looked like an Aspen resort, complete with a portable ice-skating rink and inflatable hot tub. A scratchy recording of Chopin's haunting "Polonaise in G Minor" wafted out of the cornucopia speaker of an antique cylinder phonograph. Branson indulged in warm bubbling water, joined by a bevy of bikini-clad virgins, none of whom looked the slightest bit wearied by her day's climb. The Englishman sipped champagne and consulted a map as he spoke into his high-tech, state-of-the-art walkie.

"I merely wanted to convey that, according to my lookouts, I'm camped frightfully higher than you are—about two thousand feet, I would say. Which would indicate that I am in the lead."

"Yeah, well, your lookouts are nearsighted."

"On the contrary, old man, they use nothing but the highest quality Meade telescopes."

"What do you want?"

"Direct and to the point. I like that. Quite simply, I'm giving you another chance to forfeit." He glanced at his TAG Heuer. "You see, weather permitting, I plan on summitting sometime in the next forty-eight hours."

"Don't bullshit me, Branson. You have to acclimatize just like the rest of us. Unless you made the Sherpas haul a compression chamber up there? Which by the way, I'm pretty sure would be cheating."

"No, I'm not that cruel. But I do have something else rather avant-garde up my sleeve, old boy." Here Branson reached over the edge of the hot tub and grasped a Gamow suit, just like the one Agent Resnick was wearing down at Base Camp.

"Oooh, I'm so scared. What could it be?"

"You'll see. I'll leave one up at the summit for you." He sipped his champagne and nuzzled noses with the unspoiled maidens on either side of him.

Technically speaking, Gamow suits are only designed to reacclimatize a mountaineer in distress, but if you were actually to ascend in one—provided you continually adjusted the atmosphere within it—then there really wouldn't be any need to stop and acclimatize. Hypothetically, you could climb Everest in three days instead of three weeks, and Branson had brought enough suits for all his virgins as well as his Sherpas, porters, butlers, and footmen.

"How 'bout when *I* get to the summit first, I wait for you, and you can show me whatever it is you got, then."

"Cocksure as usual. Well, let's test the width and breadth of your cockiness, shall we?"

Duncan glanced demurely down at his lap.

"Since you refuse to call it quits, what would you think about upping the ante—shall we say double or nothing?"

"What are you going to do if I lose, kill me twice?"

"I was thinking about something a bit more . . . Middle Eastern."

"I don't get it."

"Let the punishment fit the crime."

Duncan again glanced demurely down at his lap, but this time a look of horror crossed his face and he swallowed hard. "You wouldn't do that, would you?"

Branson laughed. "Of course not, old boy." Duncan breathed a sigh of relief as Branson continued. "I have highly trained, unscrupulous surgeons to do that sort of thing for me." And then Duncan swallowed even harder. "And I don't believe they use anesthetic, which serves you right, for what you did."

"Okay, okay, but what if I win?" Duncan asked.

"Then I let you keep your Golden Rhombus, and any body parts I may have my eye on, and all is forgiven, including the money I fronted for your expedition. It's such a shame you haven't found that damned diamond yet, especially when you're so close. But I suppose you'll have to give it up if you really want to beat me to the summit. And I suggest you do so, otherwise . . . well, you know the rest."

"How the hell do you know where the Rhombus is?"

"Why, I passed it earlier today, old boy, nothing but a piece of rock. Totally worthless, by the way. Just as worthless as that frozen old corpse lying next to it."

Duncan became animated. "Where? Where did you see it?"

"Do we have a bet?"

"Yeah, yeah, yeah. Just tell me where the Rhombus is."

"Ah, splendid. Take the northeast corridor to the south approach. About halfway to Camp Four you'll find your Percy and the diamond, but . . . are you really willing to sacrifice your life to find this Rhombus?"

"It's worth millions. I can feel it."

"You can't have both. What's more important to you, the diamond or your life?"

Duncan let this sink in.

"The choice is yours. And so I shall say *adieu*, until the summit."

"Yeah, right—until the summit." And with that Duncan switched off his walkie.

Did Branson really know where the Rhombus was? Or was he just bluffing to slow Duncan down? Taking the northeast corridor to the south approach would add at least a day to the climb, but what if Branson was on the up and up? The one thing Duncan knew for sure was that Branson was a man of his word. If Duncan could beat him to the summit, whatever debt he owed the man would be washed away and he wouldn't have to go through life looking over his shoulder—but if Branson got there first, Duncan had no doubt that he would exercise his right to extreme surgery or worse. There had to be a way to find the Rhombus *and* to beat Branson to the summit. But how?

Duncan took out Percy's diary. He scanned its pages closely while consulting a chart, a compass, a slide rule, and any other navigational tools he had lying around to plan another route to the summit—one that would give him a fighting chance of getting there first while still putting him in the vicinity of the northeast corridor.

He came to the sober realization that not only would he have to eschew acclimatization yet again, dangerously increasing the odds of "mountain madness," (which, by the way, had not set in yet—we get way worse), but in addition, if he wanted to overtake Branson and the virgins, he would have to move more quickly up the mountain, and that meant only one thing: He was going to have to lighten his payload. And by *payload*, I mean "us." And by *lighten*, I mean "lose," and by *going to have to*, I mean . . . um . . . oh, well, you get the point.

Since he came to this realization soberly, he decided to double-check it—and after getting drunk and coming to the same realization, he was convinced that he was right.

The first beak slipped fairly painlessly into the *pectoralis major*, just beneath the skin, but when Shawloo pierced Martin's bare chest a second time, the shock wore off and was replaced by sheer, unadulterated pain. Still, the brave actor stoically refused to show it; instead, he seemed oddly insouciant for a guy standing there with vulture beaks sticking out of his breasts.

"Shbee yama frachta dee brashkee morte. Eee luna de fragmachto!"

The muckamucks chanted in unison, *"Eee luna de fragmachto! Eee luna de fragmachto!"*

Harvey leaned over to Martin. "Chief Shawloo says, 'Now that we've all had a turn riding you, it's time for your wedding.' But before you take his daughter as your bride, you must first prove yourself worthy. He says, 'The Toothless One must undergo the Rapture of the Moon-Glider!'"

"Mmmmmmm?"

Shawloo raised his hands, and bungee cords descended from the opening in the ceiling. The big muckamuck locked eyes on Martin as he attached the cords to the implanted beaks.

Harvey watched while unconsciously grooming the head of the yeti dwarf standing next to him. Fed up, the little apeman finally slapped Harvey's hands away and Harvey apologized profusely.

When Shawloo raised his arms again, the fat albino muckamuck began a slow drumbeat and the bungee cords were pulled tightly from above. Suddenly, Martin was being lifted into the air.

A bright shaft of moonlight shone down through the opening

upon Martin, whose whole body arched backward, while his arms hung behind him, his skin stretched taut, the vulture beaks threatening to tear through at any moment.

As if this wasn't punishing enough, Shawloo directed the muckamucks above to let the bungee cords slack off just a bit, and then pull them up hard, causing Martin to bounce up and down. The tribe went berserk, chanting, hooting and dancing, and Harvey gave Martin the thumbs-up.

Dana Harding was still following the sounds of the bacchanalia through the cold, dark catacombs. She had paused only to call Norgay at Base Camp to inform him of her whereabouts, but neither her walkie-talkie nor her cell phone worked *inside* Chomolungma. (Which by the way, is a good title for the sequel.)

She rounded a corner and was met with the beaded curtain marking the entrance to the antechamber. This was it! She cocked her .45 and approached cautiously. She crawled on her belly, inching her way closer and closer. At the opening, she pulled two strands of beads aside and peered in. The image she saw would stay with her for the rest of her life, however long or short that might be.

Okay, Dana, you're not crazy, She told herself. *You're not seeing things. It is what it is: TV's President Josiah Bartlett is hanging by his man boobs in an igloo full of bigfoots.*

She watched, stunned, as Martin flew from one side of the hall to the other, ricocheting off the walls and bouncing up and down like a marionette at the mercy of its muckamuck puppeteers. Oddly enough, he didn't seem to be in any pain—in fact he had a look of peaceful serenity, as if he were under some sort of spell.

Dripping cold sweat and shaking with fear, Dana leaned back

Moon-Glider

against the ice. *Okay. Okay. Get ahold of yourself. You have to do something. You can't just leave him hanging there . . . Well, you can, but you might feel guilty about it for a couple of days. You're going to just bust in there shooting, that's what you're going to do. But wait, who knows what those big apemen are capable of ? They could easily overpower you. You're only one person, for crying out loud.*

She took another look at the mayhem inside and prudently decided to wait until the yetis were fast asleep before making her move.

CHAPTER TWENTY-EIGHT

Dear Diary,

Mark my words: Mounting Chomolungma is not just about one looking adversity straight into the eye and saying, "Go take a long walk on a short pier." One would have to be a dunderhead to believe it is as simple as that. It is far more complicated, and one only knows the answers once one stands on one's own personal tip-top.

Percy Brackett Elliott
Northeast corridor, Everest, 1924

My sleeping bag crackled as I sat up. Everything was frozen inside our tent. Icicles hung down like stalactites, while horny old Jack Frost chased funky old hoarfrost around and around in a never-ending cyclone of perverted ice capades.

Wendell was already awake. He glared rancorously at me as he tried to thaw his corrective socks over his butane lighter. In medical terms, frostbite—or *congelatio* (which they serve on cones in Italy and is absolutely dee-lish)—is nothing more than the slow death of living cells. And on that morning, it felt like the whole expedition was just one big snow cone full of multiflavored congelatio.

I sneezed and my blackened nose blew off in my hands for the first time, prompting Wendell to chortle so hysterically that he cracked his sternum in two places. Serves him right.

At six o'clock, Flip Flop stuck his head into our tent. Speaking softly, due to a frozen epiglottis, he said Duncan wanted everyone to gather out on the col.

Outside, Max was miserable, coughing and shivering violently, his skin purple and raw. Michael sat disheartened in the snow. The extreme cold had made it impossible for his body to metabolize the excess uric acid in his system, and his gouty feet were now too swollen to fit into his boots. Kirsten's eyes were half-frozen shut with tears, while Mr. Pop-eyes looked like a frozen bunny on a stick. Yorgi seemed panic stricken, as if he had just comprehended for the first time that he was a blind man climbing Mount Everest, and he clung to Wendell's elbow.

Only Lauren had her shit together—bundled up against the cold, coifed and perfumed as usual, and smoking a cig. Man, she was one tough cookie.

Tzing Tzang and Duncan were scanning the surrounding ridges with binoculars.

"We've got a problem," Duncan announced.

"What?" I asked. "Everyone looks great to me."

"Look for yourselves." He pointed up at Baldwin's Five-o'clock Shadow. Even without binoculars we could see that at least three feet of snow had fallen during the night. Tony was nowhere in sight.

"Could he maybe be foraging for wild berries?" I asked.

Kirsten broke into fresh tears. "Only if there are wild berries . . . in heaven!"

"So what do we do now, brave captain?"

"Well, I think there's only one thing to do. We split up. Half of us looks for Tony and the other half continues on to Camp Three."

Pamma and Flip Flop joined us. Flip had a needle and thread in hand and he began sewing my nose back on.

"No acclimatization again?" Pamma asked, sliding her gun into its holster.

"Um . . . I think we can catch up with our acclimatization process at Camp Three."

"And just how would you suggest dividing up the group?" Pamma asked.

"Well, I think we should, ah . . . you know . . . um . . . do it evenly. How 'bout this: Lauren, Chris, Michael, Kirsten, Max, and Yorgi go with you and Flip Flop to look for Tony, and Tzing Tzang and I take the northeast corridor to Camp Three?"

"Fair enough," I said.

"Do we have any reason to believe that Tony is still alive?" Pamma asked. "He's not answering his walkie-talkie."

"It's probably just out of batteries," Duncan said.

Kirsten sobbed. "Out of batteries . . . in heaven!"

"Our search will be futile, and you know it." Pamma gave her whip a snap to emphasize her point. Duncan seemed a bit intimidated.

"I don't think our consciences would allow us rest if we didn't give it a shot, right?" he said.

"So our brave captain has suddenly grown a conscience," Lauren said.

Pamma added, "And without us slowing him down, he'll have a much better chance of catching up with Branson and his virgins." Again she whipped the air dramatically, and Duncan flinched.

"Our brave captain may be an unscrupulous rat, lacking in all the social graces, not to mention covered with mouse ticks—plus he smells—but I don't believe he would actually *abandon* us."

"Thanks, queenie," said Duncan, "at least someone here trusts me."

"I wouldn't go that far. But I couldn't believe you would do such a thing, when we all have high-powered agents and lawyers that could take you right to the cleaners."

"That's right," I said. "I can get Joe Bornstein on the phone any time I want!"

"Now look," said Duncan, rubbing the outsides of his gloves with Purell, "you guys find Tony, and we'll look for the Rhombus on our way up . . . so that we can . . . um, resuscitate Martin with it . . . and Tony too, and whoever else dies on our way down. Tzing Tzang will get Camp Three ready, and we'll all meet up there, later in the day. That's all." A blast of Dust-Off was clearly in order.

"Sounds like a plan," I said. "I mean, it sounds like one. Is it a plan? I'm not good at that sort of thing."

Michael suddenly cried out, "There's no way I can make it!" He was rubbing his feet. "I can't even walk. I'm going to die on this mountain! We're all going to die on this mountain!"

"Don't you say that," I said. "We're only halfway there. So we've hit a little bump in the road, so what? We can get by this. You can do it, Michael. I know you can." And then I took center stage with my half-sewn-on nose dangling grotesquely over my lips. "Listen people, this is what climbing Mount Everest is all about. It's not about being the first 'this' or the first 'that' to the summit, and it's not about the homeless, or global warming, or bunnies or pasta carbonara. That's all just window dressing. The real reason we're on this mountain is to find out what we're made of as men! Or women! Or both! That's why the great George Plimpton sparred with Sugar Ray Robinson and played quarterback for the Detroit Lions. That's why my great-uncle climbed Everest—not just because of some rare diamond. He wrote in his diary that mounting Chomolungma is about looking adversity straight in the eye and saying, 'Go take a short walk on a long pier.' It's just that simple. You'd have to be a dunderhead not to see that."

"Didn't your uncle die on this mountain?" Wendell asked.

"Thank you, Wendell. Yes, he didn't make it, so maybe he's not the best example, but other people have climbed it, and most of them made it. And most of us are gonna make it too. We have to. Because if we don't, we'll all die!"

I knelt down next to Michael. "Yes, Michael, it's difficult, but as you holier-than-thou people often say, 'It takes a village.' So, let's show this damned mountain that this village is going to kick her fat ass!"

"So you'll carry me then?" he asked. "That's, uh, what a village would do."

"On second thought, maybe you should call it quits."

Duncan hooked himself into his climbing harness, doing his best to avoid Pamma and Lauren's fixed glares. Nervously, he said, "We'll all meet at Camp Three, I . . . promise."

About a half an hour later Duncan and Tzing Tzang headed off through the northeast corridor while the rest of us began ascending Baldwin's Five-o'clock Shadow.

Below the icefall, Harding sensed the time was right to make her move. She had remained ever vigilant during the night-long joviality, merrymaking, and gaiety (during the gaiety she was extra vigilant), but now the fire in the great hall was out, and the muckamucks lay about, snoring and farting and yammering in their sleep.

"It's now or never, girl," she told herself.

Martin lay with his new bride, Maita Schlaby, on a bed of straw atop a wooden scaffold.

Harding cautiously approached, tiptoeing through the prone bodies of the muckamucks toward the honeymoon suite. At one point, the crampons on her boot caught the hairs on the chest of an apeman sprawled on the floor, and when she pulled her boot free, the creature sat straight up, its eyes wide open. Harding readied herself to do battle, but it just gobbled like a turkey and plopped back down. She breathed a sigh of relief and continued on.

She climbed the scaffold and whispered into Martin's ear.

"Sir? Captain Harding, CIA." He didn't respond, so she huffed and then flashed her badge. "I'm legit. I'm here to rescue you. You have to come with me. Wake up!"

He still didn't respond. Perhaps whatever spell had kept him from feeling any pain the night before still had a grip on him. Maita Schlaby rustled and rolled onto one side, throwing her hairy arm over Martin's chest.

"Damn it." Harding held her breath and deftly lifted Maita's arm off the actor. The muckamuck bride grunted but then rolled over. Harding slid Martin off the scaffold. Straining, she struggled to carry him, fireman-style, out of the hall.

She was just about to the exit when a nasty schnauzer noticed her and started to bark.

"Shhhhhhh!"

"Hey, hey, hey. Now . . . now . . . now, where do you . . . you . . . you think you're taking our Toothless One?"

Harding whipped around and saw Harvey standing in front of her with an injured expression on his face. (At that moment he actually looked a little like Jimmy Stewart.) The agent's reflexes kicked in, and she aimed her .45 and pulled the trigger. But nothing happened. As always, the safety was still on.

"Shit!"

Harding tiptoed through the prone bodies.

She coldcocked Harvey, sending him to the floor. But as she turned to go, Maita Schlaby sat up and let out an ear-piercing squawk.

Suddenly awake, Chief Shawloo began tramping toward Harding with huge strides, roaring at the top of his lungs and aiming his spear. The obese albino muckamuck ran to his drum and beat an alarm. In a moment, hundreds of apemen were crawling out of the holes in the igloo walls or rappelling down from the ceiling.

Harding dashed through the exit. She fumbled with her gun, trying to disengage the safety, and then she slipped and fell forward on top of Martin. She rolled onto her back, and just before the yeti mob reached the door, the gun went off into the ceiling. The muckamucks, not used to guns, all stopped short and screamed. Snow and ice came crashing down between them, trapping the hairy creatures inside their gathering hall.

With her adrenaline pumping hard, Harding threw Martin back over her shoulder and hurried through the puzzling twists and turns of the catacombs until, luckily, she found a different way back to the top of the icefall. (Actually, it was a wooden elevator marked FOR MUCKAMUCKS USE ONLY.)

Inside the gathering hall, muckamucks were frantically digging through the blocked entrance when Harvey spotted something on the ground. He bent down and picked it up. It was Martin's nuclear football. He cracked it open, revealing its contents: about a hundred rolls of spare duct tape. A tear rolled down Harvey's cheek and Chief Shawloo gave him a consoling hug.

"Bee shackee makshee baboo, dee robie dow talaboo."

"Re . . . re . . . really?" said Harvey, with a glimmer of hope in his eyes. "The flute?"

CHAPTER TWENTY-NINE

"Tony? Tony?" we called out as we attacked the menacing head-wall of the Five-o'clock Shadow.

The complex terrain forced us to use a "multipitch" climbing technique, which required Pamma to set several belaying lines at one time.

"Stay close!" she shouted down from the front of the line, "flaking" the rope (running it through her hands to take out any tangles) as she went along. "This is nasty up here!"

"Do you need help, Max?" Lauren asked. The human polar bear had paused on a small outcropping and was breathing heavily.

"Well, that depends on what kind of help you're offering there, little lady. Hee, hee hee."

"Oh, fine. Never mind."

Lauren began to move on when Max grasped her wrist with a blue-black hand. "No, wait, wait. I apologize, ma'am. Yes, I could use a little help. I don't think I can go on. My body is turning to stone." Then he coughed.

"Well, of course it is, you silly man. You're covered with frostbite. Here."

Lauren steadied herself on the ledge, removed her parka, and wrapped it around Max.

"No, no. I'm not supposed to wear anything, 'cept my bathing suit."

"My dear man, I believe you lost that challenge a while ago. Perhaps it was a bit ambitious to begin with. Not to mention asinine. If you don't get warm now, you'll die."

"Well, maybe it's my time," he mumbled, dropping his head.

"Now, why would you say a silly thing like that?"

"I'm already dying, Betty." And he coughed again.

"Now, I don't want to hear this kind of talk. You simply have to warm up and then . . ."

"No, you don't understand. With or without Everest, I'm dying. I have a rare disease—aldosterone deficiency, stage three. The doctors in Houston say it's an 'inimical genetic disorder that adversely affects the adrenal glands' or some such hoo-ha." He went into a coughing fit for a few moments, then cleared his throat and popped some of his "vitamins." "It's a progressive disease, they say. Damned progressives! I got two to three months. But then again what do *they* know, right?"

Lauren somberly removed her oxygen apparatus. "I'm sorry, Max," she said. "I had no idea."

"No one does, sweet cheeks, and I'll thank you to keep it that way. You see, I wanted to climb Everest for the Polar Bear Club to leave behind some kind of legacy. Something the world would remember me for. But I've failed, even at that."

Lauren sighed. "Why do we all want the world to remember us?" She lit a cigarette.

"When you don't have anybody else, the world's the next-best thing."

"Surely, there's family—a wife? Children?"

"Nope. Never married. Didn't have the time. Too busy wheeling and dealing, building that portfolio. Shee-it, if I had known then what I know now . . . well . . . hell . . ." He paused and seemed far away for a moment. "Well . . . never despair, right? Never despair."

"Never despair and never give up! I know the best doctors at Johns Hopkins. As soon as we get you off this goddamn mountain, I'll make one call and you'll have a bed, a private room, and a sexy young nurse to keep you company."

Max laughed buoyantly. "Gosh dang it, if you ain't just like the characters you play. A spunky, no-nonsense honest-to-goodness, can-do dame."

"And why be anything else?"

"You know, I gotta tell ya, little lady, when I heard you were coming on this climb I nearly popped a gourd. I've been a fan of yours my whole life—maybe just a little more than a fan. I think I first fell in love with you up there on that there big screen. *Key Largo*, *To Have and Have Not*, *The Rockford Files* . . . well, that was the small screen, but I loved you just the same."

"You're very kind."

"I s'pose if I had ever married, I would have wanted a fiery dame like yourself. Someone who could keep up with me—you know match me one for one."

"That would be a challenge even for me, Max. But what's life without a little challenge?"

The two smiled sweetly at each other.

"Well, I suppose we should get going," Betty said. "We don't want to get lost."

"Could I ask you a favor?"

"Certainly, Max."

He turned his charred cheek toward Lauren.

"Would you give me just a little peck on that there cheek? It would mean the world to me, Betty, it surely would."

Lauren put both hands on the Texan's face and turned him toward her.

"I'll give you more than that, Tex," and she planted her plump Hollywood lips on his. Bobbing and weaving her head to and fro, she produced the most passionate, erotic, sensuously carnal, wet and wild oscillation the man had ever experienced.

"Ooooh dang!" he cried, lost in nirvana, "if that don't give a man something to live for, then I don't know what does."

"I'm glad you're enjoying it so much, but you can stop kissing me now, Max."

"I did stop kissing you."

Lauren opened her eyes and saw the Texan standing two feet away from her—without his lips.

"Oh, dear," she said, touching her mouth, where his lips were still securely planted.

Over on the northeast corridor, Duncan and Tzing Tzang had made great progress. Although they hadn't come across a single trace of Uncle Percy or the Rhombus, they were already close to Camp Three, and they assumed they were well ahead of Branson.

"Hold on a second," called Duncan, and he took off his backpack and oxygen mask and sat down in the snow, exhausted. "I just need a second."

"Sure, boss," said Tzing Tzang. "We go fast without the slow-pokes, huh? We beat Branson for sure."

"Yeah, it's easier without them, no doubt." He glanced over in the direction of the Five-o'clock Shadow. "I'm sure they're fine. That Pamma chick knows her way around." *Let me just beat Branson*

"I'm already dying, Betty."

to the summit, or find the Rhombus, and then I'll come back and help everyone else.

"Uh-oh, we gonna have to move even faster, boss." Tzing Tzang was on his belly at the edge of the ridge, peering through his binoculars at the western cwm. He could see Branson and his virgins, all in snow-white Gamow suits, already five hundred feet above them. "They use decompression suits. They don't need to acclimatize!"

"No fucking way!" said Duncan. "I don't believe it. That bastard! Come on, let's go." He grabbed his backpack.

"If they don't have to acclimatize, then he gonna make it up there before us, boss. So now we don't find the diamond and you lose bet too? Everything is shit!"

"Yeah, yeah, yeah, I know, I know. Just keep going."

"What's the point of climbing if we lose everything, boss? I mean, who cares if the movie stars make it to the summit, right? We came for diamond, right? Right? . . . Boss?" Tzing Tzang turned back to Duncan, who had stopped. Deep in thought, he was looking toward the Five-o'clock Shadow again.

"Something wrong, boss?"

CHAPTER THIRTY

"Vindall, *Yee vsnygneyt*. I scared, I scared!"

"You should be. You're blind."

"*Shto yee dymag? Tch, tch, tch.*" Yorgi shook his head.

"How the hell do I know what you were thinking, Yorgi? Probably some shit about how blind people are just as capable of climbing a mountain as seeing people." Wendell chuckled and shook his head. "Unbelievable."

"Vindall, when we summit, will you help me ski down Everest?"

"I don't think that's a good idea anymore, Yorgi. It's not even a good idea for a normal person."

"But I cannot return to my homeland a failure."

"Yorgi, you're blind, no one expects you to be successful at anything. They'll be proud of you if you manage to dress yourself. So just keep climbing, will ya?"

At the head of the line Pamma pounded pitons and snargs (tubular ice screws) into the rock. There weren't many footholds, so she used the friction of the soles of her boots to steady herself, a technique called "using the friction of the soles of your boots to steady yourself."

About an hour into the climb, Pamma reached the terrace where

Tony had presumably spent the night. Kirsten was next up, and then Lauren and Max joined them shortly after. The four of them stared at the mound of snow. Pamma and Max began to dig.

Lauren said, "Maybe you shouldn't look, child."

Kirsten said, "No, I want to see him."

Pamma said, "I found a finger."

Max said, "No, that's mine."

"Any sign of him?" I called up. I was about twenty feet below the terrace.

"Nothing yet," Lauren called back.

"You know, Chris," said Michael, "I just want to thank you for giving me the proverbial boot in the snoot down there at Camp Two. If I make it to the summit, it's gonna be all because of you, buddy."

"Yeah, that's what it's looking like," I said, because I had been carrying him and his big camera on my back since we started up, and there wasn't any sign of that changing any time soon. "Hey, Flip Flop." My faithful Sherpa was climbing beside me, as always. "Since you love me so much, you want to take a turn carrying the big guy?"

He sized Michael up with his eyes. "Uh, no, you do fine, sahib. You very strong."

Above us, Wendell and Yorgi had made it to the ledge.

"So, did you find Tony's frozen corpse, or what?" Wendell asked.

"No," said Kirsten, "but we found this."

She pointed to a small opening in the rock.

"Looks like an animal den," Max said.

Pamma snorted. "At twenty-six thousand feet? I doubt it."

Kirsten asked, "Do you suppose he went in there?" She cupped her hands and shouted into the cave. "Tony? Tony Baloney!" But no answer came back.

"Well, there's only one way to find out," said Pamma, lighting a flare.

"You can't go in there alone, little lady," said Max. "What if—"

A steely look from Pamma made it clear to Max that she wasn't about to suffer his patronizing southern chivalry. "I move more quickly on my own," she said.

"Yes, that seems to be the rule of thumb on this damned mountain," said Lauren, as she glanced in the direction where she assumed Duncan was climbing.

Pamma put her hand on Lauren's shoulder.

"You're strong. If I'm not back in five minutes, don't wait for me. Take the southern route to Camp Three. You'll pick up the trail three clicks to the east." Then she went in.

I called from below, "So, did you find Tony's frozen corpse, or what?"

"No," Lauren called back, "but there's a cave up here. Pamma went in."

Max shouted into the cave. "What do you see down there, Pammie?" But there was no answer. "Gal sure don't talk much, do she?"

"You want an Oreo cookie, Yorgi?" Wendell asked. "I gotta whole bag of 'em. Here, I'll put it in your mouth for you."

"Hey, *shto eta*? What was that sound?"

"What sound?" Lauren asked Yorgi.

"It come from cave."

"I didn't hear anything," said Wendell.

"It come from cave. I hear it, Vindall, I swear. Blind people hear things other people don't."

Wendell said, "Now, Yorgi, that's just an old wives' tale that people made up to keep handicapped people from killing themselves."

"How long has she been gone?" asked Max.

They all looked at each other.

Lauren said, "Oh, was somebody supposed to be timing?"

Kirsten shrugged. "I don't like wearing watches."

"Pamma!" Max called into the cave again. "That's it, I'm going in after her."

"You can't, Max. You heard what Pamma said. If she doesn't come back, we keep moving."

Max lowered his voice. "Betty, let me do this. I have nothing to lose, right?" He coughed as if to remind her that he was dying.

The two locked eyes. "I wouldn't say that." She took his frozen lips out of her coat, set them back on his face and kissed them passionately. When she pulled away, they were back on her face again.

"Oh, crap," she whispered, annoyed. "Just come back, all right? We'll sew you up later."

"You can count on it," he said, and with that he greased himself down with some Noxzema and wriggled into the cave.

Below I was still struggling to ascend. Flip Flop, getting bored, sat perched on an outcropping beside us, tapping his fingers.

"Michael, how are those feet of yours?" I asked, straining to pull down on my jumar.

"As swollen as a couple of bloated Cornish hens," he replied. "I don't know if I'll ever be able to walk again."

"Great, great. Just checking."

I heard a commotion coming from above.

"There it is again," Yorgi was yelling. "It getting louder."

"I hear it!" shouted Kirsten.

"Wait, I think I heard it too," said Lauren. She yelled into the cave, "Max? Pamma? Tony? Is that you?"

"How's it going up there?" I shouted. "Am I missing anything fun?"

Wendell called back, "They're just letting their imaginations run away with—"

Suddenly the opening to the cave exploded with an incredible force, blasting the side of the mountain away and sending rocks the size of microwaves flying out in all directions. Lauren and Kirsten were thrown hard onto their backs. Wendell and Yorgi were hurled over the side and only saved by the safety rope, while Michael, Flip-

Flop, and I plummeted thirty feet before the belaying line went taut and held us—dangling in midair.

When Lauren rubbed the dust from her eyes, she couldn't believe what she was seeing. Through the cloud of pulverized granite, a giant claw had appeared—and then another one, and then the entire body of a humongous green crab. It was at least six feet wide and ten feet high and covered with white speckles, and in its ugly mouth was Tony's pitch pipe. Kirsten let out a ghastly shriek. The crab's fluttering antennae and round eyes turned toward her.

Menacingly, it blew a C major.

"Hey, what the hell are you guys doing?" I yelled from below. "Having a hoedown?"

One by one, the crab's legs started to move. Its claws snapped at the air as it advanced on Kirsten, but it had only gotten to within five feet of her before another explosion rocked the mountain and an even bigger, even more menacing giant crab blasted through the wall with such force that it rammed straight into the smaller giant crab and sent it flying off the terrace.

"Michael, did you just see that?" I asked.

"I'm getting it all on film," he said.

"Hang on, sahib," said Flip Flop. "That was no ordinary giant green and white-speckled monster crab. The *yidam* is at work!"

I began to laugh uncontrollably.

"What's so funny, sahib?"

"Chomolungma has crabs! Get it? The Goddess Mother! Crabs! You wouldn't expect it, right? She seems so clean."

The new crab was all black and had to be at least twenty feet tall and fifteen feet wide. Its shell was covered with pointy spikes, and in each gigantic, craggy claw it clasped human prey. Pamma struggled for her life in its left claw, while an unconscious Max was having his rib cage slowly crushed in the other.

"Get off the terrace!" yelled Pamma, struggling to draw her revolver.

Lauren grabbed Kirsten, and together they shimmied over the side toward where Yorgi and Wendell were hanging. This infuriated the crab, which slammed Max against the rock a couple of times and then tossed him off the mountain.

"Max, noooooooo!" shouted Lauren and she covered her eyes as Max's frostbitten body tumbled head over heels, down, down, all the way down. Kirsten tried to console Lauren, but before she could pat her on the shoulder, the crab reached over the side of the terrace and snatched Kirsten by the hood. She screamed bloody murder (see, I'm not the only one).

BLAM! BLAM! BLAM! BLAM! BLAM! BLAM!

Pamma fired her revolver at the crab, but the bullets just bounced off. Startled by the noise, the monster clamped her even harder. She could actually hear her own rib cage cracking, but she was in shock and felt no pain. She pulled out her David Bowie knife and jammed it into the soft connective tissue between its knuckles and claws, but that served only to further irritate the beast. Slowly it drew Pamma toward its ugly, chomping mouth.

Kirsten had fainted and it looked as though Pamma was a goner, when suddenly the crab was zotched in the eyes with a blast of pepper spray. Duncan Carter was on its back, barely holding on and spraying for dear life. The crab reared up on its back legs and let go of Kirsten, but still held on to Pamma. Tzing Tzang caught Kirsten and laid her down behind a big boulder.

Duncan was riding the angry crab like a bucking bronco.

"Yay! Duncan came back for us!" I shouted, and at that moment he was thrown off the back of the crab. "Oops, that's gotta hurt! I'm only gonna give him a 'six' for that, because the dismount sucked."

"Run!" said Pamma in a weak voice. She unsnapped her ammunition pouch, reached in, and pulled out an old World War Two hand grenade.

"Pamma, don't!" Duncan shouted. "Don't do it!"

"Go!" she yelled, and Duncan dove behind the boulder with Tzing Tzang and Kirsten.

The crab reared up again and was about to bite into Pamma, but she pulled the pin and tossed the grenade into its gaping mouth. The demon crab swallowed it whole and Pamma held her ears, waiting for the blast—but nothing happened. Was it a dud? The crab almost seemed to smirk as it squeezed her tighter and tighter, crushing her to death.

Kirsten suddenly sat up screaming. The crab dropped Pamma, and with one giant swipe of its claw brushed the big rock aside, revealing Kirsten, Duncan, and Tzing Tzang, huddled together.

"There's safety in numbers, right?" asked Kirsten

"Sure, there's no way he can eat all three of us at once," said Duncan.

The crab roared and opened its huge mouth—plenty of room for all three.

Duncan corrected himself, "'Bye, guys. It's been nice knowing ya," but suddenly the crab stopped. It looked ill. A low rumbling sound emanated from inside it, and it seemed to convulse.

Gas? No—

KABOOM!

The ingested grenade finally detonated, and the crab exploded in a spectacular barrage of guts, shells, legs, and antennae, expelling its foul contents a good hundred feet up into the air. Everyone cheered—until a moment later, when a thousand pounds of gore came splashing down on top of us, covering us in stinking mucus, crab juice, gunky hemoglobin, rubbery entrails, green tamale, and an overpowering, oily fish-bait stench.

"Ought to keep this as a souvenir," muttered Duncan, pulling a jagged, daggerlike piece of shell out of his nappy hair. "All right, everybody up!" he cried, and one by one we were pulled to the terrace.

Although we were all grateful to be alive, the mood was glum.

Kirsten held Tony's pitch pipe and tried to blow a C major through it, but she was overtaken by hiccupping sobs. (And plus, the thing was full of goo now.) Lauren held a piece of Max's shredded Speedo bathing suit. (It was torn and just said EEDO.) Michael hobbled over and touched the fabric, a tear rolling down his cheek.

"Good-bye, my dear, sweet, carbonized right-winger." He said. "We had more in common than ye shall ever know . . ."

Lauren pressed her lips to the suit and then let it go into the wind, which picked it up and bore it away on its gossamer wings.

I knelt down and cradled Pamma's broken body in my arms.

"Pamma, I know we had our differences. You're a Tibetan, I'm a Brooklynite, I like hot, you like cold, you say tomato and I say apple. And then the biggest difference of them all—you're a woman and I'm a man, but I'm convinced we could have worked that little problem out. There was so much I wanted to show you, my potato-chip collection, my plantar warts, the Cahoots Gentlemen's Club in Yonkers. If only we had had more time, we could have—"

"Would you shut up please?" Pamma said in a weak voice.

"She's alive. Hey, everyone, she's still alive!"

She grabbed my collar and pulled me close to her.

"Listen to me." Her breath was terrible, but since she was dying I tried to ignore it.

"Yes, Pamma. What do you want to say? Just try to speak away from my face if you would."

"The medial nasal concha harbors all trespassers."

"Huh?"

"The medial nasal concha harbors all trespassers. It's the key to everything."

"Oh, yeah. Sure it is, honey. I understand." I rolled my eyes and twirled my index finger around my ear. Pamma gasped.

"The medial nasal concha harbors all trespassers. That's all I can tell you. Now I go. Tell my great-grandfather . . . to . . . to . . . to . . ."

The crab squeezed her tighter and tighter.

"Yes, Pamma, what would you like me to tell your great-grand-father?"

"Tell my great-grandfather to . . . hang ten." And with that she breathed her last.

I had no idea what the medial nasal conch shell thing was that she was blabbing on about, nor did anybody else, for that matter. We only knew that so far, this had to be the worst day of them all. Although, to be honest, none of the days since we boarded that tug in New York Harbor had been all that great. I was beginning to question whether or not this whole climbing Mount Everest idea was a smart one to begin with.

We covered Pamma's body with stones, strung a row of prayer flags from it, and all said a prayer. (I prayed for a chocolate cupcake.)

Yes, we had lost Martin, Tony, Max, and Pamma, but other than that, Duncan assured us that it had been a fairly routine climb thus far and that it was going pretty much the way most of his expeditions go. So with him in the lead we started our trek to Camp Three—two thousand feet up.

Of course, we had no idea that events transpiring both in Washington, D.C., and Nepal were about to change our climb from "routine" to cataclysmic. (I'm pretty sure, that if we had known, it really would have ruined all the fun we were having.)

CHAPTER THIRTY-ONE

Deep in the blackened bowels of the Pentagon (in Washington, DC) a young man wearing a dark suit and wingtips clip-clopped down a corridor, carrying a blue folder under his arm. His thoughts were so consumed in preparing his briefing that he blew right past the door he was looking for. He stopped, backed up, and handed his laminated identification card to the smirking sergeant at arms.

"Password?"

"Apple sauce."

"Phrase?"

The young man sighed.

"Ain't dat apple sauce yummy?"

The sergeant at arms returned the young man's card and stepped aside. The young man placed his palm on a scanner, and a blast-proof door slid open.

He continued down into a dark subterranean bunker and nodded at a guard with an automatic weapon who was guarding yet another door. The security man knocked once on the door and opened it.

"You're late, Blue Folder," said a gravelly voice from within.

The ultra-high-tech conference room had been lit so that the faces of the men and women around the table were shrouded in darkness.

All he could see were their pinstriped suits, blouses, and blazers—
and the small American flag pin on everyone's lapel.

"What do you have for us?"

The young man cleared his throat.

"The CIA's field agent reports no movement yet. To her knowledge the diamond has not been recovered."

"'To her knowledge?' What does that mean?" asked the gravelly
voice.

The young man swallowed.

"I take it to mean she doesn't know, sir."

"Goddamn it! Where are these idiot climbers right now?"

"According to our man at Base Camp, they're at least three quar-
ters of the way up."

"Jesus Christ. If they've found the diamond, do you people realize what we'll be facing?"

"We're taking all precautions to make sure that doesn't happen,
sir," said a female voice.

"Right. Just like your big 'precaution' in Labuse?"

"Our timing was off," the woman said, embarrassed.

The young man cleared his throat again.

"Yes, that may have raised a flag or two with the CIA's field agent.
She's smart. She recognized the signs of a thermobaric earthquake
bomb right away. She also recognized it as outdated ordnance."

"So?"

"So she suspects 'a rogue chef in the kitchen.'"

At that, a smattering of chuckles erupted in the room, as some at
the table ad-libbed breakfast orders: "I'll take a short stack!"/ "Over
easy please!"/ "Give me a toasted bialy with a schmeer!"/ "Boy, it's
hot in this kitchen, isn't it?"/ etc., etc. (This went on for like an hour.)

"Quiet down! What has she been told?" asked the gravelly voiced
man.

"To stop the Mountain Maniacs."

"Stop? Not 'cancel'?"

The young man consulted his blue folder again.

"The CIA has classified her as a 'B12 Incorruptible.' Her file is stamped 'Above Reproach.' And somebody wrote 'stuck-up bitch' in the margin in pencil."

"Speak English."

"She's a Boy Scout, sir. A female Boy Scout."

"Leave it to the brain trust at the CIA to put an 'incorruptible' on a special op," said another male voice, and a couple of people at the table chuckled.

"With all due respect," said the young man, who just couldn't help speaking his mind, "the original plan was to stop them *before* they reached the Himalayas. 'Cancellation' was not an option until 'intelligence' . . . um, screwed up back in New York Harbor."

Impressed with the young man's spunk, the man with the gravelly voice smiled.

The female voice spoke up. "Sir, the Tibetans believe that the power of this so-called magical diamond lies inside the idiot actor who was in that movie we all hated. If he makes it to the summit, they're certain that they can harness its energy—and with it, attempt the unthinkable. Now, we all know it's a bunch of superstitious hogwash, but faith in its power is all they need. In order to protect our interests we would have to respond militarily, and of course this would put the president in an awkward position. He's unpopular enough as it is, he can't afford to be labled 'anti-Tibet.' Cancellation of the idiot actor is our only course. He must not make it off the mountain alive."

"How?"

"The summit could be obliterated by a thermobaric 'nor'easter bomb,' and maybe we'd send in some special forces just to make sure the job was done."

"Collateral damage?"

"Whatever collateral damage is incurred would simply be chalked up to . . . a nasty weather system."

"And then the U.S. can go in and play a humanitarian role?"

"Of course, sir."

"Mmm . . . what about your field agent? She's still on the mountain, yes?" he asked. But no one answered.

Finally, the female voice spoke up again, "Agent Harding was assigned surveillance just in case anything like this ever came up. No one here believed this day would actually come. Quite honestly, we just wanted her out of our hair. She's become a bit of an embarrassment to the organization, and not just because she's always forgetting to take the safety off her damned weapon, although that really, *really* irks me." The woman paused and composed herself. "Now that she's on the mountain . . . well, whatever happens on the mountain stays on the mountain."

There was an uncomfortable chuckle in the room as the gravelly-voiced man stood up and circled the table.

"I was just a pup when I worked for Nixon, but even back then I realized the long-term implications of his visit to China. There is no question that but for a few discordant voices in the economic stabilization department, everyone saw its potential. Perhaps the notion that trade could bring democracy was a naïve one, but democracy, as we have learned the hard way, is just a word. 'Constructive engagement' is what it's all about now, baby. It's spawned billions in trade agreements, military contracts, and cheap magnetic American flags, not to mention a Wal-Mart on every street corner, and I for one don't plan on sitting back and watching it all go down the drain just because some namby-pamby, tree-hugging yogi wants his frig'n' little country back."

"We've just been waiting for the go-ahead, sir," said the woman's voice.

"Really?" said the man. "Then what are we all doing down here at four o'clock in the morning?"

"I don't know," said the woman. "You called the meeting. I thought you must have had something new to add."

"I guess I assumed you'd need convincing. People used to need, you know, a big speech for something like this. It didn't used to be so routine."

"It was a good speech, though," said another man. "And the atmosphere down here is good for this sort of thing. I don't feel like my time's been wasted."

"Ah, hell," muttered Old Gravelly, gathering his things. "Just get it done. I'm going to go grab an early breakfast somewhere."

"And the field agent?" asked the young man, closing his blue folder.

"Jeez, do we have to spell it out for you, kid?" said the man with the gravelly voice. Then the woman spoke up: "I believe I speak for all of us at the National Clandestine Division when I say that we will deeply mourn the loss of Captain Harding." And then she smirked.

Back in Nepal, among the parapets of the Rong Shu monastery, four monks blew into their *randongs* (the telescopic horns responsible for the conspicuous groan that Westerners identify as Tibetan). Another monk added the high-pitched wail of the *gyaling*, and an assembly in yellow, banana-shaped hats thumped tambourines while the less talented chanted or banged giant cymbals, and some retarded kids played hand bells. It was the beginning of a ceremony meant to appease the *yidam*.

Pong danced about the monastery in a colorful robe wearing a grotesque mask that looked like a pig with human teeth. In one hand he held the *dorje* bell that the Dalai Lama had given him, and in the other a goblet of wine. He sprang wildly about, squatting and lifting up one leg at a time, and then stamping it down furiously like a sumo wrestler. When he caught sight of Ping standing off to the side he stopped and bowed his head sheepishly.

"What you do, Pong? That not *yidam* dance!"

Pong did his best to suppress a hiccup.

"You drink too much free wine. You disgrace! Here, I make you coffee." He shoved a steaming cup into his hands. "Drink fast, we have to go to control center."

They walked together down a dark winding staircase, descending deeper and deeper into the bowels of the earth, until they finally reached a small circular chamber with no door. Ping pushed three stones and a wall opened.

"Now try act respectable," said Ping.

"Why we still speaking English?" asked Pong. "We in Nepal now."

"You shut up. You drunk. You don't understand nothing."

They stepped into a modern control center—kind of like NASA's, except that the stone walls were painted with colorful depictions of the Tibetan wheel of life, and all the men at the computer terminals were wearing orange robes and headsets.

At the front of the room was a giant illuminated map of Tibet. A monk who seemed to be in charge stood with his arms folded, frowning at his computer screen. He had a crew cut, chomped on a cigar, and was wearing a white vest over his red robe. He barely acknowledged Ping and Pong as they passed through a heavy wooden door into another hallway.

Here monks in rickety donkey carts raced up and down along a makeshift monorail system. In a glassed-in gym, hundreds of monks wearing red leather helmets practiced karate moves in perfect unison. Then Ping and Pong held their ears as they hurried past a shooting gallery, where holy sharpshooters fired outdated World War II bolt-action Winchesters at paper targets of Mao Tse-tung.

Bruno, the burly bouncer monk from New York, patted them down again, knocked three times on the door behind him and then opened it.

This time, the Dalai Lama was on his knees, hunched over a huge, intricate sand design spread out across the floor. Called a *mandala*, this labyrinth of complex geometric schemes represents the many levels of the divine universe.

He gently blew into a metal straw. A thread-thin line of yellow sand came out the bottom, and he patiently worked it around the circumference of the design.

"There, *fini*!" The two monks helped him up. "Now then, what news have you brought me, my friends?"

"A communiqué has been intercepted," said Ping, handing him a piece of paper. "It may jeopardize Operation Duhkha, unfortunately. Oh well, maybe best to call whole thing off."

The Dalai Lama adjusted his glasses and read the note. He giggled. " 'Any movement from those cute little dollies? or those wild llamas?' Ha, very clever."

He let its meaning sink in for a moment, and then he burned it over a candle. "We will proceed on schedule," he said. "I have contacted the Bodhisattva. He has identified the *yidam*. The Rhombus is safe for now."

"But such a message spells out doom, does it not?" said Ping. "Surely we should cancel the operation."

"It is disheartening, but not unexpected. The CIA stopped help-ing us many years ago. One could only hope that they wouldn't be working against us, but perhaps even that is too much to hope for. There is much at stake here, my friends." He moved to a small yel-low parrot perched on a bronze statue of Yamantaka, Lord of Death, and fed it seeds as he spoke. "Our odds are probably not very good, but we have compassion, righteousness, and love on our side. Have we not?"

Pong nodded and Ping reluctantly agreed.

"As well as a heck of a lot of chutzpah, right, fellas?" The Dalai Lama laughed heartily.

"Yes, Your Holiness," the monks said together.

"And soon the power of the Rhombus."

He walked over to a wooden canal, where candles floated in oil, and he meticulously dripped wax into the trough.

"Do you realize that it is against the law to state that you are a citizen of Tibet in our own homeland? In our *own* homeland!" he stressed, uncharacteristically raising his voice. "Our children are being taught a foreign language, our barley crops ruined, and our monasteries turned into Six Flags amusement parks. Over a million of our brothers and sisters have died of starvation, imprisonment, or monosodium glutamate poisoning. Don't get me wrong. I like Chinese food just like the next guy, but nothing is good for you if you eat it every day."

"Yes, Your Holiness."

"I have devoted my life to nonviolence, but I am coming to the end of my days, my friends. Perhaps I was wrong to have turned a deaf ear to our more . . . extreme supporters." He sighed. "For long, we have put aside our emotions and relied on our minds, our enlightened powers, and our beguiling smiles. But is it wise not to use all the means at one's disposal, especially when one faces an unenlightened enemy? With the Rhombus, and only with the Rhombus, will we succeed."

"Dharamsala reports ready and awaiting your orders," announced Pong, saluting, and then he hiccupped.

"Yeah . . . um . . . so does the Lhasa resistance," reported Ping.

The Dalai Lama opened a chest and lovingly unfolded the Tibetan national flag, which he himself had redesigned so many years

Pong danced to appease the Yidam.

before. It depicts Mount Everest decorated with two snow lions. On the tip of the mountain's summit, a bright yellow sun (the Rhombus? see, I'm not just making all this shit up) radiates shafts of blue and red light out to the universe.

He held the flag to his face, closed his eyes, and, a smile crossing his lips, smelled it. Then he sneezed.

"Mildew," he said, and returned the flag to its box. "It has been too long, my friends. This will be my last great gift to the people. When the Rhombus summits, I will transmutate, and Operation Duhkha will commence." He knelt down and put his fingers in the center of the mandala. "And with the power of compassion, righteousness, and love on our side . . . as well as a weapon of mass destruction or two, we will finally make our enemies pay for standing in the way of Truth and Light!"

Then with both hands he destroyed the extraordinary work he had labored so hard to create.

When they emerged in the monastery's garden, Pong was excited. "Come on, Ping, let's dance with the others. Our day has arrived!" and he pulled on Ping's robe. "We must celebrate!"

"You go ahead, Pong," said Ping. "There is something I must do."

CHAPTER THIRTY-TWO

Somewhere up on Lhotse Face, Captain Harding found a suitable shelf to rest upon, and lay Martin down in a powdery bed of snow. He was still unconscious, and she held her oxygen mask over his face. His eyes suddenly popped open, and he began to panic, flailing his arms about and thrashing to and fro.

"Mmmmmmmm!"

"There, there now. It's okay, it's okay. You're safe. Those yetis are all gone."

He slowly calmed down.

"How 'bout we take that tape off your mouth and let you drink some nice melted snow, huh? I can't believe those hairy monsters gagged you. What nerve! They're probably just jealous that you're a human being and they're like mythical creatures or something."

She went to pull the tape off, but he reacted violently, again flailing about.

Harding had seen her share of the Stockholm syndrome, the involuntary state in which a kidnap victim develops a strong emotional bond with his or her captors. It's said that Patty Hearst suffered from it, as well as the cast of *Survivor*, most of whom have spent the rest of their lives fretting over CBS's Nielsen ratings. She knew that the best way to deal with it was just to give the victim plenty of time and space to readjust to his newfound freedom.

"Okay. That's fine. We don't have to take it off. We can leave it on for as long as you like. But listen, would you mind giving me an autograph? I just love your work." Martin reluctantly signed her autograph book and then whimpered like an infant, pulling his knees to his chest, and curling up in a ball. As he did so, Harding noticed the small wooden flute hanging around his neck and logged it into her photographic memory.

She shook her head. "Such a shame to see such a talented guy in such pathetic shape." She picked up her walkie-talkie, switched it to Channel Three, and hit the pager button.

"Harding to Base Camp. Harding to Base Camp. Come in, Norgay, come in."

She tried several more times, but was unable to make contact.

Old Norgay couldn't answer on Channel Three because he was busy talking to Blue Folder on Channel Four (and he may have had Fidelity on hold on Channel Two, as well).

"Repeat that," said Norgay, and the young man's voice from the Pentagon came back,

"A nor'easter is headed your way. Over."

"I haven't heard anything about it on the weather station. Over."

"They wouldn't know about this nor'easter. It's a NORAD Easter, if you know what I mean—and believe me, it's headed your way."

"What should I do? Over."

"Get the hell off the mountain."

"But . . . there are innocent people climbing . . . virgins and celebrities, and there's even a CIA agent who—"

"Listen, Norgay, I know you got your fingers in a bunch of pies up there. If you want to stay, go ahead. I'm risking my own neck just telling you about this. From our end, all bets are off. Everything and every-one will be consumed by this storm, and that means even you. That's right, you're not indispensable, or indestructible, for that matter. Good luck with whatever you decide. Blue Folder over and out. Oh, wait, one more thing, Norgay. You better not warn anybody about the storm."

Norgay put the walkie-talkie down. Dazed, he shuffled out of the communal tent and into the cold.

Agent Resnick had heard the entire conversation. He sat up in his Gamow suit and glanced at his sidearm and holster, which were rest-ing on the table next to a coil of rope and climbing gear. Harding had saved his life on the glacier—now he had to save hers.

Camp Three was nothing but a few tents perched on a desolate spur of slippery ice. Our first night, Duncan had the difficult task of breaking the news to Old Norgay that his great-granddaughter, along with Max and Tony, had been crunched by a giant crab. We were all surprised by Norgay's detached reaction. "That's the way the cookie crumbles," he said, and tried once more to convince Duncan to give up the climb. Duncan refused. "We're too close now, old man," he said. "We summit in thirty-six hours. Just keep an eye on the weather."

In order to reach Camp Four we would have to climb the slick Hillary Buttress (named after the senator), then plod up a harum-scarum escarpment to the promontory just below the Hillary Step (named after the explorer), where advance Sherpas had pitched our tents on the windy south col, adjacent to the Hillary Stilettos (named after both the senator's and the explorer's fancy footwear).

Percy had penned his final diary entry at Camp Four—the one about meeting up with the "jub jub bird and nasty old Mr. Bandersnatch"—and Duncan was particularly eager to search the area.

We were about halfway there when an ominous storm cloud began to approach from the northeast. "It's just a little gully washer!" Duncan assured us. "If it were going to get bad, Old Norgay would tell us."

In fact, the storm had not escaped the attention of Old Norgay, whose high-powered Meade LX telescope had been trained on it for at least two hours now. But even though Duncan had radioed him several times during the day to report our position, Norgay had said nothing of the danger. Had he notified Duncan earlier, there is no doubt in my mind that we would have turned around and spent a peaceful night in relative comfort. But that was not to be.

A giant black cloud trundled forward in a furious, rolling boil. The massive thunderhead was supported by a bandeau of frothy, pink, cotton-candy cumulus clouds that almost seemed to be herding smaller storm systems toward it, creating an ever-increasing black blizzard. Beautiful and horrible at the same time, it pulsated violently with orange and purple lightning—unusual, even by Everest's standards. I just assumed Al Roker was judging another barbecue contest down in Katmandu. After a week of rapid ascents without proper acclimatization, "mountain madness" had set in, and a trippy phantasmagoria gripped us all.

Kirsten believed someone was following her. This is a sensation that climbers often experience, called the "I think there's an invisible man following me" syndrome. As far back as Mallory and Percy, climbers have described an unseen spiritual protector climbing alongside them, but in Kirsten's case, she said it felt more like a serial killer in a hockey mask, about to carve her to pieces. (I giggled and put away the mask.)

Duncan fell to the snow and rolled around shouting, "Get them off. Get them off of me!" I thought he was talking about his mouse

ticks, but apparently he was under the impression that he was being attacked by Branson's virgins. "Wait a second, it's okay," he said.
"You don't have to get them off me—they're fine." And a look of
serenity crossed his face.

As we climbed higher, the hallucinations became more intense.
Wendell danced a jig and spoke in a heavy brogue, claiming that he
was the scullery maid Bridey Murphy from County Cork, Ireland,
while Michael started barking and sniffing my head for truffles. Once,
when we stopped to rest, I was sure I was enjoying afternoon tea with
George Plimpton, but I think I was just talking to a snowdrift.

"You really are a silly merry-andrew, aren't you?" Plimpton said,
observing me closely as I nibbled away on an invisible cucumber
sandwich. "You *do* realize I never did any of the things I wrote about,
don't you?"

"Really?"

"Of course not. It was all doubles—pitching with the All Stars, spar-
ring with Archie Moore and Sugar Ray Robinson, quarterbacking for
the Lions—even my voice on *The Simpsons* was somebody else."

"So, you wouldn't have actually climbed Everest if given the
chance?"

Plimpton laughed maniacally. "Climb Mount Everest? Only a
dumb-ass would do something like that!" Then his visage doubled and
tripled, multiplying until there were over a hundred Plimptons spinning around me, pointing and laughing and calling me "dumb-ass."

"Don't lithen to him," said Grammy's tub of peanut butter, as it
hovered over me. "He'th jutht got a bug up hith assth 'cauth he'th
dead." Then it flew away.

I yelled, "What's happening to me?"

"You've been bitten by a mouse," said the Pope, rappelling down
the mountainside.

"Huh?"

"Chrissie, why you do this to me? Why you do this to me, Chrissie?" questioned Grammy, sitting up in an oversized hospital bed.

"You're not my Grammy!" I screamed. "You're not my Grammy!"

"Help me! Help me!" cried Lauren.

"Make it stop!" I implored, holding my head. "Make it stop!"

"No, Chris, seriously, this is no joke. I need help here!"

I looked over and saw Lauren lying on her back, jammed into a breach in the stony fortification. Her right arm appeared hopelessly stuck beneath a boulder.

I plopped Michael down and rushed to her side. "What happened?"

"Well, I was just climbing along, when it fell from above," she explained, grimacing in pain. "I think my arm's broken."

I stood back and narrowed my eyes suspiciously.

"Wait a second. How do I know you're not a hallucination?"

"The lad's got a point," said Wendell in an Irish accent. "Perhaps Darby O'Gill and the Lil' People have the answer!"

I folded my arms and cocked my head. "You could just be a product of indigestion; maybe I ate a bad piece of beef or a bit of moldy cheese."

"Oh, for Christ's sake, Christopher, I'm Lauren, and I'm real flesh and blood!"

"She does look pretty real, Chris," said Michael, down on all fours and sniffing around her. "And I think the odds of all three of us having the same hallucination at the same time are pretty slim. Besides, I had Beneful™ for lunch. *Rrrruff!*"

"Yes, well, we could all be part of *your* hallucination, Michael. Maybe Lauren, Wendell, and I aren't even here right now. Maybe we're already up at the summit!"

"Oh, I see," chirped Wendell. "Like one of them parallel universes.

They call that the 'string cheese' theory, dontcha know? Top of the mo'n'en to ya all." He tipped his hat.

"Will you idiots please shut up and help me! I'm about to pass out here."

"Forgive me. I just have to be sure." I bent over and pinched the exposed part of her broken arm.

"Aaaag! You asshole!" she screamed in agony.

This was no hallucination. Lauren was indeed real and indeed in trouble!

Michael called out, "Help! Lauren's fallen, and she can't get up!" But we had lagged far behind and now, with the first tendrils of the storm encircling us, our fellow teammates were nowhere in sight.

"Perhaps you should push your 'Life Alert' button or something?" suggested Wendell. "Hoyty titly titly tum. Weee!"

I knelt down. "Can you pull your arm out, sweetie?"

She tried, but the pain was too intense.

"Okay, well, there's only one thing we can do." I did a little drum roll with my mouth and dramatically retrieved my trusty Swiss Army knife. "Boy, this thing is getting a workout."

"You can't be serious."

"There's no other way, Betty. There's a storm coming and we're not leaving you behind."

There was a palpable pause. She knew it had to be done.

I handed the knife to Wendell. "Here, Miss Murphy, use your butane lighter to sterilize this." Then I scooped up a handful of snow and told Lauren to bite down on it. Even in her current condition, she gave me one of "those looks" that make you feel like you're two inches tall. Michael handed me one of his climbing boots.

"Use this," he said. "It won't melt."

"Good idea. Okay, now, Betty, I want you to bite on this boot." I whispered to Wendell, "We're gonna have to hold her down."

Lauren put the smelly boot in her mouth. I clamped her head firmly between my knees. Michael held her ankles while Wendell sat cross-legged on her stomach, heating up the knife right in front of her.

"Now, try to think happy thoughts," I said, "like rainbows, and frilly things—popovers and pumpkins, bebops and leelops."

"*Arrrrrrrrrr!*" she growled.

"Okay, okay, I know. You want to get this over with as soon as possible. Well so do I, sweetie. Wendell, if you please?"

He handed me the knife.

"Ow! Ow! Ow! Hot! Hot! Hot!" I was passing it back and forth from one hand to another like a hot potato when it accidentally fell—luckily flat-sided—on Lauren's forehead.

"Ooops!"

"*Arrrrrrrrrr!*" she snarled.

"Sorry, sorry." I plucked the knife off, but unfortunately it had already branded her head: DEREPMET LEETS (TEMPERED STEEL" in case you're confused).

"Okay, here we go. This is gonna hurt me more than it's gonna hurt you!" I laughed my famous hyena-esque laugh. "No, seriously, this is going to hurt you way more."

I took a deep breath, and held the knife about an inch above the exposed region of the arm. Wendell mouthed "good luck," and Lauren closed her eyes. I closed my eyes too.

"Okay, on three. One . . . two . . ."

About five hundred feet below us, Harding and Martin climbed in tandem, the leading edge of the storm already upon them. They too thought they were hallucinating when they beheld three fat bullfrogs perched on a rock.

The frogs watched Harding and Martin closely with their big black eyes, occasionally making repugnant croaks or nabbing slow-flying Himalayan monarchs with their nauseatingly serpentine tongues.

About fifty feet higher they encountered more—about a dozen of them lounging on their backs, and then a dozen more licking the ice water pouring out of a fissure. The croaking grew in intensity as the wind began to pick up. Martin's eyes went wide, and the claw wounds in his chest throbbed, a sure sign that danger was ahead.

At about 26,000 feet they turned a corner and came face-to-face with at least five hundred croaking bullfrogs perched around them on various outcroppings. Harding pulled her gun, but a huge bullfrog jumped on her hair and she screamed and dropped it. A second later, all the frogs attacked. They seemed to be swarming from every crack in Everest, licking, biting, and smothering. Martin did his best to karate them away, but there were just too many. He threw one against a rock and it exploded in a blast of gore. But more frogs appeared, taking him down and covering him with an undulating amphibious mass. Harding was on her back when a frog crawled up her oxygen mask and started licking her eyeballs. She screamed and pulled the mask off. She could barely breathe when suddenly . . .

BLAM! BLAM! BLAM!

All the toads scattered, evaporating into the fissures and fractures as quickly as they had appeared.

Harding put her mask back on and checked on Martin. He was okay. She sat up and observed an alien shape standing silhouetted against the glowing storm and holding a smoldering gun.

"Agent Resnick. What the hell are you doing up here?"

"Saving your life," he said from inside his Gamow suit. "Are you hungry? I got Triscuits."

Harding was liking her protégé more and more.

"Yeah, Triscuits, please."

No sooner had she said that when the black cloud obscured what was left of the sun, and a wild wind blew Resnick off the rock, knocking him to the ground at her feet.

"This is what I came to save you from, ma'am," he said.

"Save me from what?" Then she recognized a distinctive odor in the air, but before she could say "anionic acid," the storm hit.

". . . and three!"

"What the hell are you idiots doing?" asked Duncan, appearing out of the billowing mist with the rest of the Maniacs.

"Quiet please, you're interrupting an important amputation!"

"Get off her," he said, and as Wendell, Michael and I backed away, Flip Flop came over and casually rolled the boulder off Lauren's arm.

"Why didn't we think of that?" I said.

Luckily, Lauren's arm wasn't broken, only bruised. She sat up, spit out Michael's boot, and gave me another one of "those looks."

Duncan suggested that I take Michael and climb at the head of the queue from now on, and he told Wendell to stop talking with an Irish accent and to stay close to Yorgi.

It would be a lonely, three-hour climb through blinding snow and whipping winds before we were all reunited at Camp Four. There the squall was more powerful than a freight train, hurricane, and earthquake all rolled into one big, thunderous stink bomb. A real crisis—I mean a crisis way more deadly than anything we had experienced thus far—was set upon us. (If you read the first part of this wondrous work, you know what I'm talking about.)

After a childish argument over who ate the last Oreo, my best

"What the hell are you idiots doing?"

friend's hand slipped from mine, and as he passed into the darkness, I was sure that I would set eyes upon his cherubic—if grouchy and sometimes really sour (and come to think of it, occasionally greasy) features—nevermore. And that's when the avalanche hit and I blacked out.

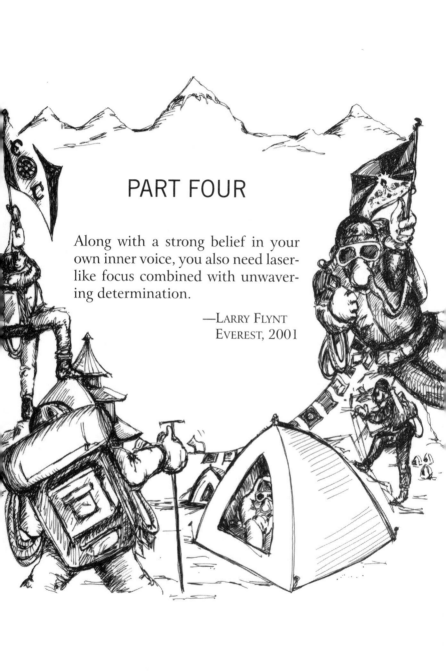

PART FOUR

Along with a strong belief in your own inner voice, you also need laser-like focus combined with unwavering determination.

—LARRY FLYNT
EVEREST, 2001

CHAPTER THIRTY-THREE

"Chris! Chris! Snap out of it!"

The wind was howling, and it was brutally cold. I cracked open my eyes and was barely able to identify Wendell hovering over me. Our Family Fun Tent had been blown completely away, and Wendell was shaking my shoulders, trying to rouse me. "Get up! We gotta go!"

I staggered to my feet and looked around. It was dark, but it seemed like Camp Four was completely gone. Only the communal tent was still pitched, and even that looked like it could take flight at any moment. The rest of the col was barren except for a few tattered bits of vinyl stubbornly holding on to their anchors.

"What happened?" I hollered. "I thought you fell into a hole and died!"

"It wasn't that deep. I dug my way out! Let's move it."

"Wait a second," I said. "Where's that last Oreo?" Then we started wrestling again. About twenty minutes later we came to our senses and decided to seek shelter.

Black snow poured from a massive black cloud and accumulated at a freakishly rapid rate. There were already drifts at least ten feet high, and visibility was next to zero. The communal tent would ap-

pear at one moment and then disappear the next. Once Wendell and
I lost our bearings completely and stood motionless in the miasma,
unable to move forward or backward, paralyzed with fear and con-
fusion. We were being buried alive, when out of the barrage of sooty
snow, two hands appeared.

"This way, sahib."

We followed the sound of Flip Flop's voice as he guided us to the
communal tent.

"Shut that damned flap!" Duncan ordered as we crawled inside.

I looked around. We were all safe now and everyone was accounted
for—at least everyone who had made it to Camp Four.

We sat on the hard, cold ground, glumly hunched over the single
kerosene lamp, rubbing our hands together and silently praying.
(I prayed for another chocolate cupcake, because the last one had
shown up smooshed.)

"What happened?" asked Kirsten, petting Mr. Pop-eyes.

"I don't know yet," said Duncan. "Some sort of freak storm,
maybe an avalanche."

"This is more than just an avalanche, brave captain. I mean, black
snow?"

"I said, I don't know yet!" Then he softened. "Sorry, queenie, I
just don't know."

Half of the tent had already collapsed, and the howling wind outside threatened to rip the rest of it from its stakes.

Duncan cleared his throat. "Okay, here's the deal. All our tents,
with most of the supplementary oxygen, sleeping bags, sweaters,
long johns, and sports bras, are gone. In addition, all our provisions
were blown over the side. We need to take stock of what we have
here. Everyone empty your pockets."

Kirsten retrieved half of a South Beach Diet breakfast bar and laid
it down. Lauren placed a jar of Noxzema next to it. Tzing Tzang
threw down an almost empty Baggie™ of hemp seeds, and Flip Flop

added some Tic Tacs. Yorgi produced a small, half-eaten container of beluga caviar and carefully placed it on the pile.

"*Pazhalista.* All the way from the Caspian Sea. Eat slow, savor flavor."

"Any toast points?" I asked, and Yorgi looked at me with one of those looks that only blind Russian people can give you.

"Have I been carrying this shit around with me this whole time?" asked Wendell, discovering the remainder of Grammy's tub of peanut oil and lard still in his backpack. The frozen glop was now as heavy as a cinder block and landed with a big thud when he tossed it into the pile.

"Is that everything, then?" All eyes went to Michael. After an awkward moment, he reluctantly surrendered his last can of baked beans, giving it a farewell kiss first.

"Oh, wait," I said, finding something worthwhile in my pocket. "I don't know how this will taste, but at least it's protein, for those of us doing the old Atkins." I chucked in Uncle Percy's schnoz. "All the way from Brooklyn Heights. *Pazhalista*, eat slow—savor flavor."

Duncan threw it back at me, and Flip Flop proceeded to sew it onto my face, adding a dollop of super glue for extra adhesive power.

"Okay, look, we're gonna have to ration what we have here."

I raised my hand, "I call the can of beans, caviar, breakfast bar, and Tic Tacs . . . oh, and the peanut butter too."

"This is just like my dream," said Kirsten. "We had to draw straws to see who'd be eaten first. It was horrible. I woke up just as Tony was eating me."

"Then that probably t'weren't a dream," mumbled Wendell.

Kirsten broke down in tears. "Oh, please, don't let them eat me!" She hugged Lauren.

"There, there now, my child, no one's going to . . . wait, are you feeling my ribs?"

"Look," said Duncan, "Nobody's going to be eating nobody, so shut up about it."

I said, "I wouldn't be so sure. Someone gets hungry enough, sleep-walks, thinks he's digging into the old ice box for yesterday's meat loaf." I looked over at Michael's stomach. His eyes went wide and he zipped up his parka.

"Maybe we should call Norgay," Kirsten said.

"Already tried," said Duncan. "Can't raise him."

"Perhaps if you try a different channel?" suggested Lauren.

"I just said I already . . . ah . . . what the hell." He switched channels and suddenly Old Norgay's voice came out. He was talking to someone else and we all strained to hear.

"I don't see the point. They dead. Over," said Norgay.

"I have to be sure."

"They not survive. You won. Come down."

"I have to be sure. Fidelity over and out."

Duncan shouted into the walkie-talkie. "Norgay? Norgay? Is that you? Norgay, we need help!"

There was no response. He switched to channel one. "Norgay?"

Silence! Again he switched channels and shouted. "Norgay, I know you're there! Answer me, you son of a bitch!"

But only static came back. After a moment or two, Duncan gave up and switched it off.

"What's up, Boss?"

"Old Norgay sold us out. That's what's up."

Flip Flop turned to Tzing Tzang. "My apologeeze, Mister Tzang. It seems Old Norgay was the *yidam*, not you, sir."

"Yeah, okay, whatever. Who was he talking to, boss?"

"It must have been Branson."

"You mean . . . ?"

"Yeah. Norgay's been working for Branson all along. That bastard!

"We just lost the summit."

He obviously didn't tell us about this storm to slow us down. Branson must have come up with more cash."

Michael mused, "What was it that Max said? 'There's enough greed in this world, but not enough need'? Why do I miss that big lug so much?" He started to tear up.

Outside, the storm pounded the mountainside, blasting huge outcroppings and ice pinnacles off its slopes, and howling murderously through the crevasses and *bergschrunds*.

"So what happens now, brave captain?"

"Well, we can't rely on Norgay anymore. The only thing to do is to wait out the storm and hope that someone else knows we're up here. I'll be honest with all of you. There's no telling how long a rescue attempt could take, if one ever comes. This may be the end of the line."

We all fell silent and suddenly felt very much alone.

"One thing's for sure, though," he said. "We just lost the summit."

CHAPTER THIRTY-FOUR

With the cold truth of our situation beginning to sink in, we sat listening to the ever-growing storm outside.

After a while, the ghostly howl of the wind and the dancing shadows from the lamp filled our tent with a sinister atmosphere. It was as though someone—or something—was in that tent with us. Obviously, I was not the only one who felt it.

"The spirits of Chomolungma are all around us," whispered Flip Flop. He glanced about the tent as if he could see them. "They are the spirits that have not passed over, and the evil ones that never will. They are here, and they are watching us."

Silence.

"If you are here. Give us a sign!"

Silence.

"Show yourselves!"

Still more silence.

"I call on you to . . ."

A sudden blast of wind extinguished our lamp, and Kirsten and I screamed.

Lauren relit it. "Okay, Flip, that's enough of that, you're scaring the children." Then she produced a single blanket. "We should all stay close for warmth." And we cuddled together, holding each other tightly, hunkering down for the night.

Hours went by, but the storm would not abate. In fact, it only seemed to grow in intensity. No one could sleep. We were all mesmerized by the flickering flame of the kerosene lamp (or maybe by the fumes), each of us seeing something different in its luminescence. Lauren envisioned herself a chiffon-gowned glamour queen, waltzing with a tuxedoed Humphrey Bogart while Jason Robards watched jealously from the sidelines; Kirsten saw an Oscar, People's Choice, Golden Globe, and MTV award. Duncan saw a shimmering diamond, Michael a flaming shish kebab, and Wendell saw me being flattened by a steamroller. I saw myself alone on the summit of Mount Everest, the whole world lying at my feet, shaped like a giant, undulating oyster. Plus I had a full head of hair and a George Hamilton tan.

More hours went by. It could have been days and nights for all I knew. There was no sunrise or sunset, only perpetual gloomy darkness and that scary, howling wind.

"We have to do something," whispered Lauren.

"I have an idea." I pulled out my cell phone and punched in a few numbers. "Hello? Yes, may I speak with Vera Wang, please?"

Wendell rolled his eyes. He was fed up. "Give it up, Chris."

"Wendell, shhhhh. I'm waiting to talk to my ex-wife."

"Chris, you don't have an ex-wife. You've never been married."

"Oh, she's busy? Well, go ahead and pull her out of the meeting, will you? It's her ex-husband, Christoff, calling."

"Chris, I'm telling you, she's not gonna take your call."

"Wendell, please . . . I'm trying to . . . Excuse me? She said what?" I paused, listening to Vera's short-tempered assistant on the other end of the line. "She's going to notify the authorities if I don't stop calling? But that's . . . yes, yes . . . I understand . . . yes, thank you." Confused, I closed the phone and slowly replaced it in my parka.

Wendell said, "Chris, you know why I don't remember being your best man and choking on a piece of orange mud cake and sleeping on the floor of your honeymoon suite at the Ogallala Day's Inn? Because it never happened. You made up the whole thing."

"But . . . I . . ."

"It was just a figment of your imagination. Your psychiatrist called it 'a kind of a post-traumatic-stress thing or something.' He said it was brought on by the closing of your one-man show. He said that you had done this kind of thing before—invented a whole other life for yourself. He said that it was the only way you know how to deal with your failures."

"What failures?"

"You made the whole thing up, buddy."

"Wow. That's freaky. But why didn't you tell me right away?"

"Your shrink said it would be better to let you come to the realization on your own. Also it was kind of fun to play along for a while. But since you've probably killed us both and all, I felt like bursting your Vera balloon. So there! Now we're even."

"Touché." I was in total shock.

Duncan held his hand out. "Let's see that cell phone."

"Don't bother," snapped Wendell. "It doesn't work, and he's not even on a plan. He wasn't talking to anybody—never has been."

Duncan took the phone and opened its back.

"It's full of gum," he said, incredulous.

I let my chin (as it were) drop to my chest. I couldn't look anyone in the face.

Michael turned off his camera and slowly put it down. "I know that this will come as a shock to all of you, but since it doesn't look like we'll ever get off this mountain, I feel compelled to confess something too. I'm . . . a Republican!"

We all gasped.

"That's right, it's all an act. And by the way, I'm not a glutton. In fact, I'm not even fat."

He reached into his parka and pulled a string. The tent filled with the sound of wheezing air as Michael's fat suit deflated. He shuffled out of it, peeled off his chin, stepped out of his "gouty feet," and stood before us, a perfectly thin—and astonishingly handsome—young Adonis.

"You bastard!" I yelled. "I just carried you up the goddamn mountain!"

"I'm sorry, Chris. It was a necessary part of the deception."

"What deception?" asked Lauren.

"I'm part of a strategy to make the other side look bad! We act the way we do so that everybody thinks liberals are nuts!"

"We?"

"Sure, there's quite a few of us—Baldwin, Robbins, Susan Sarandon—all conservatives pretending to be left-wingers. The crazier we act, the saner us Republicans seem!"

"That's brilliant," observed Lauren.

"Oh, and it's not just us. Believe me, they've got their own plants too, don't be fooled. Ann Coulter, Pat Robertson, and even Rush are all Dems trying to make us Republicans look like a bunch of racist nut jobs. The whole Fox News network is run by libs. I bet they make a bundle off us with that thing."

"But it seems like an awful long way to go."

"You're telling me—and don't get me started on what we have to sacrifice! We don't get invited to the White House when one of our boys is actually president, and we don't even get to go to our own conventions; and I'm a huge Boz Skaggs fan. But we do it all for our party—and for our country."

"Wow, and Martin?" I asked.

"No, Martin was an actual liberal, may he rest in peace—him and Sean Penn. But Max . . . Max Bullis was just like me." Michael broke down in tears. "There were so many times I just wanted to say 'Yes, Max, exactly! I agree with you a hundred percent, buddy.' But I just couldn't."

Flip Flop retrieved a goat bladder filled with *chaang* and passed it around the circle. Each one of us took a big gulp. Then Kirsten spoke up,

"I'm not wholesome!" she blurted out. "I'm not sweet and I'm not goofy. I know I act it. But I'm not. I actually belong to Mensa and I just got my advanced pilot's license. I'm certified to fly on instruments now. I do love animals though, especially bunnies. When I'm in Paris, I occasionally enjoy a nice *Coniglio con La Pinoli e Olive Nere*—rabbit with pine nuts and black olives." Mr. Pop-eyes gulped and then shot out of the tent like a bullet.

"Why do you act the way you do, then?" I asked.

"Hollywood likes its blondes skinny and ditsy. So what do I care? I make a few bucks and then retire and go back home and work on my string theory."

"That's what it's called!" said Wendell, slapping his knee.

"You came up with string theory?" I asked, astonished.

"It wasn't that hard, kid."

"But what about that affair with Tony?" Lauren asked. "If you're so smart, I hardly see how he could be your type, unless he's pretending too?"

"Oh, no, that was just for sex."

There was another pause, and Wendell lowered his head.

"Well, since we're all admitting shit . . . what the hell. Sometimes . . . around my apartment, I impersonate Diana Ross."

"I love Diana Ross," said Kirsten, and Wendell smiled at her.

"You know, I also have to admit that I don't care about PETA or global warming. I just went to that thing to see *you*. See . . . I . . . oh, forget it."

I elbowed Wendell and mouthed, "Go on."

"Well, I've . . . ah . . . always had a crush on you."

Kirsten smiled at Wendell. "Global warming is just a matter of opinion." There was a nice moment between the two. Then she added, "Who are you, again?"

"I'm Wendell, Chris's friend."

"Oh, sorry. Don't get upset, I just thought you were one of the Sherpas."

Wendell got upset. "If anybody needs me, I'll be outside freezing to death."

Outside, Everest was barely recognizable. Shrouded in a cloak of colored lightning, it looked like Mount Saint Helens, although, instead of lava, frozen detritus barreled down the mountainside in perpetual avalanches that were consuming everything in their wake. Most certainly Captain Harding, Martin, and Resnick had been enveloped (one would assume), while on the Khumbu Glacier entire Sherpa villages were being wiped away.

We were all starving (confession always works up the old appetite), so we divided up the breakfast bar. Duncan weighed each tiny morsel on a homemade scale. Then we said a prayer (I prayed for a glass of milk—not 2 percent this time, thank you) and we feasted on our meager allotment.

"Brave captain, perhaps since we're all opening up, now would be a good time to tell us the truth about your bet with Richard Branson?"

"Why don't you open up first, queenie?"

"Fine," Lauren shot back. "Let's see, I dye my hair. Now you go."

Duncan took his time finishing his part of the breakfast bar and made a point of licking the crumbs off his fingertips before speaking. "I owed him money."

"That's all?" Lauren asked.

"He hired me to track down some lowlife who had deflowered one of his precious virgins. I guess she had been his favorite. He'd wanted to make her into a star or something. She had a big future, and she threw it all away on this louse. Well, I never found the guy, but I also never gave Branson his money back. I've been looking over my shoulder ever since."

"Go on."

"Well, then the opportunity to find the Rhombus came up; if I could find that thing I'd take the money and disappear someplace far-away like South America and never bother anybody ever again. But we needed money for this expedition. So I went to Branson, and I tried to make a deal. He agreed to front the money for Mountain Maniacs, but only if I raced him to the summit. If I win, all is forgiven, but if I lose, well . . . he gets to . . . um . . . well, if not him, someone gets to . . . um . . . well, I guess maybe some unscrupulous surgeon gets to, you know, . . . cut off my . . . Oh, you know what I mean."

"Ew!" I said. "Too much information, Mr. Carter!"

"Why, that's barbaric," exclaimed Lauren. "I can't believe Branson would go that far just to reclaim a debt—unless . . ." She examined Duncan.

"So let's move on, then. Who's got something else to confess?"

"It was you, wasn't it, brave captain? You were the lowlife who deflowered the virgin."

"So what if I was?"

"But why did you take his money in the first place if you knew you couldn't do the job?" Michael asked.

"Lilly was in trouble," he said, "and she needed to get home. I wanted to float her a little traveling money. There was no other way to get it."

"Why, brave captain, you risked your life for a damsel in distress. I do believe that's almost . . . romantic." Lauren gave him a peck on the cheek. "Maybe you're not as scummy as you look . . . and smell."

"Yeah, well . . . the change from the Greyhound ticket mostly went up my nose," he added.

"Wow," I said. "You could almost say that things are not what they seem"—I paused for dramatic effect—"on top of old Chomolungma." And then I started to sing, "On top of old . . ."

Flip Flop's eyes began to tear up.

"I'm so touched. Everyone is being so honest. I feel like I must share." And then he started picking away at his face.

Bit by bit the Sherpa pulled off the prosthetic George C. Scott as Fagin makeup, until finally there before us was revealed Flip Flop's true identity.

"Richard Gere!" We all screamed. "What the hell are you doing here?"

"Yes, I am Richard Gere," he babbled through his tears, "but I'm also a Bodhisattva, a reincarnation of the chosen enlightened one— a fact that I learned after making sizable donations to the Campaign for a Free Tibet. I was charged with protecting the Rhombus."

He pointed at me, and I gave everyone a wink as if to say, "See, I'm somebody too!"

"I was to protect him from the *yidam*, a wrathful deity sent by those who would want His Holiness to fail. But now it seems that I am the one who has failed." He dropped his head in shame. "With this storm, Norgay the *yidam* has made it impossible for the Rhombus to summit. Operation Duhkha will not succeed. I am worthless."

"But why the disguise?" asked Lauren. "You're a celebrity. We're all celebrities here. I'm sure we would have been happy to have you come along."

"Not with that forehead," I whispered to Lauren and then giggled.

A stupefied look crossed Gere's face.

"Gee, I never thought of that."

"You said this *yidam* wanted His Holiness to fail," questioned Duncan. "Fail at what?"

"With the power of the Rhombus, His Holiness believes the time is right to . . ."

An astonishingly, handsome - young adonis.

Suddenly Gere's bottom lip began to quiver. His body began to convulse and tremble and then his big head shook violently. A whirring sound filled the tent, and the actor's skin glowed as if it were radioactive. The faster his head shook, the blurrier it became.

"What's happening?" I said (a perfect Spielberg-esque moment, don't you think?).

"If this is what I think it is, it should be impossible—scientifically, at least," said Kirsten. "Everyone get back."

We all inched away from Gere and huddled at the far end of the tent. His form began to change right before our very eyes. He gritted his teeth and seemed to be in excruciating pain. He flung his vibrating head backward and let out a loud primal scream, and then suddenly there was a big *BANG!* and the tent filled with blinding light.

When the light was gone and our eyes readjusted, we were all agog with dismay at what we were faced with.

CHAPTER THIRTY-FIVE

"I knew it," said Kirsten. "Faith trumps science."

"And always has, my child," said the smiling Dalai Lama, now sitting lotus-style right where Richard Gere had been sitting (actor-style). "Greetings to one and all," he said sweetly. "May the wisdom of the universe shower down upon us, and may we all know each other not by what we are not, or by what we were not, or by what we will not be, but by what we are right now—now and forever."

"Where the hell did you come from?" Duncan asked His Holiness.

"All the way from Rong Shu monastery in Makalu, Nepal," replied the Dalai Lama. Then he giggled. "And it was a bumpy ride, let me tell you!"

"Was it a transmutation?" asked Kirsten.

"It was indeed, my dear."

Lauren asked, "Transmutation?"

Kirsten explained, "The altering of complete chemical and biological elements, through the bombardment of radioactive nuclear decay, induced in this case—I assume—by pure enlightenment?"

"You're very enlightened yourself, my child," said the Dalai Lama, a little taken aback. "Do you have a twin in the movies?"

"But why transmutate?" Kirsten asked.

"You see, I was too old to make the climb myself, plus I have terrible corns and hammer toes, so Mr. Gere consented to make it for me, knowing full well that when the time was right I would transmutate here and take his place."

"But that means . . ."

"Yes. Only one soul can survive a transmutation. The other gives up his body."

"So Richard Gere is gone forever. Is that what you're saying? Tic Tac?" Lauren seemed bemused if not bored by all of this.

"At the time of death, the best parting gift is peace of mind. He had that, and I assure you, he will be reborn—and, hopefully, next time as a better actor, right?" He giggled. "Just as we all are reborn . . . right, Percy?" He was looking directly at me.

"Say what?"

"You are your great-uncle Percy Brackett Elliott reincarnated, and you possess in you a power greater than the world has ever known."

"My rompdillyiscous Rhombus?"

"You see, when your uncle was just a child he was bestowed with the Rhombus—"

"Yeah, I know, by Lizzie the homely hooker."

"But they were starving, and believing it to be rock candy, he put it in his mouth and swallowed it. It never passed. It remained inside your uncle. You are he reincarnated, so now the power of the Rhombus is inside you."

I opened my mouth really wide. "Can you see it? Can you see it?"

The Dalai Lama chuckled. "We need only to summit to experience its magnificence. You're young. I'm old and sick, but what we'll do in the next few hours will make history. It's never been done before. Not even your great-uncle would have imagined it."

Duncan rolled his eyes. "That's from *Godfather Part Two*."

"Is it?" said the Dalai Lama. "I've never seen Part Two, or Part One for that matter, but I think Part Three is dynamite!"

"Greetings to one and all."

"Perfect," Duncan mumbled. "Listen, I don't know if you looked out the window or not when you were transgendering or whatever the hell you just did, but there's a storm out there, and nobody is going to the summit. Understood?"

"One never knows, does one?" said the Dalai Lama mysteriously. "Opportunities have a way of presenting themselves on Chomolungma." Then he smiled one of his famous "my life may be simple, but it is so much more rewarding than your life is" smiles.

"Listen, Yoda, I'm in charge here and I'm telling you any push for the summit is off. Our only priority right now is getting off this godforsaken mountain—although I'd still love to find that frig'n diamond—and unless someone shows up soon to save us, we're all going to have to be reborn, if you know what I mean."

At that moment, carried on the wings of the wild wind, I was sure I detected a faint cry coming from out on the col. It almost sounded like a man calling out, "Hello?"

"And another thing," Duncan continued. "If you're gonna be a member of Mountain Maniacs, then there's a little thing called an admission fee . . ."

"Wait," I said.

"Yes, I hear it too," said Yorgi.

"Oh, don't start with that shit again, Yorgi," said Wendell, sticking his head back in the tent.

But then we all heard it: "Hello? Is anyone alive? Hello?"

We rushed outside. We could barely distinguish two thin beams of light slicing through the blackness. Two figures wearing helmets with Petzl Zipka headlamps approached.

We jumped up and down. "Over here! Over here!" we all called out.

The figures followed the sound of our voices to the communal tent. I didn't recognize them at first, but once they removed their helmets and oxygen masks, there was no mistaking them.

"Good evening, all," said Sir Edmund Hillary. "Nurse Matilda and I are here to rescue you."

CHAPTER THIRTY-SIX

"Om mani padme hum."

"Om mani padme hum."

Standing atop the parapets of the Rong Shu monastery, Pong held up the *dorje* and danced around, imploring the good spirits of Chomolungma to clear the skies.

It took but a moment before a slight break in the clouds could be discerned and Pong rushed to a copper horn and shouted into it.

"It clearing. You start now! You start now!"

Down in the control center the monk with the crew cut and the white vest received the message through a similar horn.

"Got it," he said. He turned and addressed everyone in the room. "All right, listen up, people. This is it."

Now Pong ran frantically through the monastery,

"Ping? Ping? Where are you, Ping? It all about to start. Where are you?" He stopped to catch his breath. *"Tch . . . tch . . . tch . . .* Oh, Ping. What you up to?"

At Camp Four, conditions weren't that much better, but still there was enough of a reduction in wind for Sir Hillary to put his rescue plan into effect.

Mount Pumori sits adjacent to Mount Everest and is the second-tallest mountain in the Himalayan "Five Peaks" range (its summit is five hundred feet below Camp Four). A twenty-thousand-foot-deep chasm separates the two. Sherpas who live on Pumori had shot lines of rope across the chasm, rigging a pulley system connecting the two mountains with the ropes and a sling chair that was similar to the one Michael had used earlier in the climb. The idea was to sit in the sling chair and be pulled over from Everest to Pumori by the Sherpas standing on Pumori's summit. Presumably, this is how Hillary and Nurse Matilda made it up to Camp Four in the first place. Then, since Pumori is far less treacherous, it would be an easy climb back down to the Khumbu Glacier, which spills out between both mountains.

All in all, this plan was way more dangerous than just waiting out the storm, but everyone was anxious to get off Everest, and Hillary seemed especially concerned that we leave before the weather cleared.

"Women and children first," he shouted, and of course I ran to the front of the line. He pushed me aside and then knelt down and cupped his hands. "Come on, child, this is the only way out."

Kirsten put her boot in Hillary's hands, and he hoisted her up into the chair. Duncan and Nurse Matilda strapped her in. "You sure this will work, Hillary?"

"I'm sure, Mr. Carter."

"Don't worry, Duncan," said Kirsten. "True, it's just a crude compound pulley device, but as long as the lead rope stays affixed to the sling seat, then the system should allow an object attached to the axle—that would be me—to travel at a rate commensurate with the length of the device itself. In other words, keep your fingers crossed."

"Good luck, Kirsten!" shouted Lauren, then added in a whisper, "And I've always known you were smart."

"Thanks, Betty," said Kirsten. "I'll see you at Bowling for Beluga for a Booker Noe's in one day!"

"Make it straight up for me, child!"

Duncan signaled the Sherpas on Pumori Peak with a flashlight, and they began to pull.

"Don't look down, Kirsten!" I shouted. "If you do, you might get scared and then you might lose your balance and fall off. And you'd probably die, because we're really high up."

Everyone shot me the same disdainful look. "Oh, sorry. I mean, may the good spirits of Jomolungbo or whatever be with you!"

Kirsten closed her eyes and held on. The wind blew the sling seat wildly back and forth. At one point a large pinnacle was blasted away from the side of Everest, showering Kirsten with shards of ice, but she squeezed her eyes even tighter and held on for dear life.

Eventually, she reached Pumori, and the Sherpas signaled us with their flashlights.

"That's it," said Duncan. "She made it!" We all cheered. "Let's pull the chair back."

Finally, it seemed like we were going to make it off the godforsaken mountain. (Have I mentioned that it's godforsaken?) I looked back at what was left of Camp Four and felt a bit melancholic—after all, I had only succeeded in finding Uncle Percy's nose. Being rescued now, when we were so close to the top, was bittersweet, to say the least. As I turned my attention back to the rescue efforts, I thought for sure I saw those damned little gnomes again, darting around in the black blizzard. Or were they . . . frogs?

"Okay, who's next?" shouted Duncan, as the storm began to rage again.

"Me. I'm next," said a strange voice. A woman with a shawl over her head swished to the front of the line. I scratched my whiskers.

Was there another woman with us all along whom I didn't notice? (If there was, I'm afraid I'm going to have to go back and rewrite the first part of this book, which means you're gonna have to go back and reread it. Sorry!)

Just as the woman settled into the sling chair, a fedora fell out from under her shawl.

"Wait a second," said Duncan. He pulled the shawl away. "Tzing Tzang, what the hell are you doing?"

"Getting off this frig'n mountain, boss. Everything shit! No diamond! No virgins! I go now! I don't want to die."

"What a wuss," I grumbled, and then something caught my eye. They were definitely three big bullfrogs hopping amidst the black snowdrifts. Or were they . . . gnomes?

"Did you just see some frogs?" I asked the Dalai Lama, who was standing right beside me. But the holy man merely smiled.

"Tzing, get the hell out of the chair!" Duncan demanded. "It's women first! Lauren is next, and then Nurse Matilda. Now out!"

"No way, boss. Mountain falling apart. I go now!" He kicked Duncan in the face, sending him flying to the snow. Nurse Matilda sprang for the seat.

"It's not your turn, asshole!" she shouted, pulling Tzing Tzang's hair.

"Mattie, no!" called Sir Hillary.

As Tzing Tzang struggled with the nurse, his flashlight beam bounced about. The Sherpas on Pumori thought it was the "go" signal, so they started pulling the chair back.

"Mattie!" hollered Hillary. "Don't go!" He went to grab her, but Wendell held him back.

"It's too late. They're already going!"

The sling chair was hoisted out over the abyss with Tzing Tzang seated in it and Nurse Matilda dangling precariously from it. The wind blasted the contraption back and forth, and Mattie could barely hang on.

They got to about the center of the chasm, when a loud, thundering fulmination rocked everything. Lightning flashed, and suddenly there was a huge discharge of heavier, blacker snow accompanied by a powerful blast of air that caused the sling seat to twirl.

"I can't hold on," the nurse shouted, and at that moment her fingers slipped.

"Noooooooo!" cried Hillary as she fell away.

"Good-bye, Edmund," she called out. "There's fresh milk in the fridge!" And then she was gone forever.

Tzing Tzang screamed as the entire sling seat went flying, jettisoning the Sherpa. He flipped head over heels and then dropped like a cannonball.

"Goddamn it! I knew this wasn't worth it!" cried Hillary, falling to his knees and burying his face in his palms. "But I had to try. I had my reputation to protect. I would have lost all my privileges at the club!"

"What? What did you just say?" asked Duncan.

"Everyone back to the communal tent," yelled Lauren. "The storm's getting worse again!"

Duncan grabbed Hillary by the collar. "Wait a second, old man."

"You heard the lady, Mr. Carter. We have to get back to the safety of the tent! There's no way off the mountain now."

At that moment Duncan's walkie-talkie crackled to life and a familiar voice came out. "I say, old man, the weather is frightful, but the virgins and I are making a push for the summit nonetheless. Are you game? We still have a bet, you know."

Duncan held Hillary with one hand and spoke into the walkie-talkie with the other.

"Who am I speaking to? Is this . . . Fidelity?" he asked.

"Heavens, no, old chap. It's me, Branson. My handle is 'Virgins Galore'!"

"I'll get back to you, Branson." He turned off the walkie-talkie and his eyes narrowed on Hillary. "Blue is for Fidelity," he said.

"I do believe you're hallucinating, Mr. Carter," replied Hillary. "Let us make our way back."

"At the Explorers Club, you told us the red in the flag stands for courage, but you didn't know what the blue signified . . . but you *did* know, didn't you? The blue stands for Fidelity."

"Thank you for reminding me. Now, let's be on our way."

"As in your call sign. It was you Norgay was working for, wasn't it?"

Hillary sighed and dropped his head. "My old friend Tenzing Norgay died in 1986. But yes, Mr. Carter, that thing down there that you call Norgay is in my employ, and I imagine he's in any number of other people's employ as well."

"Thing?"

"It's a Disney animatron, built to entertain tourists at the Labuse Lodge—an animatron, I might add, with a taste for cash. Pamma was its creator. It was just wires and circuits—nothing like my real friend—but it was quite useful to me. You see, I could never let you people find Percy's remains. I couldn't take the chance that somehow, some way, they could prove that I was not the first person to summit Mount Everest."

"Then you really weren't?"

"The real Norgay and I never made it past the pimps and hos party at Camp Three."

"Now who's posing as a mountaineer, *Sir* Hillary? "

"Yes, yes, Mr. Carter, perhaps I am just as lowly as you are." Suddenly an altogether different personality seemed to inhabit his body. "But still quite a bit smarter." He pulled out a semiautomatic handgun.

"You bastard!"

"That's far enough, Mr. Carter," Hillary instructed. "I'm sorry it has to end this way. I tried to save you people, but now that you know my secret, I'm afraid I can't let any of you get off this mountain alive."

Hillary aimed his gun at Duncan, but then turned it on Lauren.

"Nooo!" shouted Duncan, and he jumped in front of Lauren.

BLAM! BLAM! BLAM! BLAM!

Dark red vital fluid splattered the black snow. When the smoke cleared, Lauren and Duncan both lay motionless in a heap on the ground.

Hillary stood over them, peering through the gloom to see which one was hit. Lauren was cradling the lifeless surfer dude's head at her breast. She had tears in her eyes.

Then just as Hillary took aim at Lauren, Michael and Wendell snuck up from behind and—*WHACK!*—they hit him upside the head with the frozen tub of Grammy's peanut butter.

Hillary's eyes rolled back in his head. "Say the secret word and a duck will come down and reward you each fifty dollars." Then he fell to the ground unconscious.

"This stuff never stops coming in handy, does it?" said Wendell.

Michael grabbed some bungee cords. "Quick, let's tie him up."

"Oh, brave captain, don't die," Lauren implored, caressing Duncan's head. "Yes, I know I called you an unscrupulous rat, lacking in all the social graces and, yes you're covered with ticks, and yes you do smell, quite a bit actually, but goddamn it, if there isn't something about you that reminds me of Bogie, and how the hell could a tough broad like me not find that attractive? So if you have it in your heart to forgive me, come back, brave captain. Come back."

"Who doesn't remind you of Bogie?" groaned Duncan, opening one eye. "Don't worry, queenie," he said, "It's just a flesh wound," and then he planted a kiss on Lauren's lips. She pulled away and slapped him hard, and then she pulled his head toward her and planted one right back.

The two made out passionately. Had this been a thirties movie, a romantic swell of orchestrated music would have enveloped the scene, and Lauren would have been young and hot, but Duncan wouldn't even have been born yet, so she just would have been making out with air and hugging herself, like I did all through high school—but since there was no orchestra for miles around, Wendell sang the theme from *Mahogany*.

"Ah, folks. I think we have a problem," said Michael.

All around them, black bullfrogs began transmutating.

POP! POP! POP! POP!

One by one, the frogs popped like popcorn into little gnomes wearing gray uniforms with red armbands. Each gnome had a tiny, black square mustache under his or her nose.

"What the hell is this?" asked Lauren, wrapping her scarf around Duncan's wounded arm.

"Don't hold me to it," he said, "but it looks like a bunch of bullfrogs are turning into Nazi gnomes."

"Nazi gnomes! Goddamn it!" hollered Lauren. "Let me at 'em."

"We got a bigger problem," Wendell shouted. "Look up there!" He pointed up, and through the storm, they could just make out two figures holding torches climbing up toward the summit. It was the Dalai Lama and me. (I bet you didn't even notice us leave.)

SHWAM! SHWAM! SHWAM!

A volley of arrows came whizzing past our heroes.

Lauren dropped down and unzipped the side of her snow pants revealing a sexy, black-stocking-clad leg and a small Beretta pistol stuck in a red velvet garter around her thigh. "Bogie always wanted me to carry this for safety," she explained. "The only other time I used it was on Robards."

BLAM! BLAM! BLAM!

"Take that! You dirty midget krauts!" she shouted. "Carter! Take Wendell and go bring Chris back. Michael and I will take care of the Nazis!"

"Damn Nazi Gnomes!"

CHAPTER THIRTY-SEVEN

While Pong searched the Rong Shu monastery for any sign of Ping, the monk with the white vest adjusted his headset and began a standard systems check.

"Communications."

"Go."

"Tactical warning systems."

"Go."

"Integrated Karma?"

"It's a go for integrated Karma."

"Okay. Give me a rundown on the five 'Thermobaric Preceptors.' Number One?"

"'Do Not Destroy Life' ready to make them hurt, sir."

"Number Two?"

"'Do Not Steal' unlocked and ready for launch."

"Three?"

"'Do Not Commit Sexual Misconduct' is on the pad and very much ready for launch, if you know what I mean, sir."

"Number Four."

"'Do Not Lie' reports that it's been ready for launch for at least an hour now, sir."

"And Number Five . . . Number Five? Number Five? Control to launchpad, report status of Number Five Preceptor immediately."

"Sorry, boss. I was in the crapper. Number Five Preceptor, 'Do Not Take Intoxicating Drink,' ready for launch."

"All systems report 'Go.' Commence countdown to Operation Duhkha on my mark. In five, four, three, two, one—mark! T-minus three minutes and counting!"

The monk with the white vest put a key into the control board and turned it. Then he flipped up a Plexiglas cover, revealing a big red button. He held his shaking index finger over the button as the countdown to whatever was about to happen began. Pong stood next to him with his eyes on the surveillance monitors. There was something peculiar about the monk down in the Preceptor Number Five launch room. Pong turned a knob, zoomed in close and gasped.

"Ping? What you doing down there, Ping? I have to stop him." And he ran out of the control center.

The NORAD-induced storm did not let up as the Dalai Lama and I neared the Hillary Step. The step is a treacherous formation vaguely resembling stairs and was named by Sir Edmund, though apparently he never saw it in person. It marks the entrance to the so-called Death Zone, and serves as the last major obstacle before the summit.

"Gee, Mr. Lama," I said. "It was sure nice of you to come with me. I just couldn't leave without getting to the tippy top, if you know what I mean."

"Yes, we must all find our own . . . ahem . . . tippy tops."

"Mind if we take a little breather? Climbing without oxygen is giving me gas!" I giggled. "Giving me gas, that's a good one."

The Dalai Lama looked around nervously. "Well, yes, I suppose. But just for a little bit."

"Why, what's the big hurry?"

"Um . . . nothing, but the storm is not so good, and we should go to the summit and . . . get back and . . . off the mountain soon, right?"

"Right."

He clapped his hands together. "Okay then, so have we rested long enough?"

"Hold on there, Johnny Armstrong. Give a guy a couple minutes, will ya? Want some caviar? Ripped it off from our precious food supplies."

"No, thank you." He walked to the edge and looked over.

"Oh, my," he said, scrunching up his shoulders and giggling cutely. "I'm afraid the SS gnomes are on the loose again!"

"The what?"

"They used to be called the hill people, but they've been dressing up like Hitler ever since the Nazis came to Everest in 'thirty-eight. You see, they were looking for—"

"Yes, yes, I know all about it. They were looking for their cousins from Atlantis or some shit like that, right?" I said, massaging my aching feet.

The Dalai Lama chuckled and came over and zipped up my parka for me as he spoke. "The Nazis were looking for the true origins of their Aryan race, but what they found did not make them happy. It turns out the insane hill people—or gnomes—were their true ancestors."

"Ooh, in your face, Nazis!"

"Yes." The Dalai Lama giggled. "Well, the Nazis were terribly embarrassed, as you can imagine, and the expedition refused to bring the gnomes back to Germany, so the gnomes killed the Nazis, and they've been running around claiming to be the true master race ever since. It's funny, one must wonder what the outcome of World War Two would have been had the Nazi gnomes joined the battle. I suppose we all might be leapfrogging down the Champs-Élysées right now."

"Right, right . . . Sure. Whatever that is."

"So, shall we go?"

"Okey-dokey." I stood up.

"I don't sink so," said a big man standing on top of the Hillary Step.

"*Yidam!*" declared the Dalai Lama. "Stand back. He means to thwart us!"

"It's just Yorgi," I said. "And Yorgi's not the *yidam*—Norgay is! Yorgi couldn't hurt us if he wanted to." Then I whispered into the Dalai Lama's ear. "He's blind, you know."

"I am the *yidam*, wrathful deity of all Pretans! *Eee Ya mogee vedet*—and I can see just fine!"

"Oh, my mistake."

"I'll handle this," said the Dalai Lama, rolling up his sleeves. To Yorgi, he said, "Are you the best China has to offer?"

Yorgi laughed. "China? Who said anything about China?"

The Dalai Lama struck an intimidating karate pose.

Like a caged lion, Yorgi paced back and forth on the top of the Hillary Step, eyeing his adversary closely—seconds away from attacking.

"Has he told you his plan?" Yorgi said to me. "Has he told you how he's going to sacrifice you to the *lammergeiers* at the top of the summit? How he's going to *otrexeet vas*—cut you into pieces and then use Chomolungma's power to invade the land vonce known as Tibet?"

"Don't listen to him!" said the Dalai Lama. "He is a demon, mixing lies with the truth!"

I frowned. "Well, just what about all that was actual 'truth'?" 'Cause it all kind of sounded bad to me."

"*Svo sovem noristina!* It's all true!"

"Liar!" shouted the Dalai Lama and—*wham!*—he shot an invisible shaft of pure energy from his fingertips that slammed Yorgi onto his back. Then the Dalai Lama jumped on his chest and started to bounce up and down.

The *yidam* rubber-banded back to his feet, bouncing the Dalai Lama off.

"You will not defeat the hungry ghosts!" growled Yorgi, as black snow swirled around his head. "And you and your people will never return to Tibet!"

"We'll see about that!" And the two warriors flew at each other with such violence that the whole mountainside seemed to rumble. They pounded away at one another, and the battle seemed fairly even, until at one point the Dalai Lama was thrown to the ground, the wind knocked out of his heaving chest. Sensing his moment, Yorgi straddled the holy man, and lifting a heavy boulder high over his head, he prepared to finish him off.

"Just one question," gasped the Dalai Lama. "If not China, was it Russia that sent you?"

"How naïve!" growled the *yidam* "It was Wal-Mart!" And just before he flung the stone down, a voice cried out.

"Yorgi, no! Put the rock down!"

Yorgi turned and growled at Wendell, who was now standing on the step.

"Yorgi, you're blind. You can't kill the Dalai Lama. Only a seeing man can do that!"

Yorgi snorted and shook his head. Then to the Dalai Lama he said, "Just give me a second here. I gotta teach this guy a *yeepok.*" He moved toward Wendell.

"Vindall, I have been listening to your ignorant, insulting, and degrading comments about blind people long enough. If I actually vere blind, I vould have killed you long time ago. Even a blind person vould be able to see vhat a stupid, self-satisfied, hypocritical boob you veally are!"

I giggled. "Wendell, he said 'boob!'"

"Well, if you're starting with that shit again about how blind people can see things that us seeing people can't, then I'm gonna have to beg to differ."

This enraged the *yidam*. He lifted the rock over his head and growled, running toward Wendell at a furious pace. But suddenly he was hit from behind with another powerful blast of energy from the Dalai Lama's fingertips. Wendell stepped aside and Yorgi flew past him, right off the Hillary Step and into the atmosphere. His last futile, angry cry, "*Dasvidania*, dumb Americans . . . and Tibetans," faded away as he *svodniked* (fell) to his death.

Wendell shook his head, "See what I mean? Poor thing couldn't even see where he was going."

"Thank you, Wendell, thank you so much," said the Dalai Lama, humbly offering a *gassho*.

"Oh yeah, no problem. But listen, Duncan says you guys gotta get your asses back down to Camp Four pronto. He went to tell Branson the same thing."

"Yes. Yes. Absolutely, we will," said the Dalai Lama, and then he leaned in close to Wendell and whispered, "The kid had his heart set on seeing the summit, so I told him I'd take him up there for a quick peek—you know, take a couple of snapshots, just so he could say he did it—and then we'll be right down."

"Oh, yeah, sure. No problem," replied Wendell, adjusting his goggles over his eyes.

"Um. Wendell, I'm not sure what the nice Mr. Lama just whispered to ya, but according to what Yorgi or the *yidam* was saying, I think he has kind of a weird plan to—"

"Listen, I'm not going to stop you guys," interrupted Wendell. "You have to do what you have to do, and I have to do what I have to do, right? Isn't that what climbing Mount Everest is all about—to see what we're made of as men? I want to thank you, Chris, for giving me this opportunity. I finally know what I have to do."

"What? What are you going to do?"

"It's true I can never be the first black man to summit Mount Everest—someone already has—but I *will* become the first man—black, white, or yellow—to ski down Everest! On a Tuesday!" And with that he snapped himself into Yorgi's skis.

"Wendell, don't go," I yelled. "I think the Dalai Lama is some kind of serial killer or something!"

But he couldn't hear me. "Farewell, all! See you in the history books!" Then, with a *swoosh*, he disappeared over the edge of the Hillary Step.

There was an uncomfortable pause as the Dalai Lama slowly turned back to me.

"'Some kind of serial killer'?"

I swallowed. "Well, maybe that was a bit extreme. But I think I have to get back to—"

"Stop right there," he demanded and he made his thumb and index finger look like a gun and pointed them at me. "Hands up!"

"That's not a gun. That's just your finger."

"I think you've seen what it's capable of doing,"

"Now look here . . ."

BANG!

A rock by my head exploded into smithereens.

"Okay, okay. Now hold on, we can talk about this."

"I have waited too long to have this moment screwed up by some moron actor from the United States who thinks he's a big-time writer now."

"Well, have you read any of my work? I think you'd enjoy *The Shroud of the Thwacker*—Miramax books, twenty-two ninety-five—although I think in paperback it's only—"

The Dalai Lama battled the Yidam.

"Silence!"

"Sure."

"You and I have a date with destiny." And before I could say anything, he added, "And no joke about not knowing anybody by that name. Ha ha ha, very funny, 'Mr. Lama, I don't know anybody named Destiny.' Yeah, yeah, yeah. I've heard it all before. Maybe it's a blind date, have you ever thought of that? Now, move! The vultures await!"

I held my hands high up in the air, and with the Dalai Lama's finger pointed at my back, we solemnly ascended the Hillary Step—up into the too aptly named Death Zone.

"Farewell all! See you in the history books!"

CHAPTER THIRTY-EIGHT

Wendell whizzed past Base Camp on Yorgi's skis, a fast-moving avalanche right on his heels, but Old Norgay was too busy to notice. He was frantically switching back and forth on his walkie-talkie, trying to juggle all the chatter emanating from the communicator.

"Norgay, you bastard!"

"Duncan, is that you? You s'posed to be on Channel One!"

"No, *I'm* on Channel One!"

"Who are you?"

"The Pentagon . . . er . . . I mean Blue Folder. How's our storm going? We're sending in Alpha team!"

"Get off Channel One, you're s'posed to be on Channel Three!'

"Isn't that where Captain Harding is?"

"I think Captain Harding's gone to that big Hillary Step in the sky."

"The Hillary Step *is* in the sky."

"You know what I mean."

"Hey, everyone, this is Lauren from Mountain Maniacs, on Channel Four. We're surrounded by Nazi gnomes, and can't hold out much longer . . . running out of ammunition . . . need help. Who the hell is Captain Harding?"

A muckamuck voice suddenly came through. "*Ee shlama pata boo! Ee shlama pata boo!*"

"Who's making baby sounds on Channel Three? Stop fooling around. We don't have time for crank calls."

"Who said that?"

"You tell me who you are first."

"Norgay, it's Fidelity on Channel Two. I'm hog-tied and I can't get up!"

"Hillary?"

"I say, old man, this is Virgins Galore on Channel Two as well, who am I talking to?"

"Branson, is that you? It's Hillary. There's a frightful rumor going about that I wasn't the first one to summit. Don't be fooled."

"Branson, it's Duncan. Switch channels. Go to Channel Five. Look, you have to get off the mountain. It's too dangerous to try for the summit! And queenie, switch to Channel One, I promise I'll be right down to rescue you from the Nazis."

"This is the Park Rangers speaking, whoever's screwing around up there, get off Channel Five. This channel is for emergencies only. If you don't have an emergency, get off the line."

Suddenly Norgay's confused, overheated circuits blew, and his head exploded in a blaze of sparks and smoke. A split second later, the avalanche that had been chasing Wendell slammed hard into the Mountain Maniacs' tent and buried the double-crossing robot under ten feet of black snow. (Yeah, he got his! In your face, Norgay the animatron!)

On the western approach to the summit, Richard Branson and his virgins (all still in their snow-white Gamow suits) were pinned down by the blasting wind and icy temperatures.

"Give it up, Branson!" called Duncan, coming around from the other side of the mountain. "It's impossible to make the summit!"

"Don't be a defeatist, old boy. It's just a little squall. We still have a bet, don't we?"

"No bet. I'll pay you back somehow."

"It's not the money I want. Money means nothing to me. It's the principle of the thing!" He started to sob. "You ruined one of my beauties. My favorite beauty—beauty Number Twelve, and I want my revenge. But if you won't race with me, you'll have to deal with them!"

Branson snapped his fingers and the virgins all stood up and took karate poses.

"Oh shit, don't make me wrestle your virgins here!"

"Then race with me! You owe me that much, you bastard. I'm a man of my word. Why don't you be one, for once in your life!"

Duncan weighed his options as the wind blasted his face. It's true he had never been a man of his word. He had always let greed and avarice rule his life—perhaps finding a bit of redemption on the mountain would be a greater gift to him than even the Rhombus itself. But then he thought about Lauren down there battling for her life—he had given her his word that he would come back and save her—and so he came to the only honorable conclusion.

"You're on, you John Bull, beef-eating, swishy-talk'n', bluejacket limey! On your mark. Get set. Go!"

The two began to climb furiously, flailing their ice axes and smashing their crampons into the crusty integument of Chomolungma's homely face.

Down on the south col, Lauren and Michael stood with their hands in the air—surrounded.

"Don't tell 'em anything," Lauren said out of the corner of her mouth.

The SS gnome in charge blew a whistle and called out, "*Alle truppen zur obersiete!*" And all the gnomes started to climb toward the summit. "*Gehen sie schnell!*" He ordered Lauren and Michael to climb too.

The big gnome on campus jammed the IMAX camera into Michael's arms.

"*Film alles! Film Alles!*"

"He says, 'Film everything.'"

"Where are they taking us?" Michael asked nervously.

"To the roof of the world."

CHAPTER THIRTY-NINE

"I can't go any farther!"

"Keep moving!" ordered the Dalai Lama. "And keep your hands where I can see them. I know all about you actors and your slippery hands."

We continued up, disappearing into a pitch-black cloud that concealed the last twenty feet of Everest.

A moment later, our heads popped through the cloud, and we were on the summit. The view was absolutely spectacular as far as the eye could see in every direction: snowcapped peaks, plains, Wal-Mart stores, and amusement parks.

Not only was it sunny and vibrantly clear above the cloud (the CIA's storm was wreaking its havoc below us), but it was also eerily quiet, except for what the Tibetans call the "music of the wind," a soft, mercurial lamentation that was at once charming and annoying. The air all around was gratifyingly warm, if not actually hot, and I began to sweat under my parka. I thought to myself, *Jeez, I guess there's something to this global-warming shit, after all,* and from then on, I kept a close eye on how many carbon footprints I was leaving behind.

I took a deep breath, and my lungs were scorched by the hot air.

"It's called *druk*," said the lama. "'Hot air of the mountain.' Blows in on the Santa Annas."

The air around us became distorted by heat waves wafting up from the crags, and everything went blurry.

We discerned a dark figure stepping out from behind a mound of snow.

"Who's there?" called the Dalai Lama. "What matter of spirit are you?"

I said, "Are you a good witch or a bad witch?" and the Dalai Lama smacked me on the back of my head.

"Hi yas, boys. What's happenings?"

To my great surprise, Tony was standing before us, no worse for wear, holding the *Who's the Boss* flag and eating a big bowl of pasta.

"Tony, you're alive!" I exclaimed.

"Sures I ams, kids, and watch this."

He proceeded to do a little soft-shoe for us, and I applauded. "Bravo!"

"Boy, doos I have a couple of bones to picks with yoos."

"I bet you doos—I mean does—I mean do," I said, "but hey, where did you get the spaghetti?"

"From hims."

Tony pointed to his right, and another figure stepped from behind the snow.

This person was dressed in old-time clothing, but other than that he and I were identical. It was as though I were looking in a mirror. He was I. I was he. We were the same height, boasted similar beards, shared the same noble bald head, and . . . coincidentally he was missing his nose.

"Uncle Percy, is that you?"

"Hello, my simple-minded nephew," he said in a voice that could have been mine. "You can put your finger down now, Mr. Lama. It won't be necessary. I'm a friend."

"But it's impossible," whined the Dalai Lama. "There can't be two of you." He stamped his foot. "You died in nineteen twenty-four. The crazy actor is you reincarnated! Ping and Pong said so!"

"Calms down, Dalais babys," admonished Tony.

"I admit that there is a strong family resemblance," observed Percy, looking me up and down. "Especially around the old schnozola. Is that mine? I've been looking for that for like, eighty years."

"Maybe," I said, protecting it with my hand.

"But what's impossible is that he could be me reincarnated. Because, as you can see, I never died. The power of the Golden Rhombus has kept me alive and ageless all these years."

"And he uzes its to makes killer homemades pastas!"

I pouted. "You mean the Rhombus isn't inside me, after all?"

Percy smiled. "No, great-nephew. It's still in me! In fact, it has become part of me. The Rhombus is me, and I, the Rhombus. You can just call me Uncle Rhombus from now on."

"Could you possibly explain that for me?" (And perhaps for our readers as well?)

Percy sat down on a snow mound and lit a corncob pipe, exhaling the smoke through the large hole in the middle of his face as he spoke. "Well, it all begins with a woman."

"Don'ts it always?" remarked Tony. "The dames have it all over us guys, right Dalais babys?" He elbowed His Holiness. "Just once I'd like to knows what its like to be preggers, rights?"

"Her name was Elizabeth Cady Stanton, and by all accounts she was a spitfire. She was one of the earliest leaders of the women's suffrage movement."

The Dalai Lama yawned.

"Well, Elizabeth wanted to show the world that a woman was just as capable as a man, if not more capable. So she decided to climb Mount Everest. And why not? No man had conquered it yet, so why not a woman? That's right, boys, the first flag planted on the summit of Mount Everest didn't belong to New Zealand or the Explorers Club or even a man. It was the flag of the women's rights movement, and Elizabeth Cady Stanton planted it."

"Wow," I said. "In your face . . . all men!"

"But before she climbed back down, Elizabeth noticed the Rhombus on the tiptop of the summit. Certainly it would be worth a great deal, she thought, money that could be used to further the movement. And so she took it with her."

"The dames can't resists the ice!"

"But the Rhombus was a curse, not a blessing. You see, it may be given, or bestowed, the way Mother Earth bestowed it upon Chomolungma, but woe onto he—or she—who dares steal it. Elizabeth lost everything she had. Destitute, she was forced to sell her body to survive. She hoped an adventure abroad would mark a new beginning. But alas, the curse followed her on that fateful voyage as well."

"Voyage? So you mean . . ."

"Yes, Elizabeth Cady Stanton became Lizzie the homely prostitute and before she froze to death aboard the stranded H.M.S. *Terror*, she married a sailor, and bore him one son—me."

"I heard she married a magic popular polar bear from a neighboring ice floe."

Percy looked at me like I was nuts.

"Sorry," I said. "You're right, that would be crazy. Norgay must have been screwing with me."

"She gave me the Rhombus in a locket, because she knew its power would protect me—but I was so hungry that I swallowed it."

"See, what did I tell you?" said the Dalai Lama.

"And it became lodged in my intestinal tract. And there it remains until this day."

"Until this day, indeed." The Dalai Lama retrieved an ornately decorated cleaver from underneath his robe.

"What, are we gonna doos a cooking demos now?" asked Tony.

Above, the hungry *lammergeiers* circled, eager for the sky burial to commence.

"No!" I yelled. "You're not gonna chop up my great-uncle Percy!"

"Save your strength, my queer nephew," advised Percy calmly. "I have every intention of sacrificing myself for the praiseworthy cause of the Tibetan people. For it is a righteous cause. The Tibetan flag must fly once more, and they will need the power of the mountain to assist them. But, as I said, the Rhombus and I are one. There is only one way to return it . . . I mean me . . . to its rightful place."

Percy walked stoically up to the tip of Everest and threw one leg over, straddling the peak between his legs. "So long, my obviously disturbed great-nephew. It was sure nice to know ya." Then with a dramatic flourish he sat down on the dull point of the summit—and continued to smoke his pipe.

We all waited anxiously to see what was going to happen, but after a while it just became awkward.

"Ah . . . is that it?" asked the Dalai Lama.

"Jeez, I was sure it was still inside me," said Percy.

"Look, I think my way might be quicker." The impatient Lama raised his cleaver. "Now, technically, Buddhists aren't allowed to kill, but the way I think about it, all I'm doing is cutting, right? It's the bleeding that does the actual killing. So that way I'm in the clear."

"Wait!" I said. "The medial nasal concha harbors all trespassers!"

"I like that one," said the Dalai Lama, taking out his notepad. "Mind if I use it?"

"Don't you understand? Pamma said that was the key to everything. The medial nasal concha harbors all trespassers! Nasal! That's it! The Rhombus isn't stuck in Percy's stomach. It's in his nose—the nose that's sewn onto *my* face right now!"

"Well, what do ya know?" said Percy.

I paced back and forth, putting it all together. "So when you were a child, instead of swallowing it—you must of stuck it up your nose. Grammy told me that you used to like to stick beans up your nose just like me! You must have thought it was a bean!"

Percy laughed. "You know, I wouldn't put it past me—I am crazy as a loon, you know—always have been—nuts, wacko—out there. Bad case of lead poisoning when I was an infant. Wee! Horsey, horsey he don't stop. He done let his feet go clippety clop," and then he started to dance around and slipped and banged his head on the summit and was knocked out.

I put both my hands in the snow on either side of the summit and lifted my legs up in the air so that I was standing on my head. Then I stuck my nose into the hole in the peak.

Immediately a low rumbling sound began to grow in intensity, and the summit shook as if in the grips of a massive earthquake. An aura of blue static electricity encircled me. My upside-down face glowed with every color of the rainbow, and then suddenly great shafts of light shot out of my nostrils. Beams of energy—yellow, blue, red, and green—radiated up into the heavens and down to the earth below. Explosions of pure light blasted out luminescent sparklers, and tiny glowing orbs danced about with a life of their own.

"It's beginning," shouted the Dalai Lama. "Wake, my sleeping goddess! Wake and join the battle!"

Below the Rung Shu monastery, Pong confronted Ping in the Preceptor Number Five launch room.

"What you do, Ping?"

"I'm putting a stop to this once and for all! I don't want to go back to Tibet. I like my life in New York. I like my apartment. I just signed new lease. I'm getting new carpet. I'm gonna pull the self-destruct lever and then all preceptors will go boom."

"I can't let you do that."

"We are old friends. I don't wish to harm you," said Ping.

"Then abandon this plan," replied Pong.

"That I cannot do."

"Then it is a battle between method and wisdom." Pong pulled out the *dorje*, which glowed with a blinding light and took a defensive pose. Ping in return produced the *drilbu*, which glowed just as brightly.

The two began an awkward sword fight, using the scepter and the bell as their weapons.

In the control center, the countdown continued ". . . thirty . . . twenty-nine . . . twenty-eight . . ."

The Dalai Lama held up the cleaver. "Come, my goddess, let pure enlightenment push aside all ignorance, and let us all find glorious Nirvana in the path of the true 'cam sutra'! Wake! Wake! Wake my Chomolungma! Wake!"

Lightning bolts flashed about in all directions, converging down on me. The mountain swayed back and forth and I had a hard time holding my position.

Down on the Hillary Step, Lauren and Michael and the gnomes were thrown to the ground.

"Now's our chance!" said Lauren, and they scurried up into the black cloud, escaping their Lilliputian SS captors.

On the west side of Everest, amidst the chaos surrounding them, Duncan and Branson continued their battle for the summit. They were climbing neck and neck when Branson flailed his ice axe, but instead of hitting the mountain, it went straight into Duncan's hand. Duncan screamed in agony. "So sorry, old chap, honest mistake." Branson kept crawling upward and was about three feet above Duncan when the mountain vibrated with a thunderous shudder and he fell, grabbing hold of a rock just below Duncan.

"Take my hand, Branson!"

The Englishman grabbed Duncan's bloody flipper, but a maniacal look crossed his face. "You can't pull me up, Carter," he growled, "you're not strong enough. And if I go—you're going with me!"

Boulders were tumbling down on either side of the men. About thirty feet below them, all the virgins huddled together to shelter themselves from the cascading rubble. (I know it seems like it would be really hot, but remember they're all in those Gamow suits. It was about as sexy as watching a bunch of lesbian Pillsbury Doughboys.)

"Don't be an idiot, Branson. We can do this." Duncan strained to pull him up.

"No. You took my Number Twelve from me. So we die together!"

Duncan just smiled blissfully at Branson.

"I said, 'We die together.' Duncan? Are you even listening to me?"

Duncan shook his head. "Oh, sorry, spaced out for a second. Bad case of altitude sickness. Meant to say, 'So long, sucker!'"

Suddenly Duncan swung at Branson with something jagged—the piece of the giant crab that he had pocketed as a souvenir. The shard punctured Branson's decompression suit. A look of horror crossed Branson's face, as he was shot off the mountain and into the universe, the escaping hot air from his suit jettisoning him around and around like a popped balloon, exuding a high-pitched shriek as it went. He flew up and circled the summit several times before the shriek dissipated to a hiss, and then he just floated gently down like a feather into the storm clouds below.

Lauren and Michael and Duncan all reached the summit at the same time.

"What in the hell is going on up here?" Lauren asked, "and why is Chris standing on his head?"

The Dalai Lama was in a state of frenzied rapture. He fell to his knees and cried out, "I call on all *Kshatriyas*—warriors of the righteous—to join the great battle against ignorance and unenlightenment."

"Hi ya, everybodys! Wants some pastas?"

"Tony! Now just where in the hell have you been, young man?" Lauren asked.

"Why don't we debrief later?" suggested Duncan.

Lauren looked around. "So this is the summit, huh?" She shrugged her shoulders. "You get a better view from the Rainbow Room."

"Breathe! Breathe, Chomolungma, Goddess Mother of the world! Breathe!"

Suddenly the mountain seemed to groan as if it were a fairy-tale giant waking from a long slumber. I toppled off my perch.

"Chomolungma . . . angry!" said the mountain in a booming bass almost as deep as Lauren's.

"There, there, my Goddess Mother," said the Dalai Lama, stroking the ground.

322   *Chris Elliott*

"Everybody want climb Chomolungma! Nobody want love Chomolungma! Nasty explorers stick flags in Chomolungma's head!"

"It's okay now, it's okay. Your lama is here now. We're going to make all those nasty bad people sorry, aren't we?" He tossed a ginger snap on the ground, which opened up and swallowed it with a titanic *GULP*. "She's alive!" exclaimed the Dalai Lama, throwing his arms up in the air. "Let Operation Duhkha commence!"

"Then I stuck my nose in the hole."

CHAPTER FORTY

Ping and Pong continued to wrestle on the floor of the launch room. Pong held Ping back, but Ping stretched out his hand and was about to pull the self-destruct lever on the panel.

"Ping, don't do it. Please," begged Pong. "We are brothers. We serve the ocean of wisdom. We no need HBO, or hot dogs, or wall-to-wall carpet. We walk the righteous path—always have and we must continue to do so."

Ping's hand hovered over the lever, shaking. He looked at his brother monk and then at the lever. After a tense moment, he finally pulled his hand away.

"You always know how to get to me," he said.

"It ain't that hard, kid," replied Pong, and they smiled their beguiling smiles at each other.

". . . three, two, one."

In the control center, the monk in charge pushed the red button and a big explosion was heard. Up on the parapets, Ping and Pong emerged just in time to watch as the five thermobaric preceptor missiles were launched into the sky, soaring up past them, and then zooming off toward their chosen destinations.

"Oh, well," said Ping. "The chicks in Tibet are hotter than the ones in the States anyway."

"Yeah, white girls have such small butts!" said Pong, and the two gave each other high fives.

At that moment in Dharamsala, India, the great wooden doors of the ancient Center for Tantric Studies creaked open and battalion after battalion of red-robed Tibetan monks armed with outdated World War II rifles, pitchforks, rakes, shovels, and axes swarmed out. Brigades of horses, old tanks, Humvees, personnel transports, and a thousand mutton-on-a-stick carts backed them up. The same happened in Lhasa, Makalu, and Bhutan, and on Minya Konka. From every Buddhist monastery in China and Nepal and every Buddhist village scattered across the entire region, hordes of the devoted emerged to take back Tibet.

Of course, China was unprepared for all this, the People's Army having only a few thousand troops strategically placed along the Tibetan Plateau. Still, the Red nation quickly mustered its forces and readied themselves to quell the uprising.

"We have to get down!" yelled Duncan

"I'm not leaving without Percy," I hollered, and I went back and picked him up and threw him over my shoulder. "Also, I'd love to take a couple of snapshots." We all paused and took turns taking pictures of each other.

"Chomolungma lives!" shouted the Dalai Lama, and the mountain roared like a lion. "Soon, the whole world will know the pure, simple satisfaction of living a peaceful life, free of divisiveness, terrorism, plagues, and pestilence—a world where mankind cares for one another, where compassion is the law of the land, where life is not measured by the size of your wallet—or the size of anything else for that matter, ladies—but by how much love and kindness you share with one another. And where I, the lovingest and kindnessest of them all, will rule this totalitarian state of enlightenment with an iron fist! Yes, Chomolungma," he said, patting the mountain like it was his dog, "we shall first shower our old homeland with love and harmony, and then . . . we shall shower the world!"

"*Vraarrrg!*" howled the mountain. "Shower world! Shower world!"

"You're mad!" I said (with an English accent, for no apparent reason). "Nobody would want to live in a world like that! I'll shower with love when I want to!"

"Perhaps, but nothing can stop me now!"

A huge explosion rocked the summit and the Dalai Lama fell on his butt.

"Except for maybe big bombs," he muttered. "Yes, definitely, big bombs might."

"Let's go!" commanded Lauren.

Another blast hit the mountaintop.

"Who the hell is bombing us?"

From above F-14 Tomcats and F-18 Hornets were laying down suppressing fire, clearing the way for the arrival of the Alpha special forces unit, who were HALO jumping (high-altitude parachuting) from "Herc" cargo planes forty thousand feet up.

At the Hillary Step, we encountered the Nazi gnomes, who seemed stunned by the concussion bombs.

"*Zie blitzkrieg?*" asked the Nazi in charge rather timidly.

"Oh, not these assholes again," griped Lauren. Adrenaline took over and the elderly actress commenced kicking gnomes right and left, sending them flying off Everest like footballs.

"Get down," shouted Duncan as another bomb hit. "Jesus Christ!"

"Beautiful," said Michael, filming everything. "This will go a long way to making our government look like a bunch of warmongers . . .

er . . . I mean . . . But ultimately I'll look really silly, so in the end it will reflect positively on our government—I think."

Below, the Alpha team, who were armed with M-16 rifles and wearing jet-black Gamow suits, parachuted onto the mountain, where they were immediately met with a barrage of rocks thrown at them by the virgins.

Up on the summit, the Dalai Lama whispered into the dirt, "Now! Now! Now, Goddess Mother of the world!"

Suddenly the base of the mountain began to break apart. Rock formations that had taken billions of years to establish separated from one another and were blasted into smithereens in just mere seconds. The Khumbu Icefall shattered and then crashed into pieces like a broken vase. Everest actually began to pull up stakes and thunder forward.

We retreated down the mountain only to run smack into the skirmish between the virgins and the Alpha team.

"Take cover," called Duncan and we all ducked into a hole just as the Alphas sprayed us with automatic gunfire.

"Guys, I think this is the end of the line," said Duncan.

"You've said that before," I pointed out. "I don't believe you."

"No, I really think this time it's it!"

"What do you mean? We're gonna die?"

"Basically, yes!"

"Shit. Sure wish you had sugarcoated that one for me," I said. "I'm not good with blunt answers." And then I started screaming like I was possessed (and I may have thrown up, too).

A bomb hit above us, loosening a boulder that smashed down way too close for comfort.

"Well, everyone," I hiccuped through my hysteria, "at least I found what I was looking for up here on Everest." And then I glanced at Lauren and smiled.

"You mean your uncle Percy?" she asked.

"No," I said, squeezing her arm, "I found . . ."

Suddenly the Alpha team was all around us, aiming their M-16s into our hiding spot.

"Good-bye, everyone," I said, closing my eyes.

"What . . . what did you find?" asked Lauren, shaking me.

The Special Forces team cocked their weapons, aimed, and . . .

"I was going to say I found courage, but I just soiled myself, so I guess, uh . . ."

Suddenly a loud horn sounded from behind, and everybody turned to see what the noise was. Advancing rapidly up Chomolungma's south approach was the massive army of muckamucks, led by Chief Shawloo. The muckamucks had all taped their mouths shut with the duct tape to show solidarity with Martin. The chief carried on his shoulders our friends Martin and Captain Harding. Riding on Harvey's smaller shoulders was Agent Resnick.

"It's Martin and a bunch of yetis with their mouths taped shut. Yay!" I shouted. "Freak time on Everest!"

The Special Forces unit opened fire on the half men, half apes, and the yetis flung spears, arrows, and flaming dung balls in return.

Harding, Resnick, and Martin sprinted into our hole, and the two CIA agents commenced firing their weapons at the Alpha team.

"Martin, you're alive!" exclaimed Lauren. "Tell us what happened." She went to pull the tape off his mouth, and he shook his head violently "no."

"Oh, Christ, not this shit again," she muttered.

"Don't worry. I'll fill you in later," said Captain Harding, blasting away. "There's a lot to tell, and I do mean a lot." She nodded her head in the direction of the female muckamuck, Maita Schlaby, who was in the process of dispatching two Alpha-team attackers. She turned and batted her eyelashes at Martin, and Martin stuck his flute in his nostril and blew a couple of toots.

THWAP! THWAP! THWAP! THWAP!

"Listen," said Duncan.

THWAP! THWAP! THWAP! THWAP!

"It can't be. They're not supposed to be able to fly this high up."

"What isn't?"

Before we had a chance to guess, rising like a phoenix over the south ridge was a giant twin-rotary Chinook C-47SD cargo chopper, and at the controls was none other than our friend Kirsten. The side door slid open and our friend Wendell was there as well, waving at us. He lowered a basket on a cable and signaled us to get in.

"Okay, that's it. Everyone into the basket," yelled Duncan. "Come on, Martin!"

Harvey gave Martin a friendly knock on his chin. Martin then turned to Maita Schlaby, who had tears in her eyes. She took the tape off her mouth and kissed Martin (when she pulled away, a big red lipstick kiss was indelibly imprinted on the duct tape over his mouth). Martin saluted Chief Shawloo. Shawloo in return pounded his chest and growled appreciatively. Then Martin jumped into the cage with the rest of us.

"What about the virgins?" someone yelled, and we all looked back in time to see the virgins escaping underground with the mythical Nazi gnomes.

"I can't wait to see what kind of master race *they* come up with," said Lauren.

It only took about ten seconds before we were all up in the main cabin of the Chinook. Wendell and I hugged each other.

"I told you it would be a relaxing vacation, didn't I?"

Wendell grumbled, "I only saved you so I could kill you myself."

"Oh, you!" I gave him a little knock on his chin. And he pounded my head pretty hard.

I looked around the chopper. Sir Edmund Hillary was there, buckled into his seat, but still gagged and hog-tied. The defeated

Richard Branson, wearing both a neck brace and a sour face, sat in another seat.

"Buckle up! This is going to be dicey!" Kirsten shouted back from the cockpit as Tony went up to greet her. (Needless to say, there was an overtly mushy reunion betwixt the two, which I can't really take the time to describe here. Well, actually I did take the time to describe it, and it took about ten pages. My editor thought that it was excessively lurid so I had to cut it. But I still have it, and occasionally, on lonely nights, I reread it—over and over and over again—and I'm willing to rent it out.)

The Chinook was struggling in the thin hot air of the high altitude, and on top of that, we were also being fired upon by the F-14s and F-18s.

"Countermeasures!" Kirsten called out.

Tony, now in the copilot's seat, looked around the cockpit.

"Sures, Funny Faces, but where's would I finds those!"

"Upper left," she shouted.

BANG! We were hit.

"Got 'ems. Countermeasures deployeds."

"Okay, hang on. We're out of here!" Kirsten gunned the helicopters' two big turboshaft engines, sending us forward at maximum power.

"Good-bye, Everest!"

But just as she did, an F-14 Tomcat appeared in her windshield, heading straight for us.

"Oh, shit. Sensors up!"

The infrared display system popped up on her windshield. She tried to get a lock on the Tomcat, but it was all over the place.

"Okay, we're gonna have to play a little game of chicken here."

She put the pedal to the metal and we began to head straight for the Tomcat. We all braced for the worst.

The two aircraft hurtled toward each other at breakneck speed.

"Aaaaaahs!" yelled Tony.

"Hang on!" hollered Kirsten.

"We're all gonna die!" screamed I. (Hey, that rhymed!)

At the last minute Kirsten turned violently to the left and we disappeared into the black cloud surrounding Everest. The F-14 went crashing into the side of the mountain, exploding in a great fireball.

A moment later we flew out of the cloud and we all cheered.

"Yay!"

Tony and Kirsten kissed, Lauren and Duncan kissed, and Wendell impulsively grabbed Captain Harding and planted a nice, big wet one on her lips. Surprisingly, the normally uptight CIA agent returned the gesture. I wrapped my arm around my unconscious great-uncle Percy and rested my chin on his head—until I started smelling his scalp. The man hadn't had a shower in like, a century. I leaned him back up against the window.

As we passed over the summit, we could see the Dalai Lama sitting triumphantly astride its peak, whipping it like it was a horse. "Yee ha!" he yelled as the great mountain rumbled forward, north into China, the little holy man leading his army into battle on the Tibetan Plateau.

Across the horizon, massive explosions propelled giant mushroom clouds into the sky as the five preceptor missiles found their targets.

Our chopper was hit with one violent aftershock after another, and we were all shaken (but not stirred).

The Tibetan army—minuscule compared with the PLA—appeared like David to the Chinese Goliath, but now, with Chomolungma compassion and righteousness on the Dalai Lama's side (as well as one hell of a beguiling smile), how could the little man in the red robe and yellow sash possibly lose?

Our fearless leader, Duncan Carter, rested his head on Lauren's shoulder. He was the most beaten up of all of us, having been kicked in the mouth by Tzing Tzang, shot in the arm by Hillary, and stabbed

The great mountain rumbled forward into China.

in the hand by Branson, so he was not looking his best (although none of us had ever seen him looking particularly good). He faded in and out of consciousness, while the rest of us sat stunned, shocked, and almost comatose, the *thwack, thwack, thwack* of the rotary blades providing a hypnotic chaser to the adrenaline rush.

Occasionally we exchanged glances and half smiles with one another, acknowledging our narrow escape, but those moments, both brief and inconsequential, surrendered to a heavy, individual solace, each one of us lost in our own inner ice cave, searching our thoughts and emotions. Perhaps we were silently summing up the horrific experience, trying to make some sense out of it all. Or perhaps we were remembering our comrades whom we had left behind, and praying that such losses would not be in vain (I figured they wouldn't be, as long as my book is a best seller), or perhaps still, we were already trying to heal and recover—trying to put the nightmare of the Himalayas out of our minds completely, imagining instead the earthly pleasures awaiting us: a hot shower, a good meal, a shot of pepper spray, and perhaps a night of unrelenting debauchery at the Cahoots Gentlemen's Club.

Wherever our inner thoughts took us, we were all too exhausted, both emotionally and mentally, to focus on just one thing (especially not on how this whole ugly mess was actually all my fault).

Kirsten banked the Chinook to the left, gunned its engines, and we headed west . . . and home.

EPILOGUE

True believers contend that the Goddess Mother actually came to life that day, but cynics argue that it was nothing but a mere earthquake—triggered by the pounding of the storm, perhaps—that caused Mount Everest to move. Or maybe it was that faith trumped science yet again?

What would become known as the "Great Battle for Enlightenment" raged on for two long weeks, the "Tantric Army" growing tenfold, as those deeply committed to a free Tibet joined forces with those who were just bored and liked a good fight. The same people who had once labeled all Tibetans as "New Age, tree hugging kooks" now had no choice but to join the ranks of the righteous, and in the end (with the full support of the United Nations) even the United States agreed to help by sending aid to the affected areas. Yes, Tibet was returned to the Tibetans. But it didn't stop there.

Not only did the Dalai Lama reclaim his homeland, but he invaded all of China as well, overthrowing the brutal communist regime and replacing it with the brutal Tibetan feudal system (under which, amongst other things, thieves get their noses cut off—can you imagine?) and gaining a controlling interest in all Wal-Mart retailing.

His Holiness finally took his rightful place, back on the golden throne, flanked on either side by his two most trusted monks, Ping and Pong—and all in the shadow of the Big Bad Mama Chomolungma roller coaster at Six Flags Lhasa.

When the Mountain Maniacs expedition returned to the States, we all went our separate ways. I suppose my friends just wanted to put the dreadful experience behind them and get on with their lives, or perhaps pretend that it never happened. (In fact, most of them pretended so hard that they'd probably tell you that none of this is true and that if I had any money and didn't seem so basically pathetic they'd sue my snow pants off.)

Uncle Percy and I returned to Brooklyn Heights, and after the big parade we moved back in with my Grammy and Gramps. I immediately commenced writing *Into Hot Air*, while Percy found limited work as a carnival geek with an act that consisted of swallowing inedible objects while stripping down to nothing more than a pair of pasties and an inflatable G-string.

Life seemed to be returning to normal—that is, until late one night:

It was late one night. (Did I mention that already? Sorry, brain fart! Senior moment! They're coming to take me away, ha ha, hee hee, ho, ho.) As my uncle and I sat at the kitchen table enjoying a peanut-oil-and-lard sandwich, an ominous shadow with obvious ill intent approached me from behind.

"Um . . . Mris," said Percy. "Meer mrink mrears somemring beind moo." And he gesticulated wildly to indicate the approaching shadow. I also had a mouthful of the gunk and could only grin at my uncle.

Suddenly the back door burst open and the lights blinked on.

"Freeze!" shouted Captain Harding, aiming her .45 Magnum at my dear, sweet Grammy, who was standing over me with a butcher cleaver.

"Drop the cleaver. You're under arrest!"

"I want that Rhombus. It's still in his nose!" Grammy cackled. This left Harding no choice, so she pulled the trigger, but . . . nothing happened.

"Damn it. I always forget to take that stupid safety off."

All of a sudden Grammy dropped the cleaver and began to drool, convulse, jitter, shake, rattle, and roll. A moment later she hit the floor, revealing Agent Resnick crouched behind her with a spent Taser gun.

"Good thinking," said Harding, as the place swarmed with officers. "No reason to blow the old biddy's head off."

Gramps shuffled in. "What in the hell blazes heckfire tarnation is going on in here? I'm tying to watch Letterman. Mandy Patinkin is singing Yiddish cabaret."

"Cuff him. He's under arrest too," ordered Harding.

"Who, Mandy Patinkin?" asked Gramps.

Having cleared my palate, I was now able to speak. "For what?" I asked.

"Conspiracy to commit murder."

"But this is an outrage," Gramps said halfheartedly and then gave in. "Yeah, you're right. We're guilty. Take us away."

"Gramps?" I said, confused.

"Sorry, kid. It was your Grammy's idea. See, she was the one who sent you the diary in the first place. Years ago, Uncle Percy sent it to her from a mailbox up there on Everest—uh, I guess."

Percy nodded. "The post office used to be way more hard-core than it is today."

"See, all your Grammy ever wanted was Percy's frozen body, so she could get the diamond that she knew was still stuck in his gullet . . . which is now stuck in your nose."

"Now it all makes perfect sense."

Groggy from the electrical charge, Grammy chattered incoherently as they cuffed her to a stretcher and carried her out. "Yes, waiter, I'd like a platter of those wonderful purple balls I've heard so much about."

"Well, that wraps everything up," I said. "Now I have a real ending for my book. I can throw out that stupid crap I made up about the Dalai Lama invading China. This is so much better—and it's 100 percent real. Now I can call it a 'true story.' Or would that open me up to a bunch of libel suits?"

"Not everything is wrapped up," said Harding, as she handed her badge and .45 Magnum to Resnick. "I won't be needing these anymore, rookie."

"What do you mean, Captain?"

"Call me Dana. I'm quitting the Clandestine Division as of today. It seems that I've become a bit of an embarrassment to them anyway. And if I were you, rookie, I would watch your ass over there—not everything is what it seems." And with that she pulled off her wig and revealed herself as a man.

Resnick and I gasped.

"But why?" said Resnick, confused. (That word pops up a lot, doesn't it?)

"I wanted to be the first cross-dresser to climb Mount Everest," she—I mean *he*—said. "And I did it. Now I'm set for life. You should see the commercial offers I've been getting."

"Bravo!" I applauded. "Finally somebody makes it into the history books. I can add that to my ending as well!" Even after his harrowing descent on Yorgi's skis, Wendell couldn't even make it into the *Guinness Book*, because Slovenian Davo Karnicar had already become the first man to ski down Mount Everest—on a Tuesday, six years prior.

HONK!

"Oh, that's my ride," said Harding, throwing his wig back on.

I looked out the window and saw Wendell's yellow cab.

"Does he know?"

"It's going to be a little wedding-night surprise!" he said, and winked.

"Wedding night? That's great! Congratulations," I said, although I was a little hurt that Wendell hadn't mentioned anything to me. It brought back memories of my brief marriage to Vera Wang (which had never actually happened, but a man can still fantasize, can't he? Or does the restraining order apply to my daydreams as well? Get out of my head, law enforcement! I can imagine anything I want. Ha!).

As it turns out, the climb was not a waste of time after all. Hollywood was quick to hire homeless people as extras. Animal testing (at least on bunnies) was banned in the United States. A homemade pasta craze swept the country, and *Into Hot Air* became an international best seller.

Michael's IMAX documentary *Famous People on Everest* opened to rave reviews from the *New York Times*—and a hatchet job from the *New Republic*. The film's raw imagery not only introduced the audience to Mount Everest like never before (at least not since David Breashears's IMAX film introduced the audience to Everest about ten years earlier), but it also succeeded in trumpeting the plight of the downtrodden by exposing the low wages and wretched working conditions of the indigenous Sherpa population, as well as pointing an accusatory finger at Disney, Six Flags, Denny's, and Jon Krakauer for being leaders in a massive conspiracy to overcommercialize the Himalayas. Of course, Michael's true party—the Republicans—had a field day mocking Michael as well as his film, and in the end, the fake conservative radio hosts and Fox News pundits reduced his fine work to nothing more than "just another pile of vitriolic liberal drivel." So once again Michael had succeeded in making the opposing party look like shrill muckrakers. (I think.)

But for those of us who had really lived through it all, Michael's film was hard to watch (even harder than this book has been to read). I'm not sure any of my fellow Maniackers ever saw it. After all, everyone was busy; Lauren and Duncan were on an expedition to the Amazon to search for a rare wildflower that supposedly holds the secret to everlasting youth (watch those anacondas, guys!). Tony and Kirsten were married and living in Rome, where the brilliant actress was furthering her studies into "string theory" using Tony's homemade spaghetti in her presentations; and President Martin stayed on in Tibet, where the Dalai Lama's feudal system relegated him to nothing more than another homeless pauper. (Oh, wait. I made up all that stuff about Tibet invading China, didn't I? Oh well, forget that I made it up, because it's funny if Martin ends up homeless, right? Not that being homeless is funny. I'm just saying, if Martin . . . you know . . . who was wearing duct tape over his mouth to show solidarity with homeless people ends up, himself . . . oh, forget it.)

One day about a year later, I sneezed and the diamond finally blew out of my nose. Suddenly I was rich beyond belief. But was I happy? It's funny, you know—I had so many dreams, but once I finally had the wherewithal to achieve them, I found myself stalled, squandering my fortune by treating so-called friends and hangers-on to lavish Happy Meals at Mickey D's.

It would be a crisp fall day in Central Park when my life would be changed once more for the better. As I sat on a bench counting out my billions (all in Sacajaweas), I didn't even notice the horse and buggy pull up in front of me.

"Want a ride?" said a familiar voice. When I looked up, I saw Wendell holding the reins on top of a hansom cab.

"Wendy, what are you doing here?" I said, excited. "I thought you married Captain Harding and moved down south?"

"Yeah, well, that didn't exactly work out."

"Oh, really?" I said coyly. "Well, for heaven's sake, why not?" And then I giggled.

"It's a long story. We were just into different things, that's all. No biggy. Hop on."

"Sure. Let me just put my billions away."

I stashed my coins into my *Partridge Family* backpack. Wendell extended his hand to help me up, but of course I got into the back. (I'm a billionaire now, after all.)

"Onward, driver!" I said in my terrible English accent, and Wendell just grumbled.

"So, why are you driving one of these now?" I asked.

"I thought it was time to upgrade."

"You know, Wendell," I said, "with all this money I got, you don't ever have to work again. We could just ride off and go from one mystery to the next . . . if you wanted to."

"Ummm . . . yeah, I guess. Sure, okay."

"Yay! Back together and better than ever!"

"Gitty up," he said.

I noticed his horse had a beautiful mane of salt-and-pepper hair— as well as an unusually large forehead.

"What's your horsey's name?" I asked.

"Dickey," he said.

"Dickey? Dicky . . . Dick . . . short for Richard, right?

"That's right."

"Wait a second. You mean . . . he came back as a . . . ?"

"Yep, he sure did."

"Wow. I wonder if he's a better actor now." And I giggled like a good old-fashioned hyena.

The horse turned around and winked, and with that all three of us trotted off into the sunset . . . and on to our next adventure.

THE END

ACKNOWLEDGMENTS

A deep and heartfelt thank thank-you to my publisher, Rob Weisbach, for all his guidance and support and for that fantastic *Into Hot Air* party he threw for me at the Met—those vegan hors d'ourves were to die for! I also want to thank Richard Florest not only for his outstanding editing skills but also for keeping me off the juice just long enough to get through this hideous process. Now that it's all over, I can drink all I want, right? As usual, Kristin Powers did an amazing job putting this book together—I think most of the chapters are in the right order, but with this kind of product, it really doesn't matter, does it? My thanks to Bob and Harvey Weinstein (I just wish they'd stop calling me Cliff) and to Judy Hottensen, Katie Finch, Adrian Palacios, Chelsea Brennan, Camille March, Emily Wilkinson, Judy Hottensen (I just like saying her name), JillEllyn Riley, Melanie Dunea, and Brian Chojnowski, and anyone else at Weinstein Books who worked so hard to make this piece of . . . ah . . . gold, . . . really shine. Thank you, guys.

A special thank thank-you goes out to my friend and part part-time yogi Johnny Schmidt for all his editing work and also for suggesting that great title. I wanted to call it *Mounting Chomolungma*, but even I couldn't pronounce it.

Also for reading my rough draft and putting in their two cents, I want to thank Adam Resnick, Ethan Zweig, Eric and Justin Stengle, Steve O'Donnell, John Altshuler, Dave Krinski, Rob Des Hotel and Alan Zweibel.

Thanks to my sister Amy for her most impressive illustrating skills. Great job, sis!

Thanks to my wife, Paula Niedert Elliott, who tackled my spelling like she was wrestling a big, old, Mule-footed Iowa Landrace at the Waterloo Cattle Congress, and to my two delightful and beautiful daughters, Abby and Bridey, who during the writing process sat around being delightful and looking beautiful.

Thanks to my manager, Tom Demko, for at least "saying" that he read it, and to my literary agent, David Vigliano, for occasionally returning my e-mails or at least having someone else do it for him.

Finally, I want to sincerely dedicate this fine work to my friend and mentor David Letterman. It was his response to my last book that encouraged me to write another one—so go blame him.